CRITICS RAVE FOR
LIZ MAVERICK!

THE SHADOW RUNNERS

"If you like your heroines tough but tender, your heroes hard-edged and hungering for a better tomorrow, you'll love *The Shadow Runners*."

—Revision 14

"A winning addition to the *2176* series, *The Shadow Runners* is sure to please. Full of suspense, adventure, and an explosive romance, it is a book not to be missed."

—*Romance Reviews Today*

"This third novel in the gripping and explosive *2176* series moves along at a breakneck pace as another tough, strong woman does her part in the fight for world freedom. Ms. Maverick writes a unique, taut, exciting tale."

—The Best Reviews

"Maverick provides an excellent chapter in this ongoing adventure series....gritty and realistic, not to mention completely compelling."

—*RT BOOKclub*

A Dangerous Pair

"I'm not what you think," Dain said. "I'm not a good man."

"You wouldn't be here if you were," Fleur answered, her voice thick with emotion. "Neither would I." Her eyes shone an intense blue that seemed to penetrate his soul. Dain imagined he saw love in their depth, but he didn't dare ask. Not yet. Because he couldn't be sure of what was to come. And because he had enough emotion for both of them tonight.

"I'm warning you," he said, stalking her and pulling the jeweled combs from her hair. He crowded up to her. "I'm *warning* you."

"No more warnings," she barely had time to say. He pushed her down on the bed.

LIZ MAVERICK

CRIMSON CITY

LOVE SPELL   LOVE SPELL   NEW YORK CITY

LOVE SPELL®

July 2005

Published by

Dorchester Publishing Co., Inc.
200 Madison Avenue
New York, NY 10016

ISBN 0-505-52622-0

The name "Love Spell" and its logo are trademarks of Dorchester Publishing Co., Inc.

Printed in the United States of America.

Visit us on the web at www.dorchesterpub.com.

CRIMSON CITY

Chapter One

Fleur Dumont flung herself out of the ninety-third–floor window and somersaulted along the vertical length of the skyscraper. She quickly adjusted to the altered plane of the fighting field and leaped into the air, one leg bent at the knee; the other leg she kicked straight out into the chest of her assailant.

Her foe lost his footing, but he recovered position within seconds, foregoing any attempt at bracing himself along the slick glass of the building beneath him. Instead, hovering in the air, he gestured to someone behind Fleur. A glance at the reflection in the windows below her feet confirmed two more enemies. Sweat pouring down the back of her jacket, Fleur pulled a pair of daggers from the sheaths strapped around her thighs and whirled in a circle, her weapons at the ready, trying to make herself a little more space.

The sky blurred into a luminous rainbow as she turned, the night's darkness making the lights that streamed past much more vivid. Projected down toward the human world at street level, they originated from a fleet of flying advertisement projectors. Looped videos, holographics, multicolored skylight lasers—all touting a seemingly endless number of desires and cures. The lights were uncomfortable and distracting to vampires, but Fleur had trained outside enough to be able to ignore them when it counted.

The three vampires floating around her were, like her, armed with daggers, and she already knew firsthand of their power and skill. Well, size and numbers could not trump the strength and agility inherent in her blood, so at worst, they were equals. Fleur focused and moved in for the kill, directing a flurry of blows at all three men as she danced through the air.

Until one of the men snatched a gun from his shoulder holster and fired. Caught by surprise, Fleur lurched away and hit the top of a billboard with her knee. She cartwheeled wildly off in the other direction amid a shower of sparks as some of the bulbs exploded from the impact. She went into free fall, just missing a remote-controlled drone that hummed by projecting an all-species evening edition of the news onto the thickening smog particles.

She let herself drop and took the opportunity to catch her breath, but the splash of violet on her right sleeve spurred her back into the fight. He'd capped her, all right. That pissed her off, and immediately she reversed direction, purposely holding her left arm behind her and out of sight.

Just as she reached the three men and lunged forward with her knife, a watch chime froze all her foes in midaction. They stopped fighting immediately, and the session ended with the flat end of Fleur's blade slapping dully off Marius's chest armor. "That's time," he said. "And we're off."

Without another word, the men all turned and headed upward, Fleur on their heels. They alit gracefully on the edge of the huge picture window leading back into the training room, where the slick angles, metal, and glass wrapping the outside of the massive landmark building gave way to a completely different world: dark woods, lusciously colored fabrics and touches of gilt.

"Come on, come on . . . finish this!" Fleur looked wildly from one man to the next, but the three Protectors were already stripping off their fight gear.

"Sorry, Fleur," Warrick said, swatting her dagger away as if it were a fly. "Nice work, but next time, don't expect a reflection to save you."

Fleur knew he was right. She wasn't quite where she needed to be. She should have been training from the day she was born, but the assumption had been that she'd never be called. That hadn't really changed, but the number of vampires left between her and serious responsibility had been whittled down to two: her half-brothers, Christian and Ryan. She could have gotten away with calling them brothers, straight up, but they simply weren't close.

Her cousins, the three Protectors standing before her, were her core family now. For Marius, Warrick, and Ian Dumont had never once swayed in their loyalty, not even amidst the power struggle during the war between the species when her mother had not only fallen from grace, but had fallen forever.

Still, Fleur wasn't convinced her cousins took her training seriously. Probably no one did. But at least they humored her, and they could humor her all they wanted as long as they gave her the training she'd requested.

She sighed and threw herself down on one of the carved rosewood benches lining the training hall. "I thought it was just going to be Marius today. Nice trick calling for the others."

"You know us too well. You're able to anticipate our movements at this point," Ian said, busy flexing his chest muscles with the pleased air of a man who knew his body could not be more perfect. "And even with those damn stuffy helmets on, I'm sure you still know who is who. From movement or sense if not by sight. We should bring in some outsiders for you to practice on."

Warrick stripped off his shirt and tossed it in the corner bin, then glanced over. "You're not hurt, Fleur, are you? You took a nasty bounce off that advert."

Fleur crossed her legs to hide the rip in her training suit and quickly peeled off her jacket so they wouldn't see the violet paint. If Marius had been toting a real UV weapon, she'd be lying on the floor writhing in pain. "I'm absolutely fine. Not a bad recovery out there, I think . . . So, what are you meeting about?"

She asked them the same question every morning. It had become something of a joke, since they all knew they wouldn't say. What went on in the war room, stayed in the war room. That's the way Fleur's half-brothers wanted it, though it wasn't the candid policy vampire leaders had exercised in the past. But, then, there had been quite a few policy changes recently.

Ian gave her the look she'd been expecting and

promptly changed the subject. "Same time, day after tomorrow? We can try something new."

She shrugged and nodded.

"You're welcome to come for the beginning, you know," Warrick said, pulling a fresh shirt over his head.

Fleur managed a half-smile. Actually, she wasn't welcome. Inside the war room, they treated her as if she were still a small child; they tempered the discussion and waited until she gave up and left before letting the real discourse begin. It was a waste of time for everybody, and her presence made everyone uncomfortable, to boot. All because of her past.

The vampires of Crimson City were primarily descendants of four families who formed an organized body called the Primary Assembly, which controlled the policies of survival for the entire vampire world. Fleur had been born into the Dumont family, and thus was a key link of the most powerful lineage. The Dumonts, by tradition, controlled the Assembly. This was a legacy that should have run straight to her, and someday down to her children.

Yes, one vampire stood at the podium in the Primary Assembly meetings to report on the intricate web of relationships between the species in Crimson City. One vampire sat with the inner circle comprised of the heads of the four families and their advisors, and made final decisions on matters of defense and survival. There were other vampires who controlled matters of business and internal welfare, but it was the head of city intelligence who most impacted the survival of their species, and as the vampires evolved, it was this position that had become a kind of de facto presidency for the vampire world. And upon the death of her mother in the first major battle between the species some years back, that vampire should have been Fleur Dumont.

But Fleur had made a mistake. Though her intentions had been pure, though she'd acted in the name of love, the bottom line was that in the same month as she'd lost her mother, she'd broken vampire code. She'd been young and inexperienced, and her crime had made it convenient for the others to bypass her for the leadership circle in favor of her older half-brothers. And though the rest of the Primary Assembly had mostly forgiven her indiscretion, nobody had forgotten. Especially not Fleur. Years later, she still woke up every night with the memory of her shame.

She'd made a rogue. She'd created an enemy.

Vampires who belonged to the Primary Assembly were called primaries. All others were rogues. A rogue was a vampire who had chosen to rebel against his own kind, ignoring the Assembly's rules and way of life. Sometimes these were primaries who had chosen a life of chaos; more often, they were "made" vampires—humans who had been turned.

Which was one reason why the Assembly had decreed so long ago that humans weren't to be turned. While many humans fell prey to romantic notions about life as a vampire, not the least of which was the lure of seemingly limitless wealth and life span, the fact was that most turned humans could not—or would not, Fleur wasn't sure—accept their new fates. These unfortunates most often turned against the Primary Assembly and disappeared into the city, trying to pass as human once more. Sometimes they reappeared, often with thoughts of revenge on their minds. This had once been rare. It was not so rare anymore, and in the back of the Assembly's collective mind, a worry was brewing that the rogues had banded together and were becoming a powerful force.

Fleur reminded most of the inner circle of disaster and of failure. By legacy she should have been a key player in the security and intelligence community of Crimson City's vampire world. Like her mother before her. Instead she existed in a strange sort of limbo, unable to detach herself from a sense of responsibility and thus forever on a heightened state of alert, yet never to be called for duty. It was like playing understudy to actors who could never get sick.

Marius, Warrick, and Ian finished changing out of their gear and collected their belongings. Warrick looked over his shoulder. "Oh, and watch for hidden weapons," he said to Fleur. "You never know what someone might pull. We can work on some new evasive actions sometime, if you like."

"I'll take you up on that," she said. Warrick's advice was always good—when it came to fighting, he was the best. He might be a Protector by legacy, but sometimes she thought he had more the temperament of a Warrior like herself. Or like she was supposed to be, anyway. Fleur sighed. She should definitely start asking some of the others to train with her, if for no other reason than unpredictability.

She thought to pose the question of who, but her cousins had already turned their backs and were engaged in a discussion about the imminent business of the day. Fleur pushed away the hair plastered to her sweaty face and neck, released the clips on her chest armor and just sat, twirling a dagger in her hands while they talked amongst themselves.

Warrior and Protector—was it all so important what one was born? She supposed it was. Besides the delineation between the four families, a vampire's class was a huge part of her identity. And while as far as Fleur could tell, Crimson City's humans were just beginning to come to terms with the implications that there was a difference between vampires—rogue or primary, Warrior or Protector; the classifications were information that humans either didn't realize existed or didn't know what to do with—the vampires themselves were unfailingly aware of the differences.

Classifications were determined, for the most part, by the genetics of the parents, but they could also be affected by blood the parents had ingested or other less explicable factors. There were many classes of vampire. Protectors and Warriors were merely two, and were the most common types in the Dumont family. Protector vampires had a duty to protect their people, making full use of a heightened sixth sense that told them when those they cared about were in trouble, though Protectors seemed to connect with some individuals more than with others. Most Protectors had various psychic abilities; were sometimes capable of reading minds, sometimes were capable of other things. Protectors were trained for combat in the defense of their kind.

Warrior vampires, on the other hand, exhibited uncanny agility and strength—along with the potential for an adrenaline surge more powerful than that of any other class. Biologically it was meant to help them withstand injury, and exact it on their enemies with exponential results. Sometimes Fleur was caught by surprise by her abilities, and in the most unlikely of places. It was not uncommon for her to be reminded that she was meant for other, bigger things, like when an unpleasant incident at a crowded sales event triggered an unusual amount of rage.

"Fleur, if I could have it my way, you'd be sitting in that meeting next to us. That's how it should be," Marius said. Then her cousins left the room, and the slam of the heavy mahogany door reverberated loudly in the cavernous space.

Fleur let her dagger slip through her fingers to impale itself in the floorboards with a loud twang. "I don't know why nobody does anything about it if that's how it should be," she muttered.

Of course, *she* wasn't doing anything about it either. She wasn't barreling into the war room demanding her rights, her chance to lead. That would just make her look ridiculous. You couldn't demand anything when you hadn't a shred of power.

She replaced her training weapons in the cabinets lining the walls, then headed upstairs, passing the war room on the way. She could hear all the voices arguing loud enough to distinguish themselves through the heavy mahogany door: her three Protector cousins—Warrick, Ian, and Marius; Christian, acting as leader; Ryan reporting as the primary intelligence officer; and the other men and women representing the various clans of the Primary Assembly. The rebel groups excepted, everyone was represented in that room; all of the lines were in attendance. Everybody who was supposed to be there, was there. Except Fleur.

She took the quick route to her rooms, slipping back out the window and making quick work of the fifteen floors straight up to the residential levels. She typed in her code. Her window slid open and she slipped inside. Someone was knocking frantically on the front door of her apartments.

"Fleur? Fleur!"

Fleur dodged the shopping bags dotting her floor and opened the door.

Paulina Marakova sashayed in with an overly dramatic double take directed at Fleur's disheveled appearance. Already dressed to the nines before breakfast, the redhead flung herself into the largest chair in the sitting room and arranged her amber taffeta ballskirt around her. "We're planning a very different sort of recreation for next week. The twenties. Except—we're all going as men! The girls are having a seamstress up to do tuxedos. You must come and be fitted. Drinks, ciggies, snooker . . . it's going to be a scream!" She laughed, exposing a set of delicate, full-grown fangs that she never filed down.

Like many of her peers, Paulina never left the vampire strata—for that matter, she never even left her building, except to go shopping in the district built high above Rodeo Drive where few humans and even fewer werewolves could afford to browse. She'd taken happily to her position as a younger daughter of Marakova heritage, but underneath the materialism that seemed to consume all of her energy, there was a very real and generous spirit. Fleur counted Paulina as one of very few of her kind who'd never once let her loyalty or friendship lapse, even during the worst of what Fleur had experienced.

Already bored with sitting in one spot, Paulina leaped up and began rifling through a fortune in high-heeled shoes, party dresses, and jewelry Fleur had left strewn about the room after shopping yesterday. "Gorgeous. This one's gorgeous. Oh! I have one word for you."

Fleur unbuckled and unlaced her high boots. "Only one?" she teased.

"Ichibana," Paulina intoned. "What do you think?" She floated her arm out in front of her, waving her fingers gracefully. "The art of Japanese flower arrangement. It's going to be all the rage, and I've hired a private instructor. Can you put on something decent and join me in half an hour?"

"It sounds lovely, but I've got a meeting." Fleur frowned. "Doesn't that make me sound like a killjoy! But next week's recreation sounds brilliant. I'll try to be there."

Such recreations of past eras, which many of them had actually lived through, were a favorite pastime. Almost every night in these highest reaches of the vampire strata was filled with some sort of similar entertainment. Indulgence was encouraged, as was decadence, for in this world the population could afford to always dress fabulously and the champagne never ran out. Fleur couldn't really complain about having been forced into the life of an idle heiress. It was simply knowing that she should have been something else, and that she was capable of more, which made things difficult.

"Look, darling. I have so much to do. Decide what sort of accessories you want, and I'll order them with your tuxedo." Paulina looked her up and down as Fleur slipped off the rest of her training clothes and stood in her underwear. "Tut-tut! You exercise much too much; you're losing all your curves. And I can't believe you waste such a lovely bra and panty set on *that* kind of action. La Perla, isn't it? So pretty!" Without waiting for an answer, she blew a kiss and plowed right back out the door.

Fleur dragged a robe from her closet and slipped it on, then walked to her desk, piled high with copies of memos, research reports, photos of high-ranking werewolf and human players in the intelligence and security communities. On paper, she was more than qualified to play her rightful role in vampire leadership. They probably had no idea how hard she'd worked to keep up to speed on things even as she was shut out from meetings and forced to walk the perimeter of the inner circle.

I've got to do something. I've somehow got to make them understand that I belong in that room. Marius is right. I must talk to Christian and Ryan about my situation.

They had to listen. She'd *make* them listen, if that's what it came down to. It was the principle of the thing. Her legacy eroded a little more with every passing day. It was time to do something about that.

Chapter Two

Dain Reston always walked to work fully armed. But whether his hands held a cup of coffee and a doughnut or a silver dagger and a pistol depended on instinct. Each day when he woke, he gave himself five seconds before rising to stare up at the stark white paint peeling off his ceiling; did his instincts tell him it was a dagger-through-the-heart sort of night, or an enjoy-your-coffee sort of night?

He actually liked the walk at dusk, halfway across town to the satellite office from his flat in The Triangle, a sort of DMZ for the vamps, wolves, and humans who'd chosen not to cluster in one of the three strata dominated by their own kind. He was one who'd made that choice, and everyone always asked why. Why did he insist on living in the relative hellhole he'd chosen when he could easily live in relative comfort on the base?

Bottom line: It was here or the base, and the base made you soft. There was a reason the divisions headquartered out there were grouped under the umbrella, "Internal Operations." The official reason was because everything outside the base and inside the City was considered the external world, or the field. But to Dain it was because life in the base was like being in a cocoon. That was the positive spin on it, anyway. Dain also believed that living in such a vacuum of safety dulled the instincts. He wanted the presence of a vamp or a wolf to be a sixth sense.

The vampires had built their skyscrapers to dizzying heights that sheared off at crisp angles into the sky, and those structures gleamed with the cold perfection of tinted glass and steel. Inside, the rooms were reputed to be a riot of color in sumptuous fabrics, gold detailing, and hand-polished woods. Yes, the world above was intimidating to most, as it was meant to be. There weren't many humans—or werewolves, for that matter—up there. To go up to Crimson City's highest elevation, you needed either a serious purpose or a serious death wish.

Naturally, humans had remained where they'd always been, at midlevel, clustering in neighborhoods throughout the valleys, beach cities, and downtown areas that hadn't been razed by the fires.

The werewolves were left to make use of the underground. The psychology of this arrangement wasn't lost on anybody, and it all made for a nice cocktail of strained relations. That was why Dain made his home in The Triangle—it was one of the few places in town where he could really gauge interspecies tension. Didn't exactly make for great block parties, but this wasn't exactly a block party era, now, was it?

He was later than usual today, and as he stepped outside he was hurried by a honk from one of the chauffeured transports sent around to collect the members of the "Battlefield" Operations team for work. As usual, he passed on the ride with a friendly wave. Then, after strapping his bag across his back, double- and triple-checking his weapons for readiness, he walked into the gray mist and headed for the station, the transport trailing behind him in the street.

As a senior field intelligence officer, he knew full well that he wasn't supposed to refer to his team as B-Ops or to the city streets as a battlefield anymore. B-Ops was just supposed to be Field or External Operations, and the city was supposed to be back to being plain old Los Angeles, not Crimson City. That was the party line. But the slang coined long ago when the wolves and the vamps first came to town and the streets ran red with blood—well, that wasn't going to disappear just because the suits sitting behind the walls of their base liked to cover reality with a thick layer of gloss.

What was the reality, anyway? As far as his superiors were concerned, Dain and his field teams owned the night. Out of their satellite station in the middle of downtown, whatever was going to go down in Crimson City, B-Ops either knew about it or was planning it. But as far as Dain's counterparts amongst the vamp and the wolf populations were concerned, the streets—day or night—weren't owned by anybody anymore, least of all humans.

Two blocks from the station, a cross-eyed mutt barked from behind a chain-link fence. Dain heard a thin buzz ramp up from the transport behind him as it switched on an electrical defense system, and he had to laugh a bit. This was what he thrived on, what he lived for: the charge in the air, the too-delicate nature of the peace that had been forged. He couldn't remember a time when a sense of being on the edge of chaos wasn't the norm. All the same, he was grateful for the constraints of law and order that his job provided.

Since he could remember, he'd had little opportunity to think about anything else save his work, the state of the city, and the rest of his team. Some might call it too insular a life. Dain called it just as well. He and most of his teammates had chosen Battlefield Operations for a reason.

Battlefield Operations and Internal Operations were two divisions established at city level under the jurisdiction of the Feds to address the tricky issue of human survival in a city now sharing space with a melting pot of other species. While the the city's regular police department was still responsible for keeping the peace on the streets on a day-to-day basis as they always had, B-Ops and I-Ops concerned themselves with big picture matters of intelligence and strategic defense.

B-Ops contained teams of combat-trained field agents, spies, military personnel and intelligence hunters. I-Ops contained teams of information analysts, researchers, policy wonks, and other management types. If you had your head on completely straight, a past without at least one personal arrest, and your personality under complete control, you worked for Internal Operations. If you were a bit of a wildcard, you worked for B-Ops.

Dain fit the latter mold in spades. He'd once been a bounty hunter working dangerous, and sometimes illegal jobs. Oddly, he didn't remember any of it. He didn't remember a lot of his past, and what memories still lurked in his mind were blurry. He tried to remember the good things, the helpful things—like his wife Serena. Truth be told, he didn't care about remembering much except her, and some days he would just lie awake in bed trying to force those images to come into focus. All he had left were a few pictures and the scars on his arms from the chemical burns he'd received while trying to save her.

The vampires had killed her. There was a file on the whole thing, of course, but it was pretty slim. Just a cursory description of events filed by some hack who'd apparently had better things to do than to document the turning point of Dain's life.

Serena had worked for a consumer products company that was trying to expand operations into the vampire realm. They'd negotiated a tentative deal to build a factory up in strata +1, a very rare arrangement. Apparently, the vampires had played the humans for fools.

The deal had imploded along with the factory; Dain had received a call from his wife that she was in trouble. He'd kept the message on his cell phone for months. He could remember the exact intonation of her voice, the exact words she'd used, the way she'd formed her sentences. He just couldn't remember anything that wasn't on tape. Apparently he'd responded to her call for help and traveled up to the vampire strata . . . and by the end of the night he was in a hospital bed being treated for severe burns to his arms, with no memory whatsoever of what had gone down. All he knew was that he'd failed his wife and that there was no one person to hunt down and no simple way to seek revenge.

Thus, when chaos had threatened the city and the government called for recruits, Dain had nothing to lose and everything to gain by answering. It had been a blessing in a way, for people like himself, his partner Cyd, and others like them who now formed the nucleus of B-Ops—real fighters with real street savvy to personally monitor and respond to the primitive violence perpetrated by the fangs and the dogs. This gave them a purpose.

Dain shook his head. Humans always accused the vamps and the dogs of trying to "pass," trying to successfully play themselves off as human. Well, in a funny way, some humans were trying to pass, too. After he'd woken up in that hospital bed with no wife and no memory, he'd nearly lost it. He'd been tempted back into his former occupation, felt himself sucked toward taking out his anger and sorrow and confusion on everybody by killing them—by killing everything in his path. But the recruiters at Battlefield Operations had saved him. They'd given him a second chance at a life. And it was only fair that he stepped up now with every last ounce of his strength to keep what he'd received and to defend the people who'd finally, after so much time, given him a membership card as a respected part of society.

Today certainly seemed quiet enough. City security was humming along nicely at normal levels, and for the last month he'd had all his teams on two-day status, with full-blown station meetings only every other day. He turned the corner, the transport finally peeling off and pulling away into an adjacent parking lot. He'd arrived.

This downtown station was a night-shift outpost

also used as a satellite office for the base out at LAX. His partner Cyd probably would have preferred working the day shift—less chance of bumping into something you didn't want to bump into—except, this way she didn't have to go out to the base much. Cyd refused to go unless it was a direct order; Dain actually liked to get out there once in a while.

The station before him was riddled with graffiti and defended by a set of old-school iron window bars that clashed with the high-tech security equipment built into the structure. Dain turned and hoisted his coffee in a gesture of thanks to the driver over in the parking lot, then turned back to the door.

Highly guarded, the station house looked deceptively small from the street. It actually housed rooms for interrogation, incarceration, research, conferencing, and more. After a retinal scan and a blood prick test, the doors unlocked and Dain headed straight for the break room. He could hear the uproar from way down the hall. Through the swinging doors, it looked like the night-shift teams were all in.

JB and Trask were sitting on the lunch table playing a hand of poker. Cyd seemed to be discussing her new holster with a teammate by the coffee machine, a blue candy cigarette flopping between her lips as she spoke. And a whole slew of guys barreled in behind him, in the middle of a shoving match.

"Okay, listen up!" he called.

After a few snorts, snickers, and last-minute wisecracks, the teams quieted down. "We're on two-day check-in. I've read last night's reports"—he looked at them sternly—"and I've never been so goddamn bored in my life."

They all laughed. "So, unless you've got something

you want to discuss, we'll save the official powwow for tomorrow morning. Go ahead and download your assignments and get out in the field. Anyone have anything? No? Fantastic. Then get the hell out of here. I'll see you tomorrow. And remember—"

"Be careful out there!" the crew chimed in unison, amidst much eye-rolling. In a flurry of activity, everyone except Cyd grabbed gear and headed out.

"'Morning, partner." Cydney Brighton had the kind of smoky voice that would have made her a bona fide knockout all on its own even if she hadn't been such a natural looker. Of course, she didn't bother to work what she had. Not that Dain cared. He hadn't gotten around to shaving for two days, himself. That was B-Ops. It just took a certain kind.

"What's the temperature?" she asked.

"I didn't pick up anything unusual on the way over."

"Me neither. It should be a quiet day."

"Maybe I should bring a book."

A few hours later, he was thinking she probably wished she had. It was midnight, and the city was just hitting its stride. But as they'd dished on just about every mutual acquaintance they'd ever had, now Dain was reading some old reports while Cyd graduated to an unlit cigarette and stared out through the windshield.

Their car was like a mobile fortress. Hidden panels slid open to reveal a mind-blowing array of devices, lights, switches, and panels. GPS, video conferencing, communications center, mapping, DNA lab—everything. And that didn't count the arsenal built into side door and roof compartments. Only Dain and Cyd had the code for the car; anyone else would pretty much be incinerated if they even touched it.

In all fairness, the car would give perpetrators advance warning to back off. And besides, Dain was well enough known in the city that even his non-standard patrol car was recognized. That was one of the main reasons Cyd never took a car—she didn't want to be recognized. She was partial to the new subterranean transit system the werewolves had constructed. It was open to everyone, of course, though there still weren't too many besides the dogs who'd go down there.

Dain had been down a couple of times on business. He'd even seen a couple of young vamps on the train, once, and had to work hard not to laugh. They'd probably dared each other to do it on a lark, and had underestimated the discomfort of being surrounded by such a high concentration of opposite—and fairly antagonistic—energy.

Cyd sighed loudly. "I don't suppose you have a match on you."

"If I did, you know I wouldn't give it to you. You made me swear to it."

She sighed again and pointed to where a switch box was built into the lower part of the dashboard. "Most cars have a cigarette lighter there." This car could light up a huge radius of the night around them. Even though they had an unlimited supply of night vision contact lenses and specialized goggles, visors, and helmets, it was a nice feature to have.

Dain pushed his seat back and stretched his legs.

"Would you like me to have them swap it back out? Personally, I prefer the equipment that actually helps *save* my life."

She rolled her eyes. She'd been quitting smoking for the better part of a year. As far as Dain knew, by the time they headed back to the office for lunch, she'd be begging a book of matches off JB to start the cycle all over again.

The woman was wicked-smart. A goddamn mess, but too clever by half. Whatever else she was—and she was a lot of things—she was probably smarter than he was. But she'd had some kind of a scare working in the Paranormal Research & Development division out at I-Ops. She probably would have outranked him now if she'd stayed. She didn't talk about it, and Dain didn't ask questions.

What he did know was that Cyd had been fresh out of college when she'd joined up. There was a lot of hushed talk about her origins. One rumor had it that she'd been in a research group that had opened a portal to some demon underworld and had seen or been through "things." There had been talk of spells, curses, evil . . . whatever.

It was a bunch of crap, as far as Dain was concerned. No one had ever seemed able to describe any of those things. And frankly, the only thing Cyd seemed truly cursed with was a penchant for addictive substances. She'd spilled her purse in the car, once. Gum, mints, lozenges, real cigarettes, candy cigarettes, minibar whiskeys. And little packets of . . . stuff. Pieces, squares, random thingums. Things for days when she was on the wagon, things for days she was off.

Dain had kept his mouth shut. She was a damn good field operative, had cultivated the best network of informants in Crimson City, and therefore the contents of her purse were none of his business.

"This is getting ridiculous," Cyd finally muttered after they'd been sitting in the car for two more hours. "Maybe we should go find a section of town that the city police aren't staffing tonight."

Dain gave her a look. "You feel like creating a little trouble, do you?"

She shrugged. "There's such a thing as too quiet. I don't like it when things are too quiet."

The city police were another division entirely. They handled human crimes and human emergencies and were just as happy to pretend that werewolves and vamps didn't exist. Of course, that also meant they were just as happy to pretend that people like Dain and Cyd didn't exist, and the feeling was mutual.

"After lunch, why don't you do the rounds and visit your informants," Dain suggested. "I was thinking of stopping by the base for a meeting, anyway."

"Fun. I'll be skipping that . . . whoa. Wait." Cyd pointed to the car's GPS screen. "Do you see what I see?"

The screen showed the placement of all of the teams for which Dain was responsible. Coded by number and color, he could see their location while they were on duty. Sometimes his men turned their GPS off to avoid being traced by enemies, though that wasn't supposed to be a worry these days. And Cyd went off it more than most for the sake of maintaining her informants' privacy. But what was different about the screen today was an *extra* blip, one without a recognizable team code. It was just a symbol.

"You know anything about this?" Cyd asked.

Yeah, he knew something about it. That was the symbol for a mech. It had never been used before, and he was beyond surprised to see it being used now. Mechs—humans with mechanical features and built-in weapons systems—were developed and housed out at the base. None of them had been sent outside their barracks and training facilities. None of them had ever been out in the open. None of them had ever been programmed for a full-scale mission. "That's a mech symbol," he said.

"That's impossible," Cyd blurted. But the blip didn't fade away, and now it was moving. According to the coordinates it was on strata +1, in vampire territory.

Dain looked at Cyd darkly, jammed the gearstick in reverse and hit the accelerator. The vehicle peeled out backward, knocking over a row of garbage cans. Cyd gripped the center armrest as he flipped into forward. Fishtailing out of the parking lot, they careened toward Dumont Towers, aka "Vampire Central."

The intercom crackled. "Turn it up," Dain barked.

Cyd fiddled with the volume as Dain surfed channels on the video monitor, pausing on a view of the front door piped in by cameras mounted across the street from the tony Dumont Towers property development. There were surveillance cameras everywhere, but they revealed nothing. The streets in front of the skyscraper were empty.

Dain punched a few more controls to see what else he could find. An hourglass danced on the screen as the system searched and then finally produced what it could find. Which was absolutely nothing.

TRACKING . . .

NO DATA. INSERT CORRECT MODULE.

Dain cursed. "You drive." He took his hands off the steering wheel and the vehicle flew onto the sidewalk. Cyd calmly reached over and got them back in the street, Dain's foot still pressed hard against the accelerator as he scrabbled about in the glove compartment.

The correct module would be the one that allowed him to tap into the software used by mechs. The one he'd never used before. And the one he hadn't been expecting to use because they'd never sent a mech out on a real-life mission.

Random electronics, batteries, wires, first-aid supplies along with the ubiquitous gum, condoms, and tampons showered out of the glove compartment as something dashed across the street.

Cyd swerved. "Sorry," she muttered, her voice tense and low.

Dain found the item in question and tossed it in Cyd's lap, taking over the steering. She ripped the shrinkwrap off and plugged the module into the slot.

"Don't bother downloading it," Dain said. "Just play it straight from the cartridge."

The screen flashed a couple of times, then:

... IN PROCESS. COORDINATES: 93°NNE, 20°S,
STRATA +1. CROSSING PSR 45 SECONDS ...

"Dammit! What the hell is going on here?" Dain
raged. Cyd looked at him and he nodded. She
punched the all-call.

Dain straightened his earpiece and tapped the mic
pad. "This is Dain Reston, Field Operations. All
downtown units, please proceed immediately to
red-alert positions throughout the city. Repeat: Red-
alert is in effect. This is not an exercise."

Cyd switched off the all-call and he punched in
for a direct line to the base. "Phone. Dial 'suits.'"
Classify urgent," he instructed.

The car phone kicked in and Bridget Rothschild's
voice came on the line. "Internal Operations, red
line. What's going on, Dain?" Her voice sounded
high-pitched and thin.

"You tell me!"

"Did you send in a mech? We have no paperwork
on this!"

Dain fought hard not to lose his patience. "I have
no authority over the mechs, Bridget. Internal Ops
isn't in on this? The boss didn't send a mech out?"

"No! Not to my knowledge ... did you—"

The car swerved back and forth in the lane as Cyd
grabbed his arm. She pointed at the monitor. "Oh,
shit."

PAST PSR. MISSION LOCKED.

Chapter Three

Fleur stood in the hall before two enormous carved mahogany doors leading to the war room, absently running the toe of her boot across the supple Oriental carpet beneath her feet. She'd waited outside for a while now, turning away and walking to the window whenever someone passed by, embarrassed about her purpose here.

She looked up again, as she'd been compelled to do over and over for the last twenty minutes, gazing at the top of the doors. Carved into the wide door frame was the Latin translation of the same English engraved on a brass plaque by the street-level entrance, where the dogs and, more likely, humans passed by:

COME NOT HERE IF YOU DO NOT BELONG.

The phrase seemed to mock her, to remind her that she didn't fit in with the vampire world quite in the way that she once had. She sighed again at the idea of fitting in. Fitting *back* in. Her anxiety was such that she'd changed her outfit three times already, from a gown back into fighting gear and then into something that bridged the two styles in an attempt to achieve just the right look for her goal.

She took a deep breath and exhaled slowly, and thought about her purpose. It was to convince Christian and Ryan to give her a chance to exorcise the demons from her past. Her purpose was to make her peers want to forget about what she'd done and to make them believe that the wildness she'd exhibited that fateful night long ago was something that could be controlled.

She hadn't seen Hayden since the night she'd made him. She remembered practically every detail, every word. She remembered lying in his arms, their bodies entwined on the bed. He'd told her he loved her more than anything. He'd told her he couldn't live without her. He'd told her that he'd kill himself if she didn't take him from the human race and make him vampire, if she didn't make them of the same kind. He wanted to marry her; he wanted to live forever.

She'd believed him, though she'd been warned time and again to protect herself from those very words. From the words that would make you forget the one thing you were supposed to remember: Vampires must not turn humans. It was against code. But she'd lost her self-control in the heat of Hayden's words and the lust between them. She'd sunk her fangs deep into his neck. And then she'd lost everything.

Fleur squeezed her eyes shut and tried to focus on the idea that all she could do now was work on reclaiming what she'd lost. And the first step was to walk into that room and show that she was putting the past behind her, that she was capable of taking on the kind of role in the vampire world for which she'd been destined.

The insistent tick of the nearby antique grandfather clock measured time, driving home the fact that the meeting should have been over by now and that they would be adjourning late. But that wasn't unusual. This wasn't the first time she'd come to the war room. But the humiliation her half-brothers had doled out last time was enough to inspire her to be quite sure that she had solid arguments on her side this time.

She knew they would patronize her, try to dissuade her from her "silly" ideas, would tell her to find contentment in the riches being a Dumont vampire could provide and to forget her notions of responsibility.

But Fleur had tried that. It simply wasn't in her nature. If nothing else, she wanted to restore her good name and wipe away the shame that followed her on whispers in corridors, behind fans and between puffs of cigars. She had something to prove, and prove it she would.

Under her breath, she practiced once more. "Christian . . . Ryan . . . I respect the work you've done, but I want . . ." Fleur stopped and frowned. She sounded too weak, too uncertain . . . too whiny. She tried again: "I *should* be more involved in security matters." That was better, anyway. One more time. "I *should*—"

The door opened and the members of the inner circle filed out, giving her odd, surprised glances. Some even looked away, refusing to make eye contact.

Chin up, shoulders back, Fleur slipped into the room as the last participant filed out. Christian and

Ryan still stood by the conference table, leaning over to sign documents. Identical twins, they were nearly indistinguishable with the same black hair and pale features. Those who knew them knew that Ryan was flashier, louder, more the life of the party. Christian was the introvert and that was reflected in his dress and demeanor.

She waited quietly, knowing they could sense a presence in the room. Ryan finally looked up, his expression faltering a little as he saw who it was. "Hello, Fleur."

Christian obviously noticed his brother's tone and looked up as well, rewarding her with the same lack of enthusiasm. "Hello, Fleur," he echoed.

"Hello. I was hoping to have a word with you both." She could have sworn Christian actually cringed. It was the same old thing. She knew they didn't think much of her. She also knew that they feared her a little bit and referred to her in private circles as "the wildcard" for more than one reason. A little fear was good; she just had to be careful about how and when she exploited it.

And it wasn't as if she were trying to take anything from anyone. A power grab would only be destructive for the entire vampire world. Fleur just wanted the opportunity to participate, to serve ... and of course, to clear her name.

"Well, go ahead," Ryan said, still hunched over with his pen in midair.

Fleur wanted to roll her eyes. This wasn't the sort of thing one discussed in between autographs. But if this was as much audience as they'd offer, she'd have to take it. She stepped farther into the room and approached the opposite end of the conference table. "I wanted to first thank you for being so understanding over the last several years . . ." She'd barely managed to start her speech, when already she'd lost their attention.

Lips parted in surprise, eyes looking past her to the windows along the back wall, the two men froze. Fleur felt the chill of fresh, cold air and noted the way the brothers' hair rippled slightly in a curious breeze. Slowly, oh so slowly, she turned and looked over her shoulder.

Something . . . someone had breached the tower in complete silence. Someone who knew where to find the war room. And that someone was just standing there against the backdrop of an open window, surveying the scene.

One of the twins addressed the intercom. "This is Ryan. I'm still in the war room. We have a serious security breach. Human . . . I think. Get forces to man the perimeter of the building, get forces for this floor and outside the room. But nobody comes in here."

Turning all the way around to face the intruder, Fleur braced herself for the possibility that whatever he was doing here, whatever he had planned, it would be the beginning of something terrible. She watched the figure's gaze shift in response to the sound of fingernails against wood. Her brothers must be going for the guns in the holsters affixed under the table.

Backed up against the near end of the table, she was close enough to have a good look at the intruder, at the metal components that seemed to run in metal strips and piping and plates around his neck and radiated down underneath his clothing. He didn't appear to be armed. But that, she knew was because he was himself the weapon. His forearms shone with an overlay of polished titanium, bordered by bolts and probably filled with wireless circuitry. The part of him that was mortal flesh looked real, although almost too handsome to be a real man.

He raised his left arm, and as Fleur took a closer look, she realized with horror that it had been converted into a weapon—it held a cartridge filled with the unmistakable purple-pink glow of ultraviolet fluid.

Fleur's mouth went dry. She had no knowledge of the humans or anyone else successfully—or purposely—developing such a handheld UV weapon, much less using one in the field. "He's got UV."

"Fleur, don't move," Ryan muttered.

"He's got a UV weapon," she said, louder.

"Don't move!"

A gun discharged behind her and the bullet whizzed over her right shoulder. It bounced merrily off the intruder's chest armor and rolled across the wood flooring. The acrid smell of gunpowder floated by, dispersed by the breeze from the open window.

"They've created a mech," she said. "It's a mech."

"Shut up, Fleur!" It was Christian this time, uncharacteristically flustered. Her brothers were scared by what they saw. And they had reason to be. Fleur had heard rumors that the humans were developing something superhuman like this, some sort of creature with mechanical components who could be manipulated like a weapon. They were called mechs, but everyone had become convinced they were nothing more than a rumor meant to create fear among the vampire and the werewolf worlds.

She stood there with the hard edge of the table digging into her back as Christian and Ryan unleashed a hailstorm of bullets around her. Watching them bounce harmlessly off the intruder and roll across the floor like a spilled bag of marbles, Fleur recognized that she was looking at proof that mechs existed. And she was also looking at proof that the humans had not only gone ahead and effectively "bottled" a weapon that could easily kill vampires, but that they were willing to use it.

During the first battle between the species, the battle in which Fleur's own mother had died, the humans had been reactive, disorganized, crude. They had worked hard to broker the truce that was currently in effect—as had the werewolf and vampire leaders. But this . . . this suggested the possibility that the humans now wanted to break their truce and launch a proactive assault on the vampire world. And worse, they had a level of weapon sophistication they had not been known to possess.

Her brothers' weapons spent, the room went completely silent, thin curls of wafting smoke making Fleur tear up. Caught in the middle, she wasn't quite sure how to react. If the intruder wanted to engage in hand-to-hand combat she had some moves in mind. If he wanted to shoot her, there wasn't much she could do. And with her back to her brothers, she couldn't get a read on what they wanted. As it turned out, it didn't matter what they wanted.

The mech cocked his head, almost as if he'd been

humoring them, waiting for the ammunition to run out so those pesky bullets would leave him alone.

"Fleur, I want you to get down on the floor and crawl to the door," Ryan said.

"I can help," Fleur whispered. "I can help you."

"You'll only hurt," Christian said.

It stung, but Fleur recognized this wasn't the time to argue; she slowly knelt on the floor. Pretending to inch her way toward escape, she set her sights on a wall cabinet she hoped still contained some decent explosives.

Christian retreated from the conference table to a work desk at the far end of the room and shouted commands into the intercom, while Ryan reloaded his gun and continued blasting away at the mech. In the reflection of the cabinet glass, Fleur watched him quickly run out of bullets. Her panicked brother then tossed his weapon at the mech, but it fell harmlessly to the ground.

As she snaked one hand up and worked on the cabinet lock, Fleur could hear chaos in the halls just outside. Her hand shook and her sweaty fingers slipped on the locking mechanism. Behind her, Ryan was begging for mercy, pleading for his life.

The mech didn't answer. What was it doing? To no avail, Fleur jiggled the lock, not really caring now how loud she was. She turned one eye to the glass reflection.

The mech took a step forward and looked at Christian, who was standing bolt straight. There was a weighty silence, and then the mech raised its left hand and gracefully curled its fingers. She saw her brother wince as the bullet released from the mechanism fused to the mech's forearm, and actually felt an incongruous moment of calm watching the gorgeous violet tracer.

Christian screamed as the bullet struck his chest. It was a sound unlike anything Fleur had heard before. Blood fountained over his white dress shirt and he crumpled to the ground, still screaming at the top of his lungs. His body twitched and leaped for a moment, then he went completely silent and still.

Ryan stared at his brother in a kind of catatonic state, making no effort to run, to fight, to do anything but accept his fate.

"Run," Fleur whispered hoarsely. She got to her feet and turned to the door, but her half-brother didn't move. "Ryan! You've got to run!"

He didn't. She was nearly to him before the next bullet struck. His blood spattered her face and they fell together. Like Christian, Ryan screamed as the UV bullet penetrated his body. Fleur cradled his head, holding his face in her hands and wanting to soothe his pain. "It's okay, Ryan. You're not alone." But her words of comfort were lost; he died almost instantly, his life extinguished like a flame.

Fleur couldn't quite breathe. Gasping and choking on fear, she looked up at the mech. With his arm still suspended in midair, he surveyed the room as if cataloging its contents and looking for anybody else. Apparently satisfied that only she was left, he cocked his head and studied Fleur.

She swallowed nervously as he reached down to his leg holster. He swept his forearm down and arched it back up in one graceful movement, snapping a new attachment onto its metal rigging. Fleur's heart pounded. So this was what it was like to be at the mercy of a species you didn't fully understand.

Ryan's head still lay in her lap, and drops of his blood tickled her skin as they slid down her face. Fleur stared straight into the mech's intense aquamarine eyes and waited.

Maybe it was only what she wanted to see—in those eyes she was certain she caught a flicker of something alive, something more than just a programmed machine. But when she blinked and looked once more, there was just a dull gaze and a dead presence.

The mech raised his arm in a slow and calculated manner and shot her.

Fleur screamed in surprise and pain then realized he'd shot her with a conventional bullet. She wasn't going to die. She'd have to get some blood back into herself, but . . . Through the pain and the pounding and the roaring in her brain, she could have sworn the mech lowered his weapon and said, "Play dead." Had she misheard?

"What?"

But maybe she'd imagined it. The mech took a step backward, the same shuttered look on his face. Fleur clutched her arm to her chest and let the red blood seep through her fingers, then collapsed in a heap with her eyes closed. She heard a series of clicks and hums, then one last sound: that of a boot on the windowsill, perhaps. Then there was silence.

She was counting to ten when the door burst open. The room was suddenly in chaos, medics rushing in with Warriors and Protectors of the defense force. All at once, as if everyone simultaneously realized what she meant to them now, she felt a million hands come at her, lifting and fussing and protecting and defending . . .

"I'm fine," she whispered, opening her eyes. She sat up so the medics could properly wrap her wound before taking her to the blood banks upstairs.

But then Fleur looked over and saw them cover Christian and Ryan with cloths embroidered with the Dumont crest. The blood banks would have to wait. As if the same thought had occurred to everyone else, they turned their faces to her, one after the next.

Don't lose it. Do not lose it, Fleur. "It didn't get me. I'm fine. It ran out of UV bullets and shot me with a regular one." She shoved all offers of help away and stood up, self-conscious to the extreme. The smell of the blood was making everyone incredibly edgy, and she was no exception.

"The humans did this," someone blurted. "Didn't they? What do we do now?"

Fleur's cousins were now in the room. Marius came forward and whispered into her ear, "This is your moment, but nobody is going to give it to you. You'll have to take it."

She glanced over at the other two. "Take it, Fleur," Warrick mouthed.

Ian nodded. "Take the power."

She opened her mouth to answer, but they stepped away.

Arguments were already flaring about counterattacks, with several members of the other families discussing the transference of power. The medics attended to the bodies of her half-brothers, Fleur's cousins stood in stony silence watching her. Fleur felt in danger of being swallowed up, in danger of just disappearing.

"Wait!" She drew the hair back from her face with

blood-streaked hands. "It appears that the unthinkable has happened . . ." God, how ridiculous this must sound coming out of her mouth. She cleared her throat and turned to start giving orders. "This is what I want done: *You*—advance security measures on all of +1 to the highest level. You—get the defense teams into the skies. We're looking for at least one . . . mech. I'm pretty sure that was a mech. It looks like a human but with mechanical upgrades. It's armed and there could be more of them. If you can't bring it in, collect whatever intelligence you can. The rest of you follow standard emergency procedures and meet me back in this room in one hour."

They stared at her like stone statues. Fleur pointed at the bodies on the floor. "Do you need more convincing than this? Go!"

The room emptied, leaving the ferric smell of blood swirling in the air behind them. And when the medics finally wheeled out the desiccating remains of her half-brothers, Fleur turned to the window from which the mech had escaped, and leapt right through.

Chapter Four

"Where the hell is the audio of this mission? Try again!"

Cyd fiddled with the controls. "I think it's being scrambled." She tried again. "Whoa. The thing took pictures." She punched in her personnel code, frowned, then punched in Dain's. A hyperlink appeared on the screen and, within seconds, pictures of the bodies loaded. They were pictures of an unfamiliar female, and of two vampires Dain recognized as Christian and Ryan Dumont. The photos were time-stamped about five minutes prior.

Dain whistled, then came to a screeching halt in front of Dumont Towers.

"What do we do now?" Cyd asked.

"We wait. Either for I-Ops to give us something useful or for whatever's in there to come out. It's not like the fangs are going to invite us in. They've just been jumped."

"This place is massive," Cyd said, pointing to the compound. Massive was an understatement. Dumont Towers wasn't just one lonely skyscraper. It was a complex of buildings, a one-stop shop for all vampire work, play, and living.

Yes, the vampires comprised most of the cosmopolitan upper-class of Los Angeles these days. Designer clothes, flashy cars, serious jewelry and penthouse living were their hallmarks. They had a seemingly insatiable appetite for luxury, which was actually lucky for the rest of the city. Rather than sating themselves on other species as they had in the past, now they got their food from huge, expensive blood banks. Most of them did, anyway.

Of course, every now and then a body would turn up, indicating the code of conduct the vampires now swore by wasn't infallible. Which was bad, as the truce between the species rested on it. So far, such occurrences had been fairly rare. Dain was more concerned about the number of humans who'd gone missing only to reappear as vampires and werewolves. That wasn't supposed to be happening, either. The increased vampire and werewolf populations in town were becoming uncomfortable, and he'd had the eerie sense for some time that the entire city was approaching a tipping point.

There might even be more turnings than officials were aware of. It wasn't hard for vampires to walk amongst humans undetected. Some filed their fangs down to pass for human when they chose. High-tech protective fabrics and cosmetics could allow them to travel in sunlight, though they rarely took advantage of such scientific advances.

He wondered why. It certainly wasn't a question of cost. Purveyors and consumers of luxury goods, monopolists of art and music, evangelists for bringing the extremes of beauty and style to everyday living, the vampires as a whole could pretty much buy anything. They held power over all the accessories of life in Crimson City; the humans still controlled most of the necessities. Not surprising, the vampires looked upon the other species as beneath them socially, monetarily, and intellectually. And not surprisingly, the werewolves and humans resented them for it.

"Anything yet?" Dain asked, squinting into the dark sky.

"Nope. Still trying to find something."

Dain looked at Cyd. She shrugged. All around them the streets were empty. Silent. Dain stared straight through the windshield into the gloom and knew in his bones that it was too silent.

The dashboard screen flickered and refreshed itself, with the words glowing nice and bright in the dark interior of the car.

MISSION COMPLETE

"Something's not right. Not right at all," Cyd murmured, shifting uncomfortably in her seat. A few seconds passed. "Dain?" she drawled, as if she felt the same sense of disaster sneaking up on them both.

"Cyd?"

"Daaain?" She pointed.

He gripped the steering wheel. "Cyd?" he said again. Then he took a deep breath to clear his head and lowered the driver's-side window to look out and up where she'd indicated. He turned on the vertical night vision strobes installed in the hood of the car. The beams shot straight up into the night.

41

The green strobes swept through the air, flicking left to right.

One pass. Nothing.

Flicking left to right . . . pass two. Nothing.

Flicked left to right . . . pass three . . .

And then, like a slide show when a new image clicks into place, the sky was suddenly filled with vampires.

"Shit!" Both he and Cyd cringed back into their seats. He could feel the fangs' energy—their *angry* energy—in his body.

And then, like a ten-ton weight, something came down on the hood of the car, the weight smashing it into the pavement. The car's headlights crushed instantly and went out. Both Dain and Cyd hit their heads on the roof of the car as it rebounded from the momentum; and when Dain finally looked up next, he was staring into the eyes of a very beautiful, very pissed-off female standing on the hood of his car, the green night vision strobe illuminating her for only seconds at a time.

Dain had his gun out in a flash, pointing it at her through the windshield.

The strobe swept across her body once more, and he realized that her face was spattered with blood and she had a bandage wrapped around her shoulder. No wonder she was so hyped up. Her lips curled away from her teeth. He couldn't tell from where he sat if they were filed or human, but everything else about her screamed vampire. She held a very powerful short-nosed pistol up to the windshield between them, pointing her gun directly at his.

They looked at each other for a moment; Dain's heart pounded in his chest. Though he did his best to remain objective as far as dealing with the fangs in the context of his job, the fact remained: Vampires had killed his wife. And yet, his heart wasn't racing with intense of hate like it should have been. The way she looked at him, this angry creature who echoed Serena's blonde, blue-eyed angel looks—the way they looked at each other, it was almost as if she were staring into his soul.

Dain looked over at Cyd, who was dazed and still holding her forehead. "Stay in the car," he said, "and be ready to back me up."

Slowly, he opened the car door and got out, keeping his weapon trained on the vampire. The fang followed him with her own gun, leaping gracefully off the car to the street with just the open door between them.

"Where is it?" she asked.

"I don't know," Dain said evenly.

Her eyes narrowed. "I think you do. Are there more?"

"I don't know," he repeated. "We just got here." The adhesive on her bandage came undone and a thin line of blood began to trickle down the inside of her arm. Still holding his weapon aimed at her with his right hand, Dain slowly reached out with his left.

The vampire flinched at first, but held her ground. Her lips parted, revealing the tips of her fangs. It seemed as if they both held their breath as Dain extended his arm just a bit more and pressed the loose bandage back against her wounded arm.

When their eyes met again, he could see the surprise there. After a moment, she flipped the safety back on her gun. Dain did the same and, without referencing their actions, they simply put their weapons away.

A gust of wind rippled between them; the vamp looked up into the sky and turned to go as if she'd been beckoned by her people. Looking back over her shoulder at him, she paused, staring; she seemed to be committing Dain's face to memory. As he was hers. Then she bent slightly at the knees and leaped off into the night.

Dain inhaled sharply, stunned. The passenger side door opened and Cyd got out. She cleared her throat. "Nice to know I can still get a rush like that," she said, walking around the car to have a look at the damage. Shaking her head, she delivered a swift kick to the front of the vehicle and the armored bumper clattered to the concrete. Cyd lifted it up, walked around and heaved it into the backseat, then got back in the car. "I guess we know what I'll be doing on lunch hour tomorrow. It's cosmetic, though. Let's go."

Dain settled back into the driver's seat and put the car into drive, wincing at the metallic whine emanating from somewhere in the front. "You remember her from the files?"

Cyd shook her head. "No. Maybe she's a newly made vamp."

He stayed silent for some time, and finally Cyd punched him in the shoulder. "Hey. Snap out of it."

A flickering light indicated an incoming transmission from Internal Operations. "Dain, here," he said as he punched a button.

"It's Bridget. The boss says he'll meet you at the station."

"Already on my way." Dain cut the connection.

Cyd looked at him. "Why do I get the feeling this is the beginning of something big?"

"Either that, or we're just in the middle of something that never really ended." Dain hit the gas and they sped off into the night.

They drove the rest of the way in silence, making good time to the station where Dain turned the car over to Cyd and then made the mistake of walking up to the front doors within sight of tabloid reporter Jillian Cooper. As he reached the entrance, the woman nearly shoved her recording device up his nose in her enthusiasm for getting the story. "Mr. Reston, do you have any comment about the strange activities at Dumont Towers?"

"What activities?" he deadpanned.

"There are rumors that the mechs are real. Can you confirm this?"

"The whats?" he asked, suppressing a smile. He and Jillian had played this game a hundred times before.

Without missing a beat, she asked, "Are we headed for trouble?"

"Could you be more specific?"

Finally she showed signs of frustration, huffing a little before moving on to the next question. "Can you give me a description of the current relationship between human and vampire leadership? Vampire and werewolf leadership? Werewolf and human leader—?"

Dain entered the station, slammed the door in her face, and kept going. He knew Cyd would throw the reporter some crumbs, but she wasn't going to get squat out of him. Mostly because she had the annoying habit of writing stories that were true. If she'd actually been off the mark more or made stuff up like most of her coworkers, he might have been inclined to tell her more. *The Crimson Post* wasn't taken seriously by many people, but it was still better not to give Jillian anything to work with unless he purposely wanted a leak. Cyd was savvy about the media; she'd know what to do.

The station was a flurry of activity, and Dain headed straight for the back. The conference room was much like the man he planned to meet there: a little sterile, with too many straight edges, but with just enough in the way of personal touches to keep things from being too impossible. Richard Kippenham didn't mind going by "Kipp" on more relaxed days, but he was a suit through and through. He sported a head full of salt-and-pepper hair that was probably going to have a lot more salt before the sun came up, and a blue button-down shirt with a tone-on-tone metallic blue tie. The blandness of his gray pinstripe suit relied heavily on a huge college football ring for flash.

If Dain were ever really going to hate a guy, Kipp would have been a contender because of his position. But he was actually a good man. And a damn fine boss, if you had to have one. He trusted Dain and gave him wide berth on the job, and frankly, Dain couldn't have asked for more. Dain owed him a lot.

Kippenham was stalking the room by the windows, looking out into the street, an electronic reader tucked under one arm. He turned as Dain made his way to the empty conference table and said, "I'll get to the point. We didn't send that mech. We did not send a mech to kill those vamp leaders.

46

We didn't send a mech anywhere, for any purpose, at all."

Dain did a double take. "We *didn't* send the mech?" he asked. How was that possible?

"No."

"And yet, we created the mechs and control every single one."

Mechs were classified. The highest security clearance was required to have anything to do with them. And if his bosses hadn't sent out that mech on this assassination job, that meant there was some kind of human double agent—maybe somehow even a vampire or werewolf passing as human—operating with a game plan upon which Dain had no insight.

Kippenham put one hand behind his neck and tried to massage a crick out of it. "Right. So, to put it bluntly, if we don't figure out what happened ASAP, we've got a situation."

"I think we've got a situation either way," Dain said. "You saw the pictures of the dead?"

"Ryan and Christian Dumont. Yeah. But those aren't the pictures that matter anymore. These are." Kippenham slammed the reader down flat on the table the way the vampire beauty had slammed down on Dain's car. And there she was, staring out from the screen in a cycle of slide-show clicks.

Dain whistled and read the caption. "Fleur Dumont? She's the one who dropped in on me and Cyd earlier."

"Definitely not dead," Kipp said. "She was shot in the earlier pics, but the mech must have run out of UV or had a weapons malfunction."

"She's next in line, then?"

"Yeah. Unless they break tradition again, she's up. There's nobody else left who's a direct descendant of these particular Dumonts."

Dain flipped through some more photos, these obviously older. Oddly, none of them looked particularly businesslike. Fleur Dumont shopping in Bel Air. Fleur Dumont heading in for a UV-defense treatment at an expensive Beverly Hills skin specialist. Fleur Dumont slumming it for a dinner in the human strata at a Valley diner that Dain had actually eaten at a couple of times. It all seemed so ridiculous for a Warrior-class vampire of her lineage, he wondered how much of it was staged. "With her bloodline, shouldn't she have been offered the leadership before Christian and Ryan?"

Kippenham shrugged. "They've either been keeping her quiet because she's that important, or because she's nothing more than a pawn. Which brings me to the point. They're going to be pointing fingers right at us. Your job is to explain to her that we want to find out who sent that mech to kill their leaders just as much as they do. Keep tabs on her. Get her to confide in you if you can." He waved a careless hand in the air. "Just don't let the vamps jump to conclusions. This is a perfect opportunity to get inside their heads. We all need to figure out who the real enemy is, and you're our man in the field. Do what you need to do."

The boss tossed him a memory stick, which Dain caught neatly in one hand. "Your copy. We're done. Good luck."

Chapter Five

Two hours before dawn the next night, Dain was about ready to pass out with exhaustion. He'd sent Cyd back out on the streets to see if the dogs knew anything about all this, and had spent the rest of the night in his apartment reviewing field reports. He still had to head back to Dumont Towers for a little powwow with the beauty herself.

He'd double-bolted the doors and locked down the windows in an elevated state of uneasiness, but even in that heightened state he didn't sense the presence of anything—or anybody—unusual before he heard the knock on his living room window. His hand went by reflex for a weapon, but when he turned to look, it was just her, sitting on the windowsill. Waiting for him to let her in.

He unlocked the frame and slid the window up. She lifted her hand, gloved in long leather with emerald gemstone buttons trailing down the wrist, and placed it on his shoulder for leverage. "We haven't been formally introduced. I'm Fleur Dumont," she said, and stepped past him off the windowsill. She turned around and gave him a once-over. Looking down at his T-shirt and fatigue pants, he didn't expect her to be impressed. When her eyes finally landed back on his face, she said, "And you must be Dain Reston."

"The one." He offered his hand for a shake and she accepted it, her gaze resting briefly on the faded scar from the old skin grafts still visible on his lower arms. "Burns," he said, and when she let go, he folded his arms over his chest and changed the subject. "So, how's that shoulder?"

"It's fine, thank you." With a little more edge to her voice she added, "I heal quickly."

"Right." They shared a moment of silence. "So. Here we are. Can I get you anything? Warm beer? Cold takeout?"

"No, thank you," she said, her attention already occupied with a quick inspection of his apartment.

Dain laughed. "Feel free to have a look around." It gave him an opportunity to inspect her. The dark clothing and crimson paint on her lush mouth emphasized her pale, delicate skin. A portion of silky blonde hair peeked out from under a satin top hat carefully pinned to her head at a jaunty angle. A dusting of blue-gray under her eyes indicated Dain wasn't the only one under some pressure in this whole scenario.

Her fitted leather armor was of an expensive cut, trimmed with dark green satin accents; it did a nice job of showing off her slender, fit body. The mandarin collar of her jacket unbuttoned at the very top to reveal an enormous emerald on a choker around her neck. The ensemble was completed by tall combat boots laden with the requisite knives and handguns that everyone seemed to carry these days.

She'd dressed to awe him. Dain had never knowingly hosted a vampire at his apartment, and it was fascinating to see how they used their wealth to manipulate a given situation.

Fleur carefully removed her hat and looked around for somewhere to put it. She chose the coffee table, covered as it was by the evening newspaper and an ugly commemorative paperweight from the last campaign in the war between the species that Kippenham had gifted to the members of every field team, dead serious about it and crazy patriotic as usual. Dain had kept it because it made him laugh.

Settling on the arm of the sofa, Fleur finally gave him her full attention. "You live like a werewolf," she said, curiosity and disdain coloring her voice.

If the upper-crust lilt of her accent got to him, it had to drive the dogs insane.

Dain guessed his place unsettled her with its simplicity, and that she'd anticipated that it would—it was probably why she'd dressed to the limit, with that customary air of converted Victorian elegance in which the vamps liked to indulge when they weren't busy trying to pass as human. Of course, if she'd dressed for an interview with a werewolf, she'd probably have gone further, layering on even more jewels to highlight the class difference between them. As it was, she'd taken pains; her hair was in some sort of complicated updo that looked like it had taken hours to put together, and Dain couldn't help thinking how much he'd love to pull it apart. He also couldn't help but smile at the thought of the contrast she'd make with her elegant, jewel-adorned body lying on his plain white sheets.

"Reston," she said impatiently. "Are you still with me?"

"Can't you read my mind?" he asked.

"If I could, I wouldn't confess to it."

"If you could, you'd be blushing," he said. She'd just given away that she didn't have telepathic powers. Unless she was lying.

Her mouth parted as if she intended a retort, but she closed it again and sauntered over to him. "Well, then. Let's get on with it. Your mech murdered our top two ranking officials. If you wanted to engineer a coup, you did a rather fine job of it."

"We didn't," he said simply.

"That was your mech."

"Yes. But it wasn't sent by our command."

"Are you suggesting it malfunctioned—to such an extent that it climbed more than a hundred stories up the side of a skyscraper and shot the two most important people in our leadership?" Fleur rolled her eyes. "That's rather unlucky. And a bit embarrassing for your research department, to boot."

"I see you had time to read up on all of us."

"At least on you, Reston. You seemed relevant, given that you were at the scene of the crime." She ran a finger along the side of the coffee table, absently staring at the dust before rubbing it between her fingers. "So, you humans didn't send the mech. Hmm. Either you're lying and you sent it, you're not lying and a nonhuman compromised your secret weapon and sent it for you, or you don't know what you're talking about because you're much less informed than your position would suggest."

Dain crossed her arms over his chest, amazed that she'd actually managed to irritate him. "Sure, from your point of view it could be any of those things. But, believe me, I'm as anxious to get to the bottom of this as you are."

She gave him a long look. "You seem rather cavalier about all this. Do you realize what it means?"

"Why don't you tell me?"

"It means that once again we stand on the brink of war. What you tell me here could be extremely important as far as avoiding an immediate escalation." She stared at him.

"Meaning, you are assuming this is a sign of proactive aggression?"

She gave him an incredulous laugh. "Well, it's not as if that mech merely fired a warning shot. The two men he killed certainly wouldn't see it that way."

"Probably not. Interesting fact, though: It didn't manage to kill you."

Fleur's face flamed red, but she held his gaze. "I was lucky."

"Apparently so. I guess this puts you in charge now. Congratulations on your promotion." He gave her a hard look.

"You're a callous bastard," she said almost curiously.

"Thanks. That means I'm doing my job right."

She moistened her lips but didn't shy away. "I don't like talking in circles. Try to imagine how you'd feel if two of your team had just been murdered."

"Fair enough. But if you're already convinced we're behind this, why haven't you attacked? Wreaked revenge? You know, the usual."

"I like to be sure before I endorse catastrophe," she

said dryly. "And you said you humans didn't send the mech."

"That's it? And you believe me?" He laughed, enjoying the fact that it seemed to piss her off. A lot.

"One more time. *Did* you humans send that mech?" she repeated through gritted teeth.

"No. And my job is to figure out who did. I'd like to suggest that, under the circumstances, we try to work together on this."

Her eyebrow went up. "How do you mean, 'work together'?"

"Oh, I don't know. I'm thinking a certain spirit of open-mindedness. Sharing of any leads. Not jumping to conclusions. You get some insight into us humans, I get some insight into you vampires. That sort of thing. It's better than us just getting right to the bloodshed."

She studied his face, then suddenly narrowed her eyes. "I love how you automatically assume we are out for your blood. That's the funny thing about you humans. You'd think by your very name that you own the concept of humanity—goodness, fairness, decency. We could easily use this situation as an excuse for war. All the more reason you should show more appreciation for the restraint my visit represents."

"Well, that's a hell of a speech." And it was, though it was nothing new. The party line was always that the vamps held themselves to a higher standard. Dain knew that the real reason they hadn't attacked wasn't because they feared chaos, war, and everything that went along with it; the real reason was because they feared they'd enjoy it too much.

"Things aren't what they used to be. You humans

have lost much more power than you like to admit. You have nowhere to go but down."

She wasn't entirely off base. Except for one thing. They *all* had nowhere to go but down.

And suddenly he realized that here, underneath a substantial amount of bravado, was a young woman who might be in over her head. She was new at this; he would have known about her much, much earlier if she'd been groomed for this position of power. She'd come to size him up. Talk about home-court advantage. She needed a little shaking up.

"Don't worry," Dain said. "I get where you're coming from. I realize there's nothing more important to you vampires than hanging on to your remaining shreds of humanity. Too bad it's threatened every night by the darkness of your souls."

Fleur's mouth dropped open. "Do you try to be insulting, or does it just come naturally?"

Dain shrugged and flashed his cockiest grin. "I read up on you, too."

"You'd just better watch your step."

It was all the excuse he needed to reach out and grab her, to pull her in close and take her face in his hands. She gasped, and he pressed his thumb hard against her lips, forcing it between her teeth. She could have easily bit down and he'd be out a thumb. Not to mention that spilling any blood would probably make the whole situation even more dangerous. "First of all, if you bite me, it's not exactly going to help your case. It will only make things worse. Second, I don't appreciate it when people come into my home and make threats."

Dain lifted his other hand and wrapped it around her neck, then pushed her up against the wall. He forced her chin up and gripped her jaw until she had to open her mouth. Where her fangs should have been were perfect smooth-edged humanlike incisors. "Filed," he said. "Very pretty."

He thought about Serena and squeezed harder. The photos that dominated his wife's skimpy file showed her body drained of life, two puncture wounds in the side of her neck. Fleur twisted her head away but he forced it back.

"Now I understand you," she said. "Maybe *you're* just trying to pass for human. You live like a werewolf because you act like one."

"Hey, watch your tone, sweetheart. Some of my best friends are werewolves."

"I just bet," she said grimly.

He looked down at his thumb. Her filed-down tooth was still sharp, apparently, for it had cut him. He smeared the crimson tint against her skin. She looked sensual, ravished, and he'd barely touched her, really. He reached up and pulled a long piece of hair out of her carefully arranged updo, mussing it, and let it fall softly against her cheek. She was impossibly pretty.

"You men are all the same," Fleur said. "Don't think you can just swagger about and it means anything. This doesn't impress me."

She was strong, but he'd trapped her arms and clearly had her at a disadvantage. "Oh, but I *can* swagger about, sweetheart. After all, this is my home. Now if you're done making this social call, I have a lot more swaggering planned for the evening and I'd like to get on with it."

He released her and she stepped back, her chest heaving. She picked up her hat and quickly pinned it back on her head, pieces of her glossy hair still falling around her neck. She tried to act casual.

"Let's talk again, shall we? I think you should come to strata plus-one," she said, climbing gracefully onto the windowsill. Dain looked at her suspiciously. It was a rare invitation, to say the least. She turned and looked over her shoulder. "By the way, you might want to get a bandage for that thumb."

"Why, is my blood making you hot?" he purred.

She quirked an eyebrow and gave him a coquettish look. "Oh, absolutely. I'll likely be hounding you forever." She paused. "I'm not your enemy, Dain, but if it turns out you humans sent the mech, I *will* kill you."

He clutched his chest in a most dramatic fashion. "Now you're turning *me* on."

"How lucky. You'll die in the throes of ecstasy," she said. Then she leapt from the windowsill and was gone.

Dain stared out into the blackness, feeling an unfamiliar twinge. She'd be hounding him forever, she'd said. He raised his thumb, still wet from her mouth and his blood.

He couldn't count on forever, but she'd be hounding him for a long, long time.

Chapter Six

Fleur landed one hundred and sixty stories up the side of Dumont Towers on the balcony outside of the war room, and took a moment to compose herself. She wasn't used to humans like that—to anyone like that. People who didn't show respect, who literally manhandled her as if she had common wolf blood or something. There was something a little wild and exciting about it. She might be a good fighter, but she wasn't street smart. Not in the least. That was where her training failed her. She'd been too damn sheltered all this time.

Pressing her hand over her heart, she could feel it still beating madly. The last human who had made her heart race had been her downfall, and this one had her amped up twice as much. Flustered and even a little scared by the unfamiliarity of Dain Reston's behavior, she had to regain her balance. Inside were the Protectors, and she didn't want them to see her come undone.

Her cousins were the people she loved and trusted

most in the world. It wasn't merely because they all shared a sort of blood bond, a result of their Protector status to always watch out for her, defend her, and protect her ever since she was a baby; they could have let the bond lapse if they'd wanted. It was because, outside of Paulina, they were the only ones of the vampire world who had never let their loyalty or love flag, even when she'd done her worst. She'd sworn a long time ago that she'd never disappoint them again. She'd never put them in the position of having to justify to everyone around them that a vampire with a black mark such as herself was still worth believing in.

Taking a deep calming breath, Fleur separated the heavy silk drapes with a flourish and stepped into the room. Marius, Ian and Warrick huddled around a small coffee table in the lounge across the room from the long conference table. "Still hashing out options, are we?" she asked.

"I was about to come after you," Ian said. "When we said you should go talk to Reston . . ." He paused, looking her up and down, and the three brothers shared a look amongst themselves.

"What is it?" Fleur asked. Nobody said a word. She tossed her hat, gloves, and holster onto a side table, walked over and sank into one of the large club chairs beside her cousins. "I think it's going to take a while to figure this out."

After a pause, Warrick asked rather dryly, "He's not dead, is he?"

She looked at him in surprise. "I thought we agreed to try diplomacy first! I mean, why did we spend all that time talking the others out of fighting if you wanted me to kill Reston? Nothing's charged.

If the humans sent that mech, they'll have more. We'll never win a stand-up fight. I . . . What *is* it?" She said at last, noticing her cousin's expressions.

An arched eyebrow from Marius was the only response she got.

"Oh!" Fleur's hand flew up to her hair. She'd forgotten. Reston had rattled her and she'd completely forgotten. She must look like she'd either battled someone . . . or made love. She could still taste Dain Reston's blood on her lips and it made her dizzy to think of his thumb in her mouth. And though she'd sated her thirst prior to paying Reston a call, for exactly that reason, the delicate line she'd walked didn't escape her.

Rising and using the walk back to the side table as an excuse to turn away, she pulled a lace handkerchief from her pocket, wiped the smeared lipstick off her face, and quickly pinned up the loose hair.

"Did *he* hurt *you?*" Marius asked.

"Of course not," she said curtly. "You would have sensed it. We were just playing a game." She kept her face carefully blank.

"Who won?" Ian asked.

To avoid further scrutiny, Fleur didn't go back to her chair, choosing instead to flop down on the plush velvet couch at the other end of the room. Playing with the fringe on the matching copper brocade pillows, she smiled to herself. "We tied. But I daresay I got the last word."

She looked over her shoulder. Her cousins shared another one of those infuriating looks and joined her in the sitting area. Marius steepled his fingers. "And what's the bottom line?"

"Well . . . he's high up in the human heirarchy,

and I think he's telling the truth when he says his bosses didn't send the mech to kill Ryan and Christian. In fact, I think he doesn't know what happened and being in the dark is bothering him."

"Why do you say that?"

"It was just a sense I had. He had nothing to offer as far as information. And I really didn't get the impression that he was holding anything back." She shrugged. "I could be wrong. Still, he suggested we form an alliance on this project."

Ian rolled his eyes. "He wants to form an 'alliance' with you? Are you sure it's about finding information on the mech? What were you doing there, flirting or trying to maintain the peace?"

Fleur sat straight up. "I'm doing the best I can," she said grimly.

"We know," Warrick said. "We know."

Rubbing his temples, Marius leaned forward. "It's very important that we support each other right now. It's bad enough that we've lost Ryan and Christian. Let's not compound it."

Fleur fought back a sudden rush of tears, and nobody said a word as they gave a moment to the men they had just lost.

"Sorry about that comment, Fleur," Ian said, breaking the silence. "Just don't let Reston treat you without respect. Make sure you understand him."

She managed a smile. "I will. I plan on finding out everything he knows. I think that's something I'm capable of doing fairly well—even without the training I missed." She paused. "Look, I know this isn't something we like to think about, but have we been looking into . . . internal possibilities?"

Marius nodded. "But if someone wanted to put

you in charge by killing your brothers, it seems as though they would make themselves known. Try to get something out of it. Has anybody approached you, tried to influence you?"

"Not in the least. It's only been you three and myself since it all started."

"We'll keep our eyes open, but we feel quite sure this was an attack from the outside," Warrick said.

"Does the outside include the rogues?" Fleur asked.

"Of course," Marius said disdainfully. He hated the rogues as much as anyone she knew. "The outside includes anyone who has no allegiance to us. To you. Anyone who is not represented at the Assembly."

"So, we've got humans, rogue vampires, or the dogs," Fleur said.

"My gut says that the humans are lying. It's either that, or the werewolves are smarter than we've given them credit for," Ian said. "It's not a vampire." He gave Fleur an apologetic look. "It's just not likely a vampire would have tried to put you in power. Not after . . ."

Fleur nodded wearily. She knew. She stood up, the night's events suddenly catching up with her. "I'm exhausted. Um, you all know what you're . . . supposed to do, right?"

Ian covered his mouth and started to cough, Warrick snickered, and even Marius looked amused. "We know what we're supposed to do. Protect you and the rest of the Assembly families. And protect ourselves from ourselves."

"Right. Good. Well, I'll just go to bed." She waved. "Good night, gentlemen. See you tomorrow."

She'd gotten two steps out of the room when Marius caught up with her. "Fleur, are you all right?"

"Of course. I'm fine. It's all very new, but I'm fine."

"This is a dangerous business. The humans headed down a slippery slope with those mechs, one that's not good for anybody."

Fleur leaned against the hallway wall. "You said the same when we discovered they'd toyed with the demon underworld. Nothing came of that."

"Nothing we know of."

She just shook her head. "I still think we should have told the humans there's a possibility of demons finding their way here."

"Keep it to yourself, Fleur. We've got more immediate concerns."

"I know. It's not really relevant to the mech situation, anyway." Fleur studied Marius's face for a moment. He looked particularly dangerous tonight, and she wondered if he'd been out.

"I don't think that mech's actions were any sort of accident. Then again, I don't think humans are even prepared for what they create. Fleur . . ." Marius suddenly hesitated, looking grave and tired.

She sighed. "Say it. You know I hate it when you don't say what's on your mind. Go ahead and say it."

"I wonder if you're really ready for this. And I feel that I'm largely responsible. We didn't think this would happen. Our mission is to protect our kind, most of all those who lead the Assembly. Not only did we fail Ryan and Christian, but we have failed by not preparing you. Nothing's impossible. We should have been ready for the chance that you would be called into service."

She looked at him fondly. "You can't blame your-self for me!"

He frowned, rubbing his temple as if he'd like to erase from his mind what was bothering him. "You've not been fully trained. You should have been in on all the war room meetings for years before trying to take on this sort of responsibility. It's too much, too soon."

"Well, baptism by fire, then," she said lightly. Why were they repeating all their fears? It was time to do, not to worry. "Look, I know everyone is gossiping about me downstairs and throughout the strata for that matter, but the fact is that I'm it—I'm the one this responsibility has fallen to. And until someone can come up with a more deserving replacement, I'll serve."

"Like your mother before you . . . ," he said softly. "I can't bear to see you likewise destroyed."

"Save the sentimentality for the women you're trying to woo," she said. Looking for a change of subject she added, "There has been somebody recently, hasn't there?" She gave him a small smile.

"Let's not go there," he said, rather more grimly than she'd expected.

"Again? You picked someone who isn't a vampire *again?*" She rolled her eyes.

"It's not something one controls," he said. "Not in my case anyway."

"I'm sorry."

He shrugged. "We've got bigger problems to worry about."

"Well, don't worry about me. I don't want to see myself destroyed, either. And I'll do my best to prevent it for all of us."

He nodded and turned away.

Fleur returned to her bedroom, closed the door and slumped heavily against the wall. Good god, this business was exhausting. She made it to her bed and flopped backwards on it. Her hand crept to the gem at her throat.

"Shit." She forced the word out through her locked jaw. Fear was welling up inside of her. "Shit! I have absolutely no idea how to pull this off," she said into her pillow. "You are not going to cry, Fleur. You are *not* going to cry."

She wished her mother was there. This was all too much. Her cousins didn't believe in her, she had the fate of her people in her hands and, well, then there was Dain. She didn't want it to happen again. She couldn't let it. Not with a human. Not with Dain Reston. The immediate attraction she'd felt for him was all wrong. It had to be.

She thought of the strong line of his jaw, his lean, muscular build. . . . Under that street armor, under the roughness, he'd looked like a god. Did vampires like herself believe in myths like human gods? Green eyes flecked with copper shouldn't be so disarming, but the intensity of Dain's gaze had bored straight through her. And the way Reston touched her, the way he'd handled her as if he had a right . . . it excited her in a way she couldn't remember ever feeling. The thought of Dain taking her face in his hands, pressing his lips down on hers—there was no innocence with this man. Just that one image, that one moment, that one sensation. And thinking about it made her burn.

Fleur wrapped the sheets around her taut body and turned her face into her pillow. She'd made love to a human before, and so she could imagine what it would be like with this one, so bent on dominating her, body and mind.

Truth be told, he'd nearly finished her in his apartment. She'd nearly come undone. Being human, he probably hadn't felt half of what she had; but standing in his grasp or across the room, she had felt his desire, and it too had been powerful.

But Fleur would not be brought down by passion again. Dain Reston wouldn't be another Hayden. She wouldn't let him.

She returned her thoughts to the crisis at hand, pulled her fear back with a few deep breaths. Fear was what her cousins and the Assembly expected— fear and incompetence. The mech hadn't managed to kill her, Dain Reston had said; and while she'd told him she was lucky, that wasn't it. She obviously wasn't considered a threat. She wasn't strong enough or important enough to kill.

It was time to prove everyone wrong.

Chapter Seven

Cyd stood before the stucco wall of the station, idly tracing a graffiti tag with her fingertip. Two paper sacks lay at her feet. She looked up as Dain came down the steps, and gave him one of those chin nods requiring as little energy as possible to execute. She hadn't bothered to check in, but he'd seen her from the window and swiped her ID card for her.

"You seen your shrink lately?" he asked by way of hello.

She gave him a withering look. "Have *you?*" she asked pointedly.

Dain crossed his arms over his chest. "No. But then again, I'm not the one with the shakes," he said, gesturing. Her fingers, resting on the outline of garish neon pink paint, were trembling.

She pulled her hand away and turned to lean her body against the wall. "Maybe I was just caught off guard by having a vampire slam down on the hood of my car."

"Something wrong, Cyd?" he asked. "I'm just looking out for you."

Something in her expression softened. "I'm fine." She cleared her throat. "So, what's she like?"

"Who?"

Cyd gave him a look. "Downloaded your report from home this morning. You don't believe I actually read your reports, do you?"

Dain looked at her and grinned. "I don't always read yours."

Cyd rolled her eyes. "So . . . what's she like?"

Dain chuckled.

"Really?" Cyd drawled. "Oh, shit. Here we go."

Dain just kept grinning. "I liked her. In fact, I've got a meeting scheduled with her in Strata plus-one."

His partner did a double take. "You're supposed to hate vampires," she blurted.

"What do you mean 'supposed to'? As far as I'm concerned, everybody gets a fair shake. It's in the job description." Her words made him feel slightly uncomfortable. Dain still seemed to be caught between what he wanted to feel and what he really did. He'd never admit it to anyone but, without remembering so much of what the love between he and Serena had felt like, he still felt a sense of loss. It was much harder to feel the intensity, the will for vengeance, that he knew he should have. Loss and loneliness and a longing for a wife he didn't even know anymore—that's what he felt most of the time. Unlike when he'd stood a hair's breadth away from Fleur last night, when he'd felt a lot of other things. After she'd left, he taken out an old photograph of Serena, a little stunned at the resemblance between the two women. Apparently, he had a type.

". . . and it's not like I'm surprised," Cyd was saying. "You always like what you can't have."

"Who says I can't have her?"

With a snort, Cyd peeled herself off the wall, grabbed the paper sacks and headed toward a squad car. "Do we need to have that discussion about which body part you need to be thinking with on the job?" she asked as they settled in.

"We haven't had to have that discussion for a long, long time, have we?" He grabbed a sack. "Breakfast burritos?" he asked hopefully.

Cy nodded and took the other. "I was in the mood. Thank god they serve them twenty-four hours here. You know, out in the sticks you can only get them in the morning. OJ?" she offered.

"Yeah." He slid the dry-ice canister from the slots between the two front seats and tossed it in the well by Cyd's feet. Then he stuck their two metal juice cans in the empty slots. " 'Course, when I'm off the job, which body parts I use are my own business."

"Not if you're going to get them bitten off by vamp girl."

Dain winced, and reflexively moved his bag over the body part in question. "Damn, Cyd. Don't hold back or anything." He sniffed his burrito and grimaced.

She caught the look, sniffed her own burrito, shrugged, and swapped her sausage for his ham and cheese.

Dain bit into the sausage egg burrito and, with his mouth half-full, asked: "You jealous?" It didn't seem likely.

Cyd choked and made a point of downing half of her orange juice in one swig. "I spend more time with you than any other living being, human or otherwise. Should I be jealous?"

Dain downed all of his OJ. "Not yet," he said with a wink, then crushed the can against his forehead.

He'd hoped to a elicit a disgusted look, but Cyd only gave a shake of her head and a laugh. "Whatever," she said. "Look, you won't need the car until the afternoon. How about I take it and drop you off. I'll pick you up when you're ready to go out to the base."

"Are you planning to go out to the base with me?"

"Yeah."

He shrugged. "Okay. Your call."

They switched seats and Cyd drove him to the taxi depot. Dain got out of the car and leaned in through the open window. "I'll just be a couple of hours at most. I'll call your comm."

"Be good," Cyd called as she peeled back out into traffic.

Dain took a sky taxi to the rooftop of Dumont Towers, straight to the helicopter pad. It didn't escape his notice that Fleur hadn't simply invited him to meet her at the ground-level doors. When the taxi landed, she was already waiting for him, looking as sharp and as carefully attired as the last time he'd seen her. This time she held a large leather bag.

"I'm a little disappointed with all this," Dain said. "I figured you might fly me around yourself."

"That's a little too personal," Fleur responded.

He arched an eyebrow. "You afraid to get too close?"

She smiled wide, purposely letting her fangs show. "Aren't you?" She checked her watch and looked up into the sky. "Here we are."

A helicopter with the Dumont crest emblazoned on the side landed on the pad. The pilot waved them forward.

"Ready?" Fleur asked.

"Ready."

"Watch your head." They ran across the landing pad and slipped into the transport under the whirr of the propellers.

"We're not going far," Fleur shouted, handing Dain a headset. He slipped it on and the nimble helicopter took off immediately, whipping around in an arc and setting off in the direction of Beverly Hills.

The dropoff came not five minutes later, high above Rodeo Drive on a rooftop with no visible protective fencing, just a length of red velvet rope encircling the pavement to indicate the landing target. Fleur and Dain disembarked and ran to the safety area outside the circle, Fleur stopping for a passing word with a redhead in a lowcut party dress who waved to the pilot to hold his position.

The amused glance of Fleur's friend was nothing compared to the expressions of surprise and disdain on the faces of the other vampires who passed them. Dain ignored them and stepped toward the edge of the rooftop. His pulse raced as he swayed over the city. No safety netting, no security measures. There was nothing to stop a human from hurtling off the side to his death.

Strata +1 at its finest.

The unusually high bird's-eye view made it difficult for Dain to get his bearings at first. He looked for the landmarks, but they were hard to see; the shapes of the buildings weren't obvious in the dark and the lights from the city below were surprisingly dim. Entirely new marketing directed at the vampires cluttered the sides of buildings and were embedded on rooftops like giant television screens projecting upwards into the sky.

"Not what you thought?" Fleur asked.

"I've been to the bottom of your strata, but never this high."

She pointed to a set of colored lights dotting the four corners of just about every rooftop. "Think of that building as a sort of hub. Treat it like a compass, and think of the directional lines as similar to subway lines." Fleur swept her arm. "Like the red line there. It passes from the hub along that red line of lights."

They stood on the roof for a few more minutes, then Fleur directed him to a walkway that reached across to an adjacent building. Through the windows beyond he could see some kind of restaurant. She gestured for Dain to proceed and he started out over the city, noticing several of these casually stationed paths suspended from nearby buildings.

The walkways were ridiculously thin, like one lane zip-lines that were likely used for moments when the fangs didn't want to expend the energy to suspend themselves in the air. As Dain picked his way across, he noticed it was also particularly convenient for discouraging the presence of other species; he wasn't the type to balk from high-risk activities, but one misstep on these walkways and his mortality would definitely be showing.

Fleur led Dain through a door on the side of the building and, once they were inside, it was as he'd guessed; a bustling dining establishment dripping with massive crystal chandeliers and huge Limoges vases spilling forth freshly cut hothouse flowers. Within seconds of being seated at an emerald silk tufted booth, a gloved steward wheeled out a lacquered cart filled with bottles of champagne nestled into crushed ice.

"The usual, Miss Dumont?"

"Please."

Dain looked around while the steward opened the bottle. The men wore tuxedos, the women, simple dresses in rich, jewel-toned fabrics. And diamonds. They wore diamonds to dine though this was obviously just an ordinary midnight meal. "What is this place?"

"A caviar bar," Fleur said with a careless shrug. "Would you care for some . . . or just champagne?"

"Champagne's fine." Dain shifted uncomfortably in his chair and looked out the window. This high up, the view was pure midnight blue; there was only a twinkling of dimmed lights from the lowlight advertisements and marquee signs below.

The steward poured two flutes and left the remainder of the champagne in a small silver ice bucket. Dain turned the bottle and looked at the label. He raised an eyebrow at the vintage but Fleur didn't seem particularly concerned with price; she probably had a drink here every day.

She leaned over the table, the spicy scent of her perfume wafting under his nose. With the corner of her mouth turned up in a mischievous grin she asked, "Are you quite comfortable, Reston? Really, I thought you would get a kick out of this, but we can go if you prefer."

"I'm fine."

"I see." Fleur stared into his eyes, then let her gaze drop to his neck. He could feel his pulse beating there.

In truth, he was feeling pretty overwhelmed. Surrounded by vampires and completely isolated from his own kind, Dain wasn't fine. After all, these were the people who'd killed his wife. His adrenaline had kicked in, and he was sure the blood rushing through his body wasn't unnoticed by Fleur. Watching her stare at his neck, he had to wonder about her natural blood hunger. Everybody had a breaking point.

"Don't be nervous," Fleur said.

"I'm not nervous."

Her glance flicked to the tabletop. Tiny flecks of gold paper littered the surface. Dain hadn't even realized he'd been shredding the label off the champagne bottle.

"That's habit, not nerves," he said. Why was she trying to put him at ease? He nodded to a couple of vampires dressed to the nines heading out the door. "Is this how you live all the time? Ever have the urge to put on a T-shirt and a pair of sweatpants and just go to a burger joint?"

"Maybe. But don't pretend this isn't better. Haven't you ever had the urge to live like a prince?"

"Maybe," he admitted. "But I prefer not to have to live according to a bunch of silly expectations, either."

She rolled her eyes. "Every stratum has expectations. So . . . let me get to know you. What do you actually like?"

Dain laughed in surprise. "What do I like? Hell, I don't know. I like dancing in the rain and long walks in the park holding hands. How's that?"

"Useless lies," she said. "Though in all honesty, *I*

will admit to sneaking into the human stratum once just to smell the flowers. I suppose that counts as a long walk in the park."

"Have you ever eaten French fries?" he asked.

Fleur gave a delicate snort. "No. Fois gras?"

"God, no. Gone to the batting cages?"

"Of course not. Do you fence?" she asked. "And do you prefer saber or epee?"

"Neither. Fencing is for wimps. I prefer a weapon more like this." Dain took a severe-looking dagger out of his boot and laid it on the table.

"Oh, my. That's rather large," Fleur said in mock-horror. She looked amused. Reaching down under the table, she came back up with a knife twice the size of his. "I prefer something more like this."

They both started laughing.

Dain caught his breath. "Favorite color?" he asked.

"Red, of course," she said coquettishly. "You?"

"Black. Favorite comic book hero?"

"Easy one. Dr. Jean Gray. You?"

Dain stopped smiling. He couldn't remember reading any comic books; the old memory banks completely failed him on that one. He stared down at the table and could feel her sense the change in his mood. The lightness between them slipped away. He looked up, moistened his lips and asked, "Have you ever killed a human?"

Fleur looked at him in surprise. "That's a rather personal question."

"I know."

"Please don't ask a question you wouldn't answer yourself."

"I've killed a human," Dain said, staring at her

intently. "Several. On the job. Most of them deserved it."

Fleur seemed to need a moment to process his statement. "I have never killed a human," she finally said. "But I have taken one's soul."

It wasn't quite the answer he'd expected. Flustered, he leaned forward for clarification. "You've . . . ?" Then, realizing what she'd just admitted, he leaned back into the booth as far from her as he could get.

Fleur chewed the corner of her lip and looked away. "Yes. I made a human, vampire. It was an accident and a mistake. I regret it, and I've apologized for it."

Dain swallowed. "That's big of you."

She gave him a stony look. "Don't be a bastard. I was very young. It was horrible. And I don't intend to ever let it happen again."

"Can you help it?" He couldn't help a sort of morbid fascination.

"Of course I can help it," she said quickly. Perhaps a little too quickly. "Believe me, self-control has been an obsession of mine ever since."

"What happened?"

She took a long sip of champagne, obviously stalling. She put the crystal flute down and looked like she was about to signal the waiter, but Dain wasn't willing to let the matter go.

"What happened?" he repeated. "I need to know that I have nothing to worry about from you. I'm sure you can sympathize."

"I'd rather not talk about the specifics." Fleur gave him a pointed look. "I'm sure *you* can sympathize, having killed, yourself. But know this. While the bloodlust is unpredictable and very powerful when it hits, consider that I was young and not skilled in the art of controlling it." She looked into Dain's eyes. "I thought I was in love. I was just . . . completely swept away."

"Passion," he said.

"I'd never felt anything like it before, and I haven't since. Of course—" She reached over the table and grabbed him by the throat, mimicking how he'd handled her on his turf in the Triangle. There was a smile on her face, and she was obviously trying to make a joke, but he could feel her fingers run along the pulsing vein in his neck. "—if you play with fire, you should expect to get burned."

More unsettled than he cared to reveal, Dain dislodged her hand with a laugh. Likewise trying to keep things light even as the tension built inside him, he said. "Fire? I don't carry matches around anymore. You'll have to ask my partner."

Fleur leaned back against her side of the booth, pressed her finger into the gold paper flakes on the table until they stuck to her skin. She shrugged. "Fair enough. Anyway, we're not here to play games."

Dain nodded. At last; maybe he was going to get some information. "What *are* we here for?"

Fleur reached into the bag beside her on the seat, and pulled out a fairly wide black leather zippered case upon which her initials were stamped in gold. She laid the case on the table and unzipped it, producing a thick ream of files. Her hand hesitated for a moment, but only for a moment, and she flipped the case around toward Dain.

One glance told him these were intelligence files.

He held his palm up. "You can show me yours, but don't expect me to show you mine."

She gave him an amused look, then shrugged.

He paged through the files. "These are werewolf cases."

"They always claim we make these things up to turn the humans against them. I wanted you to understand that we have our reasons."

"Okay. So these appear—and I say *appear*, because I'm not ruling out the possibility of photo-doctoring—to be crimes against humans by were-wolves. The bodies aren't desiccating the way vampires do, and the wounds seem consistent with the usual dog M.O. What does this have to do with the deaths of your brothers?"

"They don't." She shoved the files away, and Dain was tempted to ask for them back, just to have time to look over the vampires' methods of analysis. "These are from long ago, but they show you the danger of the city. They show you how no one tells the truth. How no one works together. We could have given you this info a long time ago . . . but we didn't.

"What do you think this is about?" Fleur continued. She gestured around her, and then to them. "I bring you up here to strata plus-one. Out in the open for everyone to see, and I don't even try to dress you to pass. You walk as a human, completely safe under my watch, with my name on the line. You ask me very personal questions, and I actually answer you honestly. Then I show you classified documents."

He stayed silent and Fleur finally cocked her head to one side. "It's about trust, Dain Reston. I want us to be able to trust each other."

Trust. Dain studied her face. She was serious. And he wanted to believe her. "We forgot to toast when we drank," he said, and raised his glass. "To a new partnership. To trust."

"Trust," Fleur echoed, tipping her flute into his. The crystal sang out sweetly.

Chapter Eight

Dain called Cyd on his comm from the helicopter pad. He waited back at ground level in front of Dumont Towers for about fifteen minutes more until she finally drove up. Without giving it a second thought, she relinquished the driver's seat and settled into the passenger side.

She looked tense and withdrawn, her relatively sunny mood of earlier gone.

"Like I said, you don't have to go with me to the base," Dain said.

"They start asking questions when I'm not behaving in a partnerlike manner. Let's just go."

He nodded. "Fine. If you start . . . if you start . . . getting—"

"Weird?"

He heaved a sigh. "Yeah, if you start getting 'weird,' just give me the say-so and we'll figure something out."

She turned her face away and that was clearly an

end to the discussion. That was as much as they ever spoke about it.

Dain hit the road and they took the freeway out of the center of the city, driving in their usual companionable silence. It gave him time to think about Fleur Dumont. Dain didn't get too worked up about keeping personal things personal and business business. Life just wasn't that black and white. Personal relationships were what made business work much of the time.

Of course, that was generally the case when two humans were involved. If you started talking about having a personal relationship with a vampire or a werewolf, things weren't so clear cut. Cyd had it half-right. It wasn't that he couldn't have Fleur Dumont that added to her mystique; it was that he shouldn't.

As if on cue, Cyd muttered a string of obscenities under her breath as they pulled into the parking lot by the front gate of the base. In contrast to the dark, vertical gloom of the inner city, the base sparkled almost obscenely clean and bright. It had an aura of daylight, even at night, and was of course calculated to have that effect, being a sort of intentional psychological statement about the inherent differences between Crimson City's species.

Yes, the place was a mass of glass and white stucco, washed over and over to maintain its pristine appearance. It wasn't as if the night species would have trouble locating the place in the dark, so the idea seemed to be flaunting brightness in a kind of power play. During emergencies when the citywide UV lights went on, the white buildings of the base shone like neon beacons through the night, and what looked at first glance like decorative metal piping was actually tubing filled with liquid silver. A web of red security lasers completed the picture.

It was a glittering, gleaming, blinking mass of human will built up out of the wasteland of the California desert surrounding the LAX airport. Dain hadn't been to Vegas lately, but he'd heard the newest casino was a warped facsimile of this place, cocktail waitresses in camouflage miniskirts and drinks named after the different divisions.

Dain and Cyd alike blinked in the blazing light. He might be human, but when one spent as much time riding around in the darkness as they did, it was not an easy adjustment to make. And as they went through a plethora of security checks at the front gate, Cyd seemed to be having trouble adjusting to anything. She was taking deep, calming breaths, but there was nothing else calm about her. He didn't dare make the mistake of asking if she was okay.

It was funny. He didn't feel the way Cyd did about visiting the base. Dain actually felt a sense of comfort here, of order, of things being under control. Sometimes having parameters was a good thing, and the base had those in spades: parameters for behavior on and off the job, parameters for interacting with others, parameters for handling other species. Of course, he chose to ignore half of them under the construct that knowing the rules meant you could figure out how to effectively break them. And really, though he wouldn't have admitted it to anyone, Dain had the sense that joining the security team had saved his life, maybe even his soul. Having a framework kept him in check, for his past was becoming more and more of a blur.

It had always seemed odd that he'd managed to climb as high as he had in his current job with such a shady past. They'd certainly discussed that past during the interview process. He was impressed with what they'd managed to dig up, and by the time he'd finished, he was sure they'd only recruit him as a bruiser, someone to pummel confessions out of reluctant criminals or to delete those without good enough information to trade. But somehow they'd seen his potential. And for that he was truly grateful. It was why he still clocked in on time every night— and why he made a point to visit the base every so often, even without any official business.

What he couldn't explain was why he hadn't just up and signed with Internal Ops out here. They'd offered for him. More money. Even better housing. But he knew that no suit, no fancy house, and no money could really make him fit in. Having a purpose, having parameters, having responsibility . . . these things "took." But he'd never be like the white knights out here in Internal Ops. And he wished he could figure out why.

Why hadn't he been able to completely shake the darkness that he'd been slowly erasing from his memory over the last decade? It seemed that there was a certain amount of accumulated darkness in a person that just would never go away. And that was something with which, frankly, Dain had not yet come to terms.

In the reception area, Cyd fixated on Bridget Rothschild's face. Perfect white teeth, flawless ivory skin.

She'd once been that young, that fresh . . . that clean. While Dain signed them in and plugged the security chips into their comm packs, Cyd's mind started to wander down memory lane, a place she visited too often for her taste. Funny how things worked out. Dain would have given just about anything to remember his past; she would have given just about anything to erase her own. It wasn't clear which one of them had it better.

"Cyd? I know you haven't eaten breakfast. Do you want me to meet you in the cafeteria when I'm done?" Dain asked. He saw she was going "weird" and was giving her an out as usual. It was a miracle he hadn't gotten in trouble over her by now.

"Yeah. That would be great."

Bridget smiled and Cyd had to suppress the urge to tell her to wipe the smile off her face. She felt ugly and hard next to the girl, though they couldn't have been that far apart in age. She remembered sitting in that chair on rotation, fresh out of college. That's how it was. You worked the front desk and the commissary and basically a bunch of shit jobs while you studied for placement exams and received training.

Cyd also remembered sharing a pleasant little apartment with a couple of other trainees. And she remembered putting makeup on in the morning, carefully choosing which shoes to wear with her outfit, and curling the ends of her hair, anxious to make as good an impression in person as she did on paper. She'd finished training at the top of her class. She'd earned the right to choose her career slot before everyone else.

She would have been better off partying with the underachievers.

A tiny furrow of confusion appeared on Bridget's brow as Cyd continued to stare at her. "Do you want me to show you where the cafeteria is?" she asked hesitantly.

Cyd managed a chuckle. Sometimes it was kind of fun being known as half off her rocker; there was a certain power that went along with it. "Thanks, Bridget. But I remember."

She'd managed to avoid this place for eight months. And prior to that she'd squeaked by with just one meeting in the large conference room adjacent to the entry. She hadn't been this far inside since the day she'd transferred out of Internal Ops. At the end of the hallway was a planter filled with genetically engineered miniature palm trees. They smelled like suntan lotion, fresh air, and the beach. The engineers were getting better—there was a lack of the chemical after-scent that had attended the versions she'd seen before.

The cafeteria was to the right. And though every fiber of her being wanted to go there, to simply turn right and get a cup of coffee and wait the visit out, Cyd found that she couldn't help but turn left instead.

In the hall, she passed a couple of people she didn't recognize. Their eyes passed over her street attire and then flicked down to the comm device clipped to her waist before flashing her a tight, polite professional smile and continuing on. *If the light's blue, let 'em through. If it's red, shoot 'em dead.* That's what they used to say.

Her light was blue, of course. And even if one of the trainees in the security booth recognized her face, they probably wouldn't know enough about her story to know that it was a strange thing for Cydney

Brighton to intentionally walk back through the double doors of the Department of Paranormal Research & Development down the hall to a faded black door labeled "cleaning supplies," through that closet, and out the back into the lab for demon research.

It was absolutely empty, a far cry from the bustle and wonder and excitement that had filled the small lab when she'd worked there. A layer of dust covered the books in the small library, some of which were still open. A row of Bunsen burners, chemical testers, and forensics equipment were still plugged in. Monitors, digital equipment. Broken glass from test tubes that had rolled off the counter crunched under Cyd's feet. It surprised her that no one had either cleaned out or barricaded the place. It just looked like the entire team had gotten up to go to lunch one day and never come back.

Her own desk was still there—some of her old things, too. Sweating, her heart suddenly racing as the memories came flooding back, Cyd approached her old work space. She sat down on the chair and slowly, slowly pulled open the top desk drawer.

And that was all it took to trigger a full-blown panic attack. Her hand shaking and her nose running, Cyd managed to reach into the cargo pocket at her thigh. She pulled out a small capsule, popped the top, and clamped the point into the crook of her arm. Only then was she able to handle looking through the past.

Chapter Nine

Dain hopped in one of the smartcars parked in the narrow slots by the side door; the mech facility wasn't far but time would be sucked up by the many required security clearances. As he drove down the paved path, the pristine white of the central building faded to a dull olive. The materials here were less sophisticated, though the security was higher. Lasers and metal bars crisscrossed every window, every doorway.

Three retinal scans, two blood pricks, and a DNA mouth swab later, Dain was finally granted entrance to the barracks. He had no idea how many mechs there were here. Even the task force charged with determining when and how to use the things weren't given such information. He looked down the rows of the buildings but couldn't tell how many were actually used. He looked down at the card handed to him by the clerk at the fourth line of security, and headed for Barracks C, Bunk 14.

A sign on the barracks door said, "Disable all electronic devices." Some of the mechs had delicate wireless instruments imbedded in their bodies. This was a precaution against interference from other signals. Dain switched off his comm and opened the door.

An eerie silence greeted him, though the room was full of mechs readying themselves for some kind of workout. He nodded in greeting, careful not to reflect the too-cheerful mode probably adopted by most bureaucrats who came through on a look-see. He didn't want that kind of association. Sure, the mechs wouldn't care. They were carefully programmed and, if it were even possible, any thoughts, feelings or memories they'd accumulate over the course of a month, maybe even a week, were surely removed. But somehow, while Dain didn't think of himself as the touchy-feely sort, the possibility that these man-machines might understand somewhere deep inside and be more aware than most people believed—well, somehow that haunted him.

Maybe it seemed likely because they weren't all the same. They weren't identical, and from a visual point of view looked as though they could each have a distinct personality. The mechanical enhancements weren't the same for every mech, either. Some had faceplates, some had weaponry built into their arms and legs, some had panels with circuitry built into their backs, and some had hands so tricked out with metal they looked like gloves. And Dain figured that if you couldn't guarantee identical and consistent duplication of something, you couldn't be sure of what you were creating.

He headed to bunk fourteen. The cot was perfectly made . . . as were they all. Dain turned to the mech changing into gym shorts at bunk fifteen and gestured to the bank of lockers. "This the missing mech's stuff?"

The mech came to attention and stared straight ahead, a dead, vacant look in his eyes. "Sir, I cannot respond to questions without an associated case number, sir!"

Dain looked at the mech, surveyed the chiseled appearance of his face and body. Must have had a female designer. He glanced around the barracks. Each mech had a different but equally impressive body.

He nodded slowly. "As you were," he commanded. The mech fell out of stance and finished changing.

Though there were at least forty mechs in the room changing, complete and total silence fell. "I'm going to have a look at the locker," Dain said to no one in particular. He took out his small forensics kit and painted his hands with sterilized liquid latex. Then he dusted the surface area of the missing mech's innocuous dull metal locker, tucking swab samples into his kit for later review. Someone had been here already. He looked back over his shoulder. Not one of the mechs was watching or showing any sign of interest.

He finished on the outside and opened the locker. It was completely empty. He dusted up and swabbed the inside, then examined the locker's structure. Nothing. Looking over his shoulder, he watched some of the mechs silently file out of the barracks. The one at bunk sixteen was still tying up what looked like specialized boxing shoes. The metal embedded in his thighs and lower legs glinting in the dimly lit room.

Dain closed the locker and moved back to bunk fourteen. "Uh . . . I'm going to have to take this apart," he said gently, nonplussed by the amount of sympathy he was feeling for something he knew had no trace of human nature left. The mech from bunk sixteen froze and looked at Dain as if it were running a program to process if his statement was some kind of new command.

"As you were," Dain said, as the mech started to stand. "I'm just gonna . . . Right." He turned back to bed fourteen and took fiber samples of what was clearly pristine bedding. Then he noticed the hairline fracture in one of the bed posts. He removed the top of the bedpost and looked into the hollow tube. It was packed, absolutely packed, with scraps of paper. Scraps of blank, white paper. Dain fought off a strange sense of vertigo; he obviously hadn't been getting enough sleep. He emptied the paper into a plastic bag and stuffed it into his kit.

After one last look around, he exited the barracks and hopped back into the smartcar. While driving, he switched his comm back on, doing a double take at the number of messages that had suddenly cropped up. He immediately dialed in. "B-Ops, this is Dain. What's going on?"

JB's voice came on the line. "Things are getting pretty hairy here, man. We've got dead vamps turning up all over the place . . . and one very, very beautiful vampire girl trying to reach you."

"Is she at the station?"

"No, she asked you to meet her at—hey, can someone turn the screen a little? Thanks. Okay, the coordinates are 45 degrees south, 16 north-northwest. Strata zero."

Dain whistled. "That's human territory."

"Yeah. It's gettin' hot in here, 'cause that's not all. After the girl called, we started getting reports in from all over the Westside. The fangs may have retaliated."

"You're kidding. You're talking humans? The vamps have started killing humans out in the open?"

"I don't know any of the details, but that's what it looks like. Fair is fair, I guess. I mean, if we're killing them out in the open. . . ."

Dain hoped that wasn't the case. He hoped this wasn't the beginning of an actual war. Had Fleur decided humans were to blame for her brothers' deaths? Had her people attacked? "Shit. Tell the station clerk I'm heading out to the Westside first, and I'll go meet Dumont after."

"You got it."

Dain disconnected and sped toward the main building where he dumped the smartcar and high-tailed it on foot. A quick tour of the cafeteria produced no Cyd, but he found her at the front desk, where Bridget was paging his comm in a frantic voice, even as he headed up.

"Your station's been trying to reach you," she said. "And Cyd's . . . right here."

"No worries. I got the message. Thanks."

He took one look at Cyd, standing there covered in dust with a suspiciously vacant look in her eyes, put his hands on her shoulders and gave her a little shove toward the exit.

Bridget was staring wide-eyed at the two of them.

"Aw, don't worry about it. She hates this place." He gave her a wink and added, "You have a good lunch, Bridge."

* * *

Bridget Rothschild watched the B-Ops team head out to their transport. Lucky Cyd; Dain Reston had a really great ass. She pushed her glasses up the bridge of her nose with one carefully manicured fingernail, then went back to double-checking the output the boss had entered by voice transcription. Software wasn't perfect, but it was getting there. The mistakes were probably due more to the fact that her boss had sloppy enunciation.

The comm beeped and she picked up the receiver, thankful for the respite.

"Look under your trash can."

Bridget glanced carefully around the room, making a point not to look at the video cameras mounted high in the corners. "Colonel Billings is unavailable to take your call. May I take a message?" She used her elbow to knock the pencil off her desk, then bent over and took advantage of the opportunity to reach under the trash can. A small package of grenade bullets, highly explosive ammunition clearly designed for the gun that had shown up in her lunch pail last week, was taped to the bottom. She detached the bundle and slid it into the gym bag at her feet before sitting upright again.

"Uh-huh, I got it," she said in her best assistant singsong voice. "I should let you know that it may be a while before the blueprints for the new employee cafeteria will be discussed. We've gone on high alert today."

The voice on the phone, clearly scrambled and now resembling some sort of demonlike cartoon caricature, said softly, "Further instructions to follow." With a click he hung up.

As the all-clear tone pulsed in her ear, Bridget calmly faked the rest of the call, hung up, grabbed her so-called gym bag, and clocked out for a long lunch. She smiled pleasantly to everyone as she headed for the door. She'd be too busy to actually sit down and eat now; she'd have to grab a sandwich to scarf down on the way back.

Chapter Ten

In the dank alley, Fleur bent down next to the vampire corpse. It was dessicating quickly and its blood was congealing on the pavement beneath. He wasn't a Dumont, and she didn't know him personally. Not that it mattered.

She checked his hands, the family ring slipping off his finger into her palm. The signet crest was of the Giannini family. "Well, brother, don't you worry. I'm not going to let this pass." Somebody in the Giannini family would be crying tonight. Fleur knew all about that.

She stepped away from the corpse and let her forensics specialists do their job, pulling potential evidence, snapping pictures. "Fleur, look."

She stared down at the fingernail the technician held up between tweezers. "Werewolf?"

"Looks like it to me," the technician said, slipping the evidence into an envelope. "I'll find out if there's any UV in the claw."

"A werewolf. The dogs. That's just not really what I expected."

"Then you're just not really going to expect this either. There's more. I'm actually pulling human, werewolf, *and* vampire DNA here."

"Vampire? As in rogue vampire?"

The technician shrugged. "Couldn't say, but it's not this guy's."

Fleur frowned. "This sounds like an evidence dump. Like someone purposely is trying to obscure what species is responsible." She tucked her comm earpiece more snugly against her head and dialed Marius.

A click, then: "I'm here, Fleur."

"What do you have for me?"

"We've been chasing through the city. Two down here. We haven't gotten to any of them in time." Marius sighed. "With the one you're checking out, that's three of our kind slain."

Fleur shook her head sadly. "All right. Well, please make a concerted effort to round up any evidence we can bring to the humans—or to the dogs, if it comes to that. I've got a lot of mixed evidence here. I'm not sure who's behind this."

"Will do, Fleur." Marius paused. "By the way, one of these guys was Roddy."

Roddy? He was one of the old party crowd and Paulina's old flame, to boot. Fleur licked her lips and did her best to keep her voice steady. "Thanks, Marius. I'll see you in the war room."

From the alleyway she could see Dain Reston pull up in a transport. What were the humans up to? Or were they being set up, like Reston seemed to think?

Dain got out of the car and started walking toward her and Fleur had the sudden urge to laugh. This pretty-boy human was always doing his best to conceal his chiseled good looks under a five-o'clock shadow and some grubby body armor. The effect, of course, only made him that much more appealing.

She remembered his effect on her from their first meeting, and reminded herself not to let him get the better of her this time. Male-female attraction was the oldest trap in the book. And to say she had a bit of a weakness for human males was apparently an understatement. She could still remember the excitement she'd felt when he'd simply taken her face between his hands and . . .

Fleur ran her tongue over her teeth, noting the slight drop in her fangs. If she was planning to file them again, she ought to do it soon. Of course, things had changed. Ever since the assassinations, there hadn't been so much talk about passing for human anymore. Not like there used to be. Now it was as if among her people there was some sort of collective interest in asserting their right *not* to be human. And when word of tonight's killings got out, that sentiment would probably be felt even more strongly.

Dain hopped the curb. "Sorry I'm late," he said, looking over her shoulder down the alley. "I got caught up in a situation of our own."

"Oh?"

"How many dead vamps you got here?"

"One. Three total."

"Well, I can match you. We've got a cluster of human stiffs over on the Westside."

Fleur's mouth dropped open.

"Yeah," Dain said. "We're about to have a serious problem."

"You don't think *we're* responsible, do you?"

He shrugged. "We're still collecting evidence."

"So are we. But *our* evidence is mixed."

"What do you mean, mixed?"

"It's like a giant forensics soup. All species, it seems. It's some kind of a setup. It's just not clear who's setting what up. It could be you, of course." She stared at him, hard.

Dain exhaled loudly. "Us," he said. Then: "I can't really think straight. Show me what you've got back there and then I've gotta eat something. You hungry?" He gave her an odd look.

Fleur blinked and followed him as he passed under the police tape and headed into the alley. "You can look at a dead body and then go eat a meal?"

Dain raised an eyebrow. "I've seen it all, sweetheart. Haven't you?"

She cleared her throat. "Of course."

He studied her, his lips turned up in an infuriating little smirk. "Yeah, of course you have."

"What's that supposed to mean?" Fleur muttered under her breath.

Dain squatted down next to the slain vampire's remains. "Three of them, you say?"

Fleur nodded, shivering a little. Dain took off his jacket and, without a word, hung it around her shoulders before going on with his business.

She didn't understand him at all. And she should have been pissed off by his arrogance, the way he sort of took over when they were together, the way he showed no hesitation or uncertainty around her. She was more pissed that she rather liked it.

Dain pointed to the corpse's neck. "That's the claw mark?" He shook his head and looked more closely. "We're already losing it. You got pictures?"

"Of everything."

He sat back up on his knees and looked at her. "Okay. I gotta eat. I'll show you 'living like a prince.'"

Fleur had to laugh. She doubted they were going to a caviar bar. They headed back to his transport. It was no small feat trying to find a place to put her feet amongst all the food wrappers and newspapers, but she wasn't about to let him see her squirm.

He drove them down Ventura Boulevard and turned into the parking lot of a diner. Fleur wondered if this was really his scene or if he was trying to make her uncomfortable. Well, she wasn't uncomfortable. She got out the car and followed him inside.

The place looked as though it had once been a "classic" diner with a 1950s theme, but the current owners apparently weren't sticklers for keeping up appearances. A waitress approached, the incessant popping and smacking of her gum drawing even more attention to the two daggerlike piercings stuck through her lower lip. Almost like fangs, Fleur thought.

The frilly apron the waitress wore over her decidedly unfrilly street clothes were her single nod to the diner's erstwhile theme. After sweeping a grubby towel over the formica tabletop, she cocked her hip and waited for them to order.

Fleur looked down at the menu and didn't recognize anything. "What's good here?"

"I always get a burger," Dain said. He was watching her so closely it was beginning to make her itch.

She ordered what he ordered, smiled and said, "Sounds good." The waitress used a fingertip to punch the order into her tablet and disappeared.

Fleur had never tried a "burger" in her life. The cuisine presented at the dinner parties and assemblies in Dumont Towers consisted of complicated dishes with sauces and foreign names. She'd like to see Dain Reston navigate her world the way she was being forced to navigate his.

She could tell he was processing her every move. Yes, Dain Reston was a real pro. There was no question he was extremely good at what he did, which was collecting information people didn't want to give. And trying to imagine what he was seeing when he looked at her made Fleur very nervous. Unfortunately, he was probably beginning to pick up on that. He could probably tell she was someone who hadn't been on the city radar at all, suddenly in the spotlight in a leadership position with minimal training, nervously trying to hide her inexperience . . .

Well, she wasn't going to admit to it. "You're staring at me. What is it?" she asked.

"Why do you vampires eat food if it's blood you can't do without? The blood is what sustains you, so why those big banquets, those big Assembly meals we always hear about?"

Fleur shrugged and took a sip of water. "Because we like the feeling."

"Because it makes you feel human," he prompted.

"You'd like to think that, wouldn't you? You mortals think we eat because we want to be like you. The truth is because of the taste. We taste things differently than you. It's very beautiful. We enjoy a banquet probably more than any human could. You swallow your food without a second thought. We're much more sensual. We enjoy the beauty of the colors and the textures . . . the way foods look presented on a table. We enjoy . . . it's hard to explain. We enjoy how it makes us feel."

"You said that. What exactly do you feel?"

She couldn't find the right words.

"It makes you feel rich," Dain half-sneered, leaning forward; she wondered what she'd said to offend him. "It makes you feel powerful. You put a giant bowl of caviar next to an endless supply of expensive champagne, and it makes you feel rich and powerful. Okay, you say you don't eat and drink to feel human—admit that you do it to feel *better* than human."

Fleur flushed. He'd somehow trapped her. In the most literal sense, he was right. And yet it meant more even than that; there just wasn't any way she could explain how the sheer beauty of luscious silk-upholstered furnishings and cream-laden sauces and glittering parties and all of the rest were almost as important to vampires as the very lifeblood they siphoned from the bloodbanks upstairs in the Towers. They craved luxury and needed it. Without it, they simply did not feel alive. Or at least that was how she'd always felt.

"Why are you acting like this?" she asked in a low voice.

The waitress interrupted them with the hamburgers, plunking their plates on the table. She gave both Dain and Fleur a curious look before going on to her other customers. In turn, Fleur gave Dain a pointed look and took a huge bite out of the burger. "I feel so superior to you right now," she said sarcastically, her mouth full. "Just like a prince."

Dain loosened up and laughed, digging into his own meal. A guy in a booth on the other side of the room waved at him, and he acknowledged the salute. Fleur swallowed another bite and turned more serious.

"You know someone's going to get a picture of us together," she said.

"Yeah? Well, that's not necessarily a bad thing. Humans and vamps working together to keep the peace in Crimson City, yadda, yadda, yadda . . . Isn't that what you wanted?" Dain gave a dry laugh.

Fleur put down her hamburger. "You think this is funny? I seriously doubt that's how the papers would play it. With all those deaths? I don't know about you, but I'm trying to prevent all-out war here!"

Dain put down his hamburger and leaned close. "I don't think it's funny, but sometimes you just gotta laugh. How the hell else can anyone stay sane in this place? Look, you want to help? Maybe you need to get control of your people before you start making calls on what's happening—or what should be happening—out here in the real world. That's how you can save lives."

She flushed. "Well, thanks for telling me who you really think is responsible."

"You know as well as I do that rogue vampires have been causing problems out here for a while. What's going on with them?"

"May I remind you that we call them *rogue* for a reason? Because they aren't 'our people' anymore." Humans had a hard time understanding the difference. Fleur supposed it was because those who really knew the difference between rogue and primary vampires were either no longer human or never had been. "Look, give me a break. We've just had a major leadership change. It's a difficult ti—"

"It's a difficult time for all of us," Dain snapped. He and Fleur stared at each other for a moment and then something in his face changed; he seemed to remember they'd had a rapport. He smoothed his hair back from his forehead and shook his head. "Sorry. I, uh, don't know why I'm being such an ass."

Fleur cocked her head. "Maybe a cluster of dead humans isn't so par for the course after all. Maybe it bothers you."

Dain pushed his plate away. "You've read up on me?"

"Yes, of course."

"Then you know."

Fleur put down her food and wiped her fingers on her napkin. She wasn't sure what he was talking about.

"You know about my wife. Serena."

She almost choked. His wife? They must be separated . . . unless, of course, she was dead.

He leaned forward across the table. "You killed her."

For a second she thought he actually meant her. He said it in a familiar way. A familiar tone. *You killed me.* That's what Hayden had said after she'd made him vampire. Except he'd added rather bizarrely that she'd killed him in a way that was worse than death. She'd killed his soul.

"That shocks you," Dain said dryly. "I wonder how that can be."

102

"It m-must have been a rogue," Fleur stammered. "I've never heard anything about it. I mean, granted, I've not been privy . . . oh, Dain." Her eyes blurred with unexpected tears that she managed to hold back. Still, the emotion coursing through her was powerful. "I'm so sorry. I'm so . . . sorry."

Dain leaned away very suddenly, as far back into his chair as he could go. "I'm sorry too."

There was an awkward silence between them. Fleur was tempted to touch his hand, tempted to offer some sort of comfort. Instead, she said softly, "I know what it's like."

He cocked his head. "You know what it's like," he echoed sarcastically.

She ignored his tone. "I lost the one I loved as well."

His lips parted in surprise and he stared at her, and Fleur wondered if he was thinking the same thing she was: This strange connection between them had something more to it than just a physical attraction.

He broke eye contact first, then shook his head as if to clear his thoughts. "Can we change the subject? Why don't we . . . just go back to the way we were? I don't really feel like talking about this anymore."

Back to the way we were. Fleur would love to go back even farther. This man seemed so vulnerable, so stripped to the bone. He wanted things back where they could be controlled, where he and she could spar verbally and put their emotions and baggage on the back burner.

She nodded and took another bite of burger. She was aware that Dain was still staring at her. "Very tasty in a bourgeois sort of way," she said, indicating the food and keeping her tone as light as she could.

He cracked a smile and relaxed a little. "Glad you like it. That there's *human* food."

Fleur laughed. "I'll have to get our chefs the recipe. Anyway . . ."

"So, what's next?" Dain asked.

"There was a lot of werewolf evidence at that scene. Whether it was planted or whether there's some legitimate basis for it being there, I don't know. I think it's time we found out about the third leg of this triangle."

Dain nodded. "Good call. I'll talk to them. Cyd has some contacts."

"I'll go with you."

"You want to meet with the dogs?" he asked, clearly surprised.

"Of course. I may have a natural aversion to their kind, but our jobs are to find out the truth and react accordingly. Aren't they?"

Dain blinked. What was he thinking? "Yeah, absolutely," he said. "But are you sure you know what you're getting into?"

"I wouldn't ask otherwise."

"It's just . . . never mind." He seemed to decide this wasn't an argument he wanted to have. "You wanna talk to the dogs, you can talk to the dogs. I'll have Cyd set it up for us."

"Thank you." Fleur pushed her plate away. Dain swiped his smartcard through the table reader and they both headed for the door. Fleur looked up. It was getting quite light out. Still . . .

"Would you like me to walk you home?" she asked. "It's dangerous out there."

Dain grinned and played along with her joke. "Sure. I'll even let you tuck me in if you want."

She gave him a look. "In your dreams."

"There, too."

Fleur stopped in her tracks. "What do you think you're trying to do? Go down this path at your own risk."

She'd been joking, mostly, trying to needle him, but Dain's arms came up around her and Fleur felt a sudden shift in the intensity of the moment as his fingers brushed her arms. But he only slipped his jacket from her shoulders. Their eyes met, and she saw reflected in his face the same conflicting emotions she felt.

"Actually, my car's right there. I'll just . . . head back alone," he said. He turned abruptly away.

You're scared of me, Dain Reston. You don't trust yourself. That truth surprised her. The balance of power between them was still up for grabs, and neither of them knew what to do next.

Fleur watched him walk to his transport and disappear inside, all the while wishing against all common sense that he'd kissed her.

Chapter Eleven

With his hands full, Dain kicked on the side of the car to alert Cyd, who reached across and opened the door for him. He handed over two coffees, removed a bag of doughnuts from between his teeth and tossed it inside.

"It's never a good sign when it's this late in the shift and you're just now buying the joe and doughs," she said.

"Did you hit Santa Monica Boulevard on your rounds?"

Cyd rustled around in the doughnut bag for her favorite—white frosting with multi-colored sprinkles. "Unh-uh."

"They're back."

She looked up.

"They weren't all there yesterday, but on the way in this evening I noticed them going up."

"The lampposts? The ones from before the truce?"

"Yeah." Dain took a sip of coffee, wincing as it burned the tip of his tongue. On the way to the station he'd noticed a sudden increase in the number of black lampposts along the major avenues of the city. They'd been removed after the last truce went into effect; the electrical bills had been crippling.

"Let's go see," Cyd said, reaching for his coffee cup. Dain handed it over and started up the transport. He took a shortcut through some minor streets, then routed over to Santa Monica Boulevard and found a place to park where they could get a clear view of the work crews that had started construction. A section of normal lampposts had been removed and the new ones were already starting to go in.

The lampposts' bulbs could switch three ways: regular light, night-vision green, and UV. The lights could sweep up vertically, or out horizontally. The purpose of the UV was to keep the vampires off the main streets and away from humans. To a certain extent they also restricted airspace at lower levels, a detail guaranteed to draw some flak.

Cyd ate her doughnut, her brow furrowing; she was probably running through the same thought processes Dain had. "Did you hear the sirens earlier?" she asked.

"Yep."

"Crap. Did someone accidentally trip a switch?"

"Nope. They're testing the emergency warning system."

"Ah. Awful nice of the pols to give the general human populace in this town an idea of when to duck and cover. Don't want the dogs or the fangs getting a drop on us. Still . . . damn sirens give me a migraine."

Dain chuckled. "Yeah, and we have more to look forward to."

"Wow. So we're really preparing." After a moment of silence, she looked over at Dain. "What exactly are we preparing for?"

"I wish I knew."

Cyd did a double take. "We're preparing for what might be an attack, and you don't know anything about the specifics?"

Dain's jaw tightened. "That's pretty much it." And it was damned disconcerting to have to admit. Nothing had been in his inbox; nothing had filtered down through channels. He made another mental note to ask Kippenham about any other intended defensive implementations. This kind of infrastructure hadn't been up since the first battle between the species. At the height of that war, all of the main thoroughfares in the city had been lined with these posts.

He glanced over at Cyd. "Seriously, if I knew anything about it, I'd tell you. The fact that I don't bugs me. On a couple of different levels."

She grimaced. "You worried? About your own situation, I mean."

Dain adjusted his seat and tried to get comfortable. "It's weird. I hadn't really thought about it, but Kipp hasn't invited me to any meetings of the brass in a long time. Weeks. Out on the base or at the station. In fact, since the last time I saw him and he gave me the go-ahead to work with Fleur, I haven't heard anything from him at all. It's hard to believe there's not something going on that I should know about." He gestured to the lampposts. "For example."

Cyd gave him a sympathetic look. "It's probably not as bad as you think. You know how I-Ops gets when there's the slightest implication the dogs or vamps are on the move. They get paranoid and start closing off avenues of information. Maybe it'll all just blow over."

"I don't think so," Dain said. "They used to offer me a transfer and a promotion what seemed like every month. I'm not hearing much of that anymore."

"You never took it," she hissed. "They probably figured out you don't want it. You wouldn't leave B-Ops to go work out on the base."

The row of new lampposts suddenly flipped on. Dain and Cyd looked at each other.

"The fangs are not going to like this," Cyd said.

"No question. Not only are they not going to like it, but I doubt they will just stand by and watch."

"No way," Cyd agreed. "And if they figure out where we're probably going, we're going to have serious, serious trouble."

Both Dain and Cyd knew where the humans were probably going: full implementation of the Preemptive Defense Initiative. The lampposts were just a precursor to the crown jewel of PDI; in the hills by the Hollywood sign there were still the casings and fittings for suspension strobes, remote-controlled beams that swept higher and farther out than any before. These beams could reach the vampire strata high above and make it difficult—if not deadly—to fly.

At this point, Dain wouldn't be surprised to hear that those mechanisms were undergoing an upgrade. And if that's where the brass was going with this, they were whipping up a recipe for chaos with a side dish of inevitability.

But it wasn't too late to stop these escalations. Dain glanced over at Cyd. "Speaking of the fangs . . ."

She raised an eyebrow.

"I'd like to put Fleur in contact with one of your dogs."

Cyd stared at him and then burst out in peals of loud, overly dramatic laughter.

Dain sighed heavily. He hadn't expected her to be happy about his request; hell, he had reservations, himself. The two species were like oil and water.

"I'm serious," he said. "Can you please set it up?"

"Absolutely not," Cyd answered calmly, sticking her feet up on the dashboard. "I'm not taking a vampire in to meet one of my werewolf informants. That's asking too much."

"Watch the power pack there," Dain warned.

Cyd shifted her feet slightly to one side.

"It's in the interest of peace," Dain argued. "I think an exception could be made."

"Vampires and werewolves do *not* mix. I don't think there's any such thing as an exception," Cyd said.

The two societies were very different, Dain had to admit. And the wolves would zag if the vamps zigged, just to show them they could. Still, this seemed like a good way to get a sense of Fleur and her situation.

He tried again. "She just wants to talk."

"Tell her we can't always have what we want. I don't put my informants in situations where they can be identified later and killed. It's irresponsible at best. The answer is no."

"Well, I'm asking you to do it. Me, your partner."

Cyd slowly tilted her head, giving him a look that implied he was missing more than just a few brain cells. "My partner, eh? It's a dumb idea. So dumb, in fact, that I'm embarrassed on your behalf for asking."

"Okay, I'm not actually *asking*," he said.

Cyd's eyes narrowed.

"Don't give me that look. You owe me enough not to give me trouble on this."

"For what?"

"You know for what. For yesterday. And other days."

She quickly looked away and then shrugged. "It was just Bridget. Nobody else saw me. I wasn't that bad."

Dain cleared his throat and shifted his weight in the car seat. He felt a moment of guilt for trying to bully her. "Do you . . . uh . . . want to talk about it?"

"Do I want to *talk* about it?" Cyd asked incredulously. "What is this, The Caring-Sharing Hour? Man. What the hell did Fleur Dumont do to you? Where's the old Dain I used to know?"

He shook his head. "Maybe you could tell me," he said. "Because I still have no idea."

She stared at him, and then suddenly her face relaxed and she managed a lopsided grin. "Sorry. Geez. I'm sorry. Things have been getting so damn tense in this town, I was beginning to forget we were on the same side." When Cyd smiled for real, it was contagious and you could see a glimpse of what Dain liked to think of as her potential. The person she could be if she could ever outrun her ghosts.

"You've got to watch it, though," he warned. The brass didn't like jumpy agents—saw them as liabilities.

She knew what he meant and just stared out the windshield. Suddenly, she blurted, "I can't stop."

Dain froze, surprised, his coffee cup poised in mid-air.

She turned and looked him in the eye. "Thanks for putting up with me."

He laughed and put his cup down. "Thanks for putting up with *me*." He wanted to lighten the mood.

Cyd curled her hand and gently bumped his fist with hers. "Partner." Then she pulled away, clearing her throat and making a show of rummaging in the bag at her feet. She pulled out a box of candy cigarettes. "Care for a smoke?"

He laughed again. "Sure." He broke the cigarette in half and popped the pieces in his mouth. "Oh, shit. Is this going to turn my tongue blue?"

"Who's going to see it except me and maybe— wait a minute. Do you think the boss is booting you from the inner circle specifically because of Fleur?"

"I don't know. He knew my plan to work closely with her from the start. I think he suggested it. If he had issues, he would have said something, maybe ordered me to try something else."

She pantomimed taking in smoke, then fake-exhaled. "Maybe he can tell it's inevitable."

"I don't like the word 'inevitable.' What's inevitable?" Dain snapped. "What are you talking about?"

"We already had one argument about her this morning. Let's not go there again."

"*What's* inevitable?"

Cyd looked at her watch. "Oops, gotta run. Time to follow up on the world's dumbest meeting." She opened the car door and hopped out, slamming it behind her. Then she went and tapped on the window.

Dain rolled his eyes but hit the switch.

Cyd leaned in through the window. "I hope she's worth it. A vampire like that could really mess up a guy's—"

He hit the switch again and Cyd had to step back to avoid getting her head cut off. She blew him an exaggerated kiss, stuck out her very blue tongue, and took off in the direction of the underground.

Damn Cyd. She knew him too well. Fleur Dumont did something to him. He'd wanted to kiss her last night. Hell, he'd wanted to kiss her since the night they met. He couldn't remember being so drawn to someone . . . though of course he must have been to his wife.

After the accident, Dain had sat with Kippenham and asked him to tell what he remembered about Serena. It was one of those strange moments, one of those rare male bonding moments that never gets referred to again. Kipp had held Serena's picture and described her as sweetness with a hint of the Devil inside. For hours, he'd sat and answered every question Dain asked, told him everything he knew about the wife Dain couldn't remember. It was one reason Dain wouldn't listen to anybody talk down about Kipp, why he wouldn't participate in those watercooler grumblings about the boss.

Sweetness with the Devil inside. Fleur was more like the Devil with sweetness inside. A reverse image. It was a little disturbing, knowing how this vampire intrigued him. But maybe Fleur brought a little bit of Serena back to him. Or maybe, if he were honest with himself, he would admit that this woman, this dark princess, touched him more than the memory of his wife.

Disgusting, Dain.

It had only been two years since the accident and Serena's death. That hardly seemed enough time to give him license to compare his dead wife to someone else and find her wanting. Man. How could he think this way? He shook his head, the usual pangs of guilt stifling his thoughts. It wasn't his fault he couldn't remember much. It was an accident. He just had to try and remember that this wasn't his fault. Serena wouldn't blame him for wanting to move on. Not under the circumstances. Would she?

Dain stared out the window at the empty streets. It was dead quiet, but he wasn't surprised to see so few people around, of any species. The vampires were occupied with a meeting of the Primary Assembly, and most of the dogs were still doing their best to stay low, probably in the hope that the vamps and the humans would kill each other off all on their own.

Well, the humans seemed to be prepping for racial quarantine, and Dain had seen how the level of fear and paranoia amongst them was ramping up big time.

He got out of the car and stretched his legs, jogging over to the beginning of the boulevard to the first lamppost to see if he could find any sort of work order that would indicate who'd authorized the job. A taped-on piece of paper flapped against the metal. Dain reached out to have a look. And then he heard the sound of something in flight.

He stepped full under the glare of the lamp and hit a switch to activate the UV, figuring that if it were an enemy vampire, it wouldn't want to come any closer. It would be limited to shooting him. Not a totally comforting thought, but better than being bitten and sucked dry.

Of course from under the light, he couldn't see a damn thing. He pulled his gun from its holster and brought it up. "What do you want?" he called out. His words seemed to echo down the boulevard, the loneliest sound imaginable. A gust of wind sent a chill down the back of his shirt and he knew he was in trouble.

Dain swung his gun to and fro almost helplessly, pacing beneath the lamppost and trapped in its white-light prison. He could feel from the gusting air that whoever was there was just beyond the light. His adrenaline spiked. He fumbled instinctively for his comm pack, then remembered he'd left it in the car. "Here's the thing: This bulb's UV. You come after me and both us could end up dead. That's just stupid."

He didn't quite get the answer he wanted. Beyond the light, something moved, and suddenly an intense beam of light streamed straight into the bulb above Dain's head. The filament in the bulb expanded and flared, then changed color from UV violet to a dull orange.

Dain just stared. This had to be some new kind of weapon the fangs had developed. Fair enough. If his people were again implementing the use of these lampposts, it was only fair that the vampires had developed and were using something that had the potential to counteract them. Dain could see the glass bulb pulsing and stretching and burning, a popping and hissing sound coming from the mutating orb. The material used in these bulbs was supposed to be indestructible, but whatever the vampire used, it had a capability Dain had never before seen on the streets.

As he stared up in fascination, the bulb gave in to the pressure. It exploded above his head with a detonation that seemed exponentially greater than was possible. Dain went flying to the ground, a shower of sparks and glass raining down on him.

As the light died down, he saw the vampire's outline. All he could think was that this creature had better be one of those rogues Fleur was talking about, or she was going to have some explaining to do. It was his last thought before the bulb went completely dark and he realized the trouble he was in.

He sprinted for the next lamppost, shooting blindly over his shoulder and missing. He made it to the next post a step before the rogue blasted its bulb out.

He sprinted to the next one, losing a little more ground this time.

The rogue blasted its bulb as well, the sparks and shards burning and cutting Dain's exposed skin. Dain lost his grip on his gun, and it skittered away across the pavement.

His lungs starting to burn, Dain turned it up a notch, running as fast as he could down the boulevard along the row of lampposts. Each time he reached a light, the rogue vampire blew it up.

There was only one light left and not enough gas in his tank. There would be no outrunning the thing. The best he could do was turn and fight. Of course, there was no telling what effect the rogue's weapon would have on human flesh. But he could run no longer.

Dain put the brakes on, his body half slumped over as he tried to gather enough strength for the confrontation. He turned slowly around. The vamp was hovering in the air above him. Dain couldn't see his face. He couldn't even guess how the attack would come. And, in fact, he saw nothing after the rogue flexed his arms.

Suddenly he was on his hands and knees, wheezing and gasping as he tried to take in oxygen. But the final blow never came. From where he lay collapsed on the ground, he heard the air above him go wild.

Fleur? That was all he could think. Fleur was here!

Hearing her voice, he flipped over to watch Fleur take on the rogue vampire. The rogue flew at her, his momentum driving her up against the side of the building. Dain heard her gasp as she hit, but in the next moment, she'd lifted her boot and jammed it into the rogue's gut. He somersaulted through the air and, as he came back up, she delivered a solid roundhouse kick to the side of his head.

The rogue took a dive to the ground, stopping in thin air at the last second. He was as disoriented as Dain had been, and bleeding from the side of his face.

Fleur showed no mercy. She landed on the ground next to him and plowed him over. She locked him in a hold, his face pressed into a manhole cover. She looked as if she would have done more, but three other vampires were suddenly there next to her. Two of them pulled her away, and the other calmly walked up to the rogue, now struggling to his feet.

The primary vampire slammed his boot down on the rogue's back. The two fangs struggled, but the rogue quickly submitted. With his knee on the rogue's back while he twisted the rogue's arm behind him, the primary vampire leaned down and said something into his victim's ear.

"Go easy," shouted one of the vampires at Fleur's side.

The rogue turned to answer through a grimace of pain; Dain couldn't hear the words, but whatever he said last infuriated his captor. With a skilled twist, the primary vampire pulled the rogue off the ground, turned his body in midair and smashed his face down into a still glowing shard of the last destroyed lightbulb. Then he cut off the rogue's head.

No screams, no nothing, but suddenly the rogue was dead. It was brutal, quick, silent.

"Dammit, Marius! We should have brought him in for questioning," one of the other vampires called, his hand firmly on Fleur's arm. "What the hell did he say to you?"

The vampire named Marius wiped his forehead with his sleeve. "I asked him if rogues were responsible for sending the mech."

"Did he say yes?" the other vampire asked.

Marius shook his head. "He said he didn't know anything about who sent it, but that it was too bad it missed Fleur. And then he said . . . Never mind." Shaking his head, he walked over to where Dain lay on the ground, still dazed and not quite sold on who was friend and who was enemy. Dain flinched as a hand reached out, but the vamp was surprisingly gentle in picking him up off the ground by his collar and setting him on his feet.

"You're bleeding," the vamp said.

His chest still heaving, Dain looked down and saw that his arms were streaked with blood from the bulb shards. Then he looked at Fleur. She was held back by the two vamps on either side of her, but her eyes seemed to drill into his very soul.

He would have pushed to get to her if he'd had the strength, but between the vamp holding him back, the pain he was in, and the two vamps flanking her, it was clear there was no way. These men would see to that.

As well they should. The way Fleur was looking at him—her lips parted, her eyes dilated, the dark of her pupils dominating the blue—he'd never seen such raw desire in his life. And he felt the same.

He reached out his arm, but the vamp yanked him backward; the best he could do was keep eye contact with Fleur. He wanted to say something, to thank her—hell, he would have loved to do more than that. The desire just to touch her was nearly overwhelming, and between the adrenaline racing through his body and the look in her eyes, Dain nearly fell back to his knees.

"You're bleeding," the vamp holding him repeated harshly, obviously to drive the point home. Dain let himself be half-pushed, half-pulled back toward his car as Fleur's handlers pulled her in the opposite direction. They didn't want him near her. Not now, and probably not ever.

Aware of the vamp still waiting, watching, Dain pulled a towel from his trunk, wiped the blood off himself, and got into the car. He punched the ignition and stared down at his arms reaching for the steering wheel. The new scratches crisscrossed over the top of the old burn scars on his forearms, just as it seemed Fleur's face was beginning to obscure the last blurry images he had left of Serena.

Chapter Twelve

From her uncomfortable position trapped at the back of a garbage-strewn alley, Jillian Cooper had watched in near disbelief as Dain Reston nearly lost his life to a bad vampire—until some good vampires came and kicked the bad vampire's ass. The whole time she'd just stood there, completely frozen with fear. *Nice job, Jill. You're a real hero.*

Now she was seeing that exactly twenty-nine out of the thirty brand-new lampposts had their light-bulbs smashed on Santa Monica Boulevard, and one vampire corpse was lying in the middle of the street. So the question was: Was this a story, or a sign that Jill needed to get out of town?

She waited until it was completely silent, until she was completely sure she was alone, before she even dared move. Her sneakers were soaked with fetid water and she didn't want to think about what she'd been sitting in. Slowly, very slowly, she walked out of the alley and approached the body.

The night beat was creepier than it used to be, that

was for sure, and Jill had never really grown accustomed to it. Or even to being up all night. She basically survived in what felt like a permanent state of jet lag, waking up for the big story at whatever hour it happened to be. She'd decided long ago she didn't want to be the best night reporter or the best day reporter. She just wanted to be the best.

Of course, standing on a blood-spattered street with a vamp corpse at two in the morning wasn't her ideal way to collect the facts of a story. And it wasn't as if she couldn't be shocked. She turned the face toward her, leaping back with her heart in her throat as the body twitched. It would start dessicating soon.

She swallowed hard and moved forward, going on to study the rest of the corpse and noting its tattoo. So, *this* was a rogue vampire—one of the ones who didn't want to toe the party line. Being a rebel wasn't in and of itself a crime, of course. And the fading expression of surprise on the dead vamp's pale face was heartbreaking as death always was, whether Jill was staring down at a dead vamp, dog, or human.

She looked over her shoulder out of habit, then slowly brought her camera up to her eye. She took a shot, a close-up, the flash like a bolt of lightning in the dark. Then she turned the camera for a full-length shot, and as the flash went off, the figure of a man cloaked in darkness became visible in the temporary light.

Jill dropped her camera, ignoring the pain in her neck from the strap. She staggered backward, falling to the damp pavement, one hand outstretched with its palm toward the stranger. "I was just taking picture. Just taking a picture, that's all," she said, her voice shaking.

She flinched as his hand stretched out to her and her heart beat double-time.

"Take my hand," he said. She stared up, trying to make out his face. The voice was the same as one of the "good" vampires who'd just helped Dain.

Jill licked her dry lips and tried not to think about the vampire abduction piece her tabloid had run a week ago. All lies, of course, but one had a tendency to believe anything in this sort of situation.

She didn't take the proffered hand, but tried to stand up. When the vamp reached out again, her knees buckled. As she slid back toward the ground, he caught her around the waist and pulled her up.

"I'm scaring you," he said rather sulkily.

"Yeah," she croaked.

"It's not my intention."

"What is your intention?"

He actually laughed a little. Oddly, it helped her relax enough to take a full, deep breath. She forced herself to look long and hard at his face, in case she was alive enough to identify him in a lineup later. He looked like a Dumont, but she couldn't place which one.

His laughter vanished as his gaze swept over her, dark and brooding. His lips parted, the sharp, un-filed fangs proving him vampire if there'd been any doubt. And as she stared up into eyes so dark they were nearly indistinguishable from the night, she found herself caught in a vortex of sensation, as if his subconscious were reaching out to hers.

He looked down at her neck, but all Jill could focus on was the black fringe of his eyelashes and that sensuous mouth. He was so, so *beautiful*. And she knew without a doubt that he wanted to bury his fangs in her. Somehow, the sheer desire in his thoughts made her almost wish he would. For once in her life, Jill was absolutely speechless.

And it was at that moment that he let her go, leaning her up against the lamppost, one hand lightly at her waist to prevent her from sliding back down. "Go home, Jillian," he said.

She nodded. He let go and took a step back. Jill found her footing and without looking back ran as fast as she could.

"I've been waiting for you," Fleur said, fighting back anger. She watched Marius step through the open windows lining the sitting room behind the Assembly hall. He looked at her, wearier and sadder than she'd seen him in a while.

"I had some other business," he answered. But Fleur had seen that look before, and she knew where he'd been.

"Are you all right?" she asked.

He waved the question away. "Ian and Warrick?"

"Already here."

"Shall we go in, then?"

"I want to talk to you first."

Her cousin sighed and sat down on the sofa.

"Why the double standard for everything?" Fleur asked, working hard not to raise her voice. "Why the higher standard for *me*? Why did you hold me back from Dain only to kill that rogue in front of my eyes, then go off to woo some human female you'll be tempted to bite? Where is the control in that?"

Marius leaned his head back and closed his eyes. "I wasn't wooing. I was protecting."

Fleur rolled her eyes. "I know you. You only look like this when you're busy breaking your heart."

He sat up, and his gaze bored through her. After a moment he said, "Broken hearts aren't illegal or immoral."

"You acted as if I was completely incapable of controlling myself!"

"You *looked* incapable of controlling yourself. I know what that's like. I understand the pull of . . ." He raked his fingers through his hair. "I didn't want you to do anything you'd regret. Not when—"

"I wasn't going to do anything, for god's sake. I was in control. I was just going to rough that rogue up a bit . . . and then I was going to bring him in for questioning. But you go and kill him! Christ, Marius—you act like just being near Dain Reston might send me over the edge, and then you go nuts yourself. Killing that rogue? Jeezus. And then not even letting me near Dain. . . ."

"The difference between you and I, Fleur, is that I don't have a history," Marius said a little coldly. "You haven't proven anything. Not to me, not to anyone in the Assembly. And the others don't have to listen to me, don't have to believe I can lead them competently. . . ." He raised his arms in a helpless gesture. "And that rogue . . . well, he crossed the line. As far as Jillian was concerned, Fleur, I was 'protecting.' We can't allow human-vampire relations to get any worse." Fleur saw the haunted look in her cousin's eyes, but he spoke no more about it. He stood. "We've kept the others waiting long enough. Are you ready?"

Fleur shrugged. Marius's vote of no-confidence had made her sick to her stomach. "I'd like to go and change first."

"You look fine."

"This isn't the right image. If you don't take me seriously, I don't know why anyone else would. I shouldn't have worn this. I don't know why I did." She hadn't had much time after the street fight to get ready. With her mind on Dain and the way he looked with that blood everywhere ... she'd just dressed in her old clothes, done what still came naturally. The expensive clothes felt silly after all she'd just been through.

Her cousin surprised her: "It doesn't matter what you wear. You'll be fine."

She'd be fine. She needed to believe that.

She managed a smile for his sake, nodded, took a deep breath and stepped into the room.

The Primary Assembly meetings were serious discussions about political strategy, masquerading as some of the biggest dinner parties of the year. All of the action happened after the meal, but sitting with Paulina and her other friends as she had in the past, the meal and the after-parties were all she'd really seen. It had been an opportunity to dress up and have fun, and Fleur had hardly paid attention to what anyone was saying about other vampires or werewolves or humans. High up here during truce time, the politics of the city hadn't seemed to matter. But they mattered now, and now Fleur was at the center of things. She only hoped she didn't look like a fraud. She wasn't feeling quite so much the fraud anymore, anyway.

She was definitely getting used to things. She was

getting used to being involved. And she was starting to understand how all the pieces fit together in this very fragile world all the species had built up here in Crimson City. She just hoped that everyone could see that.

There was a long, awkward silence as she maneuvered her enormous skirt around the tables leading up to the podium. She tipped over a chair and winced as someone giggled. *Thank you, Paulina.*

When she finally made it to the lectern and looked out at the assembled crowd, she suddenly felt a sense of calm. She smiled at her audience and poured herself a tall glass of water from the crystal pitcher. Then Fleur took a long drink, leaned forward and addressed her people.

Kippenham stood on the stoop with his hand gripping the neck of a bottle of whiskey. Dain opened the door wider to let him in. Kipp hoisted the bottle in the air. "It's been a while. I thought you could use a refresher."

His words had a double meaning. He and Kipp hadn't had a "refresher" in a long, long time. When Dain had emerged from his comalike haze in the aftermath of Serena's death, his boss had been there. He wasn't ashamed to admit that they'd cried over her together, though they'd not spoken of that time much since. When Serena was still alive, she and Dain had apparently been quite social; they'd spent a fair amount of time with Kippenham and his dates. That Dain hadn't been able to remember any of his dates hadn't fazed Kipp much; that Dain hadn't remembered Serena as his wife had bothered him to no end. For weeks after her death, Kippenham had come over to Dain's apartment to talk about Serena, trying to help Dain remember. He'd tried to bring those happy times back.

Eventually, Dain had decided he would have to come to terms with the fact that his memory might be permanently damaged. Kippenham's presence had begun to feel like a burden; his stories just induced guilt. He'd begun to have dreams—that he was a murderer, a killer, someone beyond all saving. How could he not remember someone he had loved so well? How could he watch Kippenham tear up over a story about him and Serena, while he himself sat there, dry-eyed and shell-shocked as if Kipp were reading a page out of a book?

Kippenham had eventually sensed this disconnect and after a few last awkward evenings, he'd stopped coming over and became once more just a boss. But Dain appreciated what Kippenham had tried to do for him when he'd needed it most. And there had been a few times since when he'd been tempted to call him up and ask for another story, if only to be reminded that once in his life he'd had it all.

For that reason, Dain was glad Kipp had come today. His boss headed to the kitchen and took a couple of glasses out of the cupboard, then returned and placed them on the coffee table next to the whiskey. He poured out two generous servings and then, as if they'd done this only yesterday, raised his glass. "To Serena," he said.

Dain raised his own and they clinked them together. "To Serena."

Kippenham sipped his drink in silence for a moment. "I wasn't sure if you were ready, but it's been a long time." He paused for a moment. When Dain didn't say anything, he reached into his breast pocket and took out an envelope which he placed on the table and slid in Dain's direction. "I got this out of storage for you."

Dain swallowed hard and looked at the envelope, then looked up at Kippenham. "I'm ready. I'm actually ready to see all of it." While he was still in the hospital nursing his burns and dealing with the news of his wife's death, he'd asked his boss to box everything up. It seemed a strange request for someone who was having trouble remembering things, but it had been too hard to look at the effects of a woman he couldn't remember and know that when he touched her nightgown or smelled her perfume he was supposed to feel something. Kippenham had done as he'd asked, and when Dain had returned from the hospital, there was nothing of her left. But now . . . now . . . he just wanted to know. Had he loved her the way he should have? Would seeing her things give him the answers he was looking for?

Dain looked up at Kipp, who still hadn't answered. "I'm ready to see all of it," he repeated. "I want Serena's things."

Kippenham nodded and took a sip of whiskey, a faraway look in his eyes. "It's been a long time. I'll have them find out where they're all stored and have them delivered."

"Thanks." Dain picked up the envelope. It wasn't sealed, and inside was a gold heart-shaped locket. Dain felt his heart pound as he took the delicate necklace in his rough hands. He remembered this piece. He definitely remembered seeing this on her. With trembling fingers he examined the locket, inscribed "Forever Together." He opened the clasp and the two sides fell open to reveal a picture of him with a devilish grin on his face on the one side and a picture of a young, beautiful Serena on the other.

Tears welled up in his eyes. He fought them back and looked up in muddled embarrassment, but Kippenham had tears in his eyes, too. If Kippenham only knew that they weren't choked up for the same reason.

Kippenham rolled the whiskey glass between his hands. "There was this one night. Four of us went out after work. We were exhausted. We thought we'd just pick up burgers or pizza or something. We went into this pizza joint and the place was just dead. Absolutely dead. Within five minutes, Serena had everyone singing songs and ordering up beer for a long night. That was Serena. She'd turn just about anything into an occasion." He stared at the wall, but it was obvious his mind was focused on a different time, a different place. "She was wearing that old light blue sweater you gave to her as a joke because you couldn't afford Tiffany's at the time." He turned back and looked at Dain. "Do you remember that?" His voice became a little more insistent. "Don't you remember any of that?"

Dain downed the rest of his whiskey, grimaced at the burn, and poured himself another. Enough time had passed. He had to know. He hadn't had the courage to ask before. He hadn't cared. But there had to be some explanation. "Kipp, man to man . . . did *you* love Serena? Did you go out with her before she and I became a couple?"

Kippenham paled. "We've talked about this before. Don't you remember?"

Dain couldn't. He gritted his teeth, shaking his

head. "I don't remember, Kipp. I don't remember anything. I hate it, but that's—"

"Hey, stop. Dain, just stop, it's fine. I apologize. I shouldn't have said that. Or about remembering. I'm sorry. This isn't your fault. I forget what you do and don't remember and what we've talked about. It's been a long time since we talked about . . ."

Dain tried to relax, but he suddenly wanted Kippenham out of his apartment. He remembered now why they had stopped reliving the past together. He remembered those dreams, and his failures. He couldn't handle it. He couldn't handle watching his past mean more to someone else than it did to him. "Did you love Serena before me?" he asked again.

"I loved her . . . as a friend," Kippenham said stiffly. "She was my very dear friend."

Dain dropped his head in his hand. "My god." He took a moment to collect himself, then raised his head. "I'm so sorry. This is just unbelievable." He looked Kipp head-on. "I don't remember her. When I don't look at her picture I don't remember her at all. And when I do look, I don't know how much is just me thinking of all the great stories you've told me—if it's just me forcing myself to believe something I desperately want to believe."

The look on Kippenham's face was one of intense pain. He leaned across the coffee table. "She was so alive. So vibrant. And you loved her so much. It's not possible for her to have died and not have some part of her still living within you somewhere." He sounded angry, almost irrational. A tear slipped from his eye and trickled down his cheek.

Dain wanted to scream. *That's my anger.* My *sor-*

row. He stood up. "There is a part of her inside me. A small part," he lied. "You're right. I just wish there was more."

Kippenham visibly relaxed. "I'll have her things sent to you," he said, and then he too stood up.

"Thanks," Dain said. He put down his glass and moved to the door. Kippenham followed suit.

As Dain opened the door, Kippenham turned around. "If you ever want to hear more—"

"Thanks," Dain said.

Kippenham nodded, then took a deep breath and wiped the tears from his cheek. He turned around again and Dain had to suppress the urge to push him over the threshold. "Dain, I want you to know that I never made a play for her after you and she married. You were both my good friends, and I respected that."

When he finally stepped out and was gone, Dain shut the door, wheeled around, and looked around the living room. This was the same furniture he'd had during his marriage. That much hadn't changed. He went to the desk and took out the drawers, patting down the wood, looking for secret compartments, old letters stuck behind in cracks. The bureau, the bed, the bookcase . . . same thing. What he was looking for, he couldn't really say. They'd taken everything way back when, like he'd asked. But they'd been more thorough than he'd expected. There was nothing left of her in his possession. Nothing at all.

What kind of a love had they had? Was it safe and sweet? Or had they burned with desire? He thought of Fleur. Of her face and body and the way she made him lose control. She was the one who was vivid and alive for him, now, and that disloyalty to Serena swept a wave of shame through him.

He stumbled back to the coffee table and crouched down on the floor. Taking the locket in his hands, he started to shake. He covered his head in his arms and began to sob. *She was my wife and I don't feel half of what Kipp does. Where the hell is my heart? Where is my love?*

What's wrong with me?

Chapter Thirteen

It had been a few days since she'd seen Dain Reston, and for that Fleur was actually rather glad. She'd needed some time to cool off.

Stepping into his apartment looking like she'd just walked out of a movie premiere wasn't meant to stir things up again. Certainly, she'd planned this appearance carefully, partly to make the right impression on the dogs—but if she were honest about it, partly to see Dain's reaction. But she'd had no conscious intention of heating things up between them. The unpredictable part of her, that subconscious part which had gotten her in trouble with Hayden, was something Dain was clearly capable of bringing out in her. Fleur couldn't pretend she didn't want to know how far she could take things; she only knew she couldn't take things there.

In any case, she'd dressed primarily for what might lie ahead in werewolf territory.

Her hair was entwined in an intricate updo, out of her face. Her striped satin showed off a lot of cleavage, but it concealed a couple of small weapons fastened along the seams of the hem, and the ribbons and laces up the front hid comm wiring. Her black satin tunic cigarette pants were lined with a thin layer of armored fabric, and the sides of her high-heeled leather boots featured an assortment of travel-sized weapons. Granted, the footwear might not be the easiest to run in, but when you knew how to fly, that wasn't such a concern. And men always underestimated the power of a stiletto heel to the eye.

Dain looked up, apparently speechless. "Wow. Incredible."

He didn't look so bad himself. He'd had a few days for his bruises and cuts to heal, but humans didn't heal as fast as vampires, and he showed just enough wear and tear to make him even sexier. Fleur liked her men a little dangerous, which Dain definitely was.

He was still staring at her, his expression cycling between admiration and disbelief.

Fleur couldn't help smiling. That is, until Dain leaped up from his chair, crossed the room and began pulling hairpins out of her perfect coiffure.

"What are you doing?" He shook his head in disbelief. "What the hell are you doing?"

Nobody . . . *nobody* dared touch her like this. At least not in vampire circles. Confused and unsettled by his roughness, his aggression, Fleur struggled for the proper response.

She settled on slapping him hard across the face. He had the nerve to look surprised. "What are *you* doing?" she demanded.

Dain backed off, running his fingers down his cheek. "Jesus H. There's no question. You're definitely Warrior class."

"And to think I was worried about you!"

"You were worried about me?" Dain grinned. "Hell, I'm fine. You thought the fight with that rogue was serious?" He held out his scarred arms. "I don't think there's much more damage that can be done to me. You, on the other hand, are a different story." He threw up his arms, gesturing to her outfit. "So, what *is* this?"

Fleur narrowed her eyes. Typical male: no appreciation whatsoever. "I spent hours getting ready for this. Hours. And if you had certain required attire, you should have made that clear."

Dain didn't answer. He just tilted his head, his eyebrow going up as his gaze shifted from her head . . . to her chest . . . to her waistline . . . to her feet . . . and back up. Fleur just glowered at him, her hair falling in her face.

He didn't say a word.

"What? What are you staring at?"

He took a deep breath and finally swept his gaze up to her face, the look in his eyes somehow sending her heartbeat into double-time. "Sweetheart," he drawled, "there is no question that you are a knockout. But you're not wearing *that* tonight. You couldn't pass for human right now if you tried. Tell me you've got something on underneath that."

And with that, he moved in and proceeded to roughly unlace her bodice.

"Do *not* paw at me," she said breathlessly. "You're like a beast!"

She swatted at him, barely able to breathe properly with his fingers tickling her collarbone, his hands brushing her breasts. It was horrifying how much this man affected her. Completely ridiculous. Impossible. Inappropriate. But so, so exciting.

"You can't wear this—this . . . what is this called?" he was saying. "This bows-and-laces-and-low-cut business . . . what is it, 'frippery,' or something?"

Her hands had stilled as she fixated on the way his fingers slipped against her skin, and Dain simply batted them away. He finished the job, slipping the expensive tunic from her shoulders and leaving her with only a completely plain, fitted black camisole underneath. Exposed and excited, Fleur couldn't suppress the small sound that escaped her throat as he pulled one strap back up and smoothed it flat against her shoulder. He cleared his throat, noting a little hoarsely that "this" would do with a jacket over it; then he added, "At least you didn't wear a skirt and those little slipper shoe things." He looked down, his hand reaching out toward her waistband.

"Mules," Fleur said, her hand whipping out and capturing his wrist. "And don't even think about it."

"No?" he said with a cocky grin. "Why not? I think you like this."

"You're intolerable," she said. But she couldn't help but smile a little.

"Turn around."

She narrowed her eyes at him. He made a twirling motion with his fingers. Fleur licked her lips nervously and finally turned.

He started working on her hair again, more gently than he had at first, working the flopping pin-curled sections all back together at her neck. He seemed to be taking forever, but Fleur was used to that. She closed her eyes and relaxed into his touch.

When it finally stopped, Fleur opened her eyes and started to turn around, but Dain held her back with one hand while he reached over and fished around in his desk for a rubber band. He put her hair up in what was clearly a pretty sorry ponytail, then twirled her around to face him. "There. So I'm thinking that you should know that the last thing you want to do when you try to pass through were-wolf territory is to dress like a hot-shit vampire heiress. You've done this before, right? I mean, you've been around the dogs before in these kinds of situations?"

She answered his questions with her most super-cilious stare. "I dressed to impress. And from what I can tell . . . it works on humans, anyway."

He chuckled. "Point. But we do it my way tonight, because Cyd will have my ass on a plate if we try it any other way."

"Right. So, anything else about my appearance that needs addressing? Or are we done?"

"We need to do something about your makeup." Dain put his hand against her face, his thumb against her lower lip—like the first time they'd met, and yet with different emotion behind it. She could tell he was struggling to hold back. He moved closer, and she could feel his breath on her face.

"What's wrong with my makeup?" Fleur asked, her voice coming out as a whisper.

His hands slid under the edge of her camisole and across her back. "You're wearing too much lipstick," he said. Then he brought his mouth down on hers.

It was as if he'd lit a match at the end of a wick burning toward dynamite; Fleur felt the same fear and anticipation. Dain bit softly down on her lower lip, and she was struck with an overwhelming desire—to bite back, harder, and to take the one thing from him that would destroy him forever. To devour him. This was right, so right.

The lure of such an idea, the temptation of his wanting mouth burning into her made her answer back with more passion than perhaps he'd meant to draw. But Dain spun her in response, nearly throwing her up against the door. He pressed his body into hers. Fleur arched back and gave in to the sensation of his mouth trailing from her lips to her throat and down, as he caressed his way across her skin.

She closed her eyes, her mind flashing on an image of her mouth on his throat, kissing, biting . . .

Dain swept her camisole strap back down her shoulder, exposing her breasts as he went down on his knees and dragged her down with him. With her hands tangled in his hair, Fleur let herself go. His mouth moved hot and greedy over her. Wonderfully dizzy, she almost broke apart at the sound of Dain whispering her name on a soft breath.

And then someone tried to open the door. The creak of the doorknob sounded; Dain stuck his arm out as the door swung in toward the back of Fleur's head, cursed loudly as the wood cracked against his elbow.

"Dain, is that you?"

"Cyd! Uh, yeah—one sec, Cyd," Dain growled, managing to pull Fleur's camisole back up as he got them both off the ground. "You okay?" he asked.

Fleur nodded and pulled away, quickly trying to straighten herself up. The door opened and a sort of grubby, unkempt woman stood on the other side, legs braced apart, arms folded across her chest. In short, Cydney Brighton looked completely unamused and, by any estimation, less than thrilled to see her.

"Well." Cyd looked from Dain to Fleur and back again. "I'll be in the car. When you two kids feel like getting back to saving the world, you just come on down to the curb." She disappeared and Dain closed the door behind her.

"Something tells me I'll be hearing more about this." He turned back to Fleur and pulled up his T-shirt, using its hem to wipe the smeared lipstick off her mouth. "You know I'm not really good at this sort of thing, but about yesterday . . . it's not often that I get my ass saved. It was looking pretty grim."

Fleur looked down at his abs. "Marius normally would have let the rogue go, you know." Unable to stop herself, she reached out and ran her hand across his muscles.

He took a hasty step backwards, out of range, and said, "We should get going. Put this jacket on over that slip thing. It's too big, but it'll work better than what you came with."

Fleur slipped into Dain's armored jacket and followed him out the door.

As promised, Cyd sat in the driver seat of the transport, idling the engine. "Play nice," Fleur overheard Dain whisper in her ear as he got in. She shot him a look but to Fleur's surprise, the woman gamely stuck out her hand through the open window.

"Any friend of Dain's," she said.

"I'm so pleased to meet you," Fleur said.

"Don't worry, I'll get over it." She shrugged. "I'm naturally suspicious, and while it's strange for Dain to ask me to reveal an informant to him, it's really strange for him to ask me to reveal an informant to someone else. Not to mention someone like you."

"I think if we work together—," Fleur began.

Cyd quickly showed her a palm. "Save it. If we work together we can all be one big happy city and blah, blah, blah. Whatever. Dain wants me to take you to see one of my informants, that's really all I need to know."

Fleur gave her a frosty look. "I see. Fine."

Dain blew out an exasperated breath. "Let's just get going."

Cyd nodded and opened the back car door, pointing with her thumb into the tiny backseat where the criminals normally sat. Fleur raised her chin and made a point of climbing in with no hesitation.

"I'll have to call out shotgun, next time," she said.

"Not unless you want a bullet through your head, too," Cyd responded under her breath, though clearly intending Fleur to hear. "Destination Dogtown," she said more loudly. "Upon request."

In spite of the close quarters, Fleur was relieved for the opportunity to collect herself in the privacy of the backseat. She ran her index finger over her slightly swollen mouth. Oh, this was something. It wasn't the first time she'd been physical with a man, but it was the first time she'd felt such emotion from a man behind his touch. Even Hayden . . . She'd heard such longing in Dain's voice and she'd felt it on his lips. . . .

Fleur stared out the window as they drove. Was this the sort of thing that tormented Marius? He was forever involving himself with human women he could never have. From the beginning, as it would be to the end, he'd given in to them only to give them up. Which was what she should have done with Hayden.

All the more reason to remember why she was here. She'd lied, of course, when she'd said that stuff about working together. As it had been for centuries, it was her people versus everybody else. Always. Why was it so hard for her to remember that?

Chapter Fourteen

Crimson City's underground, flippantly referred to as "Dogtown" by those who didn't actually have wolf blood, belonged to the werewolves as much as the sky belonged to the vampires. That Fleur had never been down there wasn't strange: she'd never seen a dog in Dumont Towers, either.

Cyd parked the transport in some godforsaken part of the city somewhere near the Triangle. Fleur didn't recognize where she was and, judging from the general squalor and decay of the area, it didn't look like she'd missed anything. Dain's partner, on the other hand, appeared to know the area like the back of her hand.

Dain put his finger to his lips as Cyd started to walk. She seemed to be counting something off in her head as she led them through a maze of narrow streets. Finally, in the shadows by the intersection of an alley and a larger side street lined with abandoned shops plastered with faded FOR LEASE signs, the woman stopped and pointed at a manhole.

Through a manhole? She had to be joking. "This makes us look guilty of something," Fleur protested. Dain just shook his head in warning.

Fair enough—him trusting his partner. But Fleur didn't like it. She didn't like sneaking into an unfamiliar subterranean werewolf god-knew-what when they should have been walking in through the front door as equals. As diplomats.

Cyd reached down to her boot and unclipped a metal rod with a hook on the end. She used the hook to pry the manhole cover free as if she'd done so a million times before. The heavy lid clanged as she dropped it to the side. Fleur gave Dain a look, but he just shrugged.

"Stay here until I give you a signal," Cyd said, putting her boot on the first rung and then starting down without hesitation. They could hear her boots on the metal rungs for what seemed like a ridiculous amount of time. Then came a bang and a yelp, more heels on metal rungs, then silence.

Dain's hand suddenly went up to the earpiece of his comm device. Cyd was softly tapping out code on her microphone pad. Dain looked around, then stepped over to the first rung and motioned for Fleur to fall in behind him.

She did. As they made their way down, she realized with disgust that this hole was exactly what it looked like. An overwhelming stench filled the tube and a horrible claustrophobia began to set in. Fleur was used to wide open airspace, freedom to fly, and this smelly tube was almost unbearable. Sweating already, she focused on slow and steady breathing, silently swearing not to make it an issue.

Farther and farther down, she climbed—god, it seemed to take forever. As she slid against the sides of the narrow tube, cold and grimy sludge smeared over her clothes and her face. *Get over it, Fleur. Just get over it.* She gritted her teeth. If this was what it took to do her duty to her people, she'd do it. She wasn't going to let either of these humans see she wasn't up to the task, especially because of such a silly thing as this. It almost made her wonder if Cyd had taken this route for the sole purpose of trying to beat her down. But she had too much respect for Dain to think that someone he cared about would be so petty in such a critical situation.

At last, Fleur's boot moved down but there was no rung to place it on; she felt hands around her waist and saw that it was Dain at the bottom, ready to help her down. Cyd was standing there with her arms folded across her chest, a slightly amused expression on her face.

Okay, maybe Dain's partner could be that petty. After all, Fleur could probably be that petty if the situation was reversed. And suddenly Fleur wanted to laugh.

Cyd's eyebrow flew up, but then a smile broke out over the woman's face. She chuckled softly. "Nicely done," she said.

Fleur just smiled back and shrugged.

"Ready for the meeting?" Cyd asked.

"Absolutely," Fleur replied.

Cyd turned around, moved some rocks on the wall, flipped up a well-camouflaged hinged metal flap and revealed a tiny keypad. She typed in a code; there was a clicking sound and then she just took her fist and pounded once as hard as she could against the wall. The noise startled Fleur nearly to death, but even that wasn't as surprising as the sudden entrance to the werewolf's transit system.

They walked through the door and Cyd quickly closed it, sealing the stench and the squalor of the sewers behind them. Then they continued along a fairly slim riser running alongside a set of train tracks. Fleur looked around as she carefully picked her way over the uneven ground.

To one side, the tracks started to trend upward through the tunnel—clearly, that was where the train broached the ground level of the city on the werewolf side of the Triangle. To the other side, the tunnel widened for a boarding platform that was not far around the bend; Fleur could feel the vibrations in the ground from the passengers milling about as they waited for the next train, and she could certainly sense who—and what—they were.

The dogs. Dozens of them, just around the bend and down through the tunnel. Fleur stopped short, nearly overcome as a wave of dizziness swept her.

"You okay?" Dain whispered.

"I'm fine," she said, forcing herself to follow Dain's partner even closer down the line. But Fleur wasn't fine. She'd never in her life put herself in the unfamiliar territory of the dog lairs. This many dogs at once would be hard to handle. The animal in her felt the presence of its natural enemy. The feeling was incredibly strong.

Cyd led them straight toward a platform labeled for train car maintenance. It branched slightly off from the main track and housed an off-duty train car parked to one side. The cars and the architecture of the subway were as much a work of art as a service. Everything was technologically prime, sleek and fine in its aesthetic. It was nothing like the rest of the werewolf territory, and nothing like what Fleur would have expected of the dogs. She'd heard their Grand Dame was clever, but this showed an ingenuity that was positively terrifying. And that fact scared her more than if she'd walked into the most dangerous, squalid dump of a neighborhood. She felt a brief moment of gratitude that the dogs were still oppressed—at least, if they were as untrustworthy as she'd been taught. Her body seemed to believe they were.

"Stay behind me for a moment," Cyd said. She continued on ahead of Fleur and Dain, and a figure suddenly emerged from where it had been camouflaged against the grayish tint of the tunnel.

Fleur's adrenaline surged; she lost her footing and Dain had to reach out to keep her from falling. "That's him?" she asked.

Dain nodded and they watched the informant walk down the tracks toward them. He was tall and skinny, walked with his shoulders hunched over and had a habit of looking behind him every third step. He looked like a typical down-on-his-luck human. In other circumstances, she might not have guessed his species at all. Not by sight alone. As it was, he must have been scared or angry or both, and the smell of him, the sense of him as "other" was strong. Too strong.

Cyd met him in the middle of the tunnel on the tracks. She put her arm around the guy's shoulder and was taking her time explaining something to him. The informant looked up at Fleur, and she felt her skin crawl as his nostrils flared. He was taking in her scent, evaluating her.

Dain put his hand on her shoulder and gently pushed her toward Cyd and the dog. "C'mon. We have to talk to him."

Fleur's panic spiraled; she couldn't even concentrate on what Dain was saying—nor what the werewolf was saying, however valuable the information might be. The dog looked about as uneasy as she felt, undoubtedly beginning to sense her internal struggle. He suddenly looked her square in the face.

Fleur gasped . . . and he saw her half-grown fangs.

The dog gave Cyd a look of utter contempt. "You bitch. You brought a vamp." He leaned forward and snapped his teeth together in Fleur's face. He reached out and—

That was all it took. Fleur's animal nature sliced through her in an uncontrollable wave. She put her hands up on the dog's chest and shoved him back. She bared her fangs and hissed, proud of the fear appearing in his eyes.

The informant was as far gone as she, and he squared off with her, beginning to cycle toward the Change.

"Oh, shit." Suddenly Cyd was between them, struggling to get the informant to turn around. "Get her out of here, Dain. Now!"

Dain put his arm across Fleur's chest, trying to drag her backwards, but she'd discovered the true inherent strength of her Warrior nature. Feeding off each other's energy, vampire and werewolf pulled free of the restraining humans. And as the werewolf moved further from man and closer to beast, Fleur's own deepest instincts surged.

The dog lashed out first, his claws slicing her arm. Fleur saw Dain and Cyd in the blur of her peripheral vision but they meant nothing to her anymore. Her emotions were completely out of control. She struck back, unaware of any pain in her bleeding arm, expert efficiency behind her furious yet precise attack. Right hook, left jab, reverse pattern, uppercut . . .

The dog roared in pain and leaped forward with what looked like the Devil in his eyes, saliva dripping from his mouth. He fended off her blows, driving her back, but Fleur came at him again in a flurry and she could tell that she was wearing him down.

Then she made the mistake of pausing to catch her breath. He saw the opening and backflipped in the air, finishing his Change. By the time he came up from the landing, he had twisted into a more monstrous form; his body had taken on greater musculature and strength.

Fleur saw she had less of an advantage, and tried to get off an attack before he did. They both leaped into the air simultaneously, each with a jumpkick aimed at the other's chest. Fleur was slightly more on target and she caught the werewolf almost square, knocking him off balance. He fell, landing hard against the tracks.

Fleur might have delivered a solid blow then, but she landed askew, the high heel of her right boot tripping her up on the tracks. As she fell to the ground, the werewolf took his opportunity. It was his turn to give her what she'd given him—blows rained down on her, and she caught a glimpse of horror on Dain's face.

On the sidelines, as it were, Dain was nearly going mad watching Fleur fold before the dog's attack. He pulled his gun and checked that it still had silver bullets loaded.

"Don't do it, Dain." Cyd yanked on his arm. "I'm telling you. If you get involved, it's no longer one-on-one. He's gonna call his pack. Then we'll all be sorry."

Dain looked over to see the werewolf rake his claws down Fleur's thigh, ripping through the armored layer of her pants. He almost had to cover his ears when she cried out in pain. Pacing the narrow ledge above the tracks, nearly sick to his stomach, he said, "I can't take it. I just can't."

"We can't help," Cyd said darkly. "It'll cause another incident. Besides, maybe this is good for her highness. She obviously had no idea what she was getting herself into. Let her get a taste of reality."

Dain gave his partner an incredulous look. "What if he kills her?" Of course, that wasn't the point, and he knew it. The fact of the matter was, as far as his job went, his partner was completely right. This was a one-on-one between the two nonhuman species. They should stay the hell out of it and let the species settle things between them. Yet, even though it was unlikely the werewolf had the materials to kill Fleur, Dain just couldn't stand by and watch him tear her apart.

Not to mention, when Dain was in trouble, she and the Protectors had defended him against their own kind. This wasn't right.

He jumped down and kicked the werewolf away from Fleur. Just as Cyd had warned, the dog delivered a war cry to his pack. The howl reverberated down the tunnel.

"Damn it!" Cyd cried. She jumped down and pulled Dain back, and the vampire and werewolf faced off anew, seemingly oblivious to them.

If Dain had had any doubts, the rumble suddenly generated at the back of the transport shaft made things very clear. He had no idea how far away the dog's reinforcements were, but there were clearly enough of them to make it sound like an earthquake coming down the tube.

Dain moved closer to Fleur, who was in some kind of trance as she sparred with the dog. "Fleur, it's Dain. We need to go."

As if in slow motion, he watched from little more than a handshake away as Fleur drew a tiny silver dagger from her boot and jammed it into the dog's heart. In a kind of fascination and disgust, he watched her follow up the dagger blow by digging her fangs under the werewolf's jaw and snapping its neck in some sort of otherworldly fury.

Dain reeled back onto the platform in horror. Aside from the rumbling getting closer in the tunnel, everything went silent. Fleur was just staring down at the body at her feet. Cyd was probably in shock behind him. Dain managed to release the breath he'd been holding. And when he finally collected his thoughts, he was insanely pissed. "What kind of rookie move was that, Fleur? You're the goddamn head of vamp street intelligence. You're supposed to be trained for this . . ." His words trailed off as he remembered the truth of the matter.

She finally looked up at him, and they stared at one another for a moment. A couple of different emotions passed over her face, and then all Dain could see was her shame. Fleur dipped her head to her hand and just looked at her fingers wet with blood.

"They didn't train you for this," Dain reminded himself softly. "Oh, man. You had no idea what you were getting yourself into."

He stood up straight and looked over his shoulder. Cyd had her hands on top of her head and was pacing the length of the platform, her eyes like saucers. "Oh, Jesus. Oh, shit. Oh, man. Oh, I'm not believing this."

Dain wheeled around. "You didn't help me break them up. What the hell did you think was going to happen?"

She stopped in her tracks, her arms flailing out. "I thought they'd beat each other into a bloody pulp and leave it at that! I figured she'd know enough not to go and kill him."

In a kind of daze, Dain turned back to Fleur. She was still silent, her eyes bright with unshed tears, her cheeks hot and flushed.

Cyd grabbed him by the arm and wheeled him around to face her. "Do you hear that? That's the patter of little paws," she said sarcastically. "Your stupid vampire girlfriend just killed my top informant and now his buddies are going to get involved. I can't wait to read your report on this one."

Dain shook off her hand. "Okay, let's figure this out." He exhaled, watching Fleur stare in shock down at the dog she'd just killed. "Let's figure this out." The pounding got louder and then suddenly it was drowned out by a whistle and the faint glow of a headlight as a train turned a corner and started toward them. It was still quite a ways away.

Fleur put her hand in front of her eyes. "Dain?" she asked.

Dain knelt over the side of the platform. "Fleur—number one, you need to keep your mouth shut right now. Just don't say anything. Number two, you need to take my hand and get off the tracks." He held out his hand and she stared at it listlessly. It was as if the kill had completely sapped her energy. He wondered morbidly if she would have been better off drinking the werewolf's blood, and for a moment he wondered why she hadn't.

"Fly out or take my hand," he ordered. He reached down, grabbed her chin and forced her to look up at him. "Take my hand." She did as he asked, and he half pulled, half dragged her over the side. She stood, then bent over like she was going throw up, but just kept her head down and, as he'd requested, her mouth shut.

Cyd had jumped down onto the tracks and was trying to get the dog's body up over the side. As he died, the dog had changed back into human form and now looked like the slightly wacked-out thug they'd first seen.

"Leave him, Cyd. Let the train take the body. You know it's just going to open a can of worms if he's found. A random vampire doing this down on dog turf is bad enough. But nobody—and I mean, *nobody*—in this city can afford to believe that Fleur Dumont just killed a werewolf. It would be a political nightmare."

"They don't have to know it was her." Cyd kept trying to pull the body up.

"They aren't going to understand what happened."

She glared at him, the werewolf's blood all over her hands. "*I* don't understand."

"I'm telling you, you gotta let him go. You know I'm right."

Cyd looked down at the body at her feet and threw her arms up in disgust. She hopped the ledge and folded her arms. "Nobody deserves this kind of end. It's a matter of honor. He was here because he was my informant."

The wolves coming down the tunnel from the passenger platform were all howling now, perhaps calling to the one who'd sent up the alarm. Once they arrived, there would be no talking or explaining. The light for the opposite track switched to green, and the train whistled again. They had two choices: train or angry dogs.

No contest.

"I've never seen one turn like that," Fleur suddenly blurted, shaking uncontrollably.

Dain put his hand on her cheek and tried to get her to focus on him. "Get ready to jump on the train," he ordered. "You hear me?"

Fleur just nodded numbly. He put his arm around her waist, preparing to haul her alongside him.

The train shot into the tunnel like a bullet. Everything seemed to happen at once; the train raced over the informant's body, and Fleur suddenly slipped out of his grasp. He turned to find her but could only watch in shock as the same three guardian vampires from before appeared and pulled her into their protective circle. Fangs fully exposed, eyes dilated, and hovering in readied fighting stance, they were clearly up for blood and ready to attack if necessary.

But with Fleur in their care, they had what they wanted; they headed straight up the tunnel toward street level ahead of the train. Dain had no time to think about anything besides jumping onto the caboose ladder as it passed. Cyd was by his side as he made the leap, shadows of the approaching dogs a flicker against the tunnel walls as they rode up to street level far behind the vampires. As soon as the train stopped, they hopped off the back and casually walked away from the station. Dain could only hope they'd gone unnoticed.

He headed back in the direction of the car.

"Where the hell are you going?" Cyd asked. "Don't even think about going to her."

Dain wheeled around, his emotions out of whack. A combination of rage, sorrow, confusion—everything was swirling inside him. He wasn't in the mood to deal with Cyd's strange behavior, that was for sure. "I'm going to get the car. Do you want me to drop you off somewhere?"

"Don't bother. I have some relationship bridges to repair ASAP," she snarled.

Dain stopped in his tracks and ran his hand through his hair. He forced himself to be rational. "Cyd. You know that I'm sorry about your informant."

She shot him a look of total disgust. "Let me tell you something. I've known you for a very long time. I also know something about coming undone. And you, my friend, are coming undone. And it's because of that girl."

He shrugged helplessly. "I knew she wasn't totally trained for her position. But I swear, I didn't realize she was so . . . green."

Cyd whirled around. "That's because you were concentrating on the wrong things, buddy. Your head was somewhere else. You're not focused on the job. You're only focused on how everything relates to Fleur Dumont, and how to keep yourself from getting to the point where you have to admit that she's a vampire and you're a human and you can't have her!"

"That's bull—"

"I'm not done." Cyd threw her arms up in disgust. "You're on a slippery slope. And if you think that *I'm* fucked up, then you already know what you have to look forward to after you mess your life up." She stared at him. "If you can come to terms with what just happened in there, then there's something very dark in you that I don't think either of us fully understands."

"Cyd—"

"I'm not done! Look, there's obviously really nothing I can do or say that's going to matter. You're blind when it comes to that chick. You think in a job like ours we can afford to be partial? That we can cover for some green fang who goes apeshit and kills one of my best informants? All that's left for me to do on this one is to remember to duck and cover when you go down. So, go see your girl and feel free to start making your excuses for what she just did. But I don't want to hear 'em. Not now, not ever. I'll see you later."

"Cyd. Do not walk away from me. Cyd. Cyd! Dammit!"

Chapter Fifteen

Fleur sat curled up in a ball on the couch with her head on Marius's shoulder. Ian and Warrick sat in club chairs facing her; they'd helped clean up the worst of her battle wounds and Warrick was now putting the supplies back in the kit while Ian finished tying the ends of the bandage around her thigh.

She'd come down completely from any high of the kill and just sort of collapsed, totally devoid of energy and more than a little shocked by what had happened in Dogtown. The leg wound had stopped bleeding and the rest of her wounds, scrapes, and bruises were beginning to heal. Some things, however, did not seem to be improving.

"Everything that could have gone wrong, went wrong," she mumbled. "I don't understand. If I'm meant to lead us, why doesn't it show?"

Marius chuckled softly. "It shows, Fleur. Believe me."

"I may come from the purest lineage of fighters

and leaders, but apparently inheriting the genes doesn't ensure I'll be any good at it."

Warrick shrugged. "It will come. You weren't trained to face the dogs."

"Why not?" Fleur asked.

"You know that. Nobody thought it would come to this," Ian said. "Nobody thought Christian and Ryan would go down during peacetime. And after Hayden . . ." He trailed off.

Fleur felt a flush fill her cheeks. She tapped her index finger gingerly against her mouth and was relieved to feel that the swelling had gone down. She gathered her courage. "Well, let me put it this way . . . if there's anything else I wasn't trained for, let's get it set up."

Eyebrows rose all around. Fleur sat up straight and searched the faces of her three cousins. "What? Is it so ridiculous? Am I such a hopeless cause?"

Ian pushed her gently back against the couch. "Relax. You're doing fine. You're doing everything Christian or Ryan would have."

"All right then. And I want to be properly trained on how to fight a werewolf," Fleur said firmly.

Warrick threw back his head and roared. The more he laughed, the more furious Fleur became. "I'm not joking. I want the roughest beast you can find. You should have seen what happened. I feel as though I've been trained as befits a lady of the house. I want to be trained as befits a man of the house—as befits the Dumont heir! Do you understand what I'm saying? Train me as you did my half-brothers."

Marius looked at her somberly. "Our training did them little good against that mech."

"Marius, get it done."

He looked a little surprised by the tone of her voice, and he put up his hands in surrender. "Fine. Of course. You'll get whatever training you want. You're absolutely correct. I just don't think you understand yet."

"Understand what?"

"That you did nothing wrong," Ian said.

"How can you say that? I shouldn't have killed that dog. And even after I'd stabbed him with that dagger, I bit him. I was like some sort of wild animal."

Marius looked at her a little sadly. "It's our nature. It's what we fight against."

"Then how can you say I did nothing wrong?"

The Protectors looked at each other. "Okay, it was wrong. But nothing could have prepared you. We all have the one," Warrick said. "The one, first kill. The one that makes us understand what we must stop. Until then, everything we've been taught is merely words. As you've just discovered, knowing the theory behind why we use blood banks isn't the same as experiencing why for yourself. We don't truly understand why we have to fight so hard for our humanity until we actually fight for it."

"I'm surprised you didn't drink his blood," Ian said. "That's the usual for a first kill, and it's why you feel so terrible, now."

Marius tipped his head and studied her face. "I actually think you showed admirable restraint—under the circumstances."

"Well, in all fairness, there didn't seem to be time. I don't know. I . . . don't quite remember everything," Fleur said, blowing her nose distractedly into a rather nice handkerchief she'd scrounged from Ian's suit pocket. She looked up from the cloth

with a lopsided smile. "And he was a bit...
grungy."

Ian elbowed Marius. "She didn't want to suck
werewolf blood. That's our little princess."

Marius never cracked a smile, and Fleur's own
teasing one faded away. The expression on her
cousin's face made her think of her feelings for Dain.
And suddenly she realized that, what he'd seen her
do—how could he accept it? He couldn't, and anything between them would be as impossible as Marius had always said. Vampires and humans were
different species. Period.

"So, would you like to tell us exactly what you
were doing down there?" Marius asked. "We felt
you only when we sensed your danger."

"What? Oh." Fleur shrugged. "I went to see the
dogs," she said sullenly.

"Apparently. Go on."

"I asked Dain to take me to see one of their informants. I wanted to hear from the dogs for myself."

"And?"

Fleur looked away, trying her hardest not to snap.
"I didn't get very far. It was horrible. I think I've made
a mistake that's just—I honestly thought I was ready."

"Ready?" Marius prompted.

"Ready to show everyone that I hold control. That
I know what I'm doing. That losing Christian and
Ryan as leaders and my stepping into their shoes
did not weaken us."

"That you 'hold control.'"

"Yes. Instead, the humans saw how weak I am.
Which reflects on all of us. I made us look weak tonight. I thought I knew what I was doing," she repeated.

"I don't think they'll see it quite like that. Fearlessly snapping a werewolf's neck with your teeth doesn't exactly make us look weak."

"I wasn't fearless. I was . . ." She would have said *out of control*, but she didn't want to bring up again the reputation she'd gotten after making Hayden a vampire. Ironically, she'd deserved that reputation.

Warrick waved off her words. "You'll probably have the dogs analyzing what you did for weeks. They'll never figure out who did it. There's too much going on in the city right now for anyone to think it was you. The dogs' investigative abilities leave something to be desired anyway, I'm sure."

She gave her cousin an exasperated look. "War, the two humans I was with will know. I was ridiculous. I completely lost my mind. And I lied."

Marius glanced up. "What do you mean, lied?"

"An omission, a fudging sort of thing. I as much as told Dain Reston that I'd been amongst the dogs before. I should have known about that strange energy we two species seem to project when we're riled up. I mean, I *have* been amongst dogs, but it was . . ." She felt herself going red. "I think it was just in a shop or something. In any case, I've never seen them so angry—and not when *I've* been so angry. I'd never even actually seen the Change. The intensity of it was incredible."

"Yes. It is when you don't know what to expect. Part of what you felt is because you're Warrior class," Marius said. "You're right about the training, though. You needed more. But then, none of us guessed it would come to this."

Fleur sat up. "Speaking of which, there's something I really want to talk to you all about. You need to stop protecting me. If I'm to recover from my past and the mistakes I've already made in the present, I'll need every advantage I can get."

There was silence all around as her cousins eyed each other.

"How are we not an advantage?" Ian asked, with some amazement.

"You're always right there, right at my back. It's got to stop."

Marius frowned. "As Protectors, we're not only intuitive, Fleur, but we have a kind of . . . holy bond, if you will, to defend the lives—body and soul—of those who lead our people. You know that."

"I don't think we need to point out that we're a little thin these days as far as who else could inherit your position," Ian added.

Fleur nodded. "I understand that. And I'm . . . grateful. Of course I'm grateful. But you're undermining my ability to see my actions through. You're undermining my ability to learn from my mistakes. It's possible you're even undermining my ability to earn the respect of the Assembly. I'm sure they believe you control my puppet strings."

Warrick sat forward. "That's ridiculous! Everyone knows—"

"Everyone does not," Fleur said gently. "Now, I love you all very much. You're my family. But you simply must let me go. You *must*. I promise I won't disappoint you."

Marius rubbed his temples as he and his brothers thought about her words. Ian shrugged. Warrick nodded.

Marius finally sighed. "Agreed. One last bit of advice, though," he said.

"I'll always welcome your advice."

"The lying about your experience is dangerous, Fleur. I can tell you that. Putting yourself in a position where your credibility is suspect . . . We can't afford to have the humans mistrust us, unless we have a good reason to believe—"

"That they ordered my brothers killed. I know. Maybe if I explained—"

"What would you say?" Warrick asked skeptically.

"That I was scared I'd reveal how untested I was."

Marius made a sound. "You'd tell the humans that?"

"Well, I'd tell Dain," Fleur said, without thinking.

Marius gave her a curious look. "Why would you tell *him*? Is he special in some way?"

Fleur started, surprised. "Well, no . . . I . . . No. It's that he's very . . ."

"Don't do it, Fleur. Trust me. Don't get involved."

Fleur gave him a long look. "*You*'ve been involved. Time and again, you've been involved. How do you dare lecture me?" She knew she was treading on thin ice, but she figured her cousin should be able to take as good as he gave. "I wonder why you're never dangerously tempted to bite them, the ones you love. It can't just be the politics, can it?"

There was a very long silence. Ian and Warrick exchanged glances.

Finally, Marius answered: "Political differences between the species are useful in that they tend to make you think twice before you act."

Fleur raised an eyebrow, disbelieving. "And that's why you didn't bite them? You just said, she's human, I'm vampire, and that's that? That's all it took?" She felt ashamed. Hayden had asked, and she had broken vampire law. Every time she looked at Dain, she wanted to bite him, devour him, bridge the gap between them. Her cousin's answer brought her up short.

"Well, Fleur, it's never really come to that, you see. The ones I've loved have never asked." Marius stood up very suddenly and left the room.

"Well," Ian said brightly to cover the silence. "Drink, anyone?"

Warrick reached for the decanter. "Definitely."

"Make mine a double," Fleur said with a sigh. "I don't think I'm going to bed anytime soon."

Kippenham looked about as tired as Dain felt, but it was nice to know the suits were working hard on this, too. Tapping his gold championship ring against the desk, Kipp surveyed Dain's latest report in the blue glow of the reader screen, then looked up, a dubious smirk on his face.

"Fleur Dumont went down to Dogtown with you and Cyd to meet a werewolf informant, and she panicked?"

"Yeah."

He broke into a broad grin. "Vamp-werewolf one-on-one. It's been a long time since we've seen that kind of action."

Dain felt more annoyed than amused.

His boss pushed the reader aside. "I'm amazed this didn't make the evening news. I thought Cooper had for-hires in the subways. Anyway, it's for the best. How's the vamp thing looking from the inside? Are you getting the picture?"

"Well, the assassination wasn't an inside job. From what I know about Fleur Dumont and her

three Protectors . . . they didn't pull it off. If anything, they're feeling more stress because of it. And
Fleur is . . ."

"Is what?"

Dain found it a little difficult to expose Fleur's
flaws to the boss. But he had to. "Okay, Fleur Dumont is weak. She's untrained. She's got a lot of
promise; it's just not all pulled together. You know
what I'm saying? I mean, she can obviously kick
some serious butt, but she just wasn't raised like
anyone ever thought she was going to take a leadership role. And these Protectors seem more concerned about keeping her alive than stirring up
trouble in Crimson City."

"Okay, so you don't think it's them. What else?"

"I don't think it's any of the vampires who are in
the Primary Assembly. It just doesn't follow that
they pulled a coup and blamed it on us. Why would
they need a scapegoat? That being said, there are always rogue groups to think about. It's possible that
any one of the vampires from a rogue group which
doesn't subscribe to the party line could have been
involved. But from the information I've collected to
date about the Dumonts and the vampires who answer to them . . ." He just shook his head. "I don't
see them commandeering one of our mechs and . . .
There's just no evidence."

Kippenham stared out the window. "This does give
us some insight into the shaky ground the vamps are
standing on right now as far as leadership."

Dain felt horrible. He didn't like the idea of letting anyone know Fleur was weak . . . but this was
his job.

"We processed the forensics material left behind

by the mech but didn't learn anything," Kippenham said after a pause. "So, that route is dead. I've got people out on the streets looking for it, but it's either been deleted already by someone we don't have a connection with . . . or it's got more of a sense of survival than we would have expected for a machine."

Dain pulled the reader toward him. "What file is it?"

Kippenham put his palm over its screen and pulled the reader back toward him. "Actually, it's classified. Suffice it to say, we didn't learn anything that would be useful for you to know."

It took a long, uncomfortable moment for Dain to process what his boss had just said. "Um, okay. Well, can you tell me what the torn paper was all about? Did it test for anything unusual?"

Kippenham waved the question away. "It was just paper. We didn't get anything from it."

Meaning, if they had gotten something, he wouldn't be telling Dain. There was a pause while Dain tried to read between the lines. He came up blank. Finally, he got to the point. "I have top clearance," he said softly. "Or has that been changed?" *And he'd thought they were friends.*

"That's not been changed," his boss said carefully. "We've just had to establish a new classification in response to the current environment."

"Would that be *extra* top clearance?" Dain asked sarcastically.

Kippenham put his hand on Dain's shoulder. "Dain, we've been friends for a long time. And I'd like it to stay that way. But the mech program is going under even higher security than ever before, because of the malfunction. We need to tighten the circle. And that means we've got to limit the number of people with access to the information."

Dain looked down at the gold ring pressing into his shoulder. "What is it exactly you expect me to do on this assignment, then? My mission is to collect intel relating to who could have wanted the Dumont brothers dead. Who set all this up? Who arranged to have the mech do it? Yet the mechs are now essentially off limits to me."

"An unfortunate necessity, but yes. Keep Cyd on the dogs; you continue to monitor the vamps. That's all we—"

"If I don't have a total understanding of how the mechs fit into the picture, it's sort of like you're running me around on a fool's errand."

Kipp's hand finally slid off his shoulder, and Dain felt an almost palpable sense of relief. He felt like slugging the guy.

"Come on, Dain. This isn't a fool's errand and you know it. We need you to keep doing what you've been doing. You're our eyes and ears on the streets. You've got an in with the vampires, and that's where we need to keep you focused. We need to make sure this doesn't blow up. We need to protect ourselves until we can find out what's going on, and we need to keep everyone calm."

Dain nodded slowly.

"Which is going to become more difficult in the near future."

"Why is that?"

"Because we're going back to the old Preemptive Defense Initiatives."

"I knew it." At least Kippenham had said something. Dain had kept his mouth shut just to see if the boss would bring it up. He needed to know just how much information they were concealing from him. He still wasn't sure.

"It's temporary. Just to get things settled down. I suppose you've read the report on the increase in species activity against humans?"

"There might be a little vice versa, too." The bureaucrat-speak was making Dain's head spin. Who was needing protection here? Everyone was being attacked—except the werewolves. "PDI is a wartime policy," he said. "We're still in a truce. Nobody has declared anything yet. And taking away freedoms for some species and not others will only stir things up."

Kippenham smiled indulgently. "Well, maybe. But this is how we're going to do it. Nobody's declared war yet, true. But this is one way to make sure our side gets an advantage."

Dain was horrified, but there wasn't any arguing.

"Under wartime restrictions, we need to up the security and close our task forces to smaller, more intimate groups of people." Kippenham tilted his head to the side. "Dain, you know it's nothing personal, but info from the top is going to get a lot harder to come by."

"Right. I know."

"Good. I'd like you to make sure you pass that information along at the next team meeting."

"Right. Got it." Dain stroked the stubble on his jaw for the sole purpose of trying to cover the vein that had started throbbing.

"Now, we haven't really covered the werewolves."

"Well, because of that incident," Dain said as he gestured to the reader, "I didn't get a chance to talk to anybody on the inside. I sent Cyd her assignment last night to have her follow up and file any findings. But I don't have to tell you she's probably not too happy with me right now. By the way, this wasn't Cyd's fault at all. I completely accept responsibility for bringing Fleur, and I should have made sure she knew what she was doing."

Kippenham studied him for a moment, tap-tapping his ring on the desk. "How is it with you and Cyd, anyways? How is she doing these days? In general."

Dain looked up in surprise. "Same as always. She's fine. Why?"

The boss cleared his throat. "Is she . . . using on the job?"

Dain kept his gaze steady. "I couldn't say," he said evenly. *What is this, some kind of interrogation? Of your own people, Kipp?*

"You have an obligation to report her if she jeopardizes the work in any way," Kippenham remarked.

"Yeah, I know," Dain replied.

"We're done, then."

Kippenham stood up, slapped Dain on the side of the arm, and headed out. After a while, Dain stood up too. He slipped his security badge from his wallet. Out of curiosity, he stuck it in the reader and selected the button to view his personal profile. He found his privileges to travel on the base at will had been revoked. Someone wanted him away from the mechs.

How he'd gone from being a member with open privileges to being completely declassified, he didn't know. Considering that he'd been hanging out with the vamps most of the time since this thing all started—Jesus, maybe that was it! Maybe they thought he'd been compromised because of his feelings for Fleur, and they were concerned he would pass on information. Hadn't Cyd suggested that? But they couldn't know what he felt. Because *he* wasn't even sure what he felt.

But maybe Cyd had—nah, not a chance. No way.

Dain got the hell out of the building and turned off in the opposite direction. He reminded himself that Kippenham was a good boss. But all it took was the smallest shift in information, in power, in perception and good was maybe not so good anymore.

Dain flagged down a hovervendor and bought a cold soda. He'd have preferred a beer. He stared at the cola, thinking that normally he'd have been fine drinking a beer on the job. No big deal—not in the battlefield. But things weren't normal anymore. And Dain was feeling paranoid.

He took a swig of soda and shivered. The night mist had evaporated as the sun began to push its way into the city like a rising crimson tide, but the air was still chill. And suddenly, Dain felt so tired he just leaned against the wall of a building. Using his free hand as a visor, he stood and watched the sun come up.

It was the kind of moment where one realized that a major shift had taken place. He'd just lost a certain amount of power. How much, he couldn't say. But somewhere, somehow, someone had made a concerted effort to take him out of the game. Without access to the mechs, he was confined to only what he could learn in the vampire and werewolf communities. And that bothered him.

It also wasn't normal for the boss to ask him about Cyd—not when there were clearly bigger things to worry about. Heck, it wasn't normal for the boss to ask him about Cyd at all! He'd have to have one of those talks with her, the kind he generally tried to avoid. If she was getting sloppy enough to attract attention and have it get back to the bigwigs, she was getting too sloppy. And if she was getting too sloppy, her personal life was creeping into her professional life, which was what she'd just accused him of. And that just wasn't going to work. Besides, he didn't like the idea that she might be slipping. Was she concealing things from him, unable to ask for help? Of course she was. He was the same way.

He punched up her code on his comm device. "Cyd, where the hell are you?"

Silence.

Sheesh. How many times did a guy have to apologize? "Cyd? Look. I'm doing the rounds today—you know, just sort of taking the pulse of the city. I thought maybe we could go see some of your informants on the way."

He punched redial on her code a couple of times, sort of the way one punched an elevator button to hurry things up even though it was obvious nothing would change. Then he had to laugh. Trust Cyd to miss out on one of his very rare, full-blown apologies.

He checked his messages on the comm pack. Fleur Dumont would like to see him at his convenience. Dain wanted to see her, too. Sure, he'd like to confirm she was still in one piece mentally and physically. And, yeah, he was definitely in the mood to perpetrate just the kind of mindless act he knew Kippenham would disapprove of. But really, he just wanted to see her again.

Fleur had screwed up royally, and he had a right to be pissed; but somehow he just couldn't hold what had happened against her. It was a sure sign of something really twisted when a guy got butterflies in his stomach just because a certain name appeared in his voice mail in-box. Cyd knew what she was talking about. He keyed in a response and sent it out. *"If you want to meet with me tonight, meet me at my apartment. I'm heading out."*

He knew he was tempting fate. He knew that putting himself in situations where Fleur Dumont could break down his defenses and give him an excuse to question his own actions was a bad idea. But at the moment, bad seemed to have a way of feeling really, really good.

Chapter Sixteen

Fleur was actually sitting on the doorstep of his apartment when Dain got home. "Hello," she said. Then she tilted her head and frowned. "You've barely slept. Is it because of me?"

Dain had to crack a smile, weary as he was. Because of her? *Not in the way she meant.* "It's been a rough week. Look, I'm just spent. I don't want to argue."

She chewed on her lower lip, her fang peeking out. "I'm not here to argue. First, I want to apologize."

"Forget it. It wasn't you. I should've known better."

Fleur frowned. "That's a load of crap and you know it. I'm the one who lost it."

He got the door open and held it for her. "Can I get you something to drink? I haven't had anything all day. I'm so damn dehydrated."

"Let me get it." She stopped him by taking his hand. It so surprised him that he just stopped and stared. She gave his hand a little tug. "Come on. I'll just put you down on the sofa. Don't worry." She led him to the sofa and pushed him down into it. "Beer? Water? Wine?"

"Beer." Dain watched her strip off her gloves and lay them carefully along the arm of the sofa. "Well, this is nice," he said. He lifted his feet up and stretched out.

"You don't have any pictures."

"What?"

"Of family. You don't have family?"

"Nah."

"I'm sorry."

Her sympathy made him uncomfortable. "Don't worry. I don't have some dark, tormented story about how they died and I never got over it."

"Then what *is* your story?"

"They died. And I got over it."

She studied his face.

"What?" he asked. "Your mother and father are both dead. Killed in the first battle between the species as I remember. So, you know how it is, right?"

She stared at him a moment longer. "Right. They died. I got over it," she echoed.

"Hmm. I don't think so." The quick flush of her cheeks was all the confirmation he needed. She seriously had to work on her poker face.

"Of course I didn't get over it. Who would? You're not over Serena, are you?"

Dain didn't answer.

Fleur shrugged. "It's a shock whenever one of us actually dies, because it's always so sudden, so violent. The story goes that my mother and father went out in tandem to handle a skirmish between humans and vampires in the Venice area. It turns out your side was trying to set up some kind of shoreline system to disrupt our shipping activities. Obviously, we took umbrage at the idea and . . . I'm sure your history books tell you the rest. I don't know what technology or weapon killed them, but they never came back. We lost many, many people that day. As did you humans." Fleur looked down at her hands, the sweep of her lashes concealing her eyes. "And my parents were just . . . gone."

"Gone?" Dain asked gently.

"After death, for us—well, we decay very quickly. As you know. The water and the dust . . . there's nothing physical left to mourn. It was tough to believe they were gone." She looked him straight in the eye. "In a strange way, I suppose it's not much different than trying to recall someone from just a photograph."

"What? Serena? I don't remember her," he leaned forward and whispered. "I don't remember my wife. I try. I swear to god, I try."

"I think it's all right, you know. The mind was made to forget. It's . . . nature."

Dain didn't know why, but she was giving him permission to forget. Maybe she *wanted* him to forget. A bad idea, either way. He cleared his throat. "So, your parents died in that battle, your half-brothers took the reins . . . and now, we end up with you. I'm going to go out on a limb and say that you weren't expecting to take the lineage so soon."

"Obviously, I couldn't have predicted the assassination."

"Obviously," he repeated, though his tone implied something of an accusation.

"I'm not as green as you think. There's more to

this than just street smarts. Otherwise, the wolves wouldn't be the ones living in the gutter."

"Some of those gutter complexes are nicer than my apartment."

She rewarded him with a sliver of a smile. "I believe you."

He had to laugh.

"Look, I really came here to apologize. About not telling you I'd never really seen the dogs before. One could say that was a lie of omission. I'm sorry about that. It was business, if you know what I mean. I had to—"

"I would have done the same thing in your position," he interrupted with a shrug. "Now, I've come to a conclusion."

"Oh?"

"Everyone's denying responsibility for directing that mech in killing your brothers, and it never reported back. We're denying it, the dogs are denying it, you're denying it. Which means . . . somebody's lying."

She handed him a beer and sat down across from him, the coffee table positioned between them like some sort of chaperone. "Well, you obviously believe that it was an inside job. You haven't even ruled me out as part of a coup attempt."

He shook his head. "I can't rule you out based on solid evidence, but I don't think you're lying."

She looked shocked. "You're telling me you believe me?"

"Yeah."

"Then, why are your bosses treating us like *we're* the ones who've done something wrong?"

Dain studied her face. "You've seen the PDI. I tried to tell them it was the wrong thing to do, but the boss has it in mind that our danger level is going up. *He* believes you vampires are ready to go on the offensive."

"But someone sent that mech at us!"

Dain raised his hands. "I know. I only wish I had the pull to do something about it, but I'm afraid I'm just a cog in the machine." He pointed his beer bottle at Fleur. "You, on the other hand, can work a little diplomatic magic."

She looked grim.

"Hey, you look like you've got the weight of the world on your shoulders," he joked. He grinned. "It's just one city."

She still didn't smile. "I don't think you understand. I *do* have the weight of the world on my shoulders. My world, anyway. Because of my lineage. If I fail, if responsibility is transferred to someone else, I will have let down my entire family. I will be shamed. My family will be shamed. It happened once before when . . ." She broke off suddenly, looking cold.

He tried to see her thoughts but couldn't. She focused on something in the distance, worked hard at preventing him from reading the emotion in her face, and ultimately was successful.

"You really have no concept of what's at stake for me, do you?" she asked. "Sometimes I think you just see this all as some sort of amusement."

"That is not true," he argued.

"I think it is. For thousands of years the Dumonts have held power in the vampire world. *Thousands* of *years*. And through each war, each wave of battle, we've been whittled down. There've been fewer and fewer of us. My mother was the last of a long line."

"You said your mother was the last. Except for you."

"Yes. Me. The failure. I . . . didn't take over when she died. My half-brothers took charge, and with good reason. I wasn't ready. But I am ready now, though they didn't train me. I am ready to step up and do my part. And I'm trying my best. If I do not step forward—if I do not help save us all, I will have made a joke of my heritage and failed my people. The history books will close on us forever. And I will be forced to live with that failure on my shoulders."

Dain slowly nodded. "I can't honestly say I understand. Not in the way you do. I've never had those sort of family ties." He shrugged. "And I've never felt so important to my people."

"Family ties." Fleur looked nervous. "Except for Cyd Brighton . . . are you with Cyd?"

"What? Well, she's my partner, so, yeah, I'm 'with' her."

Fleur gazed at him, intent. "She's not your lover?"

"Cyd? Oh, god, no. No, she's . . ." He sighed and threw up his hands. "I guess she's just about everything else. Friend, partner, sister." He shrugged. "Well, I guess if I really thought about what it meant to be family, she'd be it."

Fleur nodded and played with a trinket on the table. "You realize she can't stand me."

"She's not supposed to be able to stand you. Neither of us are."

Fleur laughed. "That's right. I remember. 'Field operatives are to cultivate a careful understanding of members of differing species, but nothing more than that, lest it compromise their integrity.'"

Dain's eyebrows flew up. "You have a copy of our training manual."

She shot him an impatient look, still half-laughing. "Obviously. As you do ours."

He reached out and tucked a stray lock of hair behind her ear. "I don't always follow the manual. I find it makes things very predictable."

"Predictable. Don't you think there might be a good reason for those rules?" Fleur asked. She leaned closer. "Don't you ever fear making yourself too vulnerable around me?" She reached out and tilted his head to the side, exposing his neck.

"Maybe I like the fear," he said.

"I hope it's not because you underestimate me."

"Oh, it isn't. And I don't."

Their lips almost touched, and Dain almost cracked. What screwed you up wasn't what you did when you couldn't stop yourself; it was what you did when you could stop yourself and chose not to. Dain fought the urge to take Fleur in his arms, carry her into the bedroom and throw her on his bed. He could visualize it all in his mind and the thought made him almost desperate with want. Instead, he pulled slowly away and stood up. "I think I need you to get out of here."

Fleur nodded after a moment. "Probably best," she agreed.

She didn't look like she thought it was best. But the bottom line was that any potential relationship was pretty much doomed between a human and a vampire. Unless the human wanted to make the change. Dain knew of humans who'd petitioned to become vampire, likely seduced by the prospect of riches. But from what he'd seen, living with forever could hurt worse than dying.

Chapter Seventeen

Dain glanced at his watch. In two hours he needed to file a report. He had some other business to attend to as well, but he decided to stop by Cyd's place first.

She lived even farther off the edge than Dain, not far from where they'd gone underground to meet with her informant. As someone whose regular job involved hobnobbing with the shiftiest of the species—the rebels, the sellouts, the embittered changeovers, and whatever species was most down on its luck—she lived in Old Hollywood, next to slum hotel housing converted from the old Mann's Chinese Theater.

The building wasn't really supposed to exist. It was the kind of place where, if you happened to want to kill someone, you were most likely to get away with it. On her salary, she could have easily lived next door to him, but Dain didn't like to dwell on what Cyd did with her money.

With PDI enacted, the green night-vision bulbs in the lampposts were being used instead of the white lights, and searchlights scoured the sky. If things started to get really bad, they'd switch again to the UV light, rending large swaths of the sky a vampire no-fly zone. Of course, that was the kind of act that went hand in hand with a declaration of war.

In spite of the fact that it was sprinkling out, the black market was in full swing on both sides of the street as Dain made it to Cyd's place and jimmied the lock. The fan was on inside, and dust swirled up in the light rays streaming through the window.

"Cyd? You home?"

No answer. A quick perusal indicated she hadn't gotten around to signing up for Housekeeping 101. Well, neither had he.

The refrigerator contained a half-empty carton of milk, a six-pack of diet soda, and a jar on which was scrawled, "honey." Dain sighed and took the jar out, opening the lid and sniffing the contents. "Honey, my ass," he muttered.

Dain glanced at his watch and backtracked to the door. Outside, the sprinkle had become rain and the smell of wet and dirty cement filled the air. As he stepped off the landing, there was Cyd, blocking his escape.

"Cyd, I—"

She hauled back and plowed her fist into his gut.

When he again managed to get a full breath, he was kneeling on the wet sidewalk in a serious downpour, being stepped around by passersby. Cyd was sitting cross-legged next to him on the ground, looking like a dissatisfied drowned rat. "What was that for?" he managed to ask.

"I thought it might make me feel better."

"Did it, I hope?"

"Not really." She stood up and offered him her hand.

Dain let her help him to his feet. "Damn. I forgot how strong you are. It's been a while since the last time I earned one of those." He gave her a wary look. "Are you sure you're not non-human and passing, 'cause that would explain a lot."

She gave him a disgusted look, but even as he made the joke, it suddenly occurred to him that it wasn't an entirely ridiculous proposition. He shook his head and headed in for her apartment, but Cyd didn't follow. He turned around and looked at her, waiting.

"It's raining, Cyd." He held out his palm. She didn't seem to notice, or care.

"I don't want to lose you, Dain," she said. "I *need* you."

Dain froze. Things were getting very deep all of a sudden. This wasn't in character for her. Not at all. He squinted through the pelting rain at her eyes, but she didn't seem to be on something—not at the moment, anyway.

She pushed a clump of wet hair out of her face. "Do you understand?"

He reached out and tried to pull her into a hug or something, but she shook him off. Dain wasn't sure how to handle her. "Cyd, you're not going to 'lose' me. No matter what happens, I swear. And I came here to apologize for what happened with Fleur. That was totally out of control, it was my responsibility, and I'm completely sorry about it. I assure you, it will not happen again."

"Fleur changes everything. I admit it." Cyd looked up at the sky, a flickering lamppost illuminating the desperation in her face.

Dain could only pray she wasn't going to say what he feared. Cyd was the closest person in his life. Like he'd told Fleur, she was his family. His only family. But he couldn't give her more than that, and he could only hope she didn't want more from him. "She doesn't *have* to change anything," he said.

Cyd cocked her head, furious. "That's bullshit. Tell me the truth . . . would you go vamp for her? Would you trade sides?"

He stared at her. "Wait a minute. This is about loyalty? My loyalty to you?" Anger boiled up inside him. "I have backed you one hundred percent, Cyd. Always. I've always been there for you and that's never going to change." His voice lowered to a whisper. "How dare you? After everything I've done for you? You know what I've been through with you . . . *for* you. The first day you got into my car. A fucking basket case, Cyd, that's what you were. I never asked. I never expected you to tell me what happened. I just accepted you. And through it all, especially those first few years . . . with the demons in your head and the drugs in your purse and the backup lies I told—"

"Okay!" Cyd blinked. "Okay." She looked down at her soaked tennis shoes. "Things are just . . . I don't even know who to trust anymore. And the thought of you going against me . . . I just couldn't . . . I just can't . . . deal."

"Come 'ere," he said gruffly, pulling her into his arms and resting his chin atop her head. "I will always be here for you. I swear. We're on the same side."

She didn't answer, but he felt her body relax into his. "Um, Cyd?"

"Yeah," came her muffled reply.

"It's raining pretty hard."

Her head popped up. "Yeah, let's go inside," she agreed.

She led the way back into her apartment, pulled a cigarette pack from her pocket, tapped out the last one and lit it, then flopped down on her bed.

Dain lay down next to her and put his arms behind his head. "I've got a question," he said.

"Mmm?"

"I'm getting a little fuzzy." He turned and looked at her. "Do you think, at its very core, that our job is to keep the peace, to keep everything in line, to keep everybody from stepping too far over the edge—or is our job to advance the human cause?"

She looked at him, furrowing her brow. "Well, I mean . . . I thought peace and equality was the point of the truce. Obviously equality was a bunch of crap, but there was that big 'togetherness' campaign which, while being totally dorky, was admittedly at the root a nice idea."

Dain nodded. "I remember when they enacted that truce. I felt like I could relax for the first in a long time." He held up his hand for Cyd's cigarette. She gave it to him and out of curiosity he took a drag, immediately wincing. "God damn, Cyd—this stuff sounds like a better idea than it is, and it never sounded that good. Serious burn."

"Street stuff." She took the butt back. "I don't even notice it anymore. What does *that* say?"

"Got me." After another moment of companionable silence he asked, "Is it progress when you're not sure whose point of view is more reasonable? Is that progress? When you start to feel that everyone's got a point?"

Cyd chuckled. "You really want to know what I think? I think this isn't anything new. You've always thought most everyone had a point of view. You never had a rock-solid allegiance. If you did, you'd see the black and white more clearly and would have gone with the I-Ops job."

"Point. And that's a good thing, right? I mean, refusing to take sides either means you want to get along with everybody . . . or you're just reserving the right to kick *everybody's* ass."

Cyd laughed. "I'll go with the latter."

Dain ruffled his hair. "You know, I think I'm having some sort of crisis of conscience."

"Oh, for god sakes, Dain. Stop with the big words and the deep thoughts. You don't have to make everything so complicated. It's really very simple."

Dain sat up. "What?"

"You fell for a vampire. Beginning and end of story."

"What?"

She shrugged. "You fell for a vampire and now you're trying to reconcile the fact that it's starting to become hard to work. Especially since we're in human defense, and we're revving up for an offensive against the very group you've discovered you don't actually dislike."

"Thank you, Dr. Freud," Dain muttered under his breath, annoyed that she had a point. "I just feel like everything's changing so fast. As if the pressure has been building and building in this city and someone's just uncorked it. I don't know." He got up, opened the door and leaned against the doorway, watching the rain pour down in the moonlight like diamonds streaking from the sky.

"Almost a full-moon," he noted. He glanced back at Cyd, who looked a bit scared.

"I didn't think it was possible for things to get more interesting than they already were," she said. "But I think we're about to find out. I . . . I think somebody's been jiggling the locks on the door to the underworld again."

"You think?"

She regained her composure and shrugged. "Somebody's always jiggling the locks. Human nature."

Dain seconded that thought. Human nature was in challenging everything. What would happen if he just stopped listening to the boss? What would happen if he just stopped showing up to work? He'd had no idea he even harbored such a fantasy. But what if he just made his owns rules, played his own game, and chose his own allies? What if, like Cyd said, he just stopped assuming allegiance to the human side.

Cyd stared out at the sidewalk, and when she finally looked up she said, "You have the soul of a wanderer, Dain."

Dain looked at her like she was insane, but she just smiled.

"I told you once that I thought there was something very dark inside of you. I think so more and more. I think it might be true of both of us. Maybe we should start getting used to it."

Dain held his hand out; the rain had slowed to a manageable level. "I'd better get back and file some paperwork. You coming with me or what?"

"Nah. I need to go off-comm for some informant stuff. I called in sick, and I'm going unofficial."

Dain studied her face. Her green eyes locked with his, careful and inscrutable. He just sighed and said, "Okay. But I expect to see you at work tomorrow, young lady."

She grinned and shrugged him off. "I'm still working, you know."

He pointed his finger at her. "Show up for work tomorrow," he commanded.

"I *will*." Suddenly, she came at him and squeezed her arms around him. " 'Night, Dain."

It took him a second to process the move and to put his arms around her as well. She hung on for a good while, long enough for him to tell from the way she clung that she was still as much haunted by the same old fear and uncertainty as ever. Oddly choked up, he kissed the top of her head and stepped away. "Good night, Cyd."

Cyd watched Dain disappear around the corner; then she turned around and went back inside her apartment. Some people were lucky. Some just weren't. Cyd figured she fell hard into that second category, like a weight flung off the side of a building.

It wasn't an issue of getting what she deserved. Yeah, she was crooked. Yeah, she'd done more illegal things on and off the job than she could even remember. But everybody she knew did, even Dain. He was a big believer of "a time and a place for everything." If any of the Battlefield Ops team had been the type to follow the letter of the law, they'd be sitting with the suits instead of the armor.

Frankly, it was a miracle Cyd was still around. Dain was that miracle. Somewhere along the way, he'd turned into her lifeline, was the only person, place or thing that really kept her alive. They both knew that. But what only one of them really understood was that it went both ways.

This was about loyalty in the way he'd assumed. But it wasn't about humans versus vampires. It was much more personal than that. Dain couldn't see what Cyd had done for him in all the years since his accident. She'd prevented Serena's memory from fading. She'd made Dain believe he had a life worth living. She'd helped him keep the fragments of his life together. He didn't understand it, and she would never explain it to him. But if he could ever really see everything for what it was, he'd see that she'd been as much his lifeline as he'd been hers.

Cyd went into the kitchen and rummaged around in the cupboard, oblivious to the packages of dry noodle soup and soy sauce packets raining down around her. She finally found what she was looking for—a carton of smokes—and ripped the thing open, not bothering to rehide the rest from herself. Her shaking, clumsy hands scattered them at her feet.

She slid to the dirty kitchen floor against the drawers and lit up, trying to take a deep drag in spite of the trembling of her lips. She wiped her eyes on her sleeve. Dain was probably disgusted with how she'd let this place go. Poor guy did his best walking her tightrope. She could see the wheels turning when he looked at her, always trying to calibrate her mood, wondering how much to say, how much to ask, how much to just let go.

It wasn't up to him, though. Everything he'd said was true. He had done right by her. In spite of this latest ripple, he'd always done right by her. She should have been dead a long time ago. She had to admit she rather liked the mystique that surrounded her, the way the others regarded her as special property—Dain's untouchable sidekick, his project.

Cyd took a last drag, jammed the cigarette stub out against the refrigerator, picked another one off the ground and indulged once more. It would be nice to have something stronger, something that would really numb her demons. She glanced at her watch, ash falling on her forearm; she let it sit there as long as she could stand, then shook it off.

Such wasted potential. Nope, she'd never been lucky. And she never would be.

Was the fork in the road that day she'd sat for entrance exams to the Academy? She'd scored high enough to submit three choices for her concentration. She'd submitted only one: R&D. Research & Development with an emphasis in demonology. If she'd submitted others—and had been assigned to one of them instead—would she still be the person she was today?

What she'd seen in that research group, over the course of what was at first considered the division's watershed year, but then was quickly dismantled in a shroud of mystery—would she have seen the same somewhere else, somehow else? Was this her destiny? Had she been *meant* to see what she'd seen?

Cyd stubbed out her second cigarette and rested her head back against the drawers. She wasn't strong enough to change anything about herself anymore. She'd waited too long, gotten herself embedded in too many difficult places. She was so damn tired, and a part of her didn't even care anymore what happened to her. She probably had more collective intel than anyone else working the streets right now. She'd had plenty of opportunities to sell out, and the thought crossed her mind a lot these days.

Could she do that to Dain, though? That was her one sticking point. She hated the idea of him having to deal with all those told-you-so's back on base, all those higher-ups who'd wanted to delete or disappear her like they'd done the rest of her team. Not officially, of course. There was no document that explained what had gone on, but you didn't have to be a rocket scientist to figure out what it meant when none of the people you'd had lunch with five days a week for the past four years answered the door anymore.

Cyd glanced at her watch again, then heaved herself to her feet and ran her fingers under her eyes to wipe away any streaking mascara. She reaffixed her ponytail, checked her ammunition, then slipped a gun and a dagger in her belt holder, plus a couple of spares and her comm device concealed inside her jacket.

After shutting off all the lights in the apartment, Cyd let the door slam behind her and headed out into the darkness.

Chapter Eighteen

A glance at his watch told Dain he wasn't late yet, but if he didn't pick up the pace, he would be. He parked the car in the far lot, guessing that the main lot at the station would already be full, then took up the block at a jog. Inside, the alert board was going nuts. Full moon, tension between the species, PDI pissing everybody off—his teams were going to be seeing more action tonight than they'd seen in recent memory.

The break room looked like the dressing room for a battle sequence at the movies. Snapping on armor, checking weaponry; everyone appeared to be present—except, of course, for Cyd, who'd clearly ignored his direct order to be at work on time tonight, probably just to prove she could. In any case, the collective energy in the room more than made up for her absence.

"Anybody catch those vamps on surveillance last night? They were flying pretty low again."

"I am *so* ready to rock n' roll on 'em."

"Who's killed both? JB, you ever done in a vamp? Or just a dog?"

"Just a dog. Couple of them, though. All legit, I swear. I'd like to get my first vamp. And I feel it's gonna happen soon. Somebody's gonna do something wrong very soon. And then . . . boom!"

Dain couldn't help shaking his head as the teams compared the sizes and weapons of their recent street adversaries. JB and Trask obviously had their hands full in Dogtown, trying to keep the peace. Outbreaks of violence were on the rise there, as they were everywhere, nearing the levels of pre-truce, though each seemed more a result of individual anger than any coordinated effort to wreak revenge.

Running covert operations, reeling information out of traitors from the other species, and preventing any species other than humans from achieving dominance in the city were some of the many items on the B-Ops charter. Inside the city break rooms of this Federal sub-agency, the monotony of the so-called peace-keeping assignments was now happily brushed aside in the preparation for action. Peace-keeping would be left solely to the city's regular police force. B-Ops was clearly ready for a fight. The only question was whether the action would come in the name of self-defense or as part of a calculated attack.

Yes, the razor-thin boundaries between the three species' worlds were weakening. And with Kippenham planning to enact even more obvious changes, it was only going to get worse.

Dain didn't really see how civil war was going to be avoided. It was beginning to feel inevitable. And if that happened, it wouldn't matter one bit how he felt about Fleur. In a wartime situation, a vampire of any classification—rebel or inner circle, murderous or human-sympathetic—would be public enemy number one. His job would be to shoot or stake to kill. It made him feel slightly ill. He forced himself to talk tough.

"So, did everybody read up on the imminent PDI measures? They're going to go into full effect soon, and when the species get pissed off enough, there's going to be a backlash. Don't think there won't." Dain had his team's attention. "It won't matter what the official werewolf and vampire leadership decisions are at first. There's going to be some kind of knee-jerk reaction on the streets before . . . well, I hope then most of them will listen to their leaders and back off.

"But not all of them will. It's going to be fast, chaotic, and unpredictable out there. We're not going to know really where we stand, so you gotta watch your back. Be ready to make some hard decisions. For those of you without a kill, you might get it this week. And I'm not saying this like it's a good thing, so don't go getting excited. Killing a vamp or a dog . . . well, it may feel stranger and more wrong than you think."

He shuffled through some of his papers. "Oh. Also this from I-Ops. The emergency warning system is still in test mode for the general populace, but as of now, *we* are to assume the sirens are not a drill. You hear them go off, you must react as if there is either an air-based fang attack or a ground-based dog attack somewhere in the city." He looked up at the team. "Got that? If you are out on the streets when they go off, head immediately to your pre-assigned coordinates and have your comms on for further instructions. And try to make sure the humans out there take it seriously. We want them ready for the real thing. Get them inside or into the light."

JB waved his arm. "Are we already under attack? What about those killings?"

"As far as I know, those humans were random deaths and not part of any coordinated assault. I believe we're just ramping up our defense. That doesn't mean that we have license to provoke either the fangs or the dogs. That's important. You all got that?"

They murmured their assent.

Some of the older guys were kind of looking at him askance. Dain faked a smile. "Not your usual gung-ho go-get-'em speech? I guess it's because I don't like the idea of seeing any of you guys hurt. Speaking of which, anybody seen Cyd this morning?"

They all shook their heads in the negative, looking a little surprised. He waved them off. "Okay. Well, if you do, tell her to check in with me. And that's a direct order." A couple of eyebrows went up, but he ignored them. "Now, unless you have any questions about your specific street assignments, get on out and—be careful out there!"

The teams filed out, Dain following behind. He punched Cyd's autodial number on his comm. No answer. He dialed her off-job voice mail and the message kicked in, Cyd's voice ringing out: *"I'm not here."* The sound of her laughing. *"And obviously, I'm not* there. *Leave a message or take your chances."* Beep.

"Cyd, it's me. Where the hell are you? Check in. That's an order. Or I'm filing you AWOL. Look, you promised. And now I'm seriously worried. Just . . . call."

Rounding the corner, he barreled into Bridget Rothschild. He caught her before she fell to the sidewalk, her sports bag flying out of her hand. "Jesus," he said. "Are you okay?"

She answered him with a brilliant smile as he helped her regain her balance, and it was hard not to notice how tightly she'd poured herself into her pristine white tennis outfit.

"Was it as good for you as it was for me? Seriously, Dain, I'm fine!" She scrambled for her bag, then put her hand to her heart and took a deep breath. "Surprised me, though. Are *you* okay?"

"I'm definitely the windshield in this one, and you're the bug. You sure you're—"

"I'm totally fine. I swear," she said with a laugh, smoothing down the pleats of her skirt.

Dain smiled back, thinking how unusual it was to see her in the city, particularly since they had fantastic tennis courts out on the base. She seemed so clean and neat and innocent in her whites. He didn't like her being out here, what with things heating up. "What brings you outside of the base? Oh, wait. You met somebody who works in the city, didn't you?"

She made an exasperated sound, but was smiling the whole time.

He gestured to her tennis outfit. "Don't tell me you've got a date on a night court out here."

She pursed her lips and did her best to look coy. "And what if I do?"

"I'd have to hope you kick his butt."

She grinned. "I'll do my best."

Dain laughed. But even as he did, in the back of his mind he was trying to put his finger on what it was about her today that seemed . . . off.

"Do I know him?"

"Uh, no. He's a civilian. And I wouldn't tell you if you did. Office gossip is the worst."

"Fair enough. You know, maybe I should take up the game. What do you think of that?" His hand reached out as if to grab the racket handle sticking out of her tennis bag. She looked taken aback, her fingers gripping her bag just a little more firmly.

"Something wrong?"

"No." She blurted out a laugh, her trademark girlish tinkle filling the air, and started walking backwards. "Just the thought of you playing tennis . . ."

"Seriously! We should play sometime."

"Oh, I don't think so. I'd send you to the cleaners, and that wouldn't be pleasant for either of us." Then Bridget twirled and headed off, her sassy little skirt swaying around her hips. "Later!"

"Hey, you're not walking there, are you? Didn't anyone tell you there's a bad moon rising?" he called.

"I'm just going around the corner. Gotta run or I'll be late. Bye!" She headed off.

Dain frowned as he watched her go. "At least keep your comm on. And be careful!"

She gave him a wave without turning back.

Dain watched her disappear around a corner. Bridget Rothschild. She only seemed to own one tennis outfit. It always looked way too tight to play in. And it was always perfectly clean.

Oh, you are so making this up, man. She's just a girl in a tennis skirt. He'd only seen her in tennis whites a couple of times, not enough to read anything into it. On top of everything else, he was becoming paranoid about his coworkers. Not good.

Dain headed across the street in the opposite direction and had his car in sight when the city sirens went off, ramping up into a full-scale wail. He froze for only a second before he turned around and starting running, calling out Bridget's name.

Bridget winced at the high-pitched screeching that pierced the air, and she cursed loud enough to cause even the cretin in front of her to raise an eyebrow. She wasn't really the sort of girl to be afraid of the dark. But on the other hand, it was difficult to stuff the proper weaponry and defense mechanisms into a little tennis skirt or a tennis bag. And there was nothing worse than being unprepared and insufficiently armed.

She heard the sound of a voice calling her name.

Reston. Goddamn it! He'd come after her because of the siren. Why the hell did he have to be such a good guy? Wasn't anyone ever just concerned for their own personal safety anymore?

Her contact slipped back into the shadows of the alley. "Someone you know?" he said testily.

Bridget ignored him, looking around wildly for an out. "Nobody can see us together. This is bad."

"Yeah, how are you going to explain this one, Miss Perfect?"

"Shut up," she growled.

"Bridget!" Reston called again. The guy was probably getting off on full SWAT team maneuvers, ducking into every alley with his gun drawn, looking for her. Bridget swore a blue streak and took her own gun out of her tennis bag. She looked at her contact, who was lolling casually against the brick wall with his arms folded across his chest, and rolled her eyes. "Do me a favor and just get out of here."

"Unseen? I don't see how that's going to happen."

"Bridget, are you there?"

"Shit! Okay . . . move all the way back into the shadows and stay there!"

Her contact gave her a look but complied, chuckling as he moved into the full cover of darkness. "How are you going to explain this, girl? Looks suspicious . . ."

It *did* look suspicious.

"Bridget!" Reston had practically found her. She tried to come up with a scenario: *I was on my way to the courts. This creep took advantage of the all-city warning and dragged me into an alley . . .*

No, that wouldn't work. There were going to be way too many questions.

Bridget looked down at her pristine tennis outfit, still perfectly white and unrumpled. With a sigh, she slipped the delicate gold watch off her wrist, tossed it into the shadows, then turned her gun, shot herself in the arm and dropped to the ground. Faking pain wasn't a problem.

A few seconds ticked by, then suddenly Dain hovered over her, immediately moving to staunch the flow of blood. "I heard the shot. What happened? Did you see who shot you?"

"Took advantage of the alert . . . he tried to rob . . . my watch . . . got scared . . ." She shook her head, her face a mask of pain, her head turned at an angle just able to see the toe of her contact's shoe peeking into view. She tried to move so that Dain's back was more to the contact, but Dain gently repositioned her as he talked to the medics over his comm.

"They're coming," he said to Bridget. "Can you give me any details?"

"I'm sorry . . . I-I didn't see. It happened so fast."

Dain looked at the wound. "Powder burn. He was really close to you."

"Yeah," she said weakly, then turned her head. "I feel sick."

"The shock. Take deep breaths. They'll be here soon. Don't worry."

Somebody else was trying to contact him. Dain kept fiddling with his comm. The light seemed to flash on and off, but no one managed to speak. He looked at Bridget and smiled. "Whatever."

"Dain!"

Both he and Bridget jumped.

He fiddled with the device some more. "Jesus, Cyd. Your timing is unbelievable. I've got a man down right in front of me, and there are crazy calls coming in all over the city. I'm sure you heard the sirens."

No answer.

"Cyd? You've cut out again . . . Cyd?" There was no answer. Dain tapped the base of his comm pack, but Cyd didn't try again. He rolled his eyes and said something about giving his partner a serious talking-to. Bridget stared at him, doing her best to look the wide-eyed innocent.

His comm beeped again and he gave her an apologetic look. She was more than glad about the distraction. Her contact was toying with her, sticking body parts in and out of the most well-lit spots behind Dain's back.

Bridget looked away. Shooting herself hadn't been the brightest idea, but she just couldn't take the chance of being discovered. Her wound was starting to hurt a lot more, and all she wanted was for Dain to leave her alone. She glanced nervously over at her sports bag, which was lying unzipped on the ground next to her. Dain leaned over her as he fussed with her injury, and Bridget could hear yet another comm come in.

"Dain Reston," said an indignant female voice on the other end. *"Are you having me watched?"*

Bridget blinked, a nauseous drowsiness dragging her down. Dain laughed and said into his microphone, "I'd do it myself if I was going to have it done."

"I'm being followed, watched. And if it's not you, it's someone I trust even less. Well, sorry to bother you."

Bridget focused on the upperclass lilt of the woman's accent. It had to be Fleur Dumont. All the brags were talking about Dain and Fleur and their supposed affair, and about how much trouble he was in.

"Where are you?" Dain asked.

"Hollywood and Vine, the night market. But I'm fine; I don't need help. I just wanted to know if it was you."

Dain abruptly hung up and looked at Bridget. He frowned and put his hand to her forehead. "You're really pale. Let's get you back to the office."

Bridget was actually starting to feel quite sick; it was getting harder to manage her emotions, her expressions—it was getting harder to pretend at all. "I'm going to be fine." But her words were so mushed together, she wouldn't have bought them. "I think the medics just pulled up. If you just get me to my feet, I'll walk over there."

He looked at her like she was insane. "Don't fight

me, Bridget. I'd say we've got about thirty seconds before you either faint or puke."

She nodded. "I need my bag," was the last thing she managed to get out before she had to close her eyes. Dain put her tennis bag on her lap. She wrapped her good arm tightly around it; then as he collected her in his arms, she finally allowed herself to relax and let the world go dark.

Chapter Nineteen

Fleur stood on the corner of Hollywood and Vine, in the middle of the night market, tapping on her comm. "Dain? Dain?" He'd already hung up. She heaved an irritated sigh. She'd bet the contents of her jewelry box that he was on his way. She hadn't wanted that—had she?

The street was clogged with people and the sidewalks were packed with the overflow from the bars and restaurants that lined either side. It was overwhelming. She'd dressed to pass tonight, and might have indulged in the anonymity for a little while, were it not for the fact that she was quite certain she was being followed. Threading her way through the vendors, the scent of oranges and cheap perfume stinging her senses, Fleur retreated into the shadows—all the better to watch rather than be watched.

Something was wrong with the city tonight. And it seemed to be closing in from all sides. Her experience in Dogtown had honed her senses where werewolves were concerned and as the old saying went, the dogs were restless. They weren't alone. The humans were trigger-happy with those sirens again, and she wouldn't have been able to hear Dain too well even if he'd stayed on the line.

If stupidity didn't kill the humans, paranoia would. Up in strata +1, the wailing sound wasn't so bothersome. More bothersome was trying to figure out why the humans were so intent on believing the vampires wanted to attack. They'd gone around and around with it in the last Assembly meeting. She knew there was tension on the vampire side as well; her people had been on high-alert since the assassinations. Everyone was uneasy. And then there were those rogues who always seemed willing to stir up trouble, whether it served a purpose or not. She was wondering when they'd make an appearance. They were whom she'd come to find.

Fleur sighed. Whom to trust? Whom to welcome as allies? And whom to keep at arm's length? She stared at the faces of those milling by the vendors in front of her and tried to guess at who was passing for human. If she didn't know them, they weren't vampires of the Primary Assembly. But she couldn't know all the rogues.

Sometimes she thought she saw Hayden's face in crowds, but at second glance could never find it. She had used to search for him in the vampire world above, even knowing he'd never be there. Now, spending so much time at human level, the possibility of seeing him again was very real. And yet, now when she searched the crowd, she wasn't looking for him; it was Dain Reston's face she sought.

Why such a connection to Dain? Why to this man—to this *human?* Why was she so drawn to him? It was more than the obvious. It was as if something were missing in each of them and the other had the ability to fill that emptiness. What had been lacking in Hayden and what Fleur sensed in Dain was something unique in a human: Dain had a darkness inside that lived in some sort of perpetual disconnect with his world. She could tell from the way that he forced himself to hold back, as if he had to work overtime to fit his human skin because he was drawn to a darker force. Fleur lived with that darkness. The vampire world knew what to make of it, accepting that part of themselves and not condemning it. That's what she'd experienced while killing the wolf. That's what made her people, her people. That's why they had to rely on a code of conduct to maintain their balance between good and evil.

It was Dain who made the two of them a perfect fit for each other. But it was also Dain who, as a human, made them an impossible combination. Fleur could never become human, and she could never go against code again and make Dain a vampire. Once was enough. Once was more than enough.

He must have been close, because it was only ten minutes since she called him before she saw him, far off in the crowd. She saw just his face at first, the face for which she'd found herself looking instead of Hayden's or other rogues. And as she watched him, any irritation about his presumption of a rescue melted away.

Something about the purposeful way he walked toward her, that he'd come to her instantly—it wasn't hard to imagine what it would be like if he were really hers. She didn't step out from the shadows, preferring to watch him look for her. There was a sweetness to it. About the way he sought her out in the crowd—a little impatient, a little excited.

He tried to mask his relief when he finally found her. "Hey," he said distractedly, looking around at her surroundings.

"I wasn't requesting a rescue," Fleur said, unable to prevent herself from smiling.

Dain focused on her, flashing a cocky grin. "Well, you got one." He tilted his head and looked at her, and she felt suddenly self-conscious in her simple black trench coat, her hair in a loose ponytail, and no makeup.

Dain didn't say anything, but he didn't have to. He just reached out and tucked a loose strand of hair behind her ear, his attention on her mouth, a very unprofessional look in his eye. He dropped his hand abruptly and turned to face the street. "So, what do you think?"

Fleur shrugged. "I don't know what to think. I was informed that . . ." Her gaze moved past Dain's face to the crowd. "Well, here they are now. Better late than never."

Dain followed her eyes to the faces of a pair of men who seemed to be craning their necks over the sea of bobbing heads to stare right back at them. Then he looked away and brought his hand up to his earpiece. "Cyd, is that you again? For god's sake, find a pay phone or something."

"Is something wrong?" Fleur asked.

"She didn't clock in this morning and has been

triggering my comm all day. When I answer, she doesn't."

"Go find her," Fleur said quietly. "I can handle this on my own." But she wanted him to stay. She had called him for a reason. She wanted to be near him. She was being selfish. She wanted him to choose her, no matter who was in danger. No matter what happened.

Dain looked into her eyes and she could see weariness. His eyes reflected thoughts unsaid, words unspoken. Which was just as well. Fleur smiled and looked away, remembering she had no right to him. No right at all. "Go to her. Go find her," she repeated, this time doing her best to mean it. She gestured to the two men separating from the crowd, now intent upon them. "This is nothing special."

"I'll stay here with you if it's all the same," he said.

Fleur was out of words. She just swallowed and pulled herself together, turning to the men she knew to be rogues. There were two of them, one dressed rather like a bastardized version of a British schoolboy, dark cosmetics smudged around his eyes and a rep tie around his neck. The other was in more traditional street attire, with tattoos covering his forearms and a jet black mohawk almost as arresting as his piercing green eyes.

"You pass well," Fleur said.

"So we're told. And what do you know? We don't just get Fleur Dumont. We get the whole First Couple of Don't Even Think About It," the schoolboy rogue said, looking between them.

"What's that supposed to mean?" Dain asked, stepping up. He stood next to Fleur, obviously itching for a fight. She could tell his blood was up. She doubted he even realized how far he disappeared within himself when the blind desire to wreak havoc took over. Of course, she'd certainly set the standard, losing control like that in Dogtown.

"Ask her," the rogue said, gesturing to Fleur.

Fleur raised an eyebrow and said in a bored voice, "If you're here to pick a fight, maybe we should just get on with it."

The answer came in the form of a left hook. Fleur ducked and threw off her trench coat. Dain reacted like lightning, lining up in front of the tattooed rogue, fists at the ready. "Give me an excuse to be bad," he said with a grin, curling his fingers to beckon his foe forward.

The fighters squared off and went at it.

It was clear the rogues weren't carrying any special weapons, not anything that could kill Fleur anyway. The most they'd be able to do was cause her pain. And yet, that didn't seem to be their intent either. Fleur stepped down her game a bit, just to see what her attacker would do. She sensed that he adjusted as well, throwing his punches a little easier, moving a little slower. This wasn't a fight so much as an exercise of some kind.

As she slowly and methodically sparred, matching fists, feet, daggers, and brute strength against those of her opponent, Fleur watched Dain fight the other rogue from the corner of her eye. There was a more serious match. After all, Dain could be killed with one well-placed thrust of a dagger. And he was fighting as she suspected he always did, assuming his life was on the line.

With Fleur's focus more on Dain's match than her

own, her opponent took advantage and slipped her up, kicking her feet out from beneath her. Fleur fell back hard to the ground, knocking her head on the cement. Stunned as she was, the rogue took the opening and came down atop her, sitting on her as if he'd bested his mate in a high-school wrestling match. His weight effectively holding her down, he stuck his dagger to her throat.

Fleur rolled her eyes. "Lovely," she said. Then both she and her captor waited for the second fight to play out.

Circling his foe, Dain glanced over at Fleur lying in surrender on the ground and reacted like a man possessed. His opponent leaped into a hard round-house kick, but Dain grabbed his ankle and sent him crashing headfirst to the ground. The rogue groaned in pain and Dain leaped on him, pounding his fist into the rogue's face as his other arm locked around the vampire's neck.

"Uncle." Fleur's captor said it sarcastically at first, but when Dain didn't seem to hear him—or perhaps chose to ignore him—he repeated the word more urgently.

"Dain," Fleur called.

Dain looked up in surprise, his fist poised in midair, then looked down at the rogue in his grasp as if seeing more clearly.

"Tell me," Fleur said, shifting uncomfortably under the weight of her captor, "Are you here because I lead the Primary Assembly now . . . or are you here because I once made one of your kind?"

He didn't answer her, just turned to his friend who'd slumped a bit in Dain's grasp. "She's not half bad," he said.

"How personal is this?" Fleur continued.

The rogue looked more self-satisfied than blood-thirsty. He knew that she felt pain just like anyone, and he could have meted out a little if he'd wanted. Instead, straddling her with a knife at her throat, he looked over at Dain and said, "Trade?"

"Sure," Dain said.

The rogue moved the blade away from Fleur's throat, flipping it over to show that he hadn't cut her. He raised an index finger. "One?"

Dain nodded, and the rogue sheathed his knife at the same time Dain holstered his own weapon.

"Two?" Dain and the rogue simultaneously stood, both still straddling their conquered counterparts.

The rogue held up three fingers. "Done." The two men stepped completely away from their victims. Dain held out his hand and helped Fleur to her feet.

The first rogue turned to Fleur and bowed. "Oh, where are my manners? I *throw down*, Fleur Du-mont," he said mockingly. He gestured to his friend and they walked away as easily as if they'd all just had lunch.

Fleur watched them retreat. "That's it?" she called. She didn't think they'd ever intended to hurt her. But they hadn't imparted any information, either. It was almost as if they'd come for sport not politics. That made it personal, but didn't shed light on the bigger picture.

Dain picked up her trench coat and brushed it off. "You okay?" he asked.

"Nothing bruised but my pride," she answered.

"But you went easy on him, didn't you?"

"Can't get 'em every time," she said obliquely.

He looked at her carefully, but didn't pursue his

point. "So . . . those are vampires, but they aren't your people. Rogues, yeah?"

Fleur wiped the sweat off her forehead. "Rogues. You handled yours nicely."

"And you let yours off easy."

"He got the better of me," she said, "but I wasn't afraid for myself. From the get-go, I knew they just wanted sport. A bit odd."

"Two on one wouldn't have been sport. You'd think your Protectors would manage to be around when you need them."

Fleur whirled around. Dain was right; there was no one there. Her cousins weren't there. She smiled to herself.

"If they had been, they would have been impressed with you," she said.

And then the city sirens wailed once more, having an instant effect. The marketplace instantly filled with people headed for home. Dain's hand went to his comm as he got a message. "This is Dain. Who is this? Hello?"

"Is somebody else requesting a rescue?" Fleur teased.

But Dain only flinched, and the blood drained from his face.

"Go," Fleur said, taking her coat back.

He nodded, took her hand and kissed it, then disappeared into the crowd. She watched him go.

When he was gone, Fleur slipped her arms into her sleeves and pulled her coat tight against her, looking over her shoulder at where the four of them had fought only moments before. The attack had seemed really personal. To her. About her. If that pair had had a message to impart in the name of the rogues as a whole, wouldn't they have communicated it? Or were they building up to something?

Fleur walked through the crowded streets, taking the pulse of things, watching the faces of the anxious passersby. She couldn't be sure of anything, but Dain had seemed quite certain that his bosses had not sent the mech to create tension between the vampire and human worlds. Everything that the humans were doing now, he claimed was in self-defense, as a reaction to the tensions the mech had triggered.

Now, she felt a sudden instinct to rule out the rogues. Those fighters hadn't seemed to have much of an agenda. Which left the dogs—but she still didn't know anything about them.

As the sirens continued to wail, Fleur knew that time was running out. She had to choose the right enemy. So it was time to see if there was a plan to set the rogues even more firmly against the primaries than they already were. It was time to track down Hayden.

Chapter Twenty

Cyd's voice was finally coming in loud and clear, saying Dain's name over and over. Screaming it.

A horrible chill swept over him. "Cyd, I need to know exactly where you are," he said into his comm. His voice sounded cracked, scared, to his own ears. He was scared. He hadn't felt this scared in a long time.

Her terrified screams couldn't tell him what he needed to know, and Dain simply drove toward Cyd's neighborhood, praying he'd guessed correctly and relying on reflex and instinct to get him as fast as possible through the maze of the streets. It took too long to get there. Dain stared straight ahead as lights blurred into rainbow streaks through the damp windshield, and the city seemed to unravel in front of him like an endless, slow-motion movie reel.

"Help me! Dain, help me!" Cyd's breath came in gasps between her words.

A total rage replaced the edge of Dain's panic. His hands clenched around the steering wheel. "Cyd, turn your GPS on," he called. He fought to keep his voice steady. "Flip your GPS on. Cyd? Flip your GPS on or give me one word. A landmark."

She just kept screaming. Then she went eerily silent and the green light of her GPS flickered. She had finally turned on her locator.

Dain's hands shook as he hit the all-call. "Emergency units to downtown. Follow the coordinates for Cydney Brighton on the GPS. She's in trouble." *In trouble on the opposite side of town.*

Dain slammed his palm against the steering wheel, tears welling in his eyes. He took a deep breath and focused on the blinking lights of the dashboard. "JB, do you copy?"

"JB, copy."

"You're closest."

"Consider me there."

"Cyd, give me something more to work with," Dain muttered, his voice already hoarse. But static on the other end of the line would have drowned her out even if she'd been talking.

Somebody's been jiggling the locks on the door to the underworld.

"No." Dain stepped down even harder on the accelerator, which was already to the floor. "No!" He dodged a scooter, overcorrected and clipped a parked car. The side mirror snapped off and hit the back of his transport, bouncing to the pavement behind him.

Away from the tonier parts of town, the "off" feeling, the tension and anticipation he'd felt back at the station was being answered. It was as if the city hung in the balance, was on the edge of chaos. Indeed, as he sped down city blocks, entire streets seemed deserted. Then in the next minute, he'd see someone running. And a pocket of activity.

It wasn't unusual for this area, except the urgency of it all. Furtive glances, fear, and always people were running from something. Or to something. The sky was filled with dark shadows, thin traces of those who weren't necessarily human—and who weren't necessarily friendly.

"Cyd, can you hear me? Cyd, if you can you hear me, go somewhere we know. Do you hear me?" One hand on the volume button, one hand on the steering wheel, Dain fishtailed around a corner and smashed the back end of his car into a group of trash cans, ignoring them as they tumbled down the street behind him.

Closer, closer . . . Cyd's apartment was just down the street, though she herself was on the move. Dain careened onward, nearly barreling into a pack of canines racing across an intersection. They scattered, barking. "Cyd, give me something. Can you hear me?" he called.

Dead silence, save for the sound of frightened, labored breathing. Then, suddenly, Cyd was speaking, loud and clear. "They're coming for me," she said, her voice oddly measured.

Dain drove out of the side streets and merged back into traffic on Main, weaving through the lanes like they were his own personal obstacle course. He passed Cyd's apartment complex, the corner store where she bought cigarettes, the side streets leading to the hidden places where her informants lived . . .

His history with Cyd, his entire friendship with her flashed through his mind, a slide show of memories more vivid than any he had left from his former life. There came the sound of smashing glass over the comm. The car lurched as Dain reacted. Cyd was screaming bloody murder at the top of her lungs. A gunshot sounded.

Dain glanced down at the dashboard; her comm light was out. Her GPS light went out. And he was left with nothing.

He screeched to stop. He wanted to get out and walk around. He found himself at the front of a line of cars at a light that had just turned green. Behind him, horns blared, muffled curses just barely penetrating the windows of his transport. But Dain sat in the car, his foot poised above the accelerator, his gaze fixated on the dashboard. He had no idea how long he sat there, idling as the cars swerved around him.

"Dain, it's JB." The voice was bleak. "Dain? I'm here, and . . . and . . ."

It's bad. He didn't need anyone to tell him it was bad. He already knew. "I'm almost there," he choked out. He put the car back in drive, rounded the corner and drove to Cyd's last GPS signal. It was all a blur.

People clustered on a street corner. Dain double-parked, turned on his hazards, and got out of the transport. Numbly assessing the scene from a distance, he could tell they were focused on what had once been a phone booth. Nearer, he saw it was now just a metal frame with a pile of glass spread out around it. The glass sparkled like gemstones in the flickering neon from the billboards above. The phone was ripped out, the black cord lying limp in the shards like a dead snake half-buried in red-speckled ice.

Most of his B-Ops teams were there, shoulders

hunched, hands to faces, arms around each other. Dain steeled himself. He tried to, anyway, knowing that they were all watching him as he approached. Nobody said a word as he stepped to the edge of the scene and stared down. Blood spattered everything in a two-foot radius.

Dain ran his hand over the stubble on his face, feeling slightly faint. Then, with the lights flashing and the sirens wailing, he removed an evidence swab from a kit in his jacket pocket and began to take samples.

"I can finish that, sir," JB said. He was uncharacteristically formal, probably just trying to keep his shit together like everybody else.

"No, I need to make sure we get everything. It's gonna rain again."

"I know. Let me do it, sir." JB actually put his hand around Dain's wrist and gently took the swab kit away.

Dain let him. He stumbled to his feet and finally focused on the faces of his teams. They were looking to him for answers. He didn't have any. "Where's the body?" he asked, his voice still hoarse.

The others just looked at each other, at the ground . . . anywhere but at him.

Dain held out his arms, palms up. "I said, where's the body?" He honed in on Jill Cooper, the reporter, standing there with her camera held loosely at her side. She looked like she'd been crying. "Where's the body, Jill?"

Jill swallowed and shook her head. "There's no body."

"What are you talking about? Where's the goddamn body?" he bellowed. "Where's the body?"

Somebody put their hand on his back. He shook it off. "Where's Cyd?" He walked around the crime scene, gesturing to the evidence of violence at their feet. "JB? Trask? Anybody? Where *is* she?"

Trask took a step forward. "We've got teams canvassing the—"

"What the hell are you talking about? Are you telling me that whoever did this, killed her and took her goddamn body?" Dain pressed his fingers to his temple; it felt like someone had stuck an ice pick through his head.

"We don't know, sir, but it looks that way. It could have been anything, anybody. Vampire, werewolf, human. And it could have been . . . something else entirely. Forensics has already been alerted—"

Dain put up his palm for silence. He didn't want to hear empty, useless theories. They didn't answer questions. What did anything matter when the people you cared about were gone? The disappearances, the deaths . . . these were supposed to make him want revenge. Especially with what he knew. His job was about protecting humans from attacks like this, and the horrible disappearance of Cyd was supposed to be an incentive for maintaining a clear line between the species. All it did was make him feel just how pointless such lines were. Who you loved was all that mattered, human or not. Fleur mattered, human or not. Right?

"I don't know if I can do this anymore," he whispered, staring down at the pile of glass and metal.

JB put out his hand. "Dain . . ."

"Just stop!" Dain bellowed, nearly blinded by the

intensity of his rage. He wheeled around and slammed his fists down on the hood of JB's squad car. Just took his fists and smashed them down again and again and again. . . .

Chapter Twenty-one

Dain stood on the sidewalk in front of Dumont Towers, staring high up at the crest etched into the glass doors. All he could think about was Fleur. If he could just get to her, find some excuse to put his arms around her and pull her in, hold her and close his eyes and shut out the reality that was his life. . . .

The world suddenly seemed so small, though really it had been getting smaller for a long time. Serena was gone, along with the promise of that future. And now Cyd was gone, who'd been his lifeline since. His memory was so spotty after the accident. Which would be better—to remember the things he'd lost more clearly, or consider himself lucky that his mind had dulled?

Losing Cyd hurt so badly that he was beginning to think having such little clarity about his past was a blessing. But at the end of the day, he wanted something real, wanted something lasting, wanted something he could touch. And it was Fleur Dumont's face he saw when he thought of those things.

The doorman, dressed in a gray silk top hat and a jaunty gray and red coat with shiny gold buttons, carried a machine gun strapped over one shoulder and an umbrella in the opposite hand. His carefully neutral expression never wavered as Dain walked toward him, but he cocked his head slightly and murmured something into the microphone on his lapel. Under a gilded plaque engraved in gothic script—COME NOT HERE IF YOU DO NOT BELONG—the vamp doorman widened his stance and made no move to open the door.

Without missing a beat, Dain stopped, pulled out his gun, and shoved the barrel into the vamp's cheek. "I'm here to see Fleur Dumont, and I don't feel like climbing up the side of this building to do it. So you can either let me in or suffer the consequences."

The doorman blinked in surprise, then spoke into the microphone once more. After a pause, the front door clicked and the vamp pushed it open. "Start climbing," he said nastily as Dain stepped over the threshold.

The dim lobby was almost impossibly magnificent, pointedly poised on the knife edge between good taste and insanity. Wet and muddy, the soles of Dain's boots slid erratically along the heavily polished parquet floor. He steadied himself with his hand against the wall and turned to look around. Satyrs, madonnas, and kings gazed down from their carefully illuminated canvases, like sentries from another time. A chandelier dipped down into the entryway, its crystal strands still tinkling faintly from the wind Dain had shut out behind him. And the centerpiece of the foyer, an enormous velvet-covered staircase cascading in a ribbon of crimson into the entryway, rose and curled its way up into the heart of the vampire world.

This was a place where everything, every detail, every object, was done with purpose, was the best of its kind and the finest in its class. And the message was not lost on Dain as his hand curled around the edge of the gilded banister and he began to climb up through the heart of the building toward the last person in this crumbling city he truly cared about.

"Dain!" Fleur looked down over the banister from way on high, and his heart just about stopped as she opened a gate in the railing and leaped down. The diaphanous silver fabric of her dress swirled around her legs as she drifted through the center hollow. "What happened?" she murmured, landing beside him.

Dain just stared at her. She looked so much like an angel, and he'd never in his life felt more like he needed to be saved than right at this minute.

He hardly paid attention to where she was taking him as she grasped his hand and led him away from the landing to an elevator in a side corridor. The doors opened immediately and she pulled him in. As they ascended up through the tower, Fleur took his face in her hands. "What's happened to you?" she whispered.

"Cyd's . . . gone." He shook his head, unable to explain all of the things that were racing through his mind. She's gone, he wanted to say, and I don't ever want you to go, too.

Her lips parted in surprise, but it was clear she understood what he meant. And when she looked deep into his eyes, he could tell she was searching for clues. Could she see what he was feeling? He felt transparent under her gaze. How could she not know even the things he hadn't said aloud?

The elevator doors opened before either one could speak again, and she led him through the doors and down the hall, just a blur of crimson and gold in his peripheral vision. He only had eyes for her.

He snapped out of his spell when Fleur brought him inside what must be her personal quarters. It was something about the whole picture—Fleur, in full dress, in context of her magnificent rooms. He remembered how different she'd looked on the street, down in Dogtown.

Dain ran his hand over his face, conscious of how dirty and damp he was, how anathema to what stood before him. Fleur looked as if she'd been called from a party, a far cry from the hard, battle-ready beauty he'd grown to respect. Delicate and lethal. She was like a doll. Perfect hair, perfect makeup, perfect dress—and he was so wrong for her and her world.

"Don't look at me like that," she said, reading his mind. "I'm the same person."

"You're beautiful. And right now . . ." He gestured to her getup. She carefully removed his jacket, and he stood there in the middle of the room, spattering mud and rain onto the ivory hardwood floor. "I'm such a mess, and you . . . you're so, so . . . I'm sorry," he whispered hoarsely. "I don't know what I'm doing here."

She smiled. "It's all right. *I* do."

"Fleur, I lied. They all die. And the truth is, I never get over it." Dain searched her face. "Tell me to leave. Tell me to turn around and walk away."

"No."

"Tell me to leave. I'm begging you."

She put her hand to his cheek and it was all he could take.

"Oh shit, Fleur. I'll buy you another dress," he said roughly as he closed his eyes and fell to his knees before her.

She pulled him hard against her and he surrendered, wrapping his arms around her body as her fingers worked gently through his hair. His soaked shirt pressed against the thin silvery lace and silk of her skirt, molding the dress to her legs. He slid his hands along her curves as he pressed his mouth against her body, streaking dirt across the exquisite fabric and marking her as his own.

For he *was* marking her. He wanted her as his own.

He stood up suddenly, curling his fingers around her neck, touching his forehead to hers, their mouths a kiss away. Fleur took a step backward. "Come here," she commanded.

Dain didn't move, his thoughts wild as she backed up toward the canopy bed. She held out her arm, her fingers reaching for him. Like a rescue. Dain swallowed hard. He desperately needed a rescue.

"I'm not what you think," he said. "I'm not a good man."

"You wouldn't be here if you were," Fleur said, her voice thick with emotion. "Neither would I." Her eyes shone an intense blue that seemed to penetrate his very soul. Dain imagined he saw love in their depths, but he didn't dare ask. Not yet. Because he couldn't be sure of what was to come. And because he had enough feeling for both of them tonight.

"I'm warning you," he said, stalking her and

pulling the jeweled combs from her hair. He crowded up to her. "I'm *warning* you."

"No more warnings," she barely had time to say as he pushed her down on the bed.

She reached out to grasp his shirt. Dain slapped her hand away and pinned it above her head. He could tell that excited her. Giving her a pointed look, warning her not to try again, he released her and grabbed a froth of skirt, slowly pushing it up to expose the tops of her stockings affixed by a white lace garter. Then his hand slid along the smooth silk of her leg.

He lifted one of her legs up, hooking it over his shoulder, and Fleur gasped and arched her back. The heel of her party shoe was sharp enough to kill with one well-placed kick, and he liked that. The danger of making himself even more vulnerable to her spurred his desire yet higher.

Her delicate panties barely covered anything at all. He slid his hand up her leg once more, and it seemed as though his fingers ignited her flesh. Watching her face, he ran an index finger over the satin, then slipped it under the fabric. She arched back, moaning his name and moving against his hand. The sound of her, the feel of her . . . It was everything.

"You rescue me, Fleur. Everytime I see your face, it's like you save me from myself."

And she did, lying there with her arms flung wantonly above her head, her hair a gorgeous mass splayed out behind her on the bedsheets. She curled her fingers, summoning him to her.

With his free hand he released his slacks and

moved up her body, landing greedy kisses along her skin as he went.

"There must be a way for us," she murmured. "Just seeing you, I feel such a connection, and when you touch me like this, it's—"

He silenced her with a kiss. She moved her hips beneath him and he could feel his body nearly join with hers. She wanted it as much as he. That was all he needed, and he drove himself inside her; Fleur arched her back with the intensity of a pleasure that showed in her smile.

And still he wasn't close enough. He pushed her farther up the bed and wrapped his arms around her, holding her as tightly as he could while taking her mouth with his mouth and her body with his body. The sense of belonging, of this being right, was so strong; and Dain held on to Fleur with their bodies joined as if she were the last thing that had any meaning at all in his life.

She opened her eyes and looked at him, her mouth full and swollen with excitement, and she put her hand behind his neck and kissed him like she owned him. He snaked his hand down between her legs once more, and she came very suddenly, her entire body clenching, her face an expression of delirious joy.

She turned her mouth away from his, setting her fangs against his throat. The feel of it was exciting, thrilling. A wave of adrenaline shot through him as she pressed her fangs down harder and drove him toward climax. Dain lost his mind, his senses reeling with the feel of his body inside hers, driving him, driving him . . . and the pain at his throat. She pressed down harder, but the pleasure and adrenaline only increased.

And on the edge of ecstasy, he opened his eyes and found a moment of clarity—her dainty teeth had just barely cut through his flesh. Like a paper cut, that's all it was. But it was enough. Dain regained reality and tried to will himself to stop pumping inside of her. "Fleur," he gasped out in a kind of agony. Aroused beyond belief yet far too aware to ignore his fear, he turned his head away, suddenly struggling.

But she didn't understand the mixed signals, and she didn't let him go.

"Fleur, stop!" Dain pushed off her, off the bed, grabbing onto the canopy gauze for some sort of support and coming away with it in his hand as he stumbled away. Fleur sat up, her eyes wide, her expression a muddle as the white fabric fluttered down around her. It was obvious his body was still hard and wanting, and she didn't understand at all.

"What's wrong?"

He shook his head, absolutely reeling, tormented in body and mind. "I'm dark, sweetheart, but I'm not *this* dark." The look on her face proved the words hurt, but he ignored what he saw. He couldn't afford to go easy.

Fleur pushed her skirts down, angry and flustered. "I wasn't going to do it," she ground out harshly. "It was play. I wasn't going to do anything."

"How do you know?" Dain snarled as he pulled his clothes on. "Your self-control is as bad as mine."

Her eyes narrowed. "Fine. Let's pretend that I was going to do it. Let's just pretend that, for a moment.

What would you expect, Dain? You know what I am. What would you expect?" She stepped forward to engage him further, but he held up his palm, effectively stopping her in her tracks.

"You came here to me," she finally said.

"It was a mistake. I'm sorry," Dain said roughly. He looked her straight in the eye. "It was all a mistake. You know it as well as I do."

Dain practically sprinted to the elevator. It arrived quickly and descended without stopping—not exactly surprising, given that he was likely the only one in the building who needed to use it. There was a reason for that; he didn't belong here. *Come not here if you do not belong.*

I don't belong here. I don't belong anywhere.

Dain stumbled out of the lobby into the hazy, raining dawn, and turned his face up to let the cold raindrops cool his blood. Rush hour was in full force, and the blaring lights, sounds, and colors combined into a pulsing pain in his temples.

He slipped down a side street and leaned against the wrought iron gate across a storefront, letting his knees bend and his body slide to the dirty ground. He put his head in his hands and tried to calm his emotions. Why had he reacted so strongly against Fleur's action? Why did the human in him still fight, even now when there was nothing left to fight for? He *wanted* to indulge. He wanted to revel in the blackest part of his soul, to let go of all that was human and just rage. He wanted revenge for Cyd, and he wanted some way to physically express all of the feelings and sensations he wouldn't allow himself. But what exactly would that do? What would it get him, and how would he accomplish it?

Humans like his bosses liked to think they owned the term humanity. They were always preaching about maintaining it, about how it separated the species. But they were all just the same—the vamps, the dogs, and the humans. It was a joke, believing humans were somehow better, that they somehow set the standard. The fact of the matter was: When you stripped away race, nobody measured up. Everyone in Crimson City was just trying to get by, trying to tamp back their own darkness, and whatever quantity of humanity Dain thought he'd held on to all this time was a joke. It was leaching out of him. The end result was nothing better than living in a sort of no-man's-land.

So, what did all that make him? What in god's name did it make him? It was time to admit that he'd given up on his wife. Blurred memory and hazy moments aside, all he ever saw in his mind anymore was Fleur. Serena's image was literally wiped away, and he actually had to take out a photograph and stare at it to revive her memory. What did that make him? He was forgetting his past. And without a past, what the hell were you?

"Narcos?"

Dain started and stood up, noting with some relief that he had a good foot and fifty pounds or so on the pockmarked individual nearly drowning in a trench coat before him. A grubby hand held out a small device that looked a bit like one of those things used to prick a hole in an eggshell—Cyd's method of choice for using. Was the universe trying to tell him something?

Dain shook his head and pushed away. He darted into the street and hailed a taxi by way of getting into the vehicle while it was just beginning to accelerate.

"Shit, man. Scared me," the driver said. He shook his head but turned his meter on, then settled in for the fare. His eyes met Dain's in the rearview mirror, and the driver smiled, but Dain imagined he saw traces of desperation and deadness there.

Dain sat forward. Silently, he took a pistol out of his boot and pointed it silently against the cracked pleather upholstery, right at the level of the driver's heart.

"Bang," he said.

The driver glanced over his shoulder. "You say something?"

Dain just lowered the gun and put it away, then turned his head and stared out the window for the rest of the ride home.

Fleur curled up in a ball on her bed, clutching the bedsheets to her body, willing her frantic heartbeat to slow and her tears to stop. Dain was gone, running from the room like the last man she'd allowed inside. Every sense still burned with his scent, his feel, his taste.

One such mistake she could have chalked up to an error in judgment, and looked forward to better luck next time. This second time, she had to admit there was something much deeper and more complicated at work. What Marius suffered, Fleur now understood. The wanting. The intense wanting and the impossibility of having. And the wish that maybe there really was just a single person out there to whom you simply belonged. Even if it was a human.

Would she have stopped her fangs against Dain's

neck? Was the blood she'd drawn truly an accident, or had she been courting the result she really wanted? What if he'd asked her to do it, to bite deep and hard?

Fleur closed her eyes and fisted her hands. Hayden had asked her to do it. He'd said he couldn't live without her. That was the ultimate fantasy: a human so besotted with love that he'd beg you to make him vampire. But he'd played with fire he didn't comprehend, and he'd burned them both.

She'd been so consumed by that fire. It had washed over her, felt so right. But it had been a terrible mistake. Fleur had lost the respect of her peers and herself, and had lost Hayden as well. Now Dain was making her come dangerously close to losing herself in that fire once more. No, that wasn't true; she already had lost herself. But just how far had she gone?

It was wrong to make humans vampire. Rogues were proof of the consequences, and her very own mistake still roamed out there somewhere, a reminder that Dain could never fully be hers. And the irony of it was that she had finally found the man who could heal the damage. Dain understood her anguish over Hayden, and she his over Serena.

What she felt for Dain made her realize that what had existed between her and Hayden could not have truly been love. Whether she did the same for Dain's memories of Serena was doubtful, but then, he and Serena had not parted in a flurry of hateful accusations and with broken hearts.

And though the thought should have been irrelevant, part of Fleur wondered whether, if it had truly been love between them, Hayden would have felt such horror after she'd turned him. For that thought alone might give hope for a future with Dain.

If he loved her . . . Fleur squeezed her eyes shut, as if she could wish away the night. Dain *didn't* love her. He was intrigued by her, aroused by her. But now he was fully aware that they'd been playing a dangerous game.

Would she turn a human to vampire again if she had the choice? No. Not Dain. Not even if he begged. For not only was it wrong, but he would end up resenting her just as Hayden had. There weren't many made vampires who hadn't ultimately turned rogue. There just weren't enough who made the transition without regret.

She would have controlled herself this time. She *would* have.

Chapter Twenty-two

As dawn began to filter through the city, Jillian Cooper was walking her beat. The sirens had woken her up again, as they had on and off for the last week—a week that she already wished she could forget, and the damn thing wasn't over yet.

She'd heard of various trouble spots in the city from an illegal scanner she'd swiped. The Crimson City Police Department had their hands full. She'd tried to hail a cab to the site of one of the disturbances, but private transport seemed to be shut down for the night, as if everyone had a sense that things were taking a turn for the worse. It was like a vacuum had sucked the life out of the city, closing the doors on all the business and letting chaos, suspicion, and fear reign.

But they called *The Crimson Post* a daily newspaper for a reason, and Jill was going to get her story. Now, as daylight crept in, she was finding out what she could.

The city looked like it had just won a major sports

championship. Except this wasn't a game. There even looked to be a couple of bodies along with the trash littering the city, but she didn't go over to check, there was an even bigger story to be had.

No, it wasn't like it had been in the old days. Back when she was in college, only starting to come out at night. Then it had been more peaceful—or at least as peaceful as Crimson City got.

Of course, it also wasn't as bad yet as they'd described the old no-holds-barred battle between the species. But things were headed in that direction. If somebody didn't do something soon, they were all going to end up dead.

Rounding a corner, she was surprised when she felt a lurking presence. She whirled around, but there was nobody there. Swallowing hard to control her emotions, Jill changed the lens on her camera to one with better contrast between light and dark. The world was all the same color right now—a soupy, hazy gray.

She wasn't provoking anyone. Her first thought had been *werewolf*, but the dogs were still lying low as the humans and fangs circled each other. That left vampire, mech or . . . something else. It wasn't inconceivable that someone would want a newspaper reporter dead. Happened all the time. But Jill wasn't investigating anything—or anyone—in particular. She wasn't uncovering a drug ring or trailing a murderer. She was just reporting on Crimson City.

"Hello?" *Oh, for god's sake, Jill. Grow some balls.* "Who's there?" she called more authoritatively. She swung around, frightening herself more by imagining sounds and shapes in the nooks and crannies of the alley.

Moistening her lips, she lifted her camera to her face and took a few shots. But the prickly feeling on her neck wouldn't go away. She put the lens cap back on and started walking. And then she knew. She just *knew*. A smile crept over her face as she stopped in her tracks. "Why are you following me? Every time I turn around lately, it's you. But you never stay and talk to me."

"I felt you needed something. I sensed you were unhappy."

She turned to face him, and the breath was nearly knocked out of her by the sight of what she'd come to think of as her own personal vampire. He was standing in the shadow of an overhang. Resplendent in a tuxedo, he seemed entirely perfect except for the worried look on his face and his white bow tie, which lay undone against his lapels.

"Dressed to kill," she murmured, then cocked her head. "So, is that how it works—I call and you come?"

He chuckled. "Something like that."

"Do I *know* you?"

The vamp studied her face but didn't answer her question. "It's not safe out here."

Jillian started to laugh. It felt good to release the nervous energy. "You're a fang. I'm supposed to believe having you follow me around the city *is* safe?"

The corner of his mouth twisted in a slight smile. "I think you should go home."

She lifted an eyebrow. "The sun's almost up. Maybe *you* should go home." Her fingers itched to take a picture of him. She'd hardly had an opportunity to really look, but there was no question he'd photograph well. Jet-black hair and blue eyes, strong features and an even stronger body. That was clear enough from the perfect lines of his tailored clothing.

Jill giggled at the thought, then suddenly remembered Cydney Brighton's blood spattered over shattered glass and nearly burst into tears. She suddenly realized how tired she was, and how vulnerable, standing here in a deserted street with somebody she didn't know and couldn't trust.

As if he'd read her mind, the vampire leaned back against the building, his face fading even further into shadow. "I'm never going to hurt you. You don't need to be afraid when I come to you."

Why *do you come to me?* she wanted to ask, but couldn't quite find the nerve. Exhaling to calm herself, she finally said, "This city has become a very difficult place. I find myself understanding fewer things every day.

"Why are you sad?" he asked.

Jill looked up in surprise. "I lost somebody recently."

"Dain Reston's partner."

She nodded. "Her name was Cydney Brighton. I'd known her forever. She gave me scoops. We weren't super close, but she . . . she was still my friend."

"I'm sorry."

She suddenly felt stupid, asking for sympathy from a vamp. She gave a shrug and said, "But I'm okay, you know. So . . . you can go."

He just watched her for a moment, running his thumb absently across his lower lip in a movement so un-self-consciously sensual it made Jill's knees a little weak. "You're okay," he echoed and took a step backwards.

"Wait!"

He stilled, and Jill walked around behind him, standing on her tiptoes to put her hands around his neck to tie his bow tie. She let her fingers graze his skin, somehow unafraid to touch him. Closing her eyes, her mouth just a breath away from the back of his neck, she felt oddly like she was somehow being sucked underwater—and that he was the one doing it.

Coming to her senses, she stepped back, quickly finished the bow tie, then walked around to his front. "There," she said.

He was just staring at her, one hand on his tie and an odd look on his face.

"Why do you care?" she asked. "I mean, about me? For that matter, who *are* you?"

His eyes searched her face. "My name is Marius Dumont," he said, backing further down the alley. "And I shouldn't care."

Jill hovered on the edge of pursuit, staring at him in bewilderment. "But, why? Hello?"

She glanced back over her shoulder, up into the coming dawn, then took a tentative step after him. But he was gone. Where before she'd felt a strange warmth around her, now there was only cold.

"Marius," Jill whispered, just to test the name on her lips. "Marius. Why me?"

Chapter Twenty-three

Fleur had to laugh as her cousin came flying onto the balcony of the cocktail lounge alongside her; they were both ridiculously late, though Marius had wisely dressed for Assembly before going out. She, on the other hand, had gone out dressed in battle gear to ask around about Hayden. Not only had she come back without the information she sought, but by her own standards, she was hardly dressed appropriately.

Fleur was actually rather glad to have Marius alone—at least, as alone as one could be in the middle of an enormous club room filled with people. He sat at their reserved table, rather gloomily nursing his customary drink while Ian and Warrick visited other tables.

Dodging a server speeding by with a silver platter laden with strawberries, Fleur deftly plucked one off the top as he passed and settled into the chair next to Marius. Without a word, her cousin handed her his cocktail napkin to discard the stem. "Delicious," she said after eating the fruit.

The club room was packed tonight. And the clink of champagne glasses and merry peals of laughter couldn't disguise the current of tension running through it. The reason, of course, was the curfew and sirens and other policies established by the humans. Fleur could feel the constant stares and whispers, and every once in a while, she'd look up and catch someone's eye. The looks were friendly enough. Nods and waves. People she knew, various friends and acquaintances—they were all wondering what she would do, what action she would propose. They were looking for signs of weakness; they were looking to see if they wanted to keep her as head of the Assembly.

Marius pierced her with a look. "Dain Reston was here last night," he said.

Fleur choked a bit on a swallow of champagne and looked around nervously. "Cut to the chase, why don't you."

"What do you plan to do about him?" Marius asked.

"Excuse me?"

"You heard."

Fleur stared right back at her cousin. "It's none of your business," she said rather stonily.

"I realize that your personal life is none of my business—except for the fact that everything you do is by default my business. But what I want to say to you is not to do anything you'll regret. Do not take without him asking. And when he asks, do not take him then, either."

"What did you hear? I was only playing," Fleur said through gritted teeth.

Marius gave her a surprised look, like he didn't know what she was talking about. Then, to her chagrin, Fleur realized that if her cousin hadn't known before, he knew now. "What did you do to him?" he asked.

"I sort of . . . nipped at his throat. I don't feel like discussing it." She sighed as Marius laughed. "I'm so glad it amuses you."

"Reston probably hasn't been that scared in years," Marius said.

"It hurts. It really bloody hurts," Fleur said, finding herself oddly close to tears.

Marius ran his index finger around his glass. "Are you in love with him?"

"I was just playing. I mean, I was playing at first, and then I suppose it was just suddenly . . . We were . . . Oh, damn." Fleur stared blankly out into the night, not wanting to answer. Such a point-blank question, but Marius was like that. And she could tell him the truth because she knew he understood. "Look, I suppose I didn't want to just play anymore. I wanted everything. Somewhere inside, I knew what I was doing when I bit him. Which is the worst everybody thinks of me. I know they think I lack control, discipline, training. I know everybody still doubts me. You doubt me. But I believe that I would have stopped myself even if he hadn't stopped me." She blinked rapidly, refusing to cry. "Of course, he saw what I wanted. I could see it in his eyes. I don't know what he thinks of me now."

She turned back to Marius, choosing not to tell him about looking for Hayden, because she knew what he would say. That she wanted the vampire she'd made against all code to give her hope about Dain—that wasn't the only reason she wanted to find him, but it would be enough to set her cousin off.

"I know how you feel," he said, reaching out and clasping her hand. "I know how you feel."

"Ah, our lovely Fleur," Paulina said, interrupting their talk, sashaying up with Warrick and Ian hooked on either side of her. Warrick pulled out a chair for her, but Paulina chose Ian's lap after he'd settled into his own chair.

"Paulie," Fleur said, truly delighted. She and her friend hadn't gotten together in ages; they used to be inseparable.

"What a pleasure to see you." Paulina's vivid red hair, heavily made-up green eyes, and exquisite sky-blue satin evening gown embroidered with butterflies was a dramatic contrast to Fleur's own garb. Paulina snuggled closer into Ian, who didn't look the least bit unhappy. "Fleur, you never come out to play anymore! The girls miss you. But of course we understand. Though you missed a fantastic rampage through Louis Vuitton last week. *Such* a crush. Oh, my god, how we spent! It was practically an orgy."

Fleur had to admit she rather missed the days when her biggest concern was making sure nobody wore the dress on the same night. Of course, she'd not appreciated her situation then. There was a certain freedom when nothing much mattered. Now everything mattered so very much.

Paulina reached out and ran her hand down the side of Warrick's face. "You boys are turning our Fleur into a positive savage! We've been hearing all about it." She looked at Fleur and made a face. "Of course, we've managed to exaggerate everything to the point where you're killing ten humans a day and sucking them dry for breakfast. At least tell me you're happy, darling. We're wondering if we must kidnap you back and take you to high tea at the Bel Air Hotel just to reindoctrinate you."

Fleur laughed. "Have I changed so much?"

Paulina made a show of looking her over. "Are you joking? Darling, you're *horrifying*." She sounded delighted. She leaned over, strategically revealing her more-than-ample assets to Marius and Warrick, then said in a loud whisper, as if the lot of them were coconspirators, "They say Fleur is gallivanting about the city with a certain very sexy human, and he's bringing out the very bad girl in her."

Warrick snorted loudly.

Paulina looked at him and uttered in faux horror, "Shocking, isn't it? I mean, *look* at her. When the rest of us fall in love, we dress *up* for it. Even her hair is down."

Fleur was annoyed to find herself blushing. "It would seem that without you, I've completely lost my style compass."

"That's an understatement. In all the years I've known you, you've never once come to the clubroom dressed like a . . . like a . . . Warrior! I don't even know *what* you've got hanging on and strapped to you, but I'm sure you could kill me in at least three different ways if I were human." She jumped up from her chair. "Darlings, I must go. And I'm sure you're busy saving us all. Fleur, honestly, though, the girls admire you so—at least the gallivanting with that human. A wild streak is always *so* attractive." She ran her palm down Ian's inner thigh and kissed him on the neck. "It's been ages. I *miss* you. Stop by anytime. Ta!"

Suddenly self-conscious, Fleur looked at Ian. "I don't look *that* bad, do I?"

He quirked an eyebrow. "You look fine. You look like you've been putting in some hard work, which you have. Frankly, I think this getup will give you added credibility tonight in front of the Assembly."

"Speaking of which," Marius commented, swirling the ice in his drink. "What do you plan to say, Fleur? What's your message to the Assembly?"

Warrick downed his drink and signaled for another. "How about we kick some serious human ass? We've been holding back longer than should have been expected."

"I want to make sure that if we go to war, we're attacking the right people." Fleur stared at the ice cubes in her drink. "Rashness is what everyone expects, and vengeance is what everyone wants, but we need to be smart about this. We need to figure out exactly what's going on. In the meantime, the trick is going to be to kill the *message*, not the messenger. Meaning that the humans are trying to take away our freedoms—but rather than killing humans, we should work on dismantling their structures and implementations. The idea is to maintain our rights and protect ourselves. That's all we'll do. Keep what is rightfully ours."

The Protectors were silent for a moment, then Ian leaned forward. "Fleur, you really *don't* think the humans are behind the assassinations. Do you?"

She looked him straight in the eye. "No, I don't. I think that's what we're meant to think."

Marius nodded. "Fair enough. But if we send out strike teams to tell the humans where to shove their regulations, it's going to devolve into a free-for-all. There's going to be killing everywhere, and on a scale much larger than what we've been seeing lately. We'll be right back where we were before the truce. Hmm. Perhaps that's what the group behind the assassinations had in mind in the first place."

"The rogue vampires?" Warrick suggested hopefully. "They might be behind it. And they could use a little attitude adjustment." He was obviously itching for a fight.

"They're my best guess. I'm looking into it." She looked down at her glass and decided to tell her cousins the truth. "I've been trying to get into contact with Hayden."

"What?" Marius asked.

"I have to know if this is personal. Maybe revenge."

"Is that all?" Marius asked, keeping his face blank.

"More or less," Fleur answered. Quickly changing the subject, she added, "That leaves the dogs. They're entirely a wild card. We're being positioned to fight a war on two fronts. We were attacked, and now all fingers are pointing in our direction. The humans are giving us trouble, the rogues are giving us trouble . . . but the dogs are so quiet I can't help wonder what's going on with them. Especially after—"

The bell chimed for dinner. Fleur stood up and faced her cousins. "So, my message to the Assembly is this:

"Someone is driving the recent chaos in Crimson City, and they seek to pin the responsibility on us. In the short term, we must quash any and all policies that seek to undermine our freedoms, and in the long term we must begin preparing for the possibility of a second war between the species."

She looked at Ian, Warrick, then Marius. "Well? Does that work for you? Do you disagree? It should quell the warmongers and lay out our best hope for the future."

After a pause, Marius nodded and offered her his arm. "Dinner?" he said with a smile.

"That's our little girl," Ian added to Warrick, his hand clutching his heart melodramatically. "Look at her now."

Fleur looked between her three cousins and broke out into a huge laugh. She could tell by their faces that they truly approved. They believed she was ready to stand on her own; they'd given her leadership their blessing. They were truly just her council, now, and nothing more. Fleur took Marius's arm and let him lead her to the dining hall, where they took their seats.

The long narrow headtable ran down the center of the room, next to a series of individual rounds. The candles were all lit; the servants began to serve, and Fleur began to slip back into the simplicity of her former life, when all that was required of her was witty repartee and the occasional well-placed compliment. But things had changed, and constant vigilance had become second nature: She noticed the charge in the air only a few moments after her cousins, who stopped eating, their cutlery frozen midair. The others in the hall eventually noticed too, the festive overlap of their conversations unraveling and dropping off one by one until there was nothing but silence.

Their world held a measure of inherent protection by virtue of their distance from the ground, but her people's defenses were by no means fail-safe—as was proven by her brothers' murders. Fleur moved her chair back from the table, the sound of its legs scraping against the floor. Her own shallow breathing seemed immeasurably loud.

It didn't escape her notice that everyone was waiting, watching to see what she would do. The tension in her body was immense, but it wasn't the tension she'd felt while interacting with that werewolf, and she felt certain it wasn't a human she sensed. What worried her was the possibility of being beseiged by mechs, who were quite possibly the most dangerous thing she'd ever seen. Would she even sense them coming?

The Assembly dining hall was an enormous space, but it was packed with the tables and chairs that made everything seem so festive and familial; there was a certain claustrophobia, and a lack of space in which to move and defend. Fitting a ball gown between the tightly spaced chairs had once been the prime complaint; it was hardly a concern anymore. With guards on the floors below and above, the room's true weakness was an assault from the sides. And without the sound of any airborne machinery, Fleur realized her sense of dread could come from only one thing.

She slowly drew her weapons and looked around. One breath, one exhale. She looked over her shoulder at the window on the far wall. One breath, one exhale. She looked over her shoulder at the window on the far wall. One breath, one exhale. Fleur looked to the right. Nothing. One breath, one exhale. To the left. Clear sky through glass. One breath, one exhale. Then she brought her head up and stared past the rows of tables to the window beyond.

Raising both hands, with a flick of her wrists she loaded ammunition into her pistols. Silence reigned, then all four windows shattered. Glass exploded with tremendous force into the room, which erupted into chaos. The Assembly followed protocol; those trained to defend going for armament, those not part of the defense seeking cover in a swirl of color.

Fleur stood her ground as four shadowy figures appeared, each flying through a frame of one of the four shattered windows, coat swirling behind him. Each moved in a picture-perfect, calculated swagger.

The rogue vampires.

Feathers and finery waved fiercely in the wind that blew in from outside. At the end of the Assembly room, Paulina shivered. Ian covered her bare shoulders with her wrap.

The rogues landed along the periphery of the chamber, glass shards raining from their clothing and sprinkling the floor. Compared to the primaries, these vampires embraced a look that spoke of roughness and rebellion. Their clothing incorporated elements of street style found down on the human and werewolf levels. And while there was little similarity amongst them in dress, they had one thing in common: the notion that anything goes. Which described their nature as well.

Fleur stood at her place at the table, along with the others heads, and the rogues honed in on her so fast it seemed obvious she was their focus—obvious not just to Fleur, but to everyone in the room. And as the object of their intentions became clear, the chaos settled and everything went still and silent once more.

One of the rogues slowly circled the room while the other three stayed back. "Go ahead and take your seats," he said, rather like a ringmaster enjoying a private joke, one outstretched arm indicating the Assembly as a whole even as he kept his eyes on Fleur.

To be honest, everyone had their eyes on Fleur. She could feel them staring, and she could tell her cousins were itching to make a move.

But everyone knew the moment was hers. Fleur held her head high, if she couldn't help the flush warming her cheeks. These rogues meant to humiliate her, did they? By reminding her people that she'd broken code and created one of them? It was a mistake that was now coming back to haunt her—to haunt them all. For she'd be willing to bet there wasn't a soul in the room who didn't think Hayden was behind this, including herself.

But this was her opportunity to make peace with the past, and she'd take it by force.

The Assembly had settled back with an obvious wariness, and the rogue sauntered toward Fleur, stopping unpleasantly close in an intentional act violating her personal space. Fleur laughed dismissively. He didn't intimidate her. Not in the least. And when he made a show of looking her over, she did the same.

"I don't know you," she said, pointedly holstering her weapons.

"I guess the one who made me didn't tell," he said, looking around at the assembly with one eyebrow cocked. "Big surprise." Nobody made a sound.

He turned back to Fleur. "Go ahead and call me Skullestad."

"Skullestad." Fleur put her hands on her hips. "So, why didn't Hayden come himself?"

The rogue gave her a quizzical look, then threaded his way toward the far end of the long center table. Fleur followed in parallel. Without warning, Skullestad stuck his dirty, lug-soled combat boot on the fiery red satin lap of a lady to Paulina's right, ignoring her cry of dismay as he used her to leap up onto the table. As her place setting smashed beneath his feet, every single vampire trained to fight made to get out of their chairs. The Protectors in particular were enraged.

Fleur settled them back with a wave of her hand.

Skullestad looked behind him, as if he could feel the rage emanating from his audience. He laughed, turned back to Fleur and started toward her, walking on the table. Delicately etched goblets, sterling, and china decorated in classic crimson-laced chinoiserie smashed beneath his feet like skulls under a tank tread, and ladies and gentlemen of the Assembly alike winced and turned away at the destruction he caused. His footprints soiled the linen, and a cloud of scent misted the air as he crushed the floral centerpieces with his boots.

He stopped in the middle of the long table and almost imperceptibly nodded his head.

Fleur shrugged carelessly. "Was there some kind of a message here?" she asked. "Or is this all? This . . . posturing?"

The rogue held his silence.

Amped up by the adrenaline pulsing through her veins, Fleur snarled, "What does he want?"

"Who?"

"Hayden," she repeated, folding her arms over her chest.

It was his turn for a careless shrug. "We don't answer to any 'Hayden.'"

Fleur frowned in confusion. "Doesn't he pay you? Don't you work for him?"

"I think you're a little confused about how we rogues operate." Skullestad advanced on her again, and the tension in her body grew once more. But Fleur realized she was feeding off the moment. There were plenty of doubters in the seats before her, and some of them actually thought she wouldn't be able to hold her own. The idea that she could—and *would*—gave her an uncustomary thrill.

"Well, then, is there anything else you wanted to say?" She swept her hand out, indicating the ruins of the table at his feet. "Or are we ready to throw down?" She knew by virtue of her words they now had to fight. He'd be hard-pressed not to back down unless he'd been ordered to.

Apparently, there'd been no such order. Which was good, because Fleur was ready to prove herself in front of her people.

The rogue knelt down and reached across the table, plucking a handkerchief from a stranger's tuxedo pocket. He held the square up, then released it to float down onto the table. "I throw down, Fleur Dumont."

Blood lust shot through her, just as it had with the werewolf in the subway, but this time she knew what to expect; she could marshal her adrenaline to best advantage. She jumped onto the table, facing him. "I throw down, Rogue Skullestad."

And it was on.

Fleur kicked out, jabbing her boot at his forehead. She caught him square, yet Skullestad backflipped along the table, gracefully alighting on the edge. Then he rushed back in for more, slamming out with his fist and catching her on the temple.

Fleur fell backward, hard, into a bed of petals and congealing wax from candles that had been snuffed in the chaos. The Assembly gasped in horror. But though she saw stars for a moment, Fleur recovered in time to roll to the side. The rogue plunged a dagger deep into the table, right where her heart had been.

As she rolled back, several dim gaslights on the walls blew out with a slight hiss like the sound of a whisper. Fleur's chest pounded. She looked up at the rogue's face and had the bizarre sensation of being in the mud pits of yore, with all of her people watching and judging. It was a strange way to win approval, but at the same time she felt she could do it.

She waited for the rogue to plunge down his dagger once more, and the minute he tried, she curled up her legs and jammed her boots into Skullestad's throat. He stumbled back and she leapt to her feet, grabbing her own knife from its sheath.

They fenced across the table, back and forth, the sound of metal scraping and clicking in Fleur's ears, the blurred faces of the Assembly watching on either side. Finally, she gained an advantage, knocking the blade from Skullestad's hand, ignoring the weapon as it cartwheeled away.

She whipped her knife under the rogue's chin. "So . . . do you have a message from Hayden or not?"

A muscle buldged in the base of his neck, and his voice was full of venom. "No."

"Then why are you here?"

"Think of it as a test." Skullestad lifted his arms in amusement, leaving himself totally unguarded.

Fleur seized the moment and kicked him; knocking him backwards onto the table in a smashup of centerpieces, plates, and candles. "That's great," she said. She tossed her knife aside, leapt on Skullestad, and wrapped her fingers around his neck. She began to squeeze. His hands moved up to hers and closed around her wrists, trying to pull her off. He couldn't.

She gripped him tighter until he began to gasp for air. It was painful, unpleasant, but of course not deadly. "Consider exam week over," she said grimly. "And be sure to post my grade."

He pulled furiously at her hands, but she had him. "Oh, and one more thing," she added. "If Hayden didn't send you, however you rogues are organized; please find him and tell him I want to speak to him. Understood?"

Skullestad glowered at her.

"Understood?" Fleur repeated more forcefully.

"Yes," he rasped.

She let go and watched him crawl backwards, gasping. "Now get out of here. All of you," she commanded.

All four rogues ran, leaped through the windows, and disappeared into the night.

Fleur jumped off the table and wiped a bit of soup from her cheek. She met Paulina's gaze. Her friend sat, saucer-eyed, one hand pressed to her chest, frozen in her seat like the others. Fleur felt an odd combination of pride and sadness for the loss of who she once had been.

"It's a bit difficult to do that in a skirt," she said with a wink, shrugging off her doubts. She was nearly giddy with adrenaline. "Ladies, gentlemen, I'm very sorry about the mess," she called. "I'll see you all at the next Assembly."

She leaped off the table, creating a musical trill behind her as the silver jumped too, gracefully bowed her head, then left. And even though Fleur knew that the night's episode was a very serious matter, she allowed herself one small private smile. No one would think her weak anymore.

Chapter Twenty-four

Dain considered the possibility of not going back to work for a couple of days. He considered the possibility of not going back to work ever. But lying in bed and staring at the ceiling gave him too much time to think, and thinking was just too damn painful. So he got up for work late and made the walk with his weapons in hand. Coffee and donuts weren't even an option.

When he arrived at the office, he felt just about enough control to face his teams. The break room was very different this day—one of those silent, uncomfortable scenes everybody hated but couldn't break down with a well-delivered joke. Some of the guys were still teared up. Some of them looked dazed. A couple of the rookies who hadn't really known Cyd just looked nervous.

The excitement they'd exhibited over going into battle mode a few days earlier had been dampened by the reality of danger. Dain knew they were expecting some sort of rallying speech, some sort of fond remembrance. Well, JB or one of the others would have to give it.

"Dain? They're actually ready to see you now," a secretary came in and said.

They? Dain looked at JB. "You wanna . . . take care of this for me?" He gestured at the others. JB nodded, so Dain slipped right back out and headed for the interrogation room at the back of the building.

Sitting down in a rickety folding chair and looking around, Dain thought the room seemed blindingly white and clean. He waited, rebelliously picking the Styrofoam off the rim of his coffee cup, letting the white shreds fall to the ground as a panel of his superiors watched. He could imagine Kippenham, staring with total dissatisfaction at the mess, dying to clean it up, a vein in his neck throbbing from the impulse to maintain order. Of course, Kipp wasn't here. At least, not in the room.

Dain slowly turned his head to the two-way mirror and raised the trashed Styrofoam cup in mock greeting. Kipp was undoubtedly watching from behind the glass, obviously keeping a distance. He wasn't the only one: Dain imagined himself watching the entire situation play out from a spot on the ceiling. A fang's-eye view, he thought with a dry smile. He also thought that he was going to try to get himself fired, and he wasn't sure how he felt about that. He'd earned a visit to the shrink, for sure.

"Captain Reston," one of his superiors said formally, leafing through a thick file.

Dain gave the man a nod.

"First, let me say on behalf of the entire department, we are sorry for your loss. We all feel Ms. Brighton's absence this morning, but I know from personal experience that it stings much more when it's *your* partner."

"Yeah, it *stings*," Dain agreed roughly.

There was a silence. The woman on the end of the table, some random executive from I-Ops, gave him a piercing stare. It was better than sympathy. Dain wasn't sure he wanted to deal with sympathy this morning. He preferred the idea of these bastards pissing him off, him doing something without thinking, making something happen and doing something about it. Only that would get this anger out of his system.

"Captain Reston, clearly we'll make the department psychologist available to you on an ongoing basis," the first man continued.

Dain just stared at him, suddenly hating the grubby feel of his crumpled clothing. He hadn't changed since last night. Odd, how everyone stopped using first names when somebody got hurt—when somebody died. Everything became so fucking formal. He let his forehead drop into his hand, his arm resting on his thigh.

"Captain Reston?" The panel looked around at each other. "Obviously, this is a very bad time to take you out of the field. We'd like to know what you'd like to do."

Wait a minute. What I'd like to do? Stop being so damn nice. I feel like I could kill somebody right now. "I'd recommend not partnering me up." He looked them square in the eye. "I think the best thing to do is to continue working with Fleur Dumont, and to try to use our collective resources to get to the bottom of this. She's been a good ally to date, and I trust her."

He cleared his throat and added, "As much as I'd trust any vampire."

There was a pause. The panelists looked at each other, and finally the woman nodded. "You'll have to speak to Major Kippenham about that. But we're glad to know that you'd like to get right back to work."

Dain looked over the assembled faces. He was developing an uneasy feeling. "Yeah, I'm just going to get right back to work. I'd like to keep following some leads ... you know, follow up on ..." His thoughts wandered. He blinked, trying to bring the too-helpful faces back into focus. "Follow up on some ... leads." There. A strong finish. Persuasive. He'd even tacked on the hint of a sad smile. The part where he wanted to strangle every one of them and wipe their angelic, sympathetic faces off the map— well, he kept those feelings to himself.

The suit on the far left, the one with the glasses, held out a slip of paper. "Why don't you just take it easy for now? We'll have JB continue to run the staff meetings. After you have a chance to share your feelings and learn how to deal with your loss, maybe then you can go back to your normal responsibilities."

"But we're not asking you to turn in your weapons or anything," the woman added quickly.

Dain almost laughed. Someone in psych had already done an assessment, figured he was the kind of guy who preferred to mend on the job. That he would react negatively to a reduction in workload and responsibility. Hell, he had to give it to them; they were right.

But . . . that meant this wasn't really a psych exam

or evaluation. This was something else. They were looking for something else in him, and it made him uneasy.

Dain got out of his chair and walked over to the guy in glasses and took the slip of paper. "Thank you for your understanding," he said woodenly.

"The report comes first, though. Just a summary of events for the file—we've got the details from JB and the rest of the team."

"Right." Dain held up the slip. "Thanks." He moved to leave; but was stopped by a clipped, "Wait, please," from the panel members. "Major Kippenham would like a word with you."

The panel filed out and Dain sat and waited for the boss.

Kippenham's almost immediate entrance confirmed he'd been watching and listening. Dain studied his boss, who entered and pulled a chair around to set it in front of Dain. Kipp always seemed like a decent man, but there was something about his calm, upbeat fraternity boy act that had a disturbing edge under the right circumstances. These were those circumstances. Everything was relative.

Kipp didn't pull any punches, just leaned back in his chair and crossed one leg over the other. "So, you want to go back to work."

"Yeah. I mentioned to the panel that I'd hoped it would be business as usual, working with Fleur Dumont to collect more information about what's going on in this city and ultimately figuring out who sent that mech . . . and why."

Kippenham watched him very closely. "You won't be working with Fleur Dumont anymore," he said. He looked directly into Dain's eyes. "The plan has changed somewhat. You'll have no direct contact with any member of vampire leadership, including Fleur Dumont. We'll take it one day at a time. I'm putting you with JB today. He's been keeping up with Cyd's old informants."

Keeping his voice even, Dain said, "Sounds like the plan has changed more than 'somewhat.' Maybe you could fill me in."

Kippenham clasped his hands together on the table and said, "There will be no more information sharing with Fleur Dumont; the Dumonts have been reclassified as enemies."

Dain leaped up, overturning his chair. "What?"

An ugly sneer appeared on his boss's face. "You seem upset. Do you have reservations about Fleur Dumont's classification?"

Dain sat back down. "I know a lot more about the vampire world than I used to. A month ago I was under the impression that there was just one group. One leader. One . . . vision. I assumed they would just as soon destroy the human race as anything else. That's not true. And I can't even say for sure which group was responsible for Serena's death. They're not *all* bad."

Kipp winced, his expression growing dark. He'd taken off his ring and was playing with it, wringing it first, turning it over and over as if his self-control were dependent on this one object absorbing all of the anger welling up inside him. "All vampires ultimately come from the same point of view, Dain. It doesn't matter who's 'hanging out' with who. They all kill humans, they all feed on innocent blood, and they all answer to a darker force within them. That darkness is something we can't even begin to fathom." He leaned forward, his voice menacing. "I wanna tell you that you drawing a distinction between different groups of vampires makes me very, very uncomfortable."

Dain chewed on his lower lip. Kipp wasn't the only one uncomfortable about this, because he knew very well that his thinking was disloyal to his training, and if he let any more of it show than Kipp was already seeing, things would get ugly. "Look, all I'm saying—"

"I know what you're saying," Kippenham said coldly. "And if that's code for telling me that your thinking has been compromised, that we can't trust you anymore, then that's a pretty serious piece of information."

Dain tried to defuse the situation with an exaggerated groan. "You're taking my words way out of proportion, boss. I've just been entertaining some theories, that's all." He rolled his eyes and tried to get the conservation back on track. "Am I going to find you've got someone tailing me?" he joked. "That that's part of PDI?"

Kippenham managed a tight smile, but he didn't quite match Dain's levity. "Watch your step, Dain. You've got a little latitude coming because of Cyd's death, but that's only going to last so long."

Dain felt a bolt of anger. "I'm not interested in using the Cyd pity card for any reason, at any time," he snarled.

The boss gave a curt nod. "Good. I'm glad to hear it. Just so we understand each other. So, I don't need to be concerned about any misplaced loyalty to the vampires, then?"

Dain stilled, trying to think three steps ahead.

"No. I know what side my bread is buttered on," he said.

Kippenham's face remained impassive. "That's an interesting statement. It implies reluctance."

Dain ran his hand over the stubble on his face. It was sharp. "There's no reluctance. I'm just surprised. I advocate a different approach than this path to war."

A tight smile was Kipp's only response, as if to say that a different approach was out of the question.

"What are we *doing*, Kipp?" Dain asked softly. "Let's cut the crap. Give me something to work with. Give me something to believe in, here. Why this changeup with the Dumonts? You've got me in the dark. It didn't used to be that way. We used to be friends—you, me, and Serena. You make me a pawn when I know I should be a major player. Give me all the information and let me play the game with you."

Kippenham wore an inscrutable look. He seemed amused, tickled by Dain's words in a way that was incredibly disconcerting. Kipp double-checked that the interrogation voice recorder was in the off position, then leaned forward. "We *did* send the mech," he said.

Dain felt the blood drain from his face.

Kippenham started laughing, a deep, dark rolling sound. "Didn't expect that, did you?"

"Not really," Dain said quietly and calmly, though he felt rocked to his core.

Catching his breath and slipping easily back into his usual offhand demeanor, Kippenham added, "To be more specific, *I* ordered the mech sent. On our behalf. On the behalf of all humans."

"You ordered the mech to assassinate Fleur's brothers?"

"Absolutely," Kippenham sneered, his expression ugly. "As encouraged by certain superiors."

"Then what the hell am I doing out there?" Dain asked almost desperately. "What has all this been for?" *And did Cyd really have to die?*

"We wanted someone on the inside of the vampire world." With some amused sarcasm, Kipp added, "I think you got about as close as any man could get."

Dain felt dizzy. "I usually find that it's a bad sign when superiors reveal a secret to someone in circumstances like these. Why are you telling me?"

"I think you're slipping. But your memory of Serena—well, if there's a chance of keeping you in the program, I've got a lot invested in you. We've learned a hell of a lot from you, Dain. You're kind of a special case."

Dain gritted his teeth. This all made him sound like a commodity. Like the program had spent so much on his training that it was a shame to lose him. The cold facts were, he knew so much that they'd either have to be assured of his loyalty or delete him. He understood that. And he was glad Kippenham had been frank.

As if reading his mind, Kippenham leaned forward and said, "Dain, so many things happen behind the scenes that you don't see. In spite of what you said, I'm going to give you a little latitude because I think you deserve it. But I'd like you to go home and rest and think about what you believe in. I'd like you to think about your wife, Serena, about Cydney, and about the others we've known and lost to the vampires over the years. Think about the fact that we didn't invite these bloodsucking monsters into our midst. And I think when you take a moment to step back and reflect, you'll remember what your purpose is here. You'll know what's right.

"Don't think we're stupid. Fleur Dumont is persona non grata in Crimson City as far as we're concerned. Whether you recognize it or not, a strike back against the vampires has been a long time coming. It's become clear that, if we don't strike first and hard, they will—and with fatal results. And if you choose to personally ally with these killers, the rest of your life is going to be lonely and short."

"Is that a threat or a promise?" Dain asked softly.

"It's just a fact, Dain. Just a fact."

Chapter Twenty-five

Dain stared out the window at Crimson City, which was flying by as JB drove like a maniac through the crowded streets. Dain wasn't in the driver's seat this time. Numb, he didn't even try to pump a nonexistent brake as they took a corner too fast and fishtailed into the opposite lane, narrowly missing a cyclist on a jetbike.

Maybe it was because he didn't fear death anymore, he thought with a wry smile. There wasn't much worth getting out of bed for these days. He and JB were responding to reports of a second vampire death cluster, and Dain couldn't muster any enthusiasm for the job. With his loyal watchdog at his side, he felt exhausted by being forced to fake caring about things. All he could think about was Fleur, and wanting to talk to Fleur, and wanting to apologize for that crazy night and wanting to have it back.

The more he thought about it, the more he wished he'd made a different choice. The only piece of him that felt alive was the piece of his heart that now hoped to see Fleur at the scene of the crime. The anticipation of that moment, of just seeing her standing there, seemed worth any consequence.

JB apparently could read his thoughts. As he parked the car and Dain went to open the door, the locks went down.

Dain looked at JB in surprise. His new partner looked slightly embarrassed. "I don't mean to get in your business, but if Dumont is there, just play it smart and don't do anything I'll have to report."

Dain looked at him keenly. "What would you have to report? As your *boss*, I recall quite a few items on you that didn't make it into my reports."

JB glanced away. "Don't make this hard on me, man. They're going to have a microscope on you right now. And that means they're looking at me too. So don't show me any dirt. Just play it smart until everything blows over."

Dain cocked his head. "Exactly what is it you think I'm going to do?"

JB looked torn. He wiped the sheen of sweat off his forehead. "Damn it, Dain. I don't care if you screw her. I really don't, and I don't think anyone else does either. But the brass think it's gone beyond that. They think you're in over your head, so just do us both a favor and make everything real clean while I'm around. I don't want to see anything, I don't want to know anything, and I don't want to have to report anything."

Dain reached over, popped the locks, and got out of the car, stalking toward the small gathering by the mouth of the alley. Since when had his juniors started talking to him like a greenie? Screw him. Screw them all.

Fleur was already there, and while Dain kept his face blank, inside his heart beat out a very different story. She turned as he approached, and he watched a number of jumbled emotions flit over her face. She looked quickly away and smiled at JB. "Hello."

"Hi," JB responded curtly. He glanced at Dain, sighed heavily, and said too loudly, "I'm going to walk way over there and look at the bodies."

As he stalked off, Dain looked down at Fleur and couldn't believe that he'd been such an ass. If only he had that night to do over. "It's . . . it's my turn to apologize. I'm sorry."

Fleur studied his face, then frowned at all of the personnel still standing close by. "Let's go somewhere else. Somewhere it's not so complicated."

Surprised she didn't seem angrier, he just shrugged. "Absolutely."

Fleur swung around and looked at the businesses lining the street, then without another word headed straight for the nearest bar, a corner dive with unfulfilled aspirations toward a Western theme. Dain followed her through the swinging doors bolted into the metal doorframe, and while she went straight to the bar and ordered, he surveyed the place and chose the most strategically sound table.

Fleur returned with the bartender, who slapped down a cocktail for her and a soda for Dain. Dain almost smiled, thinking that vamps had better working rules. He wanted to make a joke, but instinct told him Fleur wasn't in the mood. Instead, he asked, "Do you accept my apology?"

Fleur sipped her drink, then poked at the ice with her straw. "I nicked you and you got angry. I think we're even. Still, given what you said, I'm surprised *you're* not still angry."

"It's in your nature," he said, watching her face.

She looked up at him in surprise. Maybe she saw what he was thinking—that he'd had second thoughts; that maybe the second time around he let her bite him. Of course, maybe she really believed that she hadn't been about to bite him.

She might have been thinking a lot of things. All she said was, "We're getting ourselves into a bit of a mess, you and I. This is really impossible. You know that, right?"

Dain did his best to smile. "You breaking up with me?" he joked.

Fleur burst out into laughter. "I didn't realize we were dating. You never call." They both laughed at that, but after a pause she added, "I'm not your kind. And you're not mine."

Who was she trying to convince? She didn't sound very sure of herself. "I don't really know what my kind is," Dain said.

"Well, it's not mine, anyway."

Dain looked away from her, at the sparse crowd in the bar. Who was human? Who was just passing? Was anyone for real? He shook his head. "Man. Nothing's what it should be. Nothing's logical anymore. I thought I knew everything about the human defense systems and intelligence. I have security clearance at the highest levels. I share information with the leaders of all the top levels. I should know everything. *Everything.*" But all he knew was that he couldn't trust anyone.

"Maybe you do know everything—in just the way

they want you to know it. Dain, have you ever considered why you do what you do?" It seemed to take a lot for her to say that.

"What do you mean?"

"Please don't take this the wrong way, but you don't do what you do out of loyalty or allegiance to your species. You do it for the thrill of the chase. For the pleasure of finding the truth. Or something like that."

Dain blinked, a little—no, a lot surprised. A slow grin came over his face. "So . . . what? Does that make me a bad person?"

She tilted her head and studied him. "Well, I might argue that it makes you more trustworthy. You don't operate based on blind loyalty. You operate based on facts and sense. Really, if you think about it . . . you make the perfect investigator."

He stared at her for a moment and then took a deep breath. "There's something I want you to know. Something I just found out."

Fleur raised an eyebrow.

Dain leaned in so close he could smell the faint perfume of her hair. "We did send the mech. Someone high up sent that mech to kill your brothers."

He pulled away to see how she'd take it, and Fleur just stared at him. For a moment she was absolutely speechless. "You just found out?"

Dain nodded. "The boss just told me. I felt . . . I felt you should know"—he looked down at the countertop—"since the idea of us working together was to find out."

Fleur processed Dain's words slowly, trying to guess, judge, analyze . . . trying to figure out if he was lying now to set her up, or if he'd been lying before. But for all her natural suspicions, she couldn't believe that what he'd said was anything but the truth.

In part, her faith was because of something in Dain she could sense. Something had changed. Dain wasn't for his employers anymore. He wasn't for anybody. He was like a man without a country. And Fleur had to decide if that meant she could trust him, or if it meant he was simply slipping into oblivion. People like him made fantastic informants, but he knew that better than anybody.

Was he using her? She didn't think so. She had a sense that even if he couldn't be loyal to cause, to a species, to a mind-set anymore, he was loyal to her. And knowing that made her heart ache even while she determined how it could serve her people.

When he looked up and their eyes met, there was a question there: *Do you believe me?* Fleur nodded without waiting to hear the words, and she watched as something within Dain, some sort of desperate tension, released. He stretched his arm out across the table and opened his palm.

Fleur never broke eye contact as she put her hand in his. He leaned over the table and pressed his lips to hers so tenderly that it nearly broke her heart. And when their lips parted once more, there was the barest hint of sadness there.

She looked away. "You shouldn't start what can't be finished," she said, a sad smile on her lips. She looked up. "Did the bite really scare you . . . or was it just an excuse?"

Dain cocked his head. "Were you really in control of what you were doing?" he asked in return.

A silence passed between them. "You're saying you don't really know."

"I don't know what scared me, really." More softly, he added, "What I do know is that a lot can change in the span of a few days."

Fleur looked at their hands, still clasped on the table. His were strong, the texture both smooth from his scars and rough from his calluses. They were so distinct, warm, possessive around hers. "I have to go," she said. They both knew what she would do with his information. She'd take it back to the Assembly. It wasn't worth killing the moment to discuss.

"Fleur," he said, his voice urgent. "I don't want to talk like this, with one eye on the door. There are other things I need to say to you, things—"

"Dain?" JB appeared in the doorway, his arms propped up on the swinging doors, his hip cocked like that of some brash young gunslinger. "Issues?"

Dain pulled his hands away and stood up. "Nah. Just arguing about who's zooming whom," he replied, taking his smart card from his pocket and swiping it through a reader to pay for the drinks.

Then, without looking back, he waved a careless adios behind his back at Fleur.

"Catch you later, sweetheart," he said. And to JB: "Dead fangs always make me hungry. Cheeseburger?"

Fleur watched the younger man's face relax. There was no question the humans were monitoring Dain now. He'd lost their loyalty, their trust. There had to be a very good reason why Dain's boss had told him about the mech. She just hoped that good reason wasn't waiting around the corner for him. Literally or figuratively.

Dain picked his way over a bum sleeping on the walkway and stood in front of Cyd's apartment. JB was a great kid. He reminded Dain of himself in better days. But eating a cheeseburger and shooting the shit with him had made Dain miss Cyd more than ever. It wouldn't have been the same without her if things had been normal, and it definitely wasn't the same with things the way they were. It was almost ridiculous. The whole situation had been a sham. His own people—his own *boss*—had sent that mech to kill those vampires. To start the unrest that now plagued the city. He'd give a lot to talk it over with Cyd. He'd give a lot to know what she'd known.

Glancing back to make sure the guy really was just a bum, Dain stepped past the police tape. He got out his pocket knife to jimmy the lock, but found Cyd had left the apartment unsecured. Shaking his head he stepped inside, and in the smoky green gloom, sure enough, her place had all the signs of someone who'd been planning to come back.

They hadn't found a body. They wouldn't. And Forensics had found mixed blood types all over that glass. Suddenly, everything had so many possibilities. The questions were racking up, one after the next without any being answered. It was all too unfair and confusing.

Dain walked into the kitchen, noting the cigarettes on the floor and dirty dishes piled in the sink. Drug paraphernalia was out in the open in a meat-loaf pan, sitting on the phone book, both dumped uncaringly into the open garbage now moldering in the damp heat. On the bottom of the refrigerator door was a fingertip tracing that looked relatively fresh—"Cyd + ?" An arrow pointed down from the question mark to the word, "nobody."

Dain angrily wiped at his eyes, then reached under the kitchen sink and rummaged around until he found an empty cardboard box. There wasn't much in the apartment anybody would miss. The landlord would clear it out soon enough in lieu of next month's missing rent if the Triangle's squatters and down-and-outers didn't hear of it first. Leaving the kitchen behind, he went to Cyd's bedroom and opened the drawers until he found a small lockbox. He dumped the lockbox in the cardboard box, added her jewelry and the only party dress hanging in the closet that looked like it had never been worn. He also took a stuffed animal off the bed and some pictures of people he didn't recognize and had never asked about.

Maybe that was his mistake. Maybe he should have been asking. Maybe he should have been proactively trying to get her some help, someone to help her talk about whatever had happened in her past. Maybe he'd done it all wrong. He folded the box top down and surveyed the tiny apartment one last time. He'd keep the box until he didn't hurt so much. Until he was ready to accept that she was never coming back.

Strange, Dain had always thought he was the one keeping Cyd from slipping into a darker role, into some sort of sad solitude. Maybe she'd been the glue keeping him together.

This was what you got when you played the game.

Cyd + nobody. Dain + nobody. It was a lonely game. He'd thought he'd managed to fill the voids in his life. But his job and his friendships had only concealed the fact that he felt blank. Except when he was with Fleur. The blanks got filled in when he looked in her eyes.

What the hell did it mean to be human versus anything else? Mech, vampire, werewolf, human—what would it buy him if he continued working for his own race, which was moving toward crushing everybody else? The fear of losing Fleur—really *losing* her—was overwhelming. And the answer was so simple. It balanced the equation. *Fleur* balanced all equations.

He didn't know what it meant to feel human. He only knew he wanted to be whatever he needed to be to love her. Fleur was all that sparked life in him. She was the only reason to wake up in the morning anymore. And he wasn't going to hold back, resist, or conceal anything that would put that fact in jeopardy. He'd once thought his goal was a promotion to the top of the intelligence community, following Kippenham in policy and position. But Kippenham, the job, the policies of the humans for or against anyone else—none of it held interest for him anymore. It all was a handful of hollow victories. He could do better. And where all he ever really wanted was a little peace, a little joy, something to put the fuzzy memories in his brain into focus, now he had a different plan to achieve that.

He picked through the stuff in the box. "Who'd have thunk it, Cyd? I'm in love with a vampire, and I'm going to do something about it. You were right— things in this city can turn in a heartbeat."

Dain found a copy of the surveillance tape of that fateful night, recorded in their car from the mech's broadcast. He found an old reader and stuck the cartridge in, then brought the reader's goggles to his eyes. It showed the point of view of the mech.

There was Fleur, as she'd been on that eve. There was something so skittish and vulnerable in her. That something was still under the surface, but it had been hidden under the layers of experience and pain she'd found over the course of this crazy struggle. They'd all changed. And kudos to Fleur, because she'd become stronger, more powerful, more self-assured. Dain felt like he'd been falling apart all this time, and there was barely enough of him left to function.

Though he'd run this film before—before he knew all the players and understood the game—this time felt different. He felt different about watching the mech's bullets burn into Fleur's half-brothers, and he felt different watching Fleur's horror and fear as her family died before her eyes. Then she herself stared death down.

Fleur had suggested that immortality could be a curse, but in the moment where death stares you down, Dain saw you wanted to live. You'd always rather live. And from the expression on Fleur's face as the mech's arm came up once more at the bottom of the frame, pointing a weapon at her heart, he could tell that she believed she was going to die.

Dain watched every detail. He saw the edge of metal flip over. It wasn't a weaponry malfunction; the mech had switched on purpose. It was either purposeful or a mistake in orders. But as if he'd never seen the film before, this time when the bullet went into Fleur's flesh and crimson bloomed over the fabric of her sleeve, Dain's heart nearly stopped. And in a world gone mad, a city headed unstoppably toward chaos, all he knew and all that mattered to him was Fleur. He was beyond loyalty to any one species. He was beyond honor. He just wanted Fleur to be safe. To be safe, to love him back, and to give him a reason to live. Fleur was his reason, now, and he'd make every sacrifice to keep her safe. Any sacrifice at all.

Dain took Serena's picture from his wallet and ran his fingertip over her hair. "I just don't remember you. I admit it, okay? I admit it. I don't remember knowing you, sensing you, or loving you the way I do Fleur. Forgive me, but I need her." If Serena had lived instead of him, he would have wanted her to find happiness anyway she could. "I can only hope this is what you'd have wanted for me. If it's wrong, you're going to have to give me some kind of sign."

Chapter Twenty-six

Hayden Wilks looked lean, hungry and dangerous. But also he looked oddly unfamiliar. Fleur shouldn't have been surprised about that. From the moment she'd sunk her fangs into him, he'd become a stranger. Something had shut down inside of him. He'd never even tried to indulge in the rich lifestyle that being vampire offered, a testament to how wrong the transformation had felt. He'd simply opened his eyes and known it was wrong. And then, as Fleur knelt at his feet, crying and saying she was sorry, he'd screamed in horror until he went hoarse. Everything about him still suggested he felt that way; he had the look of a man who was uncomfortable in his own skin, who was searching for a solution that evaded him.

Shockingly, the rogue she'd taken down at Assembly had been true to his word; he'd passed along Fleur's message, and she'd received a cursory response. The place to meet—in the human strata—was a pointed choice.

And when Hayden stepped forward to reveal himself after all this time, it had been as much a shock as she'd anticipated.

"You're surprised to see me," he said, his voice low. If he hated her as much as he once had, it didn't show.

"I didn't think it would be this easy to get an audience."

"Who says it's easy?" Hayden shrugged. "But I don't think you've ever sent for me before."

"No, I haven't. But then, I haven't been leading the Assembly for long."

He smiled slightly. "No, you haven't."

Fleur looked keenly at him. "And perhaps that's what makes the difference."

"Perhaps," he agreed. "What can I do for you?"

"And what can *I* do for *you*, I suppose."

"Right," he said. He spread his arms, palms up. "You got me. I'd like for you to owe me."

Fleur couldn't help herself. Bitterly, she said, "I thought I'd already taken more from you than can ever be repaid."

Hayden's eyes narrowed. "Don't patronize me. I'm not here for personal reasons. We both know what I am. It's what I've always been—an informant, a mercenary, a trader of secrets. If you pay me for knowledge, you'll get the truth. I only sell the truth and I only kill if somebody deserves to die. So, let's get on the same page. I'm not here to make you feel better about yourself. I'm not here for you. I'm here for business. Period. And the currency being traded is that you'll owe me a chit. Hell, the vampire world will owe me a big chit. Do you understand? I'm trading on the future, and if I ever come to you, I'm going to expect to get what I ask for. Is that understood?"

Fleur nodded. "The truth? Okay. Have you ever been paid to lie?"

Hayden looked surprised, then laughed darkly. "Tell me what you want from me, Fleur Dumont, and then I'm going to walk away."

"Who should I be worrying about, Hayden? You've worked with some of the same people in the human Battlefield Operations division that I'm working with now. Who killed my brothers? Why is anyone trying to end the peace? Is it the obvious? Or is it something else?"

"There are no real surprises here. Just a plan long in the making whose time has finally arrived." Hayden leaned forward. "It's the humans, Fleur. It's the same as it's always been. And no matter how many times a truce is called, one of you is going to give into temptation and try to wipe out the other."

"Do you know which human sent the mech?" she asked, just to test his information.

He shrugged. "I don't think it matters. The bottom line is the same. Whether he sent the mech or not, every human wants everyone else gone. Peace between the species is a laugh. It's a nice thought, but for humans, the only thing better would be not having any other species to worry about at all. If I were you, I'd start negotiating with the dogs."

Fleur sighed and shook her head. "We're so far gone, are we?"

"Why don't you ask Dain Reston?"

Fleur whipped her head around and stared. Hayden laughed.

"I'm a professional informant, Fleur. All I do is watch, listen, and trade information. Half the people in town make money this way. And everyone knows you two have a thing. You seem to like the taste of mortals," he added bitterly.

"Next question," Fleur said, steering the conversation away from Dain and wishing she could read Hayden's mind. "Are rogues responsible for murdering the vampires we've been finding dead in the streets? They're all primaries. Are you involved? Or is there a connection between the killings and the mech?"

"You're barking up the wrong tree," Hayden said with a grin. "Those sound like werewolf murders to me. But I haven't seen the evidence."

"Part of the problem is an evidence dump," Fleur said. "Someone—or something—is purposely contaminating the bodies with conflicting DNA. If it's not the rogues, why are you giving us so much trouble?"

"What you don't understand about us rogues is a lot. We rogues aren't trying to bring *you* down," he said, giving a cocky grin. "We're trying to bring *everybody* down. But there's really no 'we.' It's still everyone for his or her self. Sort of like whoever sent that mech. Except, we didn't."

She remembered his signature bravado well. He was fond of grandiose statements, loved developing an aura of power. She knew that a small part of him was teasing her. A small part of him wasn't.

"Seriously, you need to stop thinking of us as evil, Fleur, and start thinking of us as . . . simply different. Do you understand? I don't control any rogues the way you control the members of your Primary Assembly. Some of us just like to come together for a little fun now and then—but we're not the kind of organized mob you are. We have no real leaders; we come together as we like, and part as we like. There's no misplaced loyalty to deal with and no annoying codes of honor to stop us from doing as we wish. It's much simpler . . . and much more fun. If we had any interest in following instructions and attending tea parties, we'd have joined your silly Assembly. Of course, some of us weren't given the choice."

Fleur grimaced. "If you're such equal opportunity terrorists, why go to such lengths *now* to make yourselves known?. As your brethren, we're least likely to bring you down without direct provocation."

"We're in play for two reasons. To check out the strength of the new Assembly leadership, and to have a little fun at the expense of those who made us what we are."

"All that? All those rogues popping in and fighting me . . . you're telling me that was just 'to test out the new leader?' To have a little fun?"

Hayden shrugged. "Would you believe we're just not organized enough to pull off an actual coup?" he asked.

"I don't believe you for a second," Fleur said calmly. "Implying that you're disorganized and unfocused—it's to your disadvantage to have us underestimate you. I don't buy your line, and we'll be ready for anything you try." But she did buy it. It made sense. There was a reason those rogue attacks had seemed personal; they *were* personal. But they hadn't been part of anything larger. The rogues weren't behind the mech, and they weren't up to launching a full-scale revolution. Not yet anyway.

Hayden lifted an eyebrow and, after a few seconds of silence, said, "Believe what you want. But you primaries harbor a dirty little secret of your own. Your trained executioners . . . they are basically rogues on a leash. So don't look at me with disdain. If I weren't out on my own, I'd probably be one of your leashed made rogues by now."

"That's not true and you know it. If you'd stayed, I would have spent my life trying to make you happy."

"I'm not interested in would-have-could-have-should-have, Fleur. I'll never reconcile what you did to me, and I wouldn't have no matter how long I stayed with you."

"Listen, Hayden," Fleur said softly, her hand on his shoulder. "It's not too late to come in out of the cold. Your business is a lonely one."

He flung her hand away. "It's the same damn temperature wherever I go, and it's much, much too late."

"I suppose it was too late the moment I made you," Fleur noted sadly. "Oh, Hayden. Was it just *you?* Was it something special that I didn't know enough to see? What makes others adapt and you so unhappy?"

Hayden stared at her. "Don't pretend, Fleur. For god's sake, don't pretend to such naïveté. It makes me sick."

Fleur shook her head, tongue-tied, trying to figure out how to arrange her next words, hyperaware of the silence ticking away between them. There was so much she wanted to ask, so much she needed him to know.

Hayden studied her in the silence. His eyes searched hers. "Is the other stuff really why we're here? To talk politics? Or was there something else?"

She said nothing, the question dancing on the tip of her tongue.

"Oh, Fleur." Hayden's expression changed to one of incredulity. "Oh, Fleur. Say it isn't so. Are you in *love* again?"

"I wasn't in love the first time," she snapped.

And as she stood there, she sensed a brutality come into him. "Such a lie. That's why we're really here. You want my permission to do it again. You're looking for forgiveness."

"You don't even try to make peace with what you've become," she said.

"What *you made me*," he corrected. "And no, I don't. I don't accept it. Still."

"Is there nothing you will allow yourself to enjoy?"

His grim expression softened into a smile, but the expression made her shiver. "There is one thing. I enjoy not having a conscience."

Fleur couldn't take any more. "That's something you choose, not something inherent to our kind."

"Is it?" he asked.

"You disgust me," Fleur spat. "I don't know how I ever thought I loved you."

"I can be quite charming when I choose. Don't you remember?"

She remained silent. It was true. She did remember.

"Come on, Fleur, don't you? I remember how you longed for me. My touch sent you into a thousand pieces. And you'd do anything for me. Except tell me no when you should have." He lost some of his rakish nonchalance and grabbed her by the throat. *"You should have said no."*

"You begged me to make you a vampire," she gasped out. "You begged, Hayden. You wanted it."

"I didn't know what it meant! I didn't know! Why

did you let me become . . . this? Why did you do this to me? I can hardly stand it. I'm an *animal*!"

He crowded her up to the metal bars of a closed newsstand, pressing his body against her, practically crawling onto her. "You made me into an animal, Fleur Dumont. If you loved me, you should have had the strength to give me up. Your kind doesn't deserve to know love."

"But you still draw me, Fleur," he said, grinding his pelvis into her. "You could lure anybody, anytime you wanted. You're like a siren, an invisible web of seduction. I hate that more than anything, that I still want you."

"Get off me, Hayden," she said grimly. "You've had your fun." But she didn't force him away.

"Why do you let me touch you like this?" he asked. "Why do you let me press my body into yours when you're here to ask permission to take another?" He chuckled softly, angrily. "It can only be guilt. You know you were wrong."

She stuck to the truth. "I wasn't wrong. You made me believe it would make you happy."

"But you knew better," he murmured, rocking against her. "As you know now, about Dain Reston. Do you think he would like to see you like this? If you've come here for permission, you aren't going to get it. Maybe I should just kill him and save the poor guy the misery of what you'd like to do to him."

Fleur froze for a moment, then she put her hands on Hayden's shoulders and kneed him in the gut. He flew backward and fell to his knees, gasping for air.

"Look at me, Hayden. Number one, I'm not the same girl you once knew—got that? Number two . . ." She leaned over, lifted his chin and stared directly into his glittering, hateful eyes. "If you so much as touch him, I will find a way to make your immortal life that much more miserable."

Hayden seemed to find her words tremendously amusing. "As if that were possible. And so history repeats. I don't know this Dain Reston, but I know I was like him once."

"You were never like him," Fleur ground out. "Never."

He laughed. "Who would have guessed? The Fleur I knew *was* someone else," he joked. A mix of emotions flitted over his face, and Fleur knew he still remembered what had been between them. It was as close to a compliment as she was ever likely to hear cross his lips.

He turned to go and Fleur blurted, "You really don't forgive me, do you?"

Hayden stopped in his tracks and looked over his shoulder. Turning fully around he came back to her, raising his hand to her face and softly stroking her cheek. "No. I don't forgive you," he said. Then spun and walked away for good.

Chapter Twenty-seven

Jill Cooper hesitated for a moment, which was unusual. But there was a peculiar niggling feeling inside her that just wouldn't go away.

It had been a "Big Scoop" day for her, and she should have been jazzed; she'd actually snapped proof of the alleged affair between Dain Reston and Fleur Dumont. She'd raced to the scene of the story after receiving a tip-off, and had made it into the bar just in time to get in on the action. Coming in the back door, she'd carried a concealed camera that she'd pointed at them for a full five minutes of hand-holding à la Romeo and Juliet. They'd never noticed as she captured the moment at which they'd kissed; they were completely and totally focused on each other. As a matter of fact, at one point, Jill had found herself staring at them wistfully, wondering what it would be like to have a man look at her like Dain did Fleur.

Now, standing at the front desk of the processing counter, she was beginning to feel a little ill.

The attendant took her stick as she logged in the roll. "No backlog. I'll get this processed ASAP and throw it on the server for you."

"Thanks, man." Jill tossed the touch pen back on the desk and went to her miniscule home away from home, her dump of a cubicle with its sleeping bag and floor pad under the desk. She checked her computer and tried to focus on e-mail. But the peculiar feeling in her gut wouldn't go away.

She'd been so psyched about getting such a juicy scoop. She counted lots of public figures as friends, but the understanding was always that Jill made no promises. If she got scoop, she was going to run scoop. Dain knew that, they had an understanding, and the bottom line was that a kiss between vampires and humans of their rank was bona fide, Grade A, capital S "Scoop." If Dain had wanted to keep it on the down low, he should've stayed at home and kissed Fleur under the covers. Dain keeping his job wasn't Jill's responsibility and everyone in the know was clear that he'd been chasing vampire skirt since the case started. Unfortunately, Jill was sure that as soon as her pictures were placed on the server, B-Ops would be notified—the paper got sued enough as it was.

The computer chimed and Jill pressed print, waiting for her desk printer to start production.

There was a little pause and then a message popped up on screen:

WOULD YOU LIKE TO PRINT THE AUDIO TRANSCRIPT OF THESE EVENTS?

The buzz in Jill's brain grew louder as she realized what she'd done. Very few reporters took audio, either because they were photographing something too far away to pick up, or because it was considered unlawful bugging. She'd either hit the switch or forgot to reset it from last time. She couldn't even remember what she'd been photographing last time. . . .

Her index finger hovered above the ENTER key as Jill tried to decide what to do. The files might already be saved on the network in duplicate—and because of the photos, B-Ops was going to get access.

Maybe Dain and Fleur had just talked about how much they adored each other. Maybe they just talked about sports or the weather.

Jill pressed ENTER and waited.

Photos spewed out of the printer in sheets of nine, each printed with the computer's best guess of dialogue underneath. First was the couple holding themselves away from each other. Then they were moving in close . . . away . . . close . . . holding hands . . . kissing— Jill grabbed the other sheets as they came out of the printer and squinted down at the tiny print. And the niggling feeling in her gut upgraded to sheer horror.

Dain was talking to Fleur about mechs. There *were* mechs in Crimson City. And humans had sent them to kill vampires. Her heart beating madly, Jill reread the printouts very carefully, examining the contexts in which he said things and the expressions on his face when he said them.

Jill Cooper freely admitted she'd snapped photos and, yes, captured audio, of just about everything under the sun in her days as a reporter. She had folders full of pictures that ran the gamut from people in the throes of death agony to those in the throes of ecstasy. Such came with the territory.

But this information wasn't the stuff to make the denizens of Crimson City snicker with delight; this was information that could get a person killed. And the most likely candidate was a decent person whom she knew and liked, and who didn't deserve to die.

The single best thing about working for a tabloid was not having to answer to anyone about what she chose to run and what she chose to bury. Jill looked around, assaulted by paranoia, stuck the photo sheets in the shredder, and while she was pressing the ON button with her left hand, used her right hand to maneuver the folder of processed photo files into the garbage can on her computer. She pressed DELETE. Once the shots winked away she pressed DELETE once more, almost convulsively slamming her index finger against the key. Maybe, just maybe, pressing it *this* time, would make it disappear faster or better.

She took a deep breath and sprinted the obstacle course back to the lab counter. "I need that memory stick back."

The guy looked up in surprise, then slapped a new chip on the counter. "Have a clean one. I haven't erased yours yet."

"No, I need the original." Her voice sounded squeaky. *Just calm down, Jill.*

The guy's brow wrinkled in confusion. "But the files are on the network. Didn't you get them?"

Jill plowed through the swinging door and came behind the desk, crowding behind the technician's back. "Can you show me where?"

Flustered, the kid tapped a few things out on his

keyboard and the network originals popped up. Jill reached over his shoulder and hit DELETE.

"What the . . . ?"

Jill grabbed the box next to the keyboard. It was filled with memory sticks. "Which one is mine? I need it."

His eyes suddenly narrowed. "What's the emergency?"

She looked up and caught his suspicion. "There's a virus on it. A bad one."

"Uh-huh. Well, I'll be erasing it eventu—" His words were drowned out as Jill grabbed him by the collar. Then, realizing she was totally out of line, she immediately let go and laughed. "Oh, wow. I'm sorry. I bought some of that black market cold medicine everyone's been talking about and, well, geez, I'm thinking I won't be using *that* again." She picked up the entire box of memory sticks and headed backwards out the swinging door. "Hey, no hard feelings, man. I owe you one. Boy, next time I'll just drink some orange juice!" She laughed again, amazed how well she could sound like a lunatic, and took off. The box of memory sticks in one hand, she raced by her cubicle to grab her coat and bag and left the office.

She headed down to the Venice canals, shivering from stress and the cold. Placing the box on the ledge of one of the canals, she systematically began breaking each memory stick against the cement and tossing its parts into the water below.

Her fingers were scraped and bleeding after just ten, and there were three times that many to go. Unfortunately, she was running out of time. She held the box behind her back and turned around, leaning against the bridge as she saw JB and Trask from B-Ops headed up the slope. She considered tossing the box into the water, but the damn things might still work if they were whole, even after they sank. They needed to be smashed. And there was no way she was going to let these two have them.

Super-friendly, Trask gave a wave. "Hey, Jill!" JB called.

Jill's heart was pounding. "Hi, guys," she replied.

"Whatcha doing out here?" They'd come right up to her. She shivered a little but covered it with a shrug.

"Just on assignment. The usual."

JB tipped his head to the side. "You don't have your camera." He sighed heavily. "Come on. You know why we're here. Just give us the stuff and we'll give you a ride back in a nice warm car. It'll all end fine."

"No."

Trask sniffled and rubbed his nose. "What exactly is on it, anyway?"

"Didn't they tell you?" Jill asked.

JB elbowed his partner in what was clearly an effort to keep him quiet. "Aw, Jill. Let's cut the crap. If we're here, somebody besides you already knows what's in that box. You know we don't want to hurt you. I'm serious. I don't like this business. I don't like having to mess with people I consider pals. But I have orders to get those sticks. So hand over the goddamn things and we can all get the hell out of here."

He grabbed her, his fingers clamping painfully around her wrist. Jill winced but held the box behind her back with her other arm. It was ridiculous; they were right—if they were here, someone knew what she'd printed. "JB, let go of me."

"Dammit, Jill! Don't make me do this." He swore a couple more times as they struggled. Trask came at her from the other side and the two men, clearly not wanting to hurt her if they could avoid it, engaged in an awkward dance to try to get her prize. It was like the childhood game of keep-away.

Trask was newer and a bit of a wildcard, but Jill knew JB well enough to know he wasn't enjoying this. Finally Trask just reached out and shoved her against the bridge rail, drawing his arm back to clock her. She tried to run, but Trask caught her shirt from behind and she went flying onto her hands and knees, the contents of her box spilling all over the concrete.

"JB, get the stuff!" Trask called. JB gave him a furious look, but he started collecting the sticks as his partner put his knee on Jill's back and pressed her down against the ground.

She winced as the dirt and gravel pressed into her banged-up knees. They had her and she was done. *Sorry, Dain. I tried.* "You can take your goddamn hands off me now," she growled. She looked over her shoulder at Trash just in time to see Marius Dumont come out of nowhere to land behind him.

Mesmerized by the intensity of the vampire's expression as he pulled Trask off her and smashed his fist into the B-Operative's face, it took her a moment to realize that if she didn't do something, this rescue could have deadlier consequences than anyone wanted. As Marius cocked his fist again, Jillian scrambled to her feet. "Stop! Stop it!" she cried.

Marius froze, his arm suspended in midair. Trask's lip had begun to bleed.

"Let him go . . . for my sake," Jillian said. She looked at JB, who was just standing there with the box of memory sticks. "Get him out of here," she said.

JB rushed up and threw Trask's arm over his shoulder when Marius released it. He gave Jill a grateful look and, with the box and Trask, took off into the night.

Jill looked back at Marius and followed his stare to the blood and dirt on her knees. She hurt like hell, but she'd stopped thinking about that. But the vampire was fixated. He moved in close and Jill took a sudden breath, remembering all over again what this man made her feel every time he so much as touched her cheek.

To her surprise, he lifted her up and sat her on the canal rail and started picking the gravel out of her knees. The more he touched her, the more she felt like she might faint into the water below.

"Marius, enough," she managed to say. "I can't stand it anymore."

He thought she meant the pain. He set her back on her feet, letting her lean against him for support. The blood from her cuts was still on his fingertips; she was certain he could smell it, for he tipped her head back and ran his mouth along her throat. The dangerous sensation of his fangs delicately grazing her skin set her body on fire, and the desire building within her was more intense than anything she'd ever experienced. When he pulled his mouth away and looked deep into her eyes, Jill would have given him anything he asked for.

"Oh, god," he murmured. "Why do I let you do this to me?"

"Do this to *you?*" she asked.

In a gorgeous mix of awe and desire, he raised his hand to her forehead and delicately swept his fingers over her eyelids. Suddenly drowsy, Jill pressed her cheek against his chest and let herself collapse in his arms.

When she woke, she was at home, in bed. Her coat and purse were laid neatly over the sitting chair in her bedroom, her knees were bandaged, and a vision of Marius Dumont was all that remained of her wonderful dream.

And then she remembered, it hadn't been a dream. And it hadn't all been wonderful. Jill eased herself off the bed and limped to her purse. She grabbed her cell phone and headed back to the bed, already dialing. Curling up in a ball on the covers, Jill closed her eyes and swiped at her runny nose.

"Answer your damn phone, Dain," she begged. "It's an emergency."

Wherever you are, get away from your people immediately. Your life depends on it. 20,36, Strata-1.

Dain hung up on Jill Cooper's text message, nearly dropping his comm on the ground as he broke out in a cold sweat. He was in line at Chick-O-Wich in the east quarter, and JB idled in the car outside. The whole thing was surreal. Swap Cyd for JB and everything would seem an ordinary day before the assassinations.

He stared into the dull eyes of a tattooed server wearing an incongruously jaunty white paper hat, and ordered lunch. He paid, then walked casually toward the restrooms as his order was being processed. Pushing open the garish red, yellow, and blue striped door, he stepped inside. A glance down told him the three stalls were empty, and the medium-sized window above the sink told him he had a decent chance of not dying in a fast-food restroom.

He took his shirt off, wrapped it around his fist, then gave the window three quick shots to take out the majority of the glass. The shards tinkled down the wall outside to the ground, and Dain popped out the remaining pieces and climbed up on the sink, slipping as the old equipment pulled away from the wall. He caught himself in time and heaved his body up and through the opening.

A street punk hanging out on the fire escape next door raised a lazy hand in greeting; Dain nodded back and jumped to street level, heading away from Chick-O-Wich, JB, and unfortunately, his car. He paused long enough to buy a cheap trench coat and a Dodgers cap from a street vendor, then headed for the opening to the underground below the Indiana Gold Line. Down the narrow tunnel he went once more, to Dogtown, his sunglasses already on night vision. There Dain checked his position and looked around at the crowd. Jill had sent him nearby coordinates.

He forced himself to relax, casually walking down the length of the platform and sitting down on the closest bench to a bored-looking brunette.

"It's me," she said.

Dain nearly jumped out his skin. He looked at the brunette and frowned.

"It's *me.*" She moved her sunglasses down her

nose so he could see her eyes, and Jill Cooper blinked back at him. She looked like, if she'd slept at all in the last twenty-four hours, it had been badly. She even wore colored contacts beneath the glasses, but he recognized her now that she'd shown herself.

"You've got to be kidding me, Jill. How much TV do you watch?"

"Well, you didn't recognize me."

"Fair enough. What am I doing here?"

"You're a marked man, Dain. Your bosses are looking for a fall guy and you're at the top of the list. Worse, I've given them photographic proof."

"Start from the beginning."

She took a deep breath and obliged. When she was done explaining, she apologized up and down for the photos. He appreciated the sentiment and the warning, but they both knew she'd just been doing her job. A kiss wasn't much to get excited about these days, but it helped tell a story. Trouble was, Jill had provided his bosses with evidence that allowed them to build any number of stories. All of them put Dain in an unsanctioned alliance with vampires while holding a top-security position with B-Ops.

Dain just sat, watching the dogs exit and enter the subway cars, watching life go on around him. "If I told you that I didn't feel human anymore, would that make any sense to you?" he asked.

"Not really." Jill paused and then added, "Unless you've been made a fang or a dog. Have you?"

"No.

"And it's more than the fact that my own side might want me dead. I'm just not part of anything anymore. I don't feel the way I used to. I don't feel any kinship. I just feel like I . . . like I've been fed a load of crap."

Jill nodded. "Dain, do you think your bosses had Cyd killed?"

His gaze locked on hers. "What do you know?"

"Nothing about that. I swear. It's just an idea. I just wonder if it's coincidence that out of all the people working B-Ops, you two—partners—were both somehow . . ."

"Marked?"

"Yeah."

"What do you know, Jill?"

"Like I said, nothing. But I get a lot of dirt from a lot of different sources, and I can't help wondering."

"Why call me, then? If I'm in trouble, you'll be in trouble just for helping me."

She gave him a coquettish grin. "Even soul-suckers like us journalists have a code. Besides, at the end of the day, I'm expecting you to give me the exclusive."

"If I'm still alive," Dain said darkly.

"Why do you think I just told you what I told you?" Jill asked. "The bad news is that you're compromised, and a suspect for trading top-secret information. The good news is that you're so compromised, you probably have nothing to lose by digging into what's really going on. You can stop this frame-job and massacre before it happens."

"I didn't realize you had a soft spot for vampires."

Jill blinked, a slow flush crawling over her cheeks. "I don't, really. It's just wrong what we humans are doing. We'll be back to open season soon. How could anybody want that?"

"You might ask Kippenham that," Dain said.

"I prefer to keep my distance from him," she replied.

The whistle sounded from a new train coming down the tunnel. Dain looked at Jill, but she was staring forward, reapplying lipstick that didn't need reapplying in the tiny mirror of her compact.

"What happened to the opportunistic tabloid journalist I once knew?" he asked.

The corners of Jill's mouth curved up in amusement. "Oh, she's still here, don't you worry. I'll never really be a saint as long as good copy's on the line."

"You've got a good heart, Jillian Cooper."

Her hand stilled. "Well, don't tell anybody—I've got a reputation to uphold. And you'll be pissed off at me again soon enough, when things are back to normal." She put the lipstick back in her purse. "I've told you everything I'm going to tell you. What you plan next is not something I want to know about."

Her hand slid over his, which lay facedown on the bench. He took her hand and they exchanged a squeeze. "Good luck," she said, standing up and brushing off the back of her coat. The subway car slid to a halt and the double doors running alongside slid open. Then Jill Cooper stepped inside and didn't look back until the doors had closed. Suddenly she looked over her shoulder at him, as if she realized this might be the last time they would ever meet.

Dain smiled back at her until the subway sped away, then he let the smile leach from his face.

He waited for the next train to come, took the line to Wilshire and Vermont, transferred, and finally joined those heading aboveground on the escalators, all the while doing his best to blend in. As he hit street level, he flipped his collar up and shrank into his coat. He spent five minutes walking toward his apartment before he realized that was not where he wanted to be and changed course toward Dumont Towers.

Halfway there, Dain sensed he was being followed. He picked up his pace, first to a brisk walk, then to a jog . . . and then he looked behind him. Trask and JB weren't even trying to hide. This wasn't recon—they intended to take him out.

He started to run, hoping to lose them on Wilshire Boulevard, but he knew that the two operatives had an advantage over him at ground level no matter which street he chose. He was better acquainted with strata +1 than they, and that was his best chance.

As he ran down the boulevard with his own men on his heels, he scanned the line of high-rises along Wilshire, trying to identify his best option. He could hear JB and Trask shouting to each other, and that was all he needed to spur him on. He cut away from Wilshire, chose a target building, then sprinted into the underground parking lot and out the back where he found the fire escape. He launched himself at the metal ladder and shimmied up as fast as he could, taking the metal steps two at a time in a cacophony of tinny music.

Below, JB and Trask shouted more directions at each other, then started up the ladder behind him.

Dain kept his focus forward until he finally reached rooftop, panting and sweating. He ran across the roof and jumped to an adjacent rooftop. He hit the gravel with a fair amount of distance from the edge to spare, but a huge wolflike dog on the far side killed any joy he might have felt. Was it a werewolf?

"Where the hell did you come from?" he said. The dog covered the distance between them in record time, digging his teeth into Dain's pant leg, one incisor catching the flesh of his ankle. Dain yelped in pain as he hit the ground. But he quickly got to his hands and knees, dragging the dog with him across the rooftop as he tried to get away.

"Who are you working for? Do you know Cyd? Cydney Brighton?" Dain gasped in pain as the dog clamped down. "She's my friend . . . she's tight with you guys." This was insane. It had come to this: Humans talking to dogs, unsure if they were werewolves.

Dain shook his head. Paranoia was catching up with him. And so were his men. His old teammates, because there was no longer any reason to deny that Dain didn't belong to any group anymore. A rooftop chase kind of made that official.

As he struggled with the animal, Dain saw two hands curl over the edge of the first fire escape. He heard JB call to Trask for a boost. With every bit of strength he could muster, Dain twisted his body and kicked out with his free leg. He struck the dog in the face and the animal finally let go.

"Sorry," he mumbled. As the dog regained its footing and gave its head a shake, Dain stood up, raced to the edge of the rooftop and took a flying leap. He could hear the dog barking behind him as he flailed through the air. He caught the lip of the next building with his upper body, his legs smashing down against steel and concrete.

Knuckles scraped and bleeding, Dain practically clawed his way over the edge to safety. His lungs were on fire, his knees were like jelly, and he was damned lucky this was a case of life or death, because under ordinary circumstances he might not have had it in him to keep going. But he had to keep on running, because he knew that if they caught him, there would be no turning back. He'd have to pay for something he couldn't even quite articulate. He'd have to pay for the crime of not exhibiting blind loyalty.

He could see Dumont Towers a city block away, now, even less if he crossed diagonally. He knew what he had to do. He knew what he wanted to do. If loving Fleur was the crime they'd make him pay for, he was all too happy to provide them with more evidence. He would go to her. He'd rather spend eternity with her as a bloodsucker than even one more day without her as a human. He started running.

The sound of JB and Trask landing on the very same gravel roof came much too soon. They were younger and faster than he. Dain glanced over his shoulder, looked JB right in the eyes and let adrenaline take over. As his old teammates climbed to their feet and started toward him, Dain backed up to the ledge on the far side of the current rooftop and teetered there, a hair's breadth from plunging to his death. JB and Trask froze, and Dain let them fear the worst.

Dumont Towers was kitty-corner now. He waited a few seconds for a skyadvert to pass by, jumped for it, rolled off the side and grabbed onto one of its fins. Trask swore, and the two B-Ops men ran to the edge of the building.

The skyadvert surged wildly, unable to handle

Dain's weight. He must have jolted its projector device, because an entire night's worth of adverts were scrolling at breakneck speed right into his eyes and beyond him over the building. An explosion of rainbow colors issued from the machine as Dain careened unevenly away from Trask and JB toward Dumont Towers.

He could see his men had their weapons out, that they were holding them up, aiming them . . . and then first JB lowered his arms, then Trask followed suit.

When the skyadvert made it close enough to one of the Dumont Tower balconies, Dain let go. He dropped to the stone, cringing a little on impact. The cuts and bruises didn't give him a second thought, though, nor did the alarm that sounded as he broke in from the balcony. There was only one thought in his mind. With a pounding heart, Dain made a beeline for Fleur's room.

Chapter Twenty-eight

Fleur was poring over a map of the Hollywood region at a conference table in the war room when the building security alarm sounded.

Her comm box beeped. "Fleur, it's Dain Reston," a voice said. "He wants to see you. He says it's urgent. He says it's a matter of life or death."

Fleur looked at her cousins in time to see them exchange glances.

"*I'll* go talk to him," Marius said. "We don't know that—"

Fleur frowned. "No. He asked for me. You finish up here and I'll find out what he wants." She leaned down to the comm box. "Where is he now?" she asked.

There was a pause. Then, "Your rooms."

"Thank you. I'll be right there."

Marius held on to her as she tried to stand up. "Fleur—," he began.

"What?" she snapped, shaking his hand away. "I'm not going to do anything stupid."

"Nobody's saying . . ." Ian began.

"You don't have to say anything. I swear on my mother's grave I will not compromise what we must do here tonight for anything or anyone."

Marius cocked his head, then he stepped away to open the door for her. Fleur thought she saw a look of respect in his eyes as she passed. She walked out to the stairs and jumped over the banister, soaring up to her own floor.

Dain stood outside her rooms, flanked by two sentries. "Dain, this is a very bad— My god, you look like hell." Fleur turned to the sentries. "He's not a threat. I'll handle this. But go ahead and do a security sweep before you turn off the alarm."

The sentries nodded and disappeared.

"A security sweep," he murmured. "You think I'm a diversion?"

She ignored his complaint and took a good look at him. He was wrecked. Physically and emotionally, he was just wrecked. And in spite of Fleur's bravado only minutes before in the war room, she felt her defenses slip.

She reached out to open the door to her room, and Dain actually flinched. "You're in bad shape," she said. "Come inside."

Dain followed her in but didn't sit down. She glanced at the blood streaks over what seemed like every part of his exposed flesh, and noticed the blood pooling at his ankle. Taking a deep breath, she steeled herself and looked into his eyes, then gasped. "Oh, no. *No.*"

"What?"

"You have that look."

"What look? Never mind that." He reached out

and cupped her face in his hands. "I need your help, Fleur. It's important. Please."

Stricken without even knowing why, Fleur pulled his hands away. "Don't sweet talk me, Dain," she whispered. "Just tell me what you want."

"I need you to make me a vampire," he blurted.

She pushed him backward, fighting the urge to strike him for even saying such a thing. Was he a plant? Was he trying to betray her in some way she didn't realize? "What the hell are you talking about? A few nights ago you nearly lost your mind when I nipped you for fun. Now you want me to bite you in full and make you vampire?"

"I know, I know," he said. "I couldn't fit all the pieces together. I wasn't ready for the truth."

He looked like a drowning man, and Fleur had to work hard to fight her compassion. But she owed it to herself and her people. "What truth? Why are you asking me for this?"

Dain stared at her wordlessly for a moment. He ran his hand over his mouth and Fleur had to look away from his cuts and scrapes. They created a thirst in her, but not one more powerful than she'd already felt with Dain. She caught his expression in her dressing mirror and put her hand over her heart, almost unable to breathe.

"Can't you see it?" he whispered. "It's because I love you." His gaze met hers in the mirror. "I love you, Fleur. Can you see it? It's in everything I am."

Fleur's eyes filled with tears, and she tried to hold them back. "How dare you. How could you do this to me?" She turned to face him, her chin held high though it trembled with emotion.

Dain stumbled forward, confused. She didn't

blame him for his confusion; he'd laid his heart bare. She believed him, too, but he should have believed her when she'd said that the two of them were impossible.

"What did I say wrong?" he asked. "How can telling you I love you be a bad thing?"

Fleur couldn't shy away from the truth, though it might kill her. Might kill *them*. "You don't really mean it. Even if you think you do, you'd regret it. You'd end up hating me for changing you. You told me yourself—you said you were dark, but not that dark."

"I didn't understand then," Dain said desperately. He looked wildly around the bedroom as if the right words to convince her were there somewhere. "Being human is a state of mind. And I don't feel human anymore—I'm *not* human. I don't believe what they believe, I don't feel loyal to the people I knew. I don't love anyone there. There's no one in the human world who matters to me the way you do. You're everything. Now I'm asking you—*begging* you—to make me like you. We could be together forever, and that's worth everything."

The pressure was getting to her. Fleur struggled to keep up her facade of strength. She didn't want him to see how much she wanted to just do what he asked, no explanations needed. But explanations *were* needed. And she wouldn't do what he asked, no matter what. No matter how much she wanted to.

Crumbling under his destroyed look, Fleur started to cry. Tears streaming down her face, she walked to the door. "You really don't understand what you're asking. You've created an idealized reality of what could be because your old life's not working for you anymore. That doesn't make it right."

She put her hand on the doorknob, but Dain moved quickly and put his hand on hers, holding it. "I stand a good chance of being killed by my own people."

Fleur flinched. "Oh, Dain. Couldn't you have just said that? It's immortality you seek." *Not me.*

"No!" He looked up at the ceiling as if beseeching the Heavens to grant her understanding. "It's *you.*" His hands went to her face again and his mouth was a kiss away. "I love you. I said it once, and now I feel like I could say it a million times, to anyone. It's the timing of everything that makes it sound so bad. I don't have time right now to persuade you of how I feel about you, but if you grant me this one request, I'll spend eternity proving it."

Dazed, Fleur leaned her head back against the wall. The smell of his blood was clouding her senses. "You'll spend eternity proving to me how much you love me," she said grimly. "Oh, where have I heard that before?"

Dain's face darkened with a sudden and intense rage. He let go of her and slammed a fist into the door above her head. "You know what? I realize this doesn't look good. But this is me. I'm in trouble. I'm in trouble in part because I've allied with you. And I'm hoping that you can look me in the eyes and see that when I ask this, it's a request born out of sheer desperation. I know how we operate. I've seen this play a dozen times. I'm marked, Fleur. So, how about I just take away the love crap that seems so unimpressive to you and pare down to the bottom line: If you don't help me, I know they're going to kill me. I have to fake my death and disappear. So, will you make me vampire or not? Yes or no?"

Fleur swallowed hard but held her position.

Dain just stared at her, obviously reeling. His hands slipped on the wall above as his knees buckled. "I told you something the other day that proves my trustworthiness, and now it looks like what I told you will get me killed. I'm asking for your help. Yes. Or no."

"What you're asking isn't a simple matter of yes or no. It's drenched in the thousands of years of everything we vampires are. It's—"

"Yes or no, Fleur? Do you want me to live?"

Yes? The word wouldn't come.

"Yes or no? Do you want me to live? Say it! I want to hear you say it!" Dain pounded his fists against the door, unaware of what he was doing. Fleur could hear the sentries in the hall on the other side.

Dain took her by the shoulders and threw her back against the door. "All of the questions I have, everything that I need to know can be answered the same way. Do you want me to live? Will you make me a vampire? Do you even love me, Fleur? I'm dying here, even now."

With tears streaming down her face and in utter anguish, Fleur screamed, "No! I can't!" and she dropped her face into her hands.

Dain stilled, and it was the sentries pounding on the other side of the door that she heard now. He stepped back, freeing her from the heady scent and heat of his body, and Fleur opened the door. The sentries took Dain by the forearms and hustled him out of the room. Fleur stood in the doorway and watched them lead him down the staircase.

At the bottom of the first flight, he suddenly turned around. In a voice so cold it sent a shiver down her spine, he said, "By the way, I think we're planning to trap you tonight. It's a major offensive they've got planned out in Hollywood. You might want to get some people on that."

The sentries kept moving and Dain didn't fight any longer. When he disappeared from view, Fleur ran to the banister and looked down the heart of the spiraling crimson staircase. All she could do was watch him go and cry.

"You told me yourself," she whispered. "You're dark, but you're not that dark. I won't make you something you don't understand. Hayden would be the first to tell you this is the right thing to do. And it's because I *do* love you."

She heard the main door close and ran to the window. Pulling aside the curtains and stepping out on her balcony, Fleur leaned over the stone rail and saw Dain tumble headlong onto the sidewalk. As soon as her sentries left him on the street, he was beset by his own people. Fleur watched him struggle until she couldn't take it anymore.

Dain had just barely cleared the doorway when they were all over him. They tackled him—his own men.

"Don't struggle, man," JB said. "You know the drill. Of all people, you know the drill."

"We already lost one person we care about. Don't make us lose you, too." JB wrestled Dain to the ground on his stomach while Trask handcuffed him. "I'm not trying to kill you, boss."

"Nah, you're just trying to get me to go with the nice men with the white coats."

JB raised his left palm. "You know that's not what I want. We've got a bulletin out on you, and I know that doesn't come as a surprise. Come on, man. We can come up with something. Cyd's death put you overboard, you got raked by a dog or a vamp and nearly got made . . . everything's gonna be fine. Some shrink-time and some probation, and you'll be back on the job. But you gotta pick a side."

"JB?"

"Yeah?"

"Nice job. Chapter 6, Calming a Suspect, page 15. At least it's nice to know you were listening."

JB swallowed, his fingers shifting on the handle of his gun. "That's not how it is."

With one captor on either side of him, their hands gripping his forearms, Dain struggled, if only out of principle.

"Get in the car," Trask said, shoving Dain's head down with his palm. After tossing him in the back-seat, the man got in next to him.

JB took the wheel, and Dain couldn't help but no-tice he was still driving Dain's car. His onetime friend shrugged nervously. "You're my mentor, Dain. Please don't make this worse than it has to be. What happened to Cyd is bad enough. You're gonna end up sending *me* to the shrink."

Dain watched his protégé clearly struggling, sweat dripping off his nose and into the neck of his armor, and actually felt a little sympathy. "I'm not the man I used to be," he admitted.

"I'm wondering if you're still even human," Trask growled.

Dain's eyes narrowed. "You think I've been made?"

Before he could react, Trask pressed a three-pronged cartridge into the soft flesh at the bend of Dain's elbow. "Let's find out."

Dain roared with pain as the chemical tracer diluted into his bloodstream. He closed his eyes and shut his mouth, gritting his teeth as the fluid spread through his body.

JB suddenly pulled over, throwing everyone in the backseat forward. "This is so not right. This is so fucked up."

His forehead pressed into the back of the front seat, Dain waited it out, panting. The agony in his veins lessened. "Go ahead and take your sample," he said, wishing he had the strength to put Trask in his place. He slowly eased back into the backseat of the car.

Trask tapped his watch and shrugged. He took a drop of Dain's blood from the same spot he'd stabbed and touched it to a piece of litmus paper.

Dain had just enough energy left in him to chuckle with satisfaction at the disappointment and confusion on Trask's face.

"What the hell did they tell you about me?" he asked.

"What's it say?" JB said.

"Negative. He's not a fang . . . or a dog, for that matter. Still human. One hundred percent."

JB looked shocked, then heaved a sigh. He put the transport back in drive. "First we lose Cyd, now you. I don't know what Kipp is planning to do with you, but you're about to find out. Why'd you do it, man? All you had to do was stay away from that girl when they asked you to. You dug yourself a hole."

Dain shrugged. "I could give you a million reasons."

"You're in love with her, right?"

Dain didn't answer.

"I'd rather believe that was it, you know? It would just sit better if that was it . . . and if she was in love back, you know?"

"I didn't realize you were such a romantic," Dain grunted.

"Yeah, well, guys do stupid things where women are concerned. I can buy that. And the alternative just doesn't sit good with me, where she's some kind of freaky Mata Hari or maybe you're a double agent . . . the idea of *that* shit just makes me crazy. It just ain't right . . . this whole situation is effing nuts!" JB looked at Dain through the rearview mirror. "Sorry, man. I don't know what you did to deserve this, but I'm real sorry." He heaved a sigh.

"What the hell are you sorry for?" Trask asked. "He may not be made, but he's not one of us anymore, either. He's not human, no matter what the tests show."

He meant it as an insult, a comment about Dain's loss of loyalty, but to Dain, it was nothing more and nothing less than a fact. He wasn't human anymore; he just wished he done a better job of explaining that to Fleur.

"Well, he used to be human," JB said sullenly. "And when he was, he was a friend."

Chapter Twenty-nine

Dain sat in what he had once jokingly called, "the dentist's chair." He wasn't laughing anymore. Anytime you found yourself in one of the interrogation rooms on the wrong side of the questioning, you definitely weren't laughing.

The dentist's chair had several uses, from the harmless and mundane to the downright horrifying. Once he'd sneaked into the room on a slow night, and he and Cyd had used the Virtual Reality screen to project a minichip movie onto the wall. After he'd seen a double agent die while strapped down there, he'd saved his movie viewing for bona fide theaters.

JB questioned him for hours, pleading with him to say the right things that would give him an excuse to unlock the ankle restraints that kept Dain tied down. But Dain wouldn't say the right things. He wouldn't talk to anyone but Kipp.

". . . are you sure, Dain?" JB was saying. Kippenham had finally come. JB looked at Dain again and shook his head. "He won't talk about the Dumonts."

Kippenham cocked his head and looked down at Dain. "Why don't you leave us alone, JB."

JB nodded and left the room. Dain noticed that he didn't make eye contact—another bad sign. He took a deep breath and released it slowly, trying to calm himself as he watched Kippenham pull up a chair and flip it around to seat himself with his forearms crossed over the top of its back. "Okay. Let's try something else," Kipp said.

"Like what? Like telling me what the hell is going on here? I don't know what you've got JB thinking, but the kid is going down a path I've never even been on."

"Shut up and listen carefully," Kippenham said, all traces of warmth exorcised from his face. Dain wondered if his boss was working hard to avoid showing emotion, or if treating him as if they'd never had a friendship, as if they'd never showed each other tears, was easy.

"Over the years, you've told me time and again that your memories are fuzzy. Why do you think that is?" Kipp asked.

"I was in an accident. It screwed me up." Dain turned his hands over to reveal the scars on his forearms.

Kippenham didn't even look down. "And how do you think you got burned?"

Dain was starting to feel panicked, and he wasn't sure why. "It was a chemical-based weapon. The substance spattered me in the explosion."

"That's pretty vague, don't you think? What else do you know about your 'accident?'"

"Nothing. I suffered memory loss." Dain swallowed hard but never dropped his gaze. "Why don't you just say what you want to say?"

Kippenham ignored him. If he hadn't looked so damned cold, Dain would have thought his boss was enjoying toying with him. "Ever looked up the account in your files?" Kipp asked.

"Of course." Dain tried to shift his body in the chair, but the restraints stopped him. "It's in there."

"Not very detailed, I suspect. Probably not as detailed as you would like. Your entire file is like that."

"I work on rough stuff," Dain said. "They keep our files trim for a reason—look, could I please have some water?"

Kipp studied his face, then got up and left the room, closing the door behind him. He returned in a moment with a bottled water from the break room, but kept the bottle in one hand. Dain knew that if he reached out, he'd not be able to reach across the table. It was all he could do not to lick his dry lips as condensation slid down the plastic container. Kipp was trying to humiliate him in order to break him. And in that moment, Dain knew for certain that Kipp meant for him to die.

Tapping softly on the side of the water bottle, Kippenham released a sigh. "Now, where were we? 'They keep the files trim for a reason.' Yeah, they certainly do." He unscrewed the bottle top, took a swig and swallowed. He leaned across the table, his mouth still wet from the water. In a voice so gentle it sent fear into Dain's soul, Kippenham asked, "Now, where do you think the mechs come from?"

Dain sat in silence, letting the shock of Kippenham's question sink in. He wanted a drink of water so badly he was almost willing to beg for it. Finally, he forced himself to answer. "The mechs are gene-tically engineered humans designed to accommo-date a variety of mechanical enhancements. They—"

"Says the brochure," Kipp interrupted. "Says the brochure. The nicely packaged PR answer aside, let's be frank. Some of the mechs are criminals. We erase their memories, implant the mechanicals, and voila. A *useless* member of society is reengineered for the *benefit* of society."

Dain laughed, but the sound was tinny in his ears. "This is your way of saying that I'm a criminal who was—let me get this straight—converted to a mech and then reconverted to a human?"

"I'm not suggesting it. It is a fact."

Dain wanted out of the chair. Badly. He lunged up out of the seat, fighting against the restraints until he couldn't stand the pain and flung himself back. "Give me some water, Kipp!"

The man stared at him blankly.

"Give me some fucking water!"

And his boss did. Just like that, Kipp slid the bot-tle across the table. Dain put it to his lips and chugged it down.

"Look at your arms, Dain, and think about that mech we sent to Dumont Towers."

"No." Dain shook his head. He wouldn't believe it.

"Yes. Those burn scars cover the incisions we had to make to remove your mechanicals. You were a mech. You were a beta mech. The conversion didn't go as well as we'd hoped, so we decided to use you in another way. But it all turned out a happy accident. Until recently, you've been an excellent operative."

Dain crushed the plastic bottle in his hands as

Kippenham watched with an amused expression. "A happy accident? That's how you see me?"

Without warning, Kipp's face clouded over. "We gave you a good life and a good job. You made good friends. Think about just how bad you had to be for us to justify taking you into the program."

Dain set his jaw. It was all he could do not to back-hand Kipp out of his chair and start whaling on him with both fists. "I don't know what kind of bullshit psychology you've got going here, but I am not a criminal. I am not a murderer."

"Not anymore. Because of us, you are an entirely productive member of the human race. Your original instincts, the evil with which you conducted your-self in the first part of your life . . . that's all gone." Kippenham waved his hand to indicate Dain's body. "And the mechanical implants have been removed. So you see, you've come out ahead. Way ahead."

Dain reared back. "If what you say is true, you lied to me. Everything you've ever said, everything I've ever done for or with this department, it's all a lie."

"Not precisely. We gave you a new reality. And don't insult either of us with any 'at least when I was a murderer, I was still me,' bullshit." Kippenham studied the careful buff job on the nails of his left hand. "Your life was a nightmare. You were rotten at your very core. It's something we've worked very hard to help you overcome. Without us, you'd be nothing. Worse than nothing. There's a darkness in you, Dain—ever stopped to think about where it came from?"

Every single day of my life.

Soaked with sweat, now, and clenching the arms of his chair so hard he was disfiguring the hard plastic, Dain shivered with fear. "Show me something with my wife. Show me something with me and Serena," he said almost desperately.

Kipp didn't answer, which was almost answer enough, but Dain had to know. He had to be sure. "Where's my wife?" he asked hoarsely.

"I think you've already guessed."

"I haven't guessed anything," Dain ground out between clenched teeth, watching Kippenham's fingers curl around the arms of his own chair, watching those well-tended fingernails dig into the armrest.

"You never had a wife," Kippenham growled.

Dain shook his head. "Serena was my wife."

Kippenham lunged across the table, grabbing him by the collar, clutching the shirt so tightly it began to cut off Dain's airflow. "Serena was *my* wife!" Kippenham bellowed. "You miserable son of a bitch. She was *my* wife!"

Dain struggled for oxygen, gagging as Kippenham tightened his grip. The look in the man's eyes was otherworldly; Dain had never seen such anger there. Or perhaps he'd just never noticed it, but all the pieces started to fit: Kippenham crying with Dain at his apartment, so willing to relive those stories, those anecdotes about Serena over and over, all to help Dain remember. But the hero in those stories wasn't Dain; it was Kipp. He'd been remembering his own wife in those moments. He'd been seeking solace for the death of his own wife. He was crying over his own wife. And he was craving revenge for her.

Why Dain could never cry enough, smile enough, remember loving enough—this was his answer. How ironic, that he should find peace of mind while in the grip of death.

Two seconds from blacking out, Dain felt Kippenham let go, and he struggled to gulp air in giant wheezing inhales. The boss understood. It was as if he'd been waiting for years to set the record straight. As much as Dain had wanted to understand, Kippenham had probably wanted to tell him. To tell Dain what Dain really was. What he'd made him. What was owed.

Kippenham leaned over the chair with his hands on the armrests, trapping Dain and forcing him to listen. Unburdening himself, the words just flowed. "I gave you the privilege of her. That you ever saw Serena in your mind's eye was a privilege. You were *nothing*. You were scum. You were a mercenary, a killer looking at a death sentence. I won't even begin to tell you what you've done. And I took everything that could have haunted you all these years and erased it. I gave you peace. I gave you the memories of a most precious, innocent life. I saved you, Dain Reston. I saved you from hell. And you should be thanking me. You should be *thanking* me." Overcome with emotion, he tore himself away and moved to the window.

Dain struggled to wrap his mind around the information. Maybe Kippenham was telling the truth—that they'd taken him, erased his sins, and created a machine. Then they'd wiped his actions and mind clean once more, and two times removed they'd acquired a better man. Except for one thing. They hadn't been able to recalibrate his impulses and, somewhere in the depths of his mind, his subconscious held on to elements of his past life. The darkness Kipp spoke of could never be erased. That was why he was so drawn to Fleur.

But then it hit him. "The vampires never did anything to me, then. They never did anything to anyone I ever loved," Dain said numbly. "That was yours, too."

"The fangs killed Serena, all right. She went to the corner market to get me aspirin." Kippenham laughed hollowly. "She never came back. They killed her, Reston. The vampires killed someone so beautiful, so innocent, for no reason at all. You've lived with her in your mind for years. You know what she was. Can you deny that to murder her was a work of pure evil? Can you deny that whatever took her life lacked humanity?"

"No," Dain said. "I don't deny it."

Kippenham seemed surprised by the answer, but Dain meant it. Every word. A rogue. Serena must have been killed by a rogue. There was no one in Fleur's sphere who would kill an innocent. Vampires weren't evil by nature, they simply had the same balance of good and evil as a human—except with more power came more responsibility. The Assembly had been designed to protect vampires from themselves, as well as from other species. This he now knew without a doubt.

Looking at Kippenham, Dain thought of Fleur and the love he felt for her. What would a man do for a love like that? What kind of love was it that you would keep your memories alive in the mind of another, just to fuel revenge against an entire species? What kind of love was so strong it made you think all of what had just happened was right, that such an end justified the means.

"What happens now?" Dain asked.

"Knowing what you know, can you deny that the

vampires must be stopped at all costs? That to allow them to continue to multiply will mean an end of the humanity still in Crimson City? Yours is a debt of honor, Dain. See all of this for what it really is and do not let yourself be manipulated by Fleur Dumont."

And so it had come back to Fleur. "What exactly do you expect from me?" he rasped out.

"You don't want to follow the darkness. You know that. You don't want to become what you once were."

"No," Dain agreed weakly. What else was there to do?

"We've got a major initiative running tonight, and I would love to have you there. We're putting on a show of power, starting to shut down vampire airspace. The question is, can I trust you? If I were to place you at the scene, whose side would you take? We're expecting some real action, and I wonder, if we sent you out there, who would you fight for, Dain? Your own kind? Or the kind responsible for soiling this city? The kind who gave you up when you went to her for help. The kind who's been using you all along. Is the answer something I want to find out?

"There are so many questions," Kipp continued. "Would it be better for both of us if I erased you again? Recrafted you into a better machine? What do you think of the idea of not remembering that you fell in love with a vampire?"

Dain flinched. "I'm not in love with a vampire," he said coldly. "And I'd prefer not to have my brain screwed with again, if it's all the same to you."

"Oh, it's not all the same to me," Kipp said. "And it's not all the same to you. You have nowhere to go. No one left who still believes in you. You've burned every bridge you had, you made us doubt your loyalty and commitment. Your old teams don't trust you. Your vampire girlfriend abandoned you. You don't have a lot of options. And just remember, Reston, wherever you go and whatever you do, we'll be right behind you. So, do the right thing. Prove you're worthy of being kept as you are."

"With everything you've just said, how am I supposed to prove myself?" Dain asked bitterly.

Kippenham looked him right in the eye, a killer stare. "Deleting Fleur Dumont would be an ideal start." He leaned over and punched a security code into Dain's restraints. They fell away and Dain stood up, nearly falling over as his sore muscles bunched up.

Chapter Thirty

Fleur stood with her cousins on the tip of a gargoyle looking out on the city below. The four of them stared in silence at the spotlights beaming out from the Hollywood Hills. The benign white rays normally associated with celebrity central were now a violet-pink—the violet-pink of UV. The human military was flexing its muscles; soldiers swarmed below, around the base of each of the lights, the drone of their copters in the distance almost melding into the rest of the city sounds. They hadn't attacked, but they were there.

Fleur understood now that this was all staged to make her people pull back. But where could they pull back to? And what had spurred this? Everything they'd done had been in response to the assassinations, which had come from the humans in the first place. It had all led to one escalation after the next. Weary in body and mind, Fleur fought her longing to talk to Dain. To try to understand his kind.

"Throughout history we can pinpoint specific moments where, if people had just stood up and said 'We won't accept this,' much evil could have been avoided," Marius said beside her.

Fleur gazed down at the city below, where the cars looked like mere matchboxes and the people like specks of dust blown through the streets. Everything always looked so harmless from way up high. "Dain said his bosses had plans. This would be just the tip of the iceberg, really. You're right. We cannot sit here and do nothing." She gestured to the night sky, to the violet streaks moving from side to side and the beams crossing over one another in a mechanized rhythm. "They intend to reduce our viable airspace. It's started. At their whim, we will not be able to fly."

"An attack disguised as a defensive act," Warrick said, nodding his head. "What's your call, Fleur? What do we do?"

"I won't wait any longer," she said firmly. "We must act. But we must act carefully. We can't give the humans any reason to hate us more than they already do. We will attack and destroy those UV lights—but no killing. We must prove the humans wrong, and that we only want to live in peace." She triggered her comm pack and put in a call back to Dumont Towers. Within moments, the safe perimeter beyond the UV lights would be swarming with her Warriors. She looked at Marius for several seconds of calm. He smiled in reassurance, and Ian placed a comforting hand on her shoulder.

And so it went. In the blink of an eye, hundreds of vampires filled the sky, landing at the base of lights to engage in battle with the guards.

Sirens and light alarms that hadn't been used in

years went wild, ramping up with a wail and adding red strobes to the colors slashing the sky. Warrick and Ian turned away from Fleur with a last good-bye glance and leaped away to join the action.

The human fleet of helicopters was quickly over-run. Vampires clung from the skids, acrobatically flipping themselves up into the vehicles to engage the fresh-faced pilots who'd still been swapping bag lunches during the last war. There was no contest. Fleur could see that. One of the copters plunged from the sky toward the streets below, recovering course at the last minute. She winced as it tore through a beam of UV. Then another copter flew through on purpose.

"We have to get those lights." Fleur moved to fly, but Marius held her back.

"We can't afford to lose you. Let your Warriors do the work."

"I'm just going down to the base," she said, shaking off his hand. "It will be fine. Go do what you're here to do."

"I thought I was," Marius said quietly. But he stepped back and let her go.

She smiled at him. "I'll see you at the next Assembly," she said. And then Fleur stepped off the building into the air.

She landed on the metal casing of one of the tall UV spotlights as it lazily moved left and right. Several human soldiers noticed her immediately, and she watched as they marshaled a team, pointing at her and beginning to rappel up the support structure toward her. Above, a pair of helicopters changed course and moved into position. She recognized the vampire standing on the skids of one, and held her breath—he leaped away just before the copter flew into the light.

The heat from the generators went straight up through the soles of her boots, making her sweat. Almost mesmerized by the nearby UV light, she knew that if she lost her balance, she'd fry. Simple as that.

She concentrated on the pattern of crisscrossing strobes. If she tried to fly, it would be a matter of timing. Rather like trying to step over the red streaks of a laser alarm—except if she botched the timing, it didn't mean an alarm; it meant her death.

The lights bucked and weaved, undulated in a rhythmic motion. Fleur dug into the tool kit at her waist and started in on removing the casing to get to the bulbs. They hadn't yet mounted all of the security devices they should have if the humans really meant to keep her people away. Of course, there was always the possibility that these lights had only been meant to lure her people into a battle in the first place.

But the whys and wherefores weren't relevant at the moment; she'd made her decision. Fleur focused on the task at hand, her fingers shaking and sweating in the uncomfortable heat. If she removed too many of the protective panels or did this too quickly, it could very well send a wide, uncontrolled sweep of light over everyone in the sky. The humans wouldn't mind, but it would be a veritable death sentence for her Warriors.

A moving beam of light swept by so close she felt her shoulder singe and her skin pull. Even such an indirect exposure was painful and she jolted back from it, losing her focus and concentration. She slipped and tumbled between two light casings, but the swooping rays parted just in time. Fleur caught herself in midair and hovered, quickly evaluating her next move. With the UV rays swooping to and fro above her, and helicopters on all other sides, she was running out of time, but she wasn't going down without a fight.

She dodged away just as the helicopters closed in, but her left leg was kicked by a propeller. A huge gash in her thigh started bleeding. The wound began to heal, of course, but any loss of blood put her at a huge disadvantage. Of course, the smell of it also made her adrenaline ramp up.

As if they'd rehearsed this maneuver a million times, each helicopter lowered a pair of soldiers, each attached to a cable clipped to the pack on his back. One man to defend against any other vampires, one to concentrate on the target—her. Each combatant also carried high-grade grenade launchers, possibly with those UV cartridges that used to be so rare.

From behind the soldier who was coming for her, a grinning brunette cutout from a hanging advert toasted Fleur with a champagne cocktail. A stiff breeze had cleared out the lower layer of smog and the neon lights of Los Angeles twinkled all around. It was a gorgeous night.

The soldier raised his weapon. Behind her, Fleur felt the wind pick up as other copters moved in even closer. Her best chance was to use them against each other. But she didn't have the angle, the leverage, or the strength to last with the wound she'd incurred. She contemplated surrender, knowing that they'd prefer to capture her alive.

But meek surrender just wasn't in her vocabulary

anymore. She hadn't completed her mission. She was the Durmont heir.

One of the helicopters floated over to her. The men inside were waving her toward them, as if offering her a ride out of the rain. She saw the weapons they had in their hands; she saw that they outnumbered her. And she leaped straight into their helicopter, grabbed a grenade launcher and pumped explosives into the nearby spotlight. The men grappled with her.

The light exploded, sending shards of stinging violet and glass into the night. Everyone cringed in the copter, and Fleur escaped the soldiers to get off another shot. She blew up the second light and threw the launcher out the copter afterward.

A blanket of darkness covered everything. Fleur's eyes adjusted quickly, but even so, the black night made the sounds of battle seem that much louder, made the chaos seem that much more frenzied. Shrieking metal and cries of pain filled the air. With the two major spotlights gone, the humans adjusted, switching on several supplemental green night-vision lights, and the battle raged on.

Fleur recognized the combatant whose weapon she'd stolen: one of Dain's old team, Trask. JB pulled her legs out from under her and threw her down on the floor of the copter. She noted with some pleasure that it took three of the big strong soldiers to hold her down, bind her wrists behind her back, and stuff a gag in her mouth. It was quite possibly the last pleasure she would enjoy. The helicopter turned sharply and headed off into the smoke clogged sky.

Oddly, nervous as she was about what was in store

for her, Fleur worried more for Dain. It was strange, not to have even seen him. Not to even know if he was still alive. The last thing she'd wanted was his blood on her hands, but that would have been better than his blood on someone else's.

Standing next to Kippenham, Dain was nearly blown off the top of the building from the wind as the helicopter touched down. His jacket flapped around him as a swirl of grit from the roof slammed into his face. The door opened and JB and Trask, on either side of a bound and gagged Fleur, led her out of the copter and across the rooftop toward him.

His teammates looked stricken, as if they'd been forced to choose loyalties and their decision didn't quite feel right. JB looked Dain in the eyes, searched Dain's face looking for the truth in all of this mess. Dain couldn't blame him for following orders. If the positions had been reversed, if he'd known as little as JB and the others about the reality of Crimson City, he'd have done exactly the same thing.

The transport copter switched to idle, and though the city was still alive with activity, the only sound that registered was the heavy thump of the blades slowing to a halt. Dain stared at Fleur. The lower half of her face was obscured by a fang-gag, a sort of overzealous mask used by humans when handling vampire suspects, but her eyes told the whole story. She was angry, she smelled blood, and if given half a chance she'd quite possibly kill them all.

Kippenham gestured to his men. "Leave Dumont and take the copter back to the fight."

JB stared in disbelief. He looked at Trask, then at Dain. His body seemed to jolt back slightly as if his boss's intention had suddenly dawned on him. He pushed Fleur to her knees.

Kippenham gestured to the copter with his gun. "Take the copter back down. I'll call you for a lift."

JB marshaled his emotions, set his jaw. He tapped Trask, who let go of Fleur and started back to the transport.

"JB," Kippenham repeated in a warning voice when the other man didn't follow.

"Yes, sir." He looked at Dain. "See you around man," he said softly. He raised his hand in a formal salute, the kind the B-Ops team had all but forgone these days. Then he quickly turned and jogged to the chopper.

Kippenham looked at Fleur, still bound and gagged. Her gaze darted to Dain, questioning. Dain felt as though he could almost feel the pounding of her heart in time with his.

"I think we're out of words," Kippenham said as he cocked his weapon. It was a UV gun. "I wish you knew how sorry I am."

As Dain's mind raced, Kipp checked his ammunition. Fleur struggled up from her knees, jumping to her feet and running to the edge of the rooftop. Kippenham swore, as if this inconvenience were all he needed on a day already long turned for the worst.

He waved Dain to follow and drew a second weapon. This he kept pointed at Dain, while the first was aimed at Fleur. Fleur hopped to the ledge but just froze there, like a bird with a broken wing. Dain knew she couldn't fly bound like that, with her balance off and her arms tied at the wrists. The only thing she could do was throw herself off, knowing she'd sustain physical injuries but hoping to outrun or dodge the fatal UV bullet in the process. She'd be helpless as she healed on the cement below.

She seemed to be weighing her options as Kippenham raised his gun in mock salute. "This is for Serena. And for the future of the human race. I'm sorry it comes to this, but there you are."

Fleur looked wildly between Dain and Kippenham. "Jump!" Dain yelled. He couldn't figure out any other solution.

Fleur didn't move, but Dain's yell surprised Kippenham enough to make the man hesitate. Dain leaped at Fleur, throwing his body in front of her. Kipp's gun discharged.He didn't pause to look, just wheeled around.

Kippenham reloaded his weapon with a practiced flick of his wrist and raised the gun once more to point it at Fleur. Dain kicked out hard, planting his boot squarely in Kipp's chest. The blow was as much as he could muster.

It worked: Kippenham flew backwards toward the side of the building, the gun flying out of his hand. In an arc, it tumbled down into the street far below. Kipp's shirt billowed out in a white cloud around him as he flailed, then he went over the edge too. His knees hooked on the ledge and the back of him smashed into the window on the top floor below, sending glass shards tinkling to the sidewalk. There was no way he'd have the strength to hold on for long.

Conscious of Fleur struggling upright behind him, Dain headed for Kippenham, his hands catching the man's ankles, holding him steady. Panicked gasps came from the man. And Dain was just about to unleash the full intensity of his fury when a wave of nausea overtook him. He let go of Kipp's ankles and stared down at his own chest, where blood bloomed red across his white shirt. Kipp's bullet had gone through.

"Dain," Fleur called weakly from behind him. "Dain?"

"Help me up," Kippenham begged.

Dain clutched his chest and stared at the man's boots hooked around the ledge. One had already slipped. Kippenham didn't have much more time.

But he himself had even less.

"I saved you!" Kippenham cried. "You were my experiment."

Dain didn't have the strength to answer, let alone the strength to help. "A failed experiment," he whispered. He watched helplessly as Kippenham lost his grip on the ledge and fell. The man didn't cry out as he disappeared, which made the sound of the impact that much more jarring.

Collapsing on the rooftop overlooking Crimson City below, Dain dropped his chin to his chest and surrendered to the darkness.

"Dain! Please wake up. Please, please wake up." It had taken Fleur precious minutes to work free of her bindings and release the gag. She ran to Dain. "Why did you do that?" she whispered, battling tears. "Why?"

Her fingers pressed down on his wound in a futile attempt to staunch the flow of blood, but it was seeping out fast; his face was already pale. The pressure seemed to revive him for a moment. "Why did you do that, Dain?"

His eyes searched hers. "You know why."

She shook her head, unable to make a sound except a desperate sob. "I can't let you die. Maybe . . . If . . ."

He frowned and held on to her hand weakly. "Don't even think about it. That bullet was UV. If you drink my . . ." He broke off, unable to go on. "I love you, Fleur. It was worth it. All of it . . . was worth it. . . ."

"Dain!"

His head rolled to the side. He was nearly out of time.

Fleur felt the presence of her cousins behind her, but she didn't glance back. She could feel them will her away from Dain. She thought she could hear Marius's voice in her head: *Let him go. You know what you have to do. You're a Warrior vampire, a leader of your people. Don't make the same mistake twice.*

Fleur let her tears stream down her face and fall silently over Dain's body. She felt his pulse fade.

"Lay him down and come back with us," Marius said.

Flashes of Hayden struck Fleur, of the fateful night when she'd taken his blood in a bite of passion and love. But the love hadn't been true. If it had, if he'd stayed, if he'd believed, she would have been forgiven.

But this love between her and Dain *was* true. It was the most real thing she'd ever known, and if she had to choose between him and everything else, she'd take her chances and suffer whatever consequences her actions might bring. *You'll have to trust me, Marius,* she thought. *You and everyone else.*

"I love you, too," she whispered to Dain, stroking the hair away from his forehead.

Dain's pulse dropped to the cusp of oblivion, and Fleur leaned over, fangs bared, and made him one of her kind.

Chapter Thirty-one

Fleur had no idea how long she'd been in bed. Her mouth tasted sour, as if she'd been sick. Sitting up, she realized she was still sick. Her head spinning, she stumbled off the mattress to the bathroom, and had to collapse on the floor and roll herself into a ball just to fight the nausea. UV poisoning.

Well, she wasn't dead. She felt way too bad to be dead. The cool marble revived her a bit. She reached out and pulled a towel off the rack, using the plush fabric as a blanket. If Dain could only see her now. Dain! Fleur sat bolt upright on the bathroom floor. She had to find out about him. She had to find out about *them*.

She stood up, using the sink to support her weight as she did, head bowed over the basin. She ran some cold water and washed her face, then looked into the mirror, nearly scaring herself to death. The face was that of a stranger. Her hair was limp and matted, plastered to her cheeks.

Cuts marked the corners of her mouth where

they'd gagged her, dried blood trailed down her neck. Dain's blood? Fleur squeezed her eyes shut for a moment, then took another look. A fat lip, bruises at her cheekbones, along her collar—if she stripped down she was sure she'd find the same all over her body. Her eyes were bloodshot, circles beneath. A weary look filled the depths of her blue irises.

This is who I am, now. I'm a fighter. I'm a leader. If her people ever questioned that, they need not question it now.

She smiled suddenly at a thought: *If I ever questioned that, I need not question it now.* Maybe the dirty, embattled face in the mirror wasn't such a stranger after all. Fleur was a champion of her people. Whether they'd see it that way remained to be seen, especially if Dain was still alive as a vampire. But she didn't really care. Because she had no regrets. The only regret she'd have was not making him sooner if he hadn't survived the change.

And she knew for sure who the enemy was now. Certain humans in the military had sent that mech. The next step was figuring out what to do about it, and with the least loss of innocent life.

Fleur looked down at her hands, their fingernails broken, the knuckles cut . . . She could change before approaching the others, make herself more presentable, but that hardly seemed appropriate. This was as much who she was now as the woman in satin ball gowns and jewels. She was finally everything she'd been meant to be.

She wiped the rest of the water off her face and turned for the door. Her hands weren't even shaking.

The hall was suspiciously quiet. On a whim, Fleur tried the door on the suite next to hers. It swung open easily. Empty. Medical was in the next building; she hoped Dain was there.

She made her way to the top of the stairs, but decided that it would take too long and be too painful to walk the floors to the Assembly room. She jumped over the banister and let herself float down. Upon landing, she headed down the hall toward the noise of a gathering, steeling herself against the growing concern over how her people would accept her.

She opened the door to the back of the Assembly room and saw her three cousins at the podium. She knew they could sense her presence. She limped across the floor, her head held high, her back straight, her eyes making contact. She searched for Paulina, knowing her friend would instantly give away the others' mood. Marius's look was impenetrable.

The three men stepped down from the podium and Fleur silently limped up to it. Her head bowed as she fought the urge to be sick, and she cursed how bad it must look. What words to say: *I did it again, but I did this for you as well as me? Please understand? Please accept me?* Fleur licked her dry lips and looked up at them.

"Please . . ." she uttered hoarsely. Unexpected tears pricked at her eyes as she looked out at the audience. "Please," she tried again. She just shook her head.

And all at once, a smattering of applause broke out.

Fleur looked up, half afraid it was a joke. But suddenly all present took to their feet and the applause spread throughout the hall. Fleur looked to Marius for confirmation, and he gave her a mere flicker of a smile and a knowing bow.

At last. At last Fleur Dumont had been forgiven by her people. At last she'd erased her damaged past.

And at last she'd been accepted for all that she had to offer—as a leader, as a fighter, and as one who knew true love.

Dain stood at the back of the room, his right side bandaged, his strength sapped, leaning on a sweet-smelling redhead who had insisted he attend some sort of assembly. He'd been in a kind of fever, felt as though he could have stayed in bed for the rest of his life, but this Paulina had promised him he'd eventually see Fleur. And after hearing that, it would have taken a whole army to keep him down.

For you could manufacture, rewind, black out, or manipulate the past, but the future was untouched, pure. It was *his*. In a city where loyalty seemed always for sale and allegiances could be changed with a bullet or a bite, there was only one thing left. There was only one thing that was true. One thing that was real. There was only one thing is his heart that he knew for sure mattered and counted, and it always would: Fleur.

Yes, his past might belong to the humans, or even with the mechs, but his future in the vampire world was all his own to craft and create. There would be no more manipulation. And as long as he had Fleur, he had everything he could want.

When he'd seen Fleur stumble out to the podium, he'd wanted to run to her. She didn't know that Marius and the others had told the Assembly every-thing. That their response had been one of thankfulness, of loyalty, of acceptance. But then her friends and family responded with fervor, with nat-ural acceptance, and he didn't want to get in the way of her moment.

As she stood there at the podium and looked out amongst the cheering vampires, he saw she was searching the audience. What did she seek? Then her eyes met his, and he knew. It was as if they were the only two people in the room. She started toward him, pushing past the compliments, the pats on the back, the handshakes and the airy kisses. Paulina's hand dropped and she moved away, letting Dain go as he allowed himself to be drawn where he wished. The crowd separated, a glittering mass of color down either side with an aisle straight to Fleur.

He met her in the middle; Dain just pulled Fleur into his arms, the pain in his side fading in the face of such intense joy. He put his lips to her ear and closed his eyes. "I love you, Fleur. I'm not the least bit sorry any of this has happened, if it means I'll be with you."

Fleur laughed. "You say that now . . ."

He laughed too, and he meant his next words more than he could express: "I'll say it forever."

Chapter Thirty-two

Dain's preference for doughnuts and coffee didn't change once he became a vampire. Sure, he had to concentrate hard not to keep running his tongue over his fangs in a giveaway manner, but for all anyone knew, he was still human. He could easily pass for one, anyway, having been one all his life—and it'd be even easier once he had his fangs filed. He still liked to go down to the lower strata once in a while, though he stayed away from his old haunts.

Stepping into a corner market on the opposite side of the city from his old apartment, Dain headed to the counter and asked for a pack of smokes, a copy of *The Crimson Post*, and a bouquet of blood-red dahlias for Fleur that caught his fancy. As he loaded his purchases into a flimsy plastic sack, a hand reached over, pulled out the smokes, then dropped them back in the bag.

"That crap will kill you," a familiar voice said.

From behind him, JB reached out and grabbed a handful of bite-sized candy bars from a warped bin

339

on the counter and tossed them down next to the register. He added a handful of change. "So, how's it going?"

"Fine," Dain said, glancing out the door to see if JB had any backup. An empty squad car was parked in front of the store. "You?"

JB nodded to the clerk and unwrapped one of the candies on the counter. "I'm good. I'm getting a promotion." He looked up at Dain. "What with you gone and the boss dead, it's kind of cleared the way."

"And here I thought I owed you a favor," Dain said dryly.

"Oh, you definitely do." JB laughed, his mouth full. "And I can always use a good informant."

Dain smiled. "Let me know when you plan to stop by and collect. I'm sure Fleur would love to have you for dinner."

JB's chewing slowed as he stared at Dain's fangs. "Yeah. . . ."

"Question." Dain pulled the newspaper out of his bag and pointed to the lead article. "How much of this is bullshit?"

JB arched an eyebrow. Taking the newspaper from Dain's hands, he said, "Let's see . . . both the Feds and the Crimson City governments are apologizing up and down for unsanctioned covert activities contrary to the truce between the species. . . ." He looked at Dain. " 'Unsanctioned covert activities.' Well, I guess the big dogs at I-Ops are definitely using Kippenham as the scapegoat. I thought so. They sent around a memo. They say he pulled that untested mech from the research facility and sent it out to kill vamps as an act of personal vengeance, and that any further such actions will be met by severe disciplinary action, blah, blah, blah."

"Now that Kipp's dead," Dain said, "we can all go back to normal, eh?"

JB nodded. "Exactly. Everything should be back to normal shortly." He didn't comment on how much he believed that. He looked down and continued reading from the paper. "Blah, blah, blah . . . 'Both national and city governments are doing what they can to stabilize vampire-human relations . . .' more blah, blah . . . 'and Kippenham's mech has been taken offline and deleted.' Oh, for god's sake . . . who *wrote* this?" he asked.

Dain understood what he was talking about. "Didn't you bring in the mech and delete it?"

JB looked up and shook his head. "No. I was going to ask you if you knew anything about it . . . er, one way or another. It was programmed to return to the base right after its mission. It's still not back. Something tells me not to expect it to walk up and knock on the station door anytime soon." He shrugged and tossed the newspaper back in Dain's bag. "That article's fifty-percent bullshit. Of course, maybe it'll keep the brass from doing anything stupid for a while." He didn't look very hopeful.

"Okay, thanks. So . . . is anything new?" Dain asked lamely. It seemed odd to be so far out of loop. Of course, he was out of one loop and into another; in the interest of full disclosure he could have told JB that the vampires were planning to pursue better vampire-werewolf diplomacy, particularly with respect to plans for defense against future human attacks. That they'd approached the Vendix to help set it up. That they'd already approached the Grand Dame Alpha for a meeting. He said nothing.

JB gave him a careful look. "Well, with things back to normal, the only things left to deal with are the killings not directly related to Kipp's orders. Most of them were individual . . . you know, because of the tension—but you knew that. Of course, there have been a few . . . well, there are a few recent killings of vampires that we haven't been able to figure out." He looked like he didn't want to talk about them.

"You think they're random?"

"Yeah. Random. But to be honest, it's not a real high priority for us to find out right now. And I wouldn't expect much help from the cops." He looked a little sheepish.

"Well, we're not going to close the case on our side," Dain said. "Either way, we're keeping an eye out."

JB tossed his empty candy wrapper in the trash bin. "I would expect you to. Look, I've gotta go." He hesitated for a moment, then stuck out his hand. "I just wanted to say that you don't have to worry about me. I mean, I'm not going to tell anyone where you are. No one's going to come looking for you."

Dain paused, then shook JB's hand. "Thanks."

JB nodded. "Yeah. I'll be in touch." He exited the store and turned left.

Dain made a point to turn right.

Taking the long way home, he sought out the mangled phone booth where Cyd had disappeared. The area was quiet and deserted. He put a cig in his mouth, lit it, then took it between his fingers and watched smoke curl up from the clean white paper. A moment later, he dropped it gently into the metal skeleton of the defunct booth. "Good-bye, Cyd," he said. "Maybe we'll meet again in another lifetime. You've got a lot of explaining to do."

Then Dain turned around and headed home.

Fleur waited on the window ledge of the forty-second floor of Dumont Towers. She offered an unguarded smile as he handed her the flowers, took her in his arms and felt that same flood of emotions rush through him. He would always feel this way, and for that he was very grateful: It was good to no longer be alone.

The *Post* fell to the floor and unfurled. It would be another hour before they were summoned to the war room on account of Jill Cooper's latest scoop:

SECRET WAR VS. VAMPS REVEALED

Of course, to Dain and Fleur, there'd been nothing secret about it.

"Gorgeous," Fleur said, looking at the dahlias. She tossed them behind her onto the bed, and the petals showered across the fresh white satin. "But not as gorgeous as you." She drew a finger along Dain's jaw.

He kissed the hollow of her neck, trailing upward. Her mouth was warm as he gently bit her lower lip. He pulled her closer, the thin silk of her emerald-green slip molding against her curves like water, and his body responded in an instant. He sucked in a quick breath. "Oh, man . . . it's definitely worth it."

"What is?"

He closed his eyes as Fleur's hands slipped under his shirt. He groaned as she unbuckled his belt and slid her hands down his hips.

"Being one of us?" Fleur guessed. "There are compensations."

"Yeah. Oh, yeah." Heightened sensations filled him, sensations that weren't described in any manual he'd seen back at the station. Probably because they weren't something a human could fathom.

"And I feel everything more than ever," she said. "It's because of you. You make everything so much . . . more."

He knew exactly what she meant. The way Fleur's skin felt beneath his fingers. The way her eyes were bluer and brighter than ever, even here and now, in the dim light. The way his blood burned . . . Maybe it was just the change in his body, but as Fleur led him to the bed, Dain knew it was something more. He'd been a blank page, alone, and with a scatter-shot of memories not even his own. Fleur completed his story. She completed him, in body and mind. And she'd been meant to all along.

"We have some unfinished business," she murmured into his ear as she pulled him down onto her. They sprawled out in a sea of red petals.

"By all means," Dain said, smoothing the silk away from Fleur's body. "Forever is a long time, and I don't plan to waste a second of it."

Bridget Rothschild lay on her bed, reading the Sunday paper and thinking that things kept getting more and more interesting in this city, no matter what the higher-ups at the base thought. With her brunette locks free of that damned ponytail that was like a perma-headache, she looked nothing at all like the girl everybody thought they knew. But that was what she loved best about living here: Nobody was the person you thought you knew.

She reached over to the side table and opened the drawer, pulling out the picture of what looked like a god created in the body of a man: the mech. He— make that "it," she reminded herself—was a tough one. And it was still out there.

She'd been close, so close, that night the siren went off and Dain "rescued" her, and then the mech had just changed course and disappeared. And she'd had to give herself this damned injury.

Ah, well. There was always tomorrow. She had a feeling that mech was going to haunt this city for a long time to come, and the next time it showed its face, Bridget Rothschild would be there. That was a promise. And it was almost as certain as the fact that, in Crimson City, each day brought something completely new.

*And now a special preview
of the next installment in the
Crimson City series...*

A TASTE OF CRIMSON

MARJORIE M. LIU

Coming in August 2005!

Chapter One

They are dirty beasts, but that is the way of it. We will throw the dogs a bone, Michael. Throw them a bone, and watch them lick our fingers.

"Throw them a bone," Michael murmured. He pressed his tongue against fang, tasted sweet blood. Far below him, at street level, the vampire envoys floated single-file down the narrow alley, winding around dumpsters and rusting cars. Night, a cool breeze, the scent of rain, wet concrete shining with reflected light from apartment windows—the vampires were shadows passing over slick grit and filth.

Michael scanned the path ahead of them. He sensed no movement, no scent of human or steel. Nothing of the mechs, of whom the city had so recently become aware. Nothing, even, of the wolves.

They are dirty beasts. Celestine's words still whispered in his mind, her dry-silk voice soft, damning. Michael watched the top of her head, third in line behind Frederick: the envoys' leader and Dumont's hand-chosen negotiator.

Celestine's pale hairless scalp stood out in stark contrast to her black belted robes. Michael imagined dropping on her, dislodging vertebrae with quick fingers, immobilizing her just long enough to keep her from the negotiations with the wolves. She was a bad choice for these talks—talks that had to succeed. Michael was not a man to admit weakness, but he could eat his pride this once. The humans had proven themselves strong in their first covert offensive against the vampires, and though it had been thwarted and the man who had ordered the assassinations was dead, other enemies existed. The promise was still there, the taste of violence.

They know we are vulnerable, soft in our luxury and unprepared for a hard fight. Worse yet, we have proven to them that we are aware of their existence. Now they have nothing to lose. They know we will come for them.

Michael had been alive long enough to know the dangers of calculated desperation. The danger to them all would be greater than ever, and despite mixed feelings toward his own kind, the species had to be protected at any cost.

Even if it meant an alliance with the wolves.

I would have been a better choice as an envoy, Michael thought, and almost laughed—just as Frederick had laughed outright when Michael had challenged his part of this assignment.

So, now you wish to rejoin our kind? The outsider, reclaimed? A joke, Michael. You are the Vendix, the punisher, and that is all you are good for. You are not a diplomat. You do not do well with words or tact. Simply do what is expected of you. Hunt. Watch our backs from above. Keep us safe from traps.

Be a thug. Muscle. A hired sword.

Bitterness bloomed inside Michael's mouth, down his throat and into his chest. The horrors of his past, the crimes he had committed—three hundred years later he still paid. He would always pay. It might be that redemption was something he would never be allowed to find. His role in society had been burned on his body for eternity.

Michael gripped the ledge he crouched upon and jumped. An embrace—wind cushioned his body, sheathed him tight. He floated, toes pointing down-ward, arms loose at his sides. Black hair fell over his eyes; he pushed it aside, brushing metal. The gold filaments laced into his thin braids felt cooler than his skin.

He flew above and ahead of the envoys, scan-ning the shadows. Nothing at first, just the still-ness of deep night. A rare quiet for the heart of the city, without the crush of traffic and quick-paced bodies. Perfect and lovely. This was the city Michael loved best, full of peaceful solitude. It was the kind of city to get lost in, without eyes to judge or pry.

For a moment, he thought he heard singing, far-away lilting, a man's voice rimmed with shadow. Michael thought, *That does not sound human*—and then he stopped listening to the music, because less than twenty yards ahead of the envoys something large moved.

Wolf.

Michael sank swiftly, noting from the corner of his

eye Frederick's slowed movement, light flickering off
the lead envoy's rings. Silk flared around Michael's
legs as he alighted on the ground; he brought back
his right hand, brushing the hilt of his sword, and
looked deep into the gloom.

"Hello," he said quietly.

He saw sleek fur, wiry legs. Golden eyes and glittering teeth. A low growl rumbled like thunder in
the night air.

Michael did not respond. He waited, patient,
aware of the envoys behind him, the heavy weight of
their stares. He sensed their impatience. Irritation.
Immortals, in a hurry. The irony was not lost on
Michael, but it was troubling: a sign of nervousness
that the mission—and Frederick, as its head—could
ill-afford. The wolves would smell weakness.

Bones crackled. The wolf's jaw shifted, receded.
Fur smoothed into naked skin. Muscles rippled in
forelegs, expanding, elongating; paws became
sinewy, masculine hands.

Michael did not avert his eyes. Vampire and werewolf locked gazes—brown to golden—until, at the
very last, when the animal had become man and
there was nothing left but sweat and burning eyes, a
hoarse note emerged from the werewolf's throat and
became, "Hello."

"We are expected," Michael said.

The werewolf's spine popped. He was tall, with
pale broad shoulders. A faint scar ran up his left
cheek. Silver dusted his hair, although he had a relatively young face.

"The Grand Dame Alpha is waiting. I'm supposed
to lead you underground." His distaste was evident,
profound.

Michael felt breath on the back of his neck. Frederick said, "We are ready."

Michael twisted sideways, stepping close to the alley wall. The werewolf frowned as Frederick passed between them, followed closely by the rest of the envoys. The vampires each floated at least six inches off the ground, giving them a secure advantage in height. Michael heard the werewolf mutter obscenities, his feet slapping hard against the pavement as he loped ahead.

Michael watched the faces of every vampire who passed, noting their focused indifference with amused detachment. The only one who met his eyes was Celestine, and her dark gaze was sly, smug. Her thin red lips tugged upwards, and then she was gone, gliding past him down the alley. The record-keeper followed, and then the seven guards, their long embroidered robes concealing more weapons than they revealed, most of which were modern—handguns, stun rods, small explosives.

Quaint. Not very elegant.

Michael fell into a floating step behind the last guard. He sensed a tremor run through the vampire's body, and smiled grimly. Psychopath, assassin, murderer, executioner—all of these were names other vampires had given Michael. All of these were names for their fear.

He almost touched his cheek, caught himself before he could show that sliver of weakness. The tattoo hurt. Centuries old, and still it pained him. Ink laced with gold did not heal properly, even in vampire flesh, and it would never fade or be absorbed by his body. He was marked, forever. Vendix. Punisher. Condemned to be alone.

Michael drew back, drifting higher, following the envoys at a discreet distance. No more werewolves revealed themselves. He watched as the envoys were led to a wide sewer grate. The werewolf guide leapt over the rusty steel bars and in one fluid motion swept down to yank them open. The hinges were surprising quiet; Michael heard only a faint squeak.

A voice rose up from the darkness of underground—hollow as a tunnel, brittle with well-worn age, feminine in a way that might have once been lovely but now was only wise.

"Welcome, vampires. Welcome to the home of Maddox."

"Thank you," said Frederick, his bejeweled hands clasped together. He bowed his head; a strand of black hair drifted over his shoulder, caressing the pale glow of his long neck. The other vampires also bowed their heads—as they had been commanded to do—though Michael did not miss the hard line of Celestine's lips, nor the arrogance that narrowed the eyes of every vampire but Frederick.

You are not a diplomat. You do not do well with words or tact.

Maybe. But at least Michael knew enough to hide his emotions for the sake of politeness. At least he still remembered humility—or as much as was necessary to pretend at compassion.

"Jas," said the voice in the darkness. The werewolf guide took a reluctant step back and gestured at the open sewer grate. His jaw was tight, his naked body rigid, coiled. Michael thought he might be shaking, and knew it for rage.

"Don't you dare try anything," Jas said. A sharp bark from underground made him flinch.

Frederick did not answer. He stepped off the alley ledge and drifted slowly down, down into the darkness of the werewolf tunnels. The other vampires followed, with more reluctance than was courteous.

Michael watched from above, waiting until the last guard descended. Jas looked up at him. The two men locked gazes and Michael felt the challenge and questions.

Just try something. And, *Who are you?*

Michael waited, silent, until Jas pulled back his lips in a silent snarl. His eyes flashed. Michael saw the hint of fur, the shift of his chin into something narrow and sharp. Then the wolf jumped down into the waiting darkness, and several pairs of hands emerged from the tunnel to pull shut the grate. Silence descended, the weight of the night bearing down into a hush. There was no singing anymore.

Alone, at last.

Michael drifted backwards until his shoulders rubbed the alley wall. It was small comfort, to be away from his own kind. He took some satisfaction in their fear, but it truly only served to heighten his isolation, the knowledge that he could never be part of them. That even if he wanted, they would never accept his presence.

Vampires did not easily forgive those who killed their kind—especially when the killer was a vampire himself.

His assignment was not yet over. Frederick had been very clear; Michael was to stay until the envoys reemerged. There was a three-hour deadline on the talks, enough time for the envoys to return home before sunrise. Each carried a special day-pack—enough makeup and shielding to protect him or her from the sun. Not that it mattered. Despite the official statements, the human offensive had begun: it was a return of the old days, if in a different fashion. There was no more safety under the light of day, not when sunlight made it so difficult to pass as human.

We should have expected it. Michael tilted his head, struggling to see the stars beyond the glare of city lights and smog. *Humans have always feared us, for good reason. And now with their numbers dwindling, birth rates declining . . . they cannot risk our presence, our promises of self-control.*

Self-control. That was laughable.

He finally gave in and touched his stinging cheek, traced the hard round lines etched into his skin. No other Vendix was marked in this way. Only Michael.

For your past misdeeds, as well as the ones you will commit.

Michael pulled his hand away. He curled his fingers against the brick behind him.

Don't, he told himself. *Not now.*

He heard laughter, then, distinctly male. Raucous, drunk, wild. The kind to avoid, if he was weak and human. The kind to avoid, even if he wasn't. He listened carefully, but the humans had an echo in their voices that meant distance—several blocks' worth—and Michael felt little interest in investigating. As long as they did not approach the entrance to the tunnels, they could piss and vomit up their drunken stupor on any street they liked.

And then the laughter stopped. Suddenly, eerily. A curtain of silence dropped hard and fast, creating an expectant voice within the night: *Not right, not right*. Michael pushed himself away from the wall, drifting higher.

He had almost cleared the rooftops when he heard a whistle, a low catcall. Laughter, again, but lower this time. A promise. More silence . . . and then shoes slapping against concrete—hard, fast. More and more, a group of people running. Chasing.

A woman screamed.

And just as Michael shot into the sky, pursuing the sound of that terrified cry, the men began screaming, too.

Liz Maverick

Named for the angels, Los Angeles is a city of demons, a crucible of souls. It is Crimson City. Here vampires and werewolves vie for dominion, humans build soldiers of flesh and steel who seethe with fury. But alongside strife can be love—a love that cares nothing for species or origin.

"An original, dark and fascinating world!"
—*RT Book Reviews*

Yet, love doesn't always conquer. Marius and Jill have long been kept apart. Bound by destiny yet forbidden true union, he is vampire; she, human. And a marriage alliance that promises peace for all others shall separate them forever.

"Maverick grabs readers from page one."
—*Publishers Weekly* on *Wired*

As if peace might be achieved so easily. Darkness is rising: a mysterious plot shall force every inhabitant of Crimson City to take sides. Deliverance exists, but first must come a tale of impossible passion and discovery, of Marius and Jill in a race against time leading back to the city's paranormal beginnings, to Victorian London, to an era of invention and a world of . . .

Crimson and Steam

ISBN 13: 978-0-505-52779-0

✂

☐ **YES!**

Sign me up for the Love Spell Book Club and send my
FREE BOOKS! If I choose to stay in the club, I will pay
only $8.50* each month, a savings of $6.48!

NAME: _____

ADDRESS: _____

TELEPHONE: _____

EMAIL: _____

☐ I want to pay by credit card.

☐ **VISA**   ☐ **MasterCard.**   ☐ **DISCOVER**

ACCOUNT #: _____

EXPIRATION DATE: _____

SIGNATURE: _____

Mail this page along with $2.00 shipping and handling to:
Love Spell Book Club
PO Box 6640
Wayne, PA 19087
Or fax (must include credit card information) to:
610-995-9274
You can also sign up online at **www.dorchesterpub.com**.
*Plus $2.00 for shipping. Offer open to residents of the U.S. and Canada only.
Canadian residents please call 1-800-481-9191 for pricing information.
If under 18, a parent or guardian must sign. Terms, prices and conditions subject to
change. Subscription subject to acceptance. Dorchester Publishing reserves the right
to reject any order or cancel any subscription.